ONE YEAR GONE

Also by Avery Bishop

Girl Gone Mad

ONE YEAR GONE

A NOVEL

AVERY BISHOP

This is a work of fiction. Names, characters, organizations, places, events, and incidents are either products of the author's imagination or are used fictitiously. Any resemblance to actual persons, living or dead, or actual events is purely coincidental.

Published by Lake Union Publishing, Seattle

www.apub.com

ISBN-13: 9781542018708
ISBN-10: 1542018706

Cover design by Damon Freeman

Printed in the United States of America

For the missing

But she didn't know
Didn't know the truth
And now she's gone
Gone forever

—Bronwyn Hayden,
"Her Dark Secret"

PROLOGUE

Nobody just disappears.

Not like in movies. Or on TV. Or in books.

People can't just one day up and vanish. Life isn't an elaborate magic trick. There is no magician standing in the wings whose fingertips are so powerful they can make a person disappear with one simple snap.

Of course, there were times when you were younger—barely sixteen—when you wondered if that were true. If there was in fact some mysterious illusionist who had one day decided to make your father disappear into thin air.

But you knew those thoughts were silly. Foolish. Naive.

Your father was never around much in your life, even when he was there. He worked fifty hours a week. Oftentimes went to the bar at night to drink. When he was home, he spent time in his ratty recliner, the footrest cranked up and aimed at the television, a can of beer sweating on the worn coaster protecting the cheap side table your mother found at the Salvation Army.

Your mother, who was the sweetest woman in the world. The one who always had a smile for you. Who was always there when you were feeling sick. Who always took care of you when nobody else could.

Your mother who, when you turned sixteen, learned she had cancer.

Stage 4 Hodgkin's lymphoma, the doctors said. It had come out of nowhere. And it had come fast, and it had come strong, and while your mother was encouraged to start treatment, you could hear the truth in the doctors' voices that there wasn't much time left.

That was when your father decided to show his true colors.

He packed a single suitcase and walked out the front door and never came back.

You didn't even have the heart to tell your mother at first, not on your daily visits to the hospital in the cramped room with all the medical equipment and the wires and the dry-erase board with the shift nurse's name scrawled in black, erasable marker.

Your mother didn't ask where your father was. Didn't even ask if he planned to make an appearance. Somehow she just knew.

Your father never returned. Never called. Never even sent a postcard.

It took a while, but you eventually forced yourself to forget about your father. To act like he no longer existed. By the time you graduated college and decided to move with your boyfriend back to his hometown, your father was but a distant memory.

The town's name was Bowden. A rural town located in North Central Pennsylvania. The kind of town that's not big enough to have a Walmart, because there's a Walmart one town over, but still big enough to have two grocery stores, three banks, a bowling alley, a four-screen movie theater, a gun shop, a diner, and two restaurants, not to mention a McDonald's, a Burger King, and a KFC, as well as a Subway in the small strip mall that also hosts a gym and Chinese restaurant and nail salon and a Radio Shack that would one day go out of business, leaving behind the husk of a storefront sitting empty for years.

About five thousand residents, all said, scattered through the main town and then the outskirts and out into what the locals affectionately called the sticks.

And it's in Bowden that you start your life. Where you begin a business. Where you get engaged. Where you become pregnant.

Nine months later, your daughter is born.

You'd struck a deal: your fiancé would name your son; you would name your daughter.

You decide on Bronwyn. A pretty name. Welsh. You remember seeing it in a novel you had to read in college, and it's always stuck with you.

Years pass. Your business grows. You never marry, which is just as well, as your relationship with Bronwyn's father disintegrates. He meets someone else, gets married, starts a family.

Still, he remains active in Bronwyn's life. Remains active in your life too. Despite no longer being together, the two of you get along well, which helps in raising your daughter.

Bronwyn lives with you—her bedroom across the hall from yours—and there are times when the two of you laugh and times when you argue and times when you don't talk to each other for days, but she is your daughter and you would do anything for her, anything at all, because there is nobody else in the world you care for more than you care for her.

And then one day, just months after she turns seventeen, your daughter disappears.

Nobody knows where she went. The police deem her a runaway. You look everywhere, do everything you can to find her, but with no luck.

Days become weeks. Weeks become months.

No contact. Not even a text message. Or an email.

You have no idea where she's gone. Who she might be with. Who she might have become. And despite all the sleepless nights, all the phone calls, all the searching, you're told by the police that sometimes this happens.

Sometimes people just disappear.

Especially teenage girls.

Then, almost a year later, the first text comes in at just after four o'clock in the morning.

The phone on the bedside table makes its familiar ding.

The sound is so faint that anyone asleep would miss it, but as you've been drifting in and out of sleep, you take it as a welcome distraction, especially since it's come at such an odd hour.

Eyes still half-closed, you roll over in bed and reach for the phone in the darkness. Almost knock it off the table as the phone issues another soft ding.

Two text messages. In the middle of the night.

You open your eyes just enough to squint at the bright screen.

Realize after a moment you aren't breathing.

The first text says, mom

The second text says, please help

Eyes now wide, blood thumping in your ears, you wonder if it's some kind of dream.

Then the phone dings a third time, and the words that pop up on the screen cause your blood to go cold.

i think he's going to kill me

1

Jessica

Now

"Um, Ms. Moore? I think we have a problem."

Catherine Colvin says this a second after she's knocked on my office door and poked her head in. Not all the way—she doesn't want to enter unless she's been invited—but still far enough that I can see the worry on her face.

"I told you, Catherine. Call me Jessica." I pause, noting the clock on the wall near the door. "It's past midnight. What are you still doing here?"

"I was helping Nick with a couple of things. It's okay. I already clocked out a half hour ago."

Nick Jennings is a twenty-four-year-old college dropout with the looks of a *Bachelorette* contestant. He's a great bartender, no question about it, but he's also a major flirt. And seeing as how Catherine is only seventeen years old, Nick should know better.

"I don't want anybody working off the clock," I tell her. "Besides, you should be home by now."

She nods, dropping her eyes, looking crestfallen for just long enough that I glimpse a shadow of my daughter in her posture, and then I blink and remember why Catherine knocked on my office door in the first place.

"Anyway, what's the problem?"

"It's Officer Gorman."

"Why is he here?"

"He's been here for about an hour or so. He's not on duty or anything—at least, he's not in uniform—but he's been drinking pretty hard, and now he's harassing some of the other customers."

With a heavy sigh I push back from my desk, rise to my feet.

"Why am I just hearing about this now?"

"Nick's been dealing with him, trying to get him to settle down, but I don't think it's helping. Officer Gorman keeps getting louder, and he keeps getting angrier, and I just . . ."

She pauses, shrugging her thin shoulders, this beautiful young girl with a heart-shaped face and honey-blonde hair who also happens to be the daughter of the town's mayor. She's worked here for only a couple of months, since the beginning of summer, and now it's late September and she's proved to be an incredible hostess. All the customers like her, and it's not just because her father is so well regarded around town. She's naturally gifted in the way of customer service, always giving every guest her undivided attention, always with a bright smile, and she's never one to slack off, finding something to do when it's not busy, some way to help out.

Because of her age, I hired her simply as a hostess. But as I don't have much use for social media—and as my assistant manager is too busy—I've put her in charge of the Wonderwall's Facebook, Twitter, and Instagram accounts. Since she's taken over, social media engagement has gone through the roof.

Grabbing my iPhone off the desk, I start toward the door.

"All right, let's see what we can do about Mr. Gorman."

I follow Catherine down the hallway and into the dark dining room portion of the Wonderwall. We shut this section down at 10:00 p.m., so the chairs have already been stacked upside down on the tables, and somebody has swept the carpet.

We thread through the tables toward the bar, as if drawn to the music playing from the speakers situated around the large room.

When Joe and I first opened this place, we'd had long discussions on the type of music we would play. As Bowden is a rural area, country music seemed the most obvious choice.

But there were already several other bars in town, most of which played country music, so we wanted to mix things up. We knew doing so might kill business, but we were young, just out of college, and so we were at an age where taking risks was half the fun.

We'd almost decided on Top 40, the kind of pop you hear on the radio, but in the end we decided to stay true to our college roots and stick to alternative nineties rock music. We named the place the Wonderwall, because Joe and I had been Oasis fans and always loved that song, and so we played Radiohead, the Verve, Pearl Jam, Smashing Pumpkins, Green Day, and, well, practically every other band of that era. Joe put together a mix, not just of each band's most famous songs, but some of their deep tracks too.

It was a hit.

Or, at the very least, nobody complained. The first year or so, we had a mishmash of customers, all different ages and economic standings, and pretty soon we established the kind of clientele we were looking for. We wanted to be the kind of place young professionals in town could come to hang out for happy hour, and I'd played around with the decor, given the bar a more sophisticated touch, made it a little more upscale.

We added a stage. Started featuring live music, mostly acoustic sets, and we hosted a karaoke night, which became very popular.

Now, though, just over Red Hot Chili Peppers' "Under the Bridge," we can hear Kenny Gorman's deep voice. It's enough to make me pause.

Enough so that I unlock my phone, scroll through my contacts, and dial Tony Parsons.

The police chief answers on the third ring, his voice husky with sleep. By then I've followed Catherine through the dining room. We linger off to the side, watching over the tables toward the bar, where right this moment Kenny Gorman is standing tall in his stonewashed jeans and checkered shirt, his boots scuffed from years of use. He's in his midthirties, has lived in Bowden his entire life, and will probably end his days here too.

Tony whispers, "Yeah?"

"It's Jess."

"Jessica? Why are you calling at this hour? It sounds like you're still at work."

"I am still at work. And right now I'm watching one of your guys making a complete ass out of himself."

A low, irritated sigh issues through the phone.

"Who is it?"

"Kenny."

"What the hell is he doing there? The Wonderwall ain't his scene."

"Tell me about it."

There's a beat of silence on Tony's end before he clears his throat.

"So I'm guessing Kenny ain't gonna leave on his own, huh?"

"I highly doubt it. But you once told me to call you if any of your men came in here acting a fool, and since then I've never had any issues with any of your guys. Then again, this is the first time Kenny's stepped foot in here."

"Yeah, I get it." Another irritated sigh. "All right, I'll have a car come out and get him. Hopefully somebody will be there in ten minutes."

Judging by how loud Kenny's getting, I'm not sure ten minutes will do, but I thank Tony anyway and slip the phone into my pocket as I start toward the bar.

The Wonderwall has never needed a bouncer. We've always had a strict Don't Act Like an Asshole policy, and it's served us well since we first opened. Somebody gets too loud or starts showing off, they get a warning. They keep it up, we call the police, and that person gets banned for life. But it's a bar, and we expect people to have fun, so sure, people will get drunk. Some might even throw up, and that's okay. Just as long as they're not assholes. The moment they step over that line, they're done.

It's Friday night, so the place is crowded. We had a band in here earlier to perform, but they've since packed up their stuff and headed out. At least, some of the band. I spot the drummer and bass player over in one of the far booths, along with a couple of women.

They, just like everybody else, are watching Kenny.

"Oh, I'm sorry," Kenny says, his voice way too loud even with the music. "Am I making you girls *uncomfortable*?"

This question is directed toward a table of college-age girls, and even from this distance, they do appear to be quite uncomfortable.

A guy in his forties with a sharp chin and product in his hair has gotten up and started toward Kenny, but he's walking cautiously, because the guy knows—just like everybody knows—that Kenny is a cop, and so he doesn't want to piss him off too much. Too much risk of retaliation. Not that any of Tony's guys would do such a thing—he runs a pretty tight ship—but it's never wise to piss off a cop, even when he's off duty.

"Hey, man," the guy says, edging a bit closer to Kenny, "why don't I buy you a drink?"

"Hey, man," Kenny mimics, "why don't I punch you in your fucking teeth?"

Nick, who has watched all this from behind the bar (and who has since spotted me across the room), finally decides enough is enough. He motions at our other bartender to keep an eye on things as he steps out from behind the bar and makes his approach.

"Kenny, I think it's time for you to leave."

Kenny spins toward him, swaying on his feet, his bottle of Coors almost falling from his hand, and jabs a finger in Nick's direction.

"Stay out of this, pretty boy."

Nick holds his hands out at his sides, in a calming gesture, though since Kenny is a cop it almost looks like he's surrendering to him.

"I just don't want you to do anything stupid, Kenny."

"Stupid?" Kenny's voice rises even higher above the music. "Tell me, pretty boy, who's the stupid one here?"

Kenny swaps the Coors from one hand to the other. It's meant to be a distraction, I realize. To get Nick to look at the beer while, with his other hand, Kenny makes a fist. He's going to slug Nick, right here in front of everyone, and I know the moment that happens, things are going to spiral out of control.

"Kenny!"

The Red Hot Chili Peppers have faded away, and in that second or two of silence before Alice in Chains kicks in, my voice sounds like a scream.

Kenny turns toward me, a lopsided grin on his face. He's had way too much to drink, which is something I'll need to talk to Nick about, though maybe Kenny was already wasted when he came in here, having had way too much to drink at another bar or even at home in the trailer where he lives with his mom.

"Well, well, well," he drawls, still unsteady on his feet. "If it ain't the boss lady. How's it hanging, boss lady?"

I've started toward him but notice that Catherine starts to follow, so I wave at her to stay where she is. Then I keep moving, my heels tapping across the hardwood floor, holding my gaze steady with his, and when I'm about five feet away from the man, I gesture to an empty table.

"Why don't you take a seat, Kenny. I'll get you some water. Maybe we can find something in the kitchen for you to eat."

Kenny Gorman is a moderately good-looking guy. He's fit, with short hair and a cleft in his chin. I know back in the day he played football, was a pretty good player, and there had been talk of him getting a college scholarship before he got drunk one night at a party and tried to impress his friends with some silly stunt and ended up breaking his leg in the process.

Now this moderately good-looking guy who almost managed to make it out of town sneers at me like I'm an ant he's about ready to stomp.

"Yeah?" he says. "Well, maybe you can go fuck yourself."

Nick says, "Hey, Kenny, that's enough."

Kenny spins on him, raising his fist this time.

"The fuck did you just say?"

Nick doesn't say anything. He keeps his hands at his sides and takes a slow step backward.

"Yeah," Kenny says, dropping the fist, "that's what I thought."

He then seems to remember where he is, as though suddenly waking from a dream. He looks around the bar, at the people watching him—a few even with their phones out, recording the spectacle—and he focuses again on the table of college girls.

"What is it you bitches even want, huh?" He doesn't wait for a response and shouts at the rest of the room: "What is it all you bitches want? We try to be gentlemen, right, fellas? We try to be good ol' boys and say the right things and be polite and all that shit. And then a bitch starts talking to you on the app, acting like she cares, like she's actually interested in you, and she finally says she wants to meet, and then . . . she doesn't fucking show up."

I pull out one of the chairs, turn it so that it's facing Kenny.

"Stuff like that happens all the time, Kenny. It sucks, I know, but don't take it too hard. Now, why don't you have a seat?"

Again with the sneer.

"Why don't you shove that up your tight ass?"

It's clear Nick wants to say something else, do something in front of all these people (he doesn't want to look weak, especially in front of the ladies), but I shake my head at him and then glance toward the entrance door.

"I've already spoken to Tony. He's sending somebody over here to pick you up."

"Fucking bitch," Kenny mumbles as he takes a swig of his beer. "Went and tattled to the police chief, huh?"

"Nobody wants you driving in this condition. You're apt to wrap yourself around a telephone pole. Or worse, you might run somebody over."

"Yeah," he says, "that would be a god-awful shame, wouldn't it?"

Out through the front windows, a police cruiser pulls into the parking lot. The sneer slips off Kenny's face.

"Shit," he whispers.

Taking one last swig, he steps over to the bar, sets the beer on top, but he does it carelessly, and the empty bottle tips over and rolls off the side.

Snorting a laugh, he says, "Whoops," and starts for the door.

He gets only five paces before he trips over his own feet and falls flat on the floor.

Nobody moves to help him. Those filming or taking pictures don't even bother lowering their phones.

The front door opens, and James Healy steps inside. Tall with a dark mustache, his light-gray uniform looking like it could use a press, he scans the room before spotting Kenny and then starts toward him.

And that's when Kenny throws up. A little bit ends up on his checkered shirt.

A few people let out gasps. Some laugh.

"Shut up," Kenny says, wiping at the vomit with the back of his hand as he climbs to his feet. "Shut the fuck up!"

James takes Kenny's arm, starts to lead him toward the door.

"Gee, Kenny," I call out to him, "I can't imagine why anyone would stand you up."

The moment the words leave my mouth, I regret them. They're childish. Stupid. Unprofessional.

But his sneer kept replaying through my mind, the sneer of a man-child who is mean for the sake of being mean, the kind who likes to stomp on ants because he's so much bigger than they are, and when I hear a few people laughing at my comment, I feel a strange sort of pride knowing that I've knocked him down a peg.

Kenny pauses. He starts to turn around, starts to say something, but James Healy—a man several years older than Kenny, who's been on the force since he was twenty-one years old—tells Kenny to forget it and pushes him toward the door.

Kenny goes without a word, his shoulders slumped forward in shame, his head lowered.

The second both men exit the bar, a handful of people start clapping. It's just a smattering, but then a few more join in, and then a few more, until the applause is louder than the music.

I motion for everyone to quiet down, then apologize for the disturbance and ask everybody to make sure when they leave to drive home safely.

I turn back to Catherine, who says, "I'll get a mop."

Always one to help out, even when she's not asked.

"No, you won't. You'll get in your car and drive home. It's way past curfew. Thanks for all your help, Catherine, but I'll clean up this mess myself."

When I arrive home two hours later, it's to an empty house.

It has been almost a year, and I still haven't gotten used to it. I'd known the day would come, of course, the day when Bronwyn would eventually leave—for college, I'd hoped—but her leaving would be something that we both agreed upon, something that I helped her plan and not just something that happened in the dead of night when I wasn't home.

I park in the garage and let myself in through the side door, the one that goes through the laundry room and enters the kitchen.

I set my keys on the counter, turn toward the fridge, and pull out a bottle of wine.

It's cheap wine, but over the years I have found that cheap wine works just as well as the expensive stuff.

My father liked to drink, liked it very much, and he would often drink until he passed out. Sometimes he'd even pass out at the bar, and men who weren't his friends—because I don't think my father had any friends—would draw straws to decide who would take him home.

He was never abusive, my father. He'd raise his voice, sure, but he never once laid a finger on my mother or me, at least from what I remember.

But whatever sickness my father had, I'd inherited it. Maybe not as bad. For several years I managed to keep that sickness at bay. In high school, I went to parties, but I never drank too much for fear of my mother finding out.

Of course, in the immediate aftermath of my mother's death—with the world suddenly feeling vast and unruly, hell-bent on destroying me next—I'd gone to a party and gotten plastered, started making suicidal statements that landed me in a psychiatric facility. It was only two weeks, and in those two weeks I'd managed to reset, to focus again on life. But at discharge I remembered that I no longer had anyone in my life, that I was completely and utterly alone.

Fortunately, distant relatives took me in. They gave me a place to stay. They fed me, clothed me, took me on vacations, though I never really felt like I belonged, like a puzzle piece that just won't click into place no matter how many ways you twist it around. Plus, it didn't help that I'd stay out late and go to parties and come home early in the morning smelling of booze and sex. My relatives were concerned, but they remembered what all I had been through and didn't push too hard, fearing I might have another breakdown.

In college, it got worse. There were nights I'd get blackout drunk, but it was college, so nobody really thought much of it. I had no family or close friends looking out for me. At least not until I met Joe.

Then later, once we'd moved to Bowden, once Joe and I had decided to buy that empty building and turn it into a bar, I'd drink here and there on the job, sometimes just a shot to keep me going, but never once did I become drunk at work, not once.

What finally made me stop—what opened my eyes to my father's sickness that had so maliciously spread through my veins—was when I was driving Bronwyn home one night many years ago and almost passed out behind the steering wheel.

The car swerved off the road and almost hit a house, but I managed to yank the steering wheel at the last second. Because there was some damage, the police got involved, and because the police got involved, so did Joe.

By then we were no longer together. Joe had gone to work at the municipal building a few years back as the town's administrator and zoning officer. He was still a silent partner in the Wonderwall but no longer came in every day like before.

It was at the municipal building where Joe had met Emma. That was around the time it became clear to me that he and I were not destined to get married. That despite wearing the engagement ring he'd given me, five years was more than enough time to know nothing was going to come of it, and I was actually okay with that.

Marriage, I knew, would complicate things.

Plus—and this was something I realized much later, a revelation that must have been drifting just beneath the surface of my subconscious—the idea of marriage terrified me. I knew Joe and I were not my parents, but I remembered all the fights they'd had, the heavy silences that would grow between them, how it was clear that whatever love they had once shared for one another had curdled, and I didn't want our daughter to grow up in that same toxic environment.

When Joe found out I'd nearly crashed the car due to being drunk, he flipped out. Threatened to take full custody of Bronwyn.

I promised right then and there I would stop drinking. I was still running the Wonderwall and wasn't about to go into rehab—I kept telling myself it wasn't *that* bad—but I did start drinking less and less. Forgoing the morning shot of vodka to get me going.

For a couple of years, I wasn't drinking anything at all.

Then I started with a glass or two of wine every night after work. Nothing bad seemed to happen. I told myself as long as I drank at home and never got behind the wheel of a car, it was okay.

Because despite my father's sickness, I am not my father's daughter.

A glass of pinot noir or chardonnay after a long night at work? Nothing wrong with that.

So now I fill a glass and wander into the living room and turn on the TV.

I drain the glass faster than I probably should, still kicking myself for saying what I said to Kenny. I owe the man an apology, though who knows when I'll run into him. Usually, when I see him, he's driving past in his police car.

I debate whether or not I could use a second glass and then pour one without really thinking.

Soft light from the TV bounces around the dark living room, just reruns and infomercials. Marie Osmond gushing about Nutrisystem, a perky brunette in a bright-pink sports bra promising me a great work-out at home, and when an ad for Clegg & Hawthorne, a regional law firm, comes on, it's then that I realize my second glass is empty.

I could probably go for a third glass but decide to head to bed instead. I rinse the glass in the sink and set it aside and then turn off the lights and drift down the hallway.

As always, I pause outside my daughter's bedroom door. Reach for the knob, hesitant, telling myself I'm being silly but knowing that I have no choice.

Turn the knob. Open the door, enough so that a ribbon of light from the hallway falls across the bed.

The empty bed.

Of course it's empty. It's been that way for nearly a year now. Bronwyn disappeared homecoming weekend, not long after what happened at the pep rally, and nobody has seen or heard from her since.

But still, every night I hold out hope that the bed won't be empty. That one night my daughter will be there, lying on her side. That when the light streams in, it will fall on her face, and she will open her eyes and say the one word that will break me.

Mom?

I close the door with a snap, shaking my head. Just how much longer will I hold out hope that she'll come back? Just how much longer will I kid myself into thinking that my daughter wants anything to do with me or her father or this shitty town?

Soon I've stripped out of my clothes and am crawling into bed.

I connect the charging cable to the iPhone and set it on the bedside table.

I lie on my back and stare up at the ceiling and start counting backward from one hundred. I forget when, but I learned that that's more effective than taking an Ambien. Especially when you have a glass or two or three of wine in your system.

Eventually I drift off to sleep.

I don't dream—but I do wake up to a nightmare when the soft ding of my phone alerts me to the first text message.

2

Jessica

A Year Ago

One Day after the Pep Rally

Walk of shame.

Those were the words clanging around my head as I hurried out of Steven Clark's town house that Saturday morning. I was wearing the same clothes I had worn last night, my hair was a mess, and as I darted for my car, I felt like the entire apartment complex was watching me—maybe even a classmate of my daughter's, recognizing Wyn Hayden's mom scurrying to her car like some floozy.

Part of me knew I was overreacting—I was a forty-year-old woman, for Christ's sake—but another part was furious at what had just taken place.

I'd known Steven for the past several years, and when he'd separated from his wife and started the divorce proceedings, our casual acquaintance became more than friendly. That usually meant ending up back at my place, when my daughter wasn't home, or back at his place, once he'd signed the lease on the town house. We didn't date so much as hook up, and the arrangement worked for both of our busy schedules. Plus, he wasn't interested in another serious relationship, and after all those years with Joe, I had never felt the need to get into another serious relationship of my own.

Our hookups ebbed and flowed. There were times I would see him out with other women. Then a few months would pass and he would text me and we would start talking again, and soon one of us would end up at the other's place.

But I had never stayed over, not once, until last night.

I unlocked my car and slid into my seat and slammed the door shut. I glared up at Steven's town house, as though he was watching from one of the windows, but if he was, I didn't see him.

My iPhone was dead—it was an older model and the battery life sucked—so I started the car and plugged it in.

Soon it powered itself on, the Apple logo flashing on the screen, and then I saw the phone searching for service.

At once, notifications came in. A few emails, both personal (mostly daily deals from Amazon and Target and Kohl's) and work, some breaking-news alerts from CNN and the *New York Times*, but that was it.

No text messages from Bronwyn. Not even a voicemail.

I sighed and glanced back at the town house.

I wasn't sure why I was upset about what had just happened there. Steven and I had never kidded ourselves into believing we had anything real. If anything, we simply had been using each other for sex.

And so when Steven came into the bar last night, seeking me out, we had started flirting, having instantly fallen back into that familiar rhythm, and it was not long after that when I told my assistant manager I was leaving and then followed Steven back to his place.

We drank a bottle of wine, had sex, and then we drank another bottle of wine and had even more sex, and it got to the point that it wasn't safe for me to drive home, so Steven encouraged me to stay over.

So I had.

No big deal. Waking up in his bed wasn't a problem. He'd even gotten up before me to make breakfast.

And it was there, while we sat at his tiny kitchen table, the plates of bacon and eggs and toast spread out before us, freshly brewed coffee steaming in mugs, that Steven confessed to me that he and his ex-wife had been talking off and on for weeks now and it looked like they were going to get back together.

Sometimes people just keep finding each other, he said. *Even after they go through a pretty ugly divorce.*

I'd realized then what last night was. Not just any ordinary hookup. This was a one-and-done thing. Steven hadn't been to the Wonderwall in months, and then all of a sudden he'd shown up looking for me, and we eventually ended up back at his place, where I stayed the night, and then he waited until the morning to drop the bomb that he was getting back together with his ex-wife.

I'd called him an asshole. Said that he knew he was getting back together with his ex-wife and had just wanted one last fuck with somebody else. Steven denied this, trying to defuse the situation, but I'd gathered my things, quickly dressed, and then hurried out the door.

And now here I sat in my car, the engine purring, not sure what I should do next.

I was still shaking. Worried that if I started driving in my current state, I might do something stupid.

I glanced back down at my phone. Went to Messages and tapped on my daughter's name.

I often worked late, but I always came home, even if I strolled in after 2:00 a.m. If Bronwyn wasn't staying over at a friend's, she would be home, and she would see my bag and keys on the kitchen table and know that I was home and would sleep in, as I normally did on the weekends.

But the past two months had been hard on my daughter, ever since her best friend, Taylor Mitchell, had died in an accident. Bronwyn had become more distant. More closed off.

It was almost 9:30 a.m. now, which meant she would have already gotten up. I'd like to think as soon as she saw I wasn't home she would have sent me a text message asking if I was okay.

I typed out a quick text—Hey, just wanted to check in—and hit the white arrow circled in blue to send it.

I could see the message was trying to send; usually within a second or two it showed as delivered. Sometimes it took longer, depending on whether I had a good signal.

But here it looked like the message went through but wasn't delivered.

Which meant . . . what, exactly?

Maybe she'd turned off her phone. Or maybe she'd blocked my number. She'd done that once after one of our spats. And Thursday night—just two nights ago—we'd had one major spat.

I set my phone aside and closed my eyes, drew in a deep breath. I was no longer shaking so badly. My sudden fury had begun to subside.

It wasn't that I'd expected much out of my relationship with Steven. In fact, even to call it a relationship was laughable. But his knowing when he'd come to the bar last night that he was getting back together with his ex-wife and still inviting me back to his place . . .

Stop. No more thinking about it. I was done. If I really wanted to cause trouble, I would contact Steven's as-of-right-now ex-wife, let her know whom he had spent the night with, but what was the point? I never wanted to see him again. She could have him.

I put the car in gear and headed home.

Bronwyn and I lived in a ranch house near the edge of town. A woodsy area, with only a handful of homes along the road. Our closest neighbor was maybe a half mile away.

The house had one garage, and it was there that I always parked. Which meant when Bronwyn was home, she parked her decade-old Ford Escort in the pavement-cracked driveway.

Her car wasn't there that morning.

Which didn't necessarily mean anything. Maybe she was covering the morning shift at Shepherd's Market, the grocery store where she'd worked as a cashier the past year. Or maybe she had stayed over at a friend's house.

Bronwyn had friends besides Taylor, though none immediately came to mind. The older she got, the more she didn't like talking about her social life. I guessed most girls growing up experience this with their mothers, but I'd never had the chance, so I couldn't really tell whether or not this was normal teenage behavior.

I parked in the garage and let myself in through the laundry room. I wanted to strip out of my clothes immediately, throw them in the washer. I felt unclean after my time with Steven. And guilty. I kept telling myself it wasn't my fault—there was no way I could have known—but still I felt I should have known better.

I needed a shower. I headed through the kitchen and down the hallway toward my bedroom—but paused when I noticed that Bronwyn's door was slightly ajar.

In the larger scheme of things, it didn't mean anything. Sometimes doors just didn't properly shut. Especially if you were in a hurry and pulled a door closed behind you and didn't wait the extra second or two to make sure it latched.

But for the past two years, my daughter's door was always closed. Whether she was inside it or not.

I couldn't remember the last time I'd been inside. Her walls, when she was little, had been adorned with butterflies. Bronwyn had loved them as a kid. She'd had a childlike fascination about them, how they went from a caterpillar to a cocoon to a beautiful butterfly.

A butterfly, my daughter once said, was the most perfect animal in the world.

Joe had helped me paint the room with butterflies, but that had been years ago, definitely over a decade by now, and since then Bronwyn's fascination with butterflies had waned, as childhood passions tend to do.

She'd tacked posters up around the room, mostly of her music idols—Taylor Swift and Billie Eilish and Lana Del Rey and Alicia Keys and Amy Winehouse—and on the rare occasions I had looked inside, I'd caught glimpses of those fading butterflies that hadn't been covered over, forever frozen in place on the walls.

I thought of butterflies now as I pushed open my daughter's bedroom door.

Because that's what I felt inside my stomach.

A fluttering of uneasy butterflies, their wings moving so fast I had to grip the doorframe as I looked inside the room.

I may not have been inside her room in a while, but I knew what should have been there.

The laptop Joe had purchased her for Christmas last year on her desk. Her piano keyboard in the corner. Her guitar. Most of her clothes, which either hung in her closet or lay chaotically folded in her bureau drawers.

They all should have been there, all in their specific places, but they weren't.

And as those butterflies kept fluttering even more wildly, like the kind that would start a hurricane across the globe, an unsettling truth hit me smack in the face.

My daughter was gone.

3

Wyn

Day of the Pep Rally

On a typical school day, Wyn would wake up around 6:30 a.m.

When she was younger, she had no problem rolling out of bed, often excited for the upcoming school day. Of course, as was the case with most things, school had eventually lost its allure, and ever since she'd started high school three years ago, she often found herself smacking the Snooze button on her phone at least three times before finally crawling out from under her sheets to take a shower.

There had even been a few times when she skipped a shower in lieu of an extra fifteen minutes of sleep, after staying up late reading an e-book or watching YouTube videos on her phone. Her mom had been much stricter when Wyn was younger—a couple of times even having the audacity to take Wyn's phone away from her—but since then she and her mom had come to an understanding. Which was basically that Wyn stayed out of her mom's business, and her mom stayed out of hers.

Wyn loved her mom—there was no question about that—but she was seventeen years old, almost a woman, and so the less hassle her mom gave her, the better for their overall relationship.

That didn't mean they still didn't argue from time to time. Like last night, when they'd had a near blowout over her mom's favorite topic: Wyn going to college.

She knew her dad wanted her to go to college too, but he wasn't in her life as much since he had his own family. Which was fine, really, because Wyn thought he'd done everything he could when she was growing up, keeping a room for her at his house on the nights Wyn wanted to visit and stay over. At first it had been fun, going to sporting events and other activities with her half siblings, but eventually it became awkward, and Wyn stopped reaching out to her dad, always finding an excuse not to call him back or hang out with him every time he asked.

So one could assume the reason she was wide awake at 6:00 a.m. was due to the argument from last night, but that wasn't the case.

Sure, Wyn was still irritated at her mom about the whole thing—she'd gotten the sense her mom didn't believe Wyn could make it as a songwriter, that she was crushing Wyn's dreams, which, okay, seemed a bit overdramatic but that's how it felt, at least in the moment—but the real reason Wyn's sleep had been restless and why she found herself staring up at her ceiling at six o'clock in the morning was the steady drip of adrenaline coursing through her veins at the knowledge that today was the day.

The day Wyn had been anticipating for over a month.

The day she had also been dreading.

In her head, Taylor's voice whispered to her.

Nothing to worry about. You've got this, babe.

Even though she knew it wasn't really Taylor's voice, Wyn still found herself smiling. It may have just been her own thoughts, but she remembered Taylor saying the same thing at times when Wyn had grown anxious.

Taylor Mitchell. The most popular girl in school. The most beautiful. The most likable. The one everybody loved.

Taylor Mitchell, whom Wyn had known since they were in preschool, and who had stayed close to Wyn throughout the years, even when their social trajectories had begun to diverge, like two adjacent asteroids that were knocked off course, never to see each other again.

In most teenage friendships, that would have happened. Taylor would have gone her way, Wyn would have gone hers. In any other case, their friendship would have ended years ago. They just didn't move in the same circles. Not with Taylor becoming head cheerleader and always sitting with the cool kids during lunch and getting invited to all the parties.

Despite all that, Taylor had remained her close friend.

Maybe, Wyn thought, the reason Taylor had stayed so close to her for so long was simply out of principle.

That she saw herself as the more virtuous one. The popular girl who could buck the system—who could stay friends with her best friend from elementary school—and nobody would make a peep.

The idea made Wyn queasy. It sometimes popped into her head when she felt most vulnerable. Especially in the last year, when Taylor was still alive. Back when they still hung out on the weekends. Taylor had been dating Sean Heller, high school quarterback, because in high school the head cheerleader always dates the quarterback.

But still, Taylor had always found time for Wyn, even when things were going hot and heavy with Sean. *Especially* when things were going hot and heavy with Sean. Taylor had told her one night that she didn't trust anyone else the way she trusted Wyn. Her oldest friend. Her best friend. The friend she knew she could count on the most.

Which was why Wyn was extra nervous this Friday morning.

Today was the start of homecoming weekend. The pep rally was slated for later today. She'd already spoken to Principal Webber about what she wanted to do—her way to best honor Taylor's memory—and she'd been given the green light.

The entire school would be there. As would Sean, who had graduated last year and started at Penn State just last month.

As she finally sat up in bed, grabbing her phone to check her notifications, Wyn smiled because she knew Sean had no idea what was coming.

Nobody did, and that somehow made the knowledge of what she planned to do even sweeter.

But then, just as quickly, the smile disappeared.

One of the notifications was from her YouTube channel. A comment left on the most recent video she'd uploaded. A song that she had cheekily titled "Untitled."

The video had 278 views. Not a ton for a video uploaded just over two months ago—right before Taylor's accident—but she knew it wasn't terrible either.

At least, she didn't think so.

The video had eleven likes, but it had sixty-eight dislikes.

One more dislike than from yesterday.

Yesterday, there had been only one comment, which was from Taylor.

Sounds great, Wyn! ☺☺☺

Hers had been the only comment because Wyn had deleted the rest. Just as she knew she would have to delete this new comment left sometime in the middle of the night.

The username was a mishmash of letters and numbers. A troll account. Wasn't even worth reporting as harassment or bullying, which most of these comments were. Wyn had reported a few in the past, but nothing ever came of it. The troll would just delete the account and create a new one to keep leaving nasty comments on her videos.

She didn't know if it was the same person; she suspected it was a handful of the same kids from school, probably the cheerleaders who were jealous of Wyn because she'd been Taylor's best friend. Before, when Taylor was alive, those girls knew better than to mess with Wyn. They'd been on their best behavior. Even waving to her in the hallway between classes and inviting her to their parties. But now that Taylor was gone . . .

Jealousy sometimes makes people do crazy things.

Also nasty things.

The new comment had been left at just after 1:00 a.m. last night.

worst voice I've ever heard. sounds like a goat being tortured. somebody needs to put it out of its misery. the goat 2.

In her head, the Taylor voice spoke up.

They're just haters, Wyn. You do you. Crush this.

She *would* crush this. She would crush this so hard that nobody would know what hit them. Especially Sean Heller.

Wyn deleted the comment. She started to set the phone aside but then opened Twitter.

A direct message from Onyx Butterfly was waiting for her.

Good luck today! I know you're going to kill it ☺

The smile touched Wyn's lips again. Her eyes lifted to the far wall, which was plastered with posters. Many of the butterflies her parents had painted years ago were hidden behind those posters, but one in particular she'd made sure not to cover.

There was a period in middle school when she'd felt ostracized by almost everybody in the school, excluding Taylor. In retrospect, it had just been a feeling—a weird, utterly off-the-wall feeling—but for about a week or so, Wyn had felt like nobody understood her and everybody was making fun of her behind her back. And so one day at home she'd gotten mad and taken a black ink pen and started coloring in one of the butterflies. Her intention had been to color in all of them, but as soon as she'd finished the first, she'd taken a step back and gazed at the butterfly and realized it was now completely different from all the rest.

That was how she felt, she realized. Like an ugly duckling. A black swan.

One of her recent spelling tests had included the word *onyx*, and Wyn had thought it sounded cool, so that's what she decided to call the butterfly: Onyx Butterfly. Then, years later, when she began writing songs—when she felt bold enough to start posting the finished songs online—she named one of her very first songs "Onyx Butterfly."

It wasn't one of her best songs but it had been a strong early contender for sure, and so she hadn't been tempted to delete it like some of the others.

And, well, apparently one of her fans—and to even contemplate the notion that she had fans was insane—had felt so enamored by the song that they'd created a Twitter account with that username and, not too long after Taylor's death, had followed Wyn and started communicating with her via direct message.

At first, Wyn had worried that the person behind the account was another troll and that their entire purpose was to make her life a living hell, but the more they communicated back and forth—about their favorite music, their favorite movies, their favorite books, then just about their days in general—it was clear that a true connection had started to materialize.

Wyn had even hinted at the fact that she had something significant planned for the pep rally, though she couldn't bring herself to let Onyx Butterfly know even the most basic details.

Now, realizing that the morning was ticking by, Wyn replied—thanks so much i will keep you posted—and then closed her phone.

She'd sometimes skip a shower for an extra fifteen minutes, but not today. Today may very well be the most important day of her life.

Plus, before school, she needed to make a stop.

4

Jessica

Now

The house is an impressive two-story Cape Cod with brick siding and white trim and flower boxes in front of each window. Joe and Emma built it six years ago, right before Amanda was born. I had been inside only a handful of times, and every time I would marvel that the house Joe often talked about living in had become a reality.

When Joe and I moved to Bowden, we didn't have much savings, and the combined amount of our school loans was so insanely high that just thinking about it often put a sour taste in the back of my throat.

Joe's parents, who lived in town, offered to help out where they could, but they were struggling too, and the last thing Joe and I wanted to do was add more debt onto their already buckling shoulders, so we opted for the cheapest place we could get.

There was a trailer park situated on the other end of town, what the locals had christened Little Texas, as all the lanes were named after cities in the Lone Star State. We had looked at a trailer there, had almost decided to go for it, when we received word of a ranch home suddenly available toward the other end of town. A quiet wooded area with a large backyard and nice patio—it seemed perfect.

"Quaint," Joe called it, after we'd done a walk-through. Then later, after we'd signed the lease (our intention being to rent to own), he'd taken me into his arms and kissed me on the lips and whispered, "This is only temporary, Jess. One of these days we'll build a house. A big, beautiful house."

Of course, many years later we started drifting apart. I still cared for Joe, just as he still cared for me. But he eventually found someone else, someone he cared for even more, and so that was why we finally stopped pretending we would someday marry. I let Joe go, just as he let me go. He married Emma, and they had Amanda, and then, two years later, they had Trent.

A happy little family living in a happy little house with a manicured lawn that has a Colvin for Congress sign planted front and center.

I've been sitting here now in my car for the past ten minutes, just parked in the driveway, staring at the house like a stalker. I'm surprised Joe hasn't noticed me yet. Or Emma. She is the more observant of the two. I haven't had much interaction with her over the years, but I have to admit I like her.

Okay, enough. No more stalling.

My mind has been going a hundred miles a second ever since I received the first text from Bronwyn. I could have called Joe, could have told him to come to the house, but I didn't want to be there—not in that dark, sad place. So I dressed and got in my car and drove straight here.

Now I open my door, start to get out, but I realize my legs are shaking so badly that if I do attempt to stand, I'll just fall right down on my ass.

So I give it a minute. Give it two minutes. Just sitting there with the car door open, one foot flat against the driveway, one hand still squeezing the steering wheel.

The front door opens. Emma steps out.

Even at seven o'clock in the morning, she looks flawless. Still in her midthirties, slight and fit and carries herself like the confident mother she has always wanted to be.

She's wearing pajama bottoms and an undershirt, slippers on her feet, and she squints at me from the doorway.

"Jessica?"

She doesn't speak at a normal tone, not this early in the morning. The kids might still be asleep. Or not. Maybe they're already up. Maybe she's been making them breakfast. Pancakes and sausage with real maple syrup. They have always struck me as the kind of family that'll have a hearty breakfast every Saturday. Sitting around the kitchen table, no electronics in sight, while they joke and laugh.

"Jessica, are you all right?"

That's when Joe appears behind her. He, too, is wearing pajama bottoms and an undershirt. Only his bottoms are blue, while Emma's are yellow. So not quite matching. Just the thought makes me want to laugh out loud because I don't know what else to do.

Joe steps past Emma onto the porch. He tells her to go back inside. She hesitates, clearly uneasy with the situation, but she turns and retreats back into the house without a word.

I watch Joe as he comes down the walkway cautiously. I've never shown up at his house like this, especially at this time of the morning. Joe knows I typically work late and that mornings are my least favorite time of day.

"Jess, what's wrong?"

He stops only a couple of feet away. Just stands there watching me, his hands on his hips. He's a good-looking man, even at forty-one, but he has lost a lot of weight since the last time I saw him. What has it been now—five months? Six?

Suddenly I think about my mother, how the cancer had stripped her of all her strength, had turned her into a shadow of the resilient woman she once was, and I want to ask Joe if he's okay. I even take a breath, open my mouth, but I can't speak.

Joe takes a step forward, his ocean-gray eyes focused on me. There were times in the past when I loved staring into his eyes. I had once told him it was like looking into another universe. I'm pretty sure I was drunk at the time.

When I still don't speak—still just sitting there, one foot on the driveway, the other in the car, my body visibly shaking—Joe crouches down next to me, places a hand on my knee.

"Jess."

I blink. Stare back at him. Open my mouth, but again no words come out.

I don't need words, I realize. At least not yet. Not to get this started.

I open my phone and shove it at him. Joe isn't expecting it and nearly fumbles the phone, and for an instant I think it's going to slip through his fingers, that the screen will crack into a hundred little shards and that my lifeline to my daughter will be severed.

But he manages to grip the phone tight, and then stares down at the screen.

"What am I looking at?"

I reach out, tap the Messages app.

"Scroll to the top."

My voice doesn't sound like my own. It sounds like it belongs to a desperate woman. To a lunatic.

Frowning, Joe uses his finger to scroll to the very top. But those are older messages, I realize, the messages I'd sent to Bronwyn after she went missing. The ones that were never delivered.

"Here," I tell him, taking back the phone, and despite my trembling hands, I find the spot where the first text message came in only hours ago and then practically fling it back at him.

He's becoming impatient, but he has dealt with me in manic moments like this and knows that the best way to handle me is to do as I say. So he looks down at the phone and starts reading the text messages—the first three that had come through early this morning, and then all the rest.

A storm of emotion builds across his face. First confusion, then curiosity, before quickly morphing into panic and dread.

"Jesus Christ," he whispers.

I see that his hand, too, is trembling. His gaze shifts to meet mine, his gaunt face suddenly pale.

"A cop." His voice shakes, almost lost to the storm surging through him. "Our daughter . . . has been abducted . . . by a *cop*?"

5

Jessica

One Day after the Pep Rally

Fifteen minutes after I placed my first call, Joe arrived, and fifteen minutes after that, Officer Carter Redcross eased his police cruiser into the driveway.

He was a medium-size man in his fifties, with a bit of a gut and thinning hair that he kept very short. He was a decent man who had lived in town most of his life, had a wife and three children, two of whom were already in college, and he always carried himself like a man who sincerely cared about the rule of law and making sure to protect those who couldn't protect themselves.

"Tony called me," he said, standing on the front porch in his light-gray uniform, his black shoes so shiny they had probably been polished that morning.

Joe and I invited him in. We showed him to Bronwyn's bedroom, and he stood in the doorway for about a minute, his hands on his hips, staring into the room as though absorbing every detail. Then he cleared his throat, turned back around—and I saw the truth on his face before he even opened his mouth.

"You think she ran away," I said.

Carter shook his head. "I haven't made a determination, one way or another. What time did you notice she was gone?"

"About an hour ago. I called Joe, who came right over, and then he called Tony, who called you."

My voice had begun to quiver, those butterflies in my stomach still not having calmed down. I felt Joe put his hand on my back, warm and solid, holding me steady. It was almost intimate, something he would have done decades ago when we'd first started dating, just to touch me and not because he feared I might lose it.

"She deleted her social media," Joe said, almost blurted.

Carter arched an eyebrow at him. "Excuse me?"

"All of her social media accounts. Her Facebook and Twitter and Instagram and TikTok and YouTube. They're all gone."

I had to admit this was one of the more disturbing developments of the past hour. Our daughter was a red-blooded American teenager, which meant she lived and breathed on social media. Especially on her YouTube channel, where she would upload videos of the songs she wrote and performed.

A teenager's social media is practically sacred, one of the few things in life they've molded from nothing, and deleting not just one account but all of them . . . I didn't even want to consider what it meant.

"What can you do?" Joe asked, his voice ticking into desperation.

Carter lifted his hand, rubbed the back of his neck. It was clear that he wasn't quite sure how to begin. We'd known Carter for almost fifteen years, give or take, and while he wasn't necessarily a friend—at least not to me—he was friendly with us and didn't want to add any undue stress to our lives, but he also wanted to be honest.

"When was the last time either of you saw your daughter?"

Joe said, "For me, it's probably been a week or two."

There was a tinge of disappointment in his voice, a pinch of regret, as if he'd just realized it had been that long since he'd last seen his daughter and that he might never see her again.

No, a voice spoke up in my head. *Don't think that. Of course you'll see her again.*

Carter nodded at Joe's response, as though he'd expected no less—the man knew Joe had a family of his own and that our daughter lived with me—and then his gaze flicked over to meet mine, and I found myself looking away, suddenly ashamed.

"The last time I saw her was Thursday night," I said quietly. "We had an argument."

This perked up Carter's ears.

He said, "Can you tell me what the argument was about?"

I glanced over at Joe, who was now watching me curiously. I shrugged.

"It was just an argument. We had them every once in a while. But this one . . . this one got heated."

Joe shifted on his feet, folded his arms over his chest. His brow had furrowed, and I realized I was now being judged for my parenting skills.

"What?" I said to him. "The argument was about college. You've talked to her about it before, I'm sure."

"I have, but it never became . . . *heated.* What happened?"

"Well, you know how she wants to become a singer-songwriter. I told her it's great to have dreams but that she needs to have realistic dreams, especially since she still suffers from stage fright. That didn't go over well. I think she thought I was questioning her talent. I told her she needed to go to college, that she needed to at least *apply* to colleges, and that's what really pissed her off. That's what started the shouting and the screaming. I can't remember the last time we had an argument like that. Not about boys. Or her schoolwork. Or, well, anything. But this . . . this set her off. She said that she hated living with me. Said that after graduation she plans to pack her bags and leave town, go to New York or Los Angeles or Nashville or *somewhere* that's not here. And then she threw out how I never call her by her preferred name, like I'm doing it on purpose."

Carter had started taking notes on a small pad. Now he glanced up at me.

"Her preferred name?"

"Wyn," Joe said. "She likes to be called Wyn."

Carter said to me, "And what do you call her?"

"I've just always called her by her full name. But it's not like I was ever doing it on purpose." I paused, and frowned. "You don't think that's why she ran away, do you?"

"I'm not sure what to think right now," Carter said. "But you said she told you after graduation she plans to pack her bags and leave town. What's to say she didn't decide to do it sooner than later?"

Before Joe or I could answer, Tony Parsons arrived. The police chief rang the doorbell and then knocked on the screen door before opening it without invitation.

Concern filled his broad face, and for some reason seeing it here, in this home that suddenly felt so empty, I nearly burst into tears. But I tamped them down, gritting my teeth and twisting my lips up into a smile that no doubt looked like a grimace.

"How are you two holding up so far?" Tony asked.

Joe simply nodded and thanked Tony for coming out. Then Carter showed him Bronwyn's room, and Tony did the same thing Carter had done not too long ago: stood with his hands on his hips, staring into the room, taking in every detail before he turned back around and released a heavy breath.

"You both know about what happened at the pep rally yesterday, don't you?"

The question sent a shiver of disgust snaking through me. While we'd waited for Carter, Joe had shown me one of the videos posted online; he'd said that somebody had notified him of it last night and that he'd attempted to reach out to our daughter, with no answer.

I couldn't get it out of my memory fast enough. And it wasn't just Bronwyn's humiliation, which was bad enough, but the laughter that immediately followed from some of the students in the gymnasium.

Joe said, "We're aware of what happened at the pep rally, yes. What are you implying?"

Tony shifted uncomfortably in his boots, ringing a thumb through one side of his belt to hitch up his pants. The only time I'd dealt with Tony in any professional capacity had been a few years earlier, when some college kids had broken into the Wonderwall to steal liquor, and he'd involved himself personally because he and his wife used to frequent the restaurant before his wife had started showing severe signs of Alzheimer's.

"I'm not implying anything," Tony said. "But it's obvious your daughter packed up much of her belongings. I imagine you've tried calling—"

I answered before he could even complete the sentence, practically spitting the words out.

"Of course we've tried calling her. We've tried texting her, but the messages don't seem to go through."

His heavy brow creased at this. "What does that mean?"

I explained about sending text messages from iPhone to iPhone, how they'll show a user when their messages have been delivered and sometimes when they've been read (a feature Bronwyn had promptly turned off on her phone), and his eyes lit up with understanding.

"Sorry," he said, giving me a smile. "I'm an Android guy."

He was trying to lighten the mood, which I might have appreciated under normal circumstances, but the longer we stood here doing nothing, the higher my level of anxiety inched up.

"Can't you trace her phone or put out an APB or whatever on her car?"

Tony and Carter exchanged a thoughtful glance, the many years of working closely together having created a wordless bond, and Tony nodded again.

"We can certainly try to ping her cell phone. We're gonna need to get a warrant for that, of course. As for her car, we can certainly send out an alert for all officers to keep an eye out."

Carter said, "I can also reach out to Steven Clark over at First National."

Hearing the name of the man whose bed I'd woken up in this morning nearly made me jump. I certainly hadn't been expecting it, but when Carter saw the confusion on my face—what he thankfully took as confusion, at least—he elaborated.

"The ATM faces the main highway out of town. Assuming your daughter left in that direction, we can use the security feed from the camera in the ATM to pinpoint a time frame. It'll at least give us something to work with."

"Speaking of cameras," Tony said, his eyes focusing on something behind us, "it looks like you've got your own security cameras in here."

I turned and traced his gaze to the tiny camera set up on the bookcase in the living room. It oversaw that portion of the house like a gargoyle, its fish-eye always recording the interior—except when it wasn't.

I shook my head. "I know what you're thinking, and it won't help."

Both Tony and Carter looked genuinely perplexed.

"How can that possibly be?" Carter said. "I saw one of those cameras at the front door too. Don't any of them work?"

Joe said, "They work, but not when either Jess or Wyn are home."

When the police chief and officer frowned at him, Joe offered up a helpless shrug.

"That's how we set it up a couple years back," he said. Then, glancing over at me: "Unless you ended up changing the security settings."

"No," I said, wishing now that I had. Confusion still shadowed the two men's faces, so I did my best to explain. "After that break-in at the Wonderwall, I realized it would probably be good to get cameras set up in here too. I mean, it helped to figure out who'd broken into the place. But I just . . . I don't know. I get paranoid with the idea of cameras constantly watching me. It's one thing at the bar—we need those going constantly for liability and security—but at home? No way."

Tony shifted again, a little less uncomfortably now, and folded his arms over his protruding belly.

"So let me get this straight," he said. "You set it up so the cameras turn off when either you or your daughter are home?"

I nodded. "The system senses the apps on our phones. When we're close enough to connect to Wi-Fi, the cameras shut off. Well, except for the one at the front door."

Carter said, "Well, what are we doing standing here? Let's see when the cameras turned off. That'll help us with a time frame. Plus, we should be able to see when she pulls into the driveway from the door camera."

I wanted to kick myself. *Of course* we could see what time Bronwyn had come home based on when the cameras turned off.

The computer sat on the desk in the corner of the living room. I powered it up, and then a minute later I was online and accessing the security feed from last night.

At just after midnight, all three cameras—the one in the living room, the one in the kitchen, and the one in the hallway—went dark.

The cameras stayed dark for the next twenty minutes, and then they blinked back on, as if waking from a nap.

Tony said, "That didn't happen to be you, did it?"

"I was still at work," I said, staring at the computer screen. The very last thing I wanted to do was tell these men how I'd stayed over at Steven Clark's town house last night. "We get busy Friday night."

Carter asked, "What time did you get home?"

I hesitated. Wondering whether I should tell them the truth. That I hadn't returned home until early this morning.

"After two o'clock or so," I said finally.

Already I was sensing the world tilting out of my control. A drop of black ink splashing into my conscience. Soon the ink would start to spread, and the lies would pile up, and then where would I be?

Carter said, "Now how about we see the front door."

I clicked over to that screen, went back to about eleven o'clock, and then tapped the button to speed up the running time so that we were watching life breeze by.

A few cars came and went—our neighbors down the road or those just passing through—but at no point did a car pull into the driveway.

At least, the headlights of a car didn't pass over the front lawn.

From the angle of the camera by the door, the driveway was mostly obscured. The purpose of the front-door camera was to see who was standing at the front door.

When Joe and I had installed the camera—Joe having come over to help with the technical stuff because that wasn't my forte—neither of us had been worried about seeing the driveway.

"Hmm."

Tony Parsons made the noise thoughtfully, his lips pressed together, though it was clear there was something uncertain lurking just beneath it.

Carter said, "Strange she didn't have the headlights on, huh?"

Tony nodded, still watching the screen even though I'd paused the video. It had gone past 1:00 a.m. anyway. We already knew by then that Bronwyn had left.

Plus, I didn't want them to wonder why my car's headlights wouldn't eventually show around 2:00 a.m., when I told them I'd returned home.

Another drop of black ink.

Tony said, "Have you called around to Wyn's friends, to her work, to anybody she might have gone to stay with?"

I glanced at Joe, and he glanced at me. We'd been so racked with worry that the thought hadn't even crossed our minds.

"Not yet," Joe said. "But we can do that next."

Tony grunted his approval. "I think you should. Nine times out of ten in a situation like this, we find the kids staying with friends. Now, when was the last time she posted on social media? I imagine a girl her age has all different kinds of accounts."

As Carter filled him in on how our daughter had apparently deleted all her social media, Tony's face fell. He turned to look at Joe and me, and the heaviness in his expression was enough for me to feel my stomach tighten.

"Well," he said, clearing his throat, "I'm one for positive thinking, so right now I don't see any reason to get too alarmed. I've had kids run away for a day or two and then come home. Let's hope the same thing happens with your daughter."

He forced another smile, then hitched at his belt again.

"Anything else comes to mind, I don't want either of you to hesitate in calling me. Day or night. I mean it. We're gonna do what we can on our end, but I'm going to be honest with you. It's not like Wyn's a thirteen-year-old girl. She's seventeen years old—almost an adult. Now, I see it in your face, Jess, that you don't agree, and I have to admit I don't either—she's still a minor—but the way these things work, and based on what happened at the high school yesterday and the fact it looks like she's packed most of her things . . . Well, you can see why it's gonna be tough for me to make this a top priority."

Part of me wanted to shout at the man. To tell him to forget every other issue the police force in town was dealing with and focus solely on finding Bronwyn.

But then Joe's hand touched my back, and like that, the fight went out of me.

"We understand," Joe said. "Please do whatever you can."

"Oh, believe me," Tony said, "we will. We're gonna notify the state police to be on the lookout for her car. So we're gonna need the make and model and license plate number. Carter, is there anything else I'm forgetting?"

Carter was silent a moment, thinking, and then he said, "Yeah, actually there is. Do either of you have access to your daughter's bank account?"

6

Wyn

Day of the Pep Rally

The sign at the entrance to Fox Lane was stern and direct:

ROAD CLOSED

It hung off a traffic barricade. Three six-foot white-and-orange-striped boards held up by iron uprights. Two yellow LED lights had been situated on both ends of the top board, blinking lazily.

The barricade wasn't especially large, but Fox Lane wasn't a wide road, so most drivers knew better than to try to squeeze past it.

Wyn wasn't of the same mindset.

She nosed the Escort between the barricade and the edge of the road. Her passenger-side tires dug into the loose dirt and grass. Only a couple of feet, nothing more, and then she adjusted the steering wheel to get back onto the pavement.

Fox Lane wasn't even a secondary road, so it wasn't well maintained. It had probably last been paved thirty years ago. Now much of it was cracked, loose gravel smattered all throughout.

The gravel made the road especially dangerous when driving at high speeds. Kids in town—the boys, usually—would often race down the lane. Hence the reason this ragged strip of macadam had earned the name Fast Lane.

Wyn had once heard that a kid had gotten up close to ninety miles an hour for a couple of seconds before wussing out and applying the brakes.

Fox Lane was maybe a mile and a half long. It connected Frog Hollow Road and Hidden Valley Road. Frog Hollow was considered one of the main roads through town, while Hidden Valley was considered a secondary road. But a quarter mile down it led to Tobias Road, which was practically a highway in a town the size of Bowden.

The shortcut could save about a minute, but not many people bothered taking it. Mostly it was the teenagers who'd just recently gotten their driver's licenses—the lamination still warm—who tore down the road to see just how fast they could get before their nerves got the best of them and they lifted their feet off the gas pedal.

Woods surrounded Fox Lane, and there was always the threat of some animal darting out into the road. If you lost control, there was an excellent chance you'd go off the road, and since there wasn't much road to begin with, that most likely meant into a tree.

Wyn, her fingers tight around the steering wheel as the Escort coasted forward, closed her eyes.

Maybe she shouldn't have come here, after all. Not today, not with everything she had planned.

But she had to—she *had* to—and so that was why she was here, at just after seven o'clock in the morning, her car going no more than five miles an hour, the tires crunching over that loose gravel, and before she knew it, she'd reached the spot.

Fox Lane wasn't a straight shot, at least not all of it. For three-quarters of a mile or so it was, and then the road curved about thirty degrees.

Dead Man's Curve was a name Wyn had heard mentioned, though as far as she knew, nobody had actually died there. Some cars had gotten scraped when they came too close to the trees, yes, but nobody had ever flipped over or gotten smashed.

That was, not until two months ago.

As she came to the curve, her foot eased against the brake, and the car stopped.

She placed the Escort in park and then just sat there, silent, listening to the weird constant ticking of the old engine before she finally turned it off.

Morning sunlight streamed through the trees, crisscrossing shadows everywhere. Birds were in those trees, chirping their morning songs. Many of the leaves had already fallen, and those still attached to their branches were aflame with amber and gold.

She grabbed the flowers off the passenger seat. Pansies, which weren't Taylor's favorite (she had loved tulips), but they were the best Wyn could get this time of year. She'd purchased them yesterday from Shepherd's and left them in her car overnight.

Now she stepped out of the car, clutching the flowers at her side, and stared at the oak tree standing at the base of the curve.

She wondered if the tree had known when it was just a sapling that it would one day—many years later, decades later, a century later—be the cause of a young girl's death.

Of course, Wyn knew the tree wasn't at fault. It could have been any number of trees that Taylor's car might have smashed into that night. It didn't look like the tree had taken much more damage than a dent from being rammed into by a two-ton vehicle.

As Wyn approached the tree, something glinted on the ground. It was there for a second, and then it was gone. Most likely pieces of Taylor's car that hadn't been swept up after the accident. Wyn assumed the police or whoever it was had attempted to clean up as much as they could, but still slivers of glass and other pieces of the car had managed to slip through.

That glint alone nearly broke Wyn, but she pressed on. Ignoring the birds in the trees. Ignoring the part of her that wanted to second-guess her plan for today. The thing that would give Taylor's sudden and tragically premature death justice.

The soles of her sneakers crunching against the loose gravel, Wyn walked right up to the tree and placed her hand against it. She closed her eyes, listening past the birds and the quiet breeze, trying to see if she could feel anything within the tree. It had absorbed so much force, so much energy, that surely echoes of it might still be inside.

Wyn shook her head, muttered, "Don't be silly," and bent to place the flowers at the base of the tree.

That's when she heard the approaching vehicle. The quiet hum of another engine. Wheels slowly rolling over gravel.

Wyn turned and watched a red Honda Civic slow to a stop behind her car. The engine died, and the door opened, and Aaron Colvin stepped out.

Her stomach twisted at the sight of him. The boy she had known almost her entire life. The one who had always been a good friend. The one who, for the past year, had been her boyfriend.

Aaron had been her first kiss, though she'd told him that she'd kissed another boy when she was at summer camp, a total lie made up on the spot because she'd felt embarrassed thinking she was too old not to have had her first kiss yet.

And then, of course, they'd had sex. But only once. Neither of them had really known what they were doing, both having confessed to being virgins, and in the end the whole experience had been so awkward and uncomfortable that whenever Aaron tried to initiate things after that, she would always find a reason to stop.

Aaron was tall and good-looking, with wavy brown hair and blue eyes and a cute smile. But he had always been shy, and his awkwardness around girls meant that he hadn't dated much. He didn't play sports either, which was a serious blow to a high school boy's social standing, but because his father was the town mayor, he'd been accepted into the popular crowd by default. He was invited to all the cool parties, but he was never the one people hung around with, always just standing off to the side.

Taylor was the one who had gotten Aaron and Wyn together last year. Always looking for an opportunity to play matchmaker, Taylor had grinned at Wyn when she mentioned how she'd heard Aaron had a major crush on her and asked if Wyn liked Aaron too, and Wyn had said sure, she liked Aaron just fine, and the next thing she knew they were out on a double date with Taylor and Sean Heller.

"What are you doing here?" she said.

He wore jeans, his Bowden Badgers hoodie, and sneakers. And his Phillies baseball cap, the one Wyn had gotten him as a present after they'd gone down to Philadelphia to watch a game last spring. This one wasn't the traditional bright red but was instead gray, the team's logo blue and red on the front of the cap.

She still remembered the day she'd given him the hat, how excited he'd been, his eyes glowing like a kid's on Christmas morning, and how from that day forward he'd worn it every chance he got. Even now, almost two months after they'd broken up, he was still wearing the hat.

Aaron quietly shut his car door—the car in which he and Wyn had spent many a sweaty make-out session in the back seat—and walked toward her.

She said, "Did you follow me?"

Obviously he had. It was written across his face. She couldn't believe she hadn't noticed him trailing her.

"I figured you might come here," he said. "But, um, yeah, I did follow you."

Again, her stomach twisted. She didn't like being so isolated like this. Not that she didn't trust Aaron—he had always been a gentleman around her—but still she felt too open, too vulnerable.

She looked away from him, toward the trees on her left. Autumn Porter's parents' farmhouse sat on the other side of those trees. Autumn was one of the Seasons, as Wyn had dubbed her and Summer Green, both girls Wyn had grown up with and who had become cheerleaders, just like Taylor.

Autumn had admitted to seeing Taylor that night. She said that Taylor had come over to her house and that she'd appeared drunk, and that Autumn had tried to get Taylor to stay with her but that Taylor got into her car and drove away before she could stop her. Autumn said that by the time she'd gotten into her own car and tried to go after her, Taylor was long gone. Autumn told the police she'd thought Taylor had headed west, which was the direction Autumn had gone, though it turned out Taylor had gone east instead. And a quarter mile away turned off onto Fox Lane and hit the gas and drove straight into the ill-fated oak tree.

She hadn't been wearing her seat belt. The airbag, too, hadn't deployed.

The impact was enough to send her through the windshield and headfirst into the tree.

Wyn's father worked for the township. She knew that there was a chance she could have asked her father to find out exactly what had happened—how Taylor died—but she never felt comfortable crossing that particular line.

Besides, the official word was that there had been alcohol in Taylor's system. More than enough to get her drunk. She shouldn't have been anywhere near a steering wheel, let alone driving like a madwoman down Fast Lane at that time of night.

A cautionary tale. Just another sad statistic of reckless teen life. It had resulted in a school assembly the following week to remind everyone about the perils of drunk driving.

Now, watching Aaron approaching her, she said, "Stop."

He paused. Stared at her for a beat, and then frowned.

"What's wrong?"

"Your following me is what's wrong. Don't you realize just how creepy that is?"

"What do you want me to say, Wyn? I'm worried about you. You haven't returned any of my texts."

"We aren't together anymore, Aaron."

"I know that. I do. But I know it's also because of everything you've been going through since Taylor—"

He paused suddenly, his eyes shifting toward the oak tree behind her, and then shrugged.

"I just want to make sure you're okay," he said.

A flash of anger made her start moving forward, toward Aaron, though when she reached him she didn't stop and instead walked right past him.

He called after her: "Wyn, come on. I know you must be nervous about today. I thought it'd help to talk—"

That stopped her. She had already opened her door, was about to slide into her seat, but now glanced back at him.

"Why would I be nervous about today?"

"The pep rally. I know you're planning to sing."

"How do you know that?" Then, a second later: "Are you Onyx Butterfly?"

Another frown. "Onyx Butterfly? What's that? Oh, wait. Isn't that one of your songs?"

She stared at him, not sure how to respond. The idea that Onyx Butterfly was Aaron had never once crossed her mind, though in a way it made sense: Hadn't the person reached out to her right after she'd broken up with Aaron?

But right now, that was a secondary worry.

"Aaron, how do you know about me performing at the pep rally?"

He shrugged again. "I mean, there's only so much time to fit everything in. There's like a schedule. The team was told that you'd perform after the coach announces them in."

She closed her eyes. It had taken a while for her to convince Principal Webber that performing a tribute to Taylor at the pep rally was a good idea in the first place. But when he'd finally agreed, she'd stressed to him how she wanted to make her performance a surprise. Maybe he'd thought she meant a surprise to the rest of the school.

Aaron said, "I'm just worried is all."

She opened her eyes. Stared straight back at him.

He swallowed. Looked around at the trees, maybe hoping one of the birds might pause from their constant song to throw him a hint of what to say.

Finally he said, "You get stage fright. You've never performed in front of so many people before. I just . . . I'm worried."

If Wyn were being honest with herself, she was worried too. Worried about all of it. Not just her stage fright, but about what would happen later today. After the pep rally. Once the high school—the entire world—learned the truth.

"I'll be fine," she said.

She didn't wait for Aaron to say anything else. She slipped into her car, started the engine, and then drifted past him.

Wyn didn't bother looking at her ex-boyfriend as she drove past. She only glanced at the rearview mirror to see him still standing in the middle of Fox Lane, and then the road curved and he was gone.

7

Jessica

Now

mom

The word stared back at me. Not a question but a statement.

please help

More than just a statement. A plea. A plea from a daughter I hadn't seen or heard from in almost a year. A daughter whom I loved more than life itself and would do anything for.

i think he's going to kill me

That was when my sleep-and-wine-addled brain snapped itself awake. I'd been half-asleep, groggy, stuck in the no-man's-land between consciousness and unconsciousness, and those seven words were enough to rip me from that limbo.

I shot up in bed, my head pounding from the prologue of a hangover, my pulse suddenly cranked up twenty extra beats. I didn't bother responding, at least not via text message. Instead I tapped Bronwyn's name at the top of the screen, the one that gave me the options of "Audio" and "FaceTime" and "Info," and I practically punched "Audio" so hard with my finger I was surprised the screen didn't crack.

The phone to my ear, I started murmuring, "Come on, come on, come on," as the call connected.

I expected it to ring. Maybe one or two times. No more than three. And then I'd hear my daughter's voice. Her lovely, soft, familiar voice.

And I did hear her voice, but the words were the same ones I'd heard spoken more than a thousand times in the past year, every time I'd called her phone.

"Hi, it's Wyn. You know what to do."

But instead of a beep, there came an automated voice—a deeply feminine voice, as if users would better understand it, would be more likely to accept it—telling me sorry but the person I'm trying to reach has a voicemail box that was full.

The phone dinged again, and then again.

mom are you there
im scared

I typed back a reply, my fingers so frenzied and sleep heavy that I was thankful for autocorrect.

I'm here.
Where are you?

No immediate reply. I realized I was holding my breath. Staring at my phone in the dark, panic scratching its sharp claws against the inside of my skin.

Then the gray dancing dots as my daughter typed her reply.

i dont know

I closed my eyes, took a deep breath. Tried to steady my nerves. Tried to clear my mind so that I could better focus.

Who is going to kill you?

Again, no immediate reply. Ten seconds passed with just my question hanging there on the screen. And then the dots came again, and three texts shot out almost simultaneously.

i dont know his name
he never told me
he makes me call him daddy

I nearly screamed. Before I knew it, I was up out of bed, my bare feet racing across the carpet to the bedroom door. Where I was going, I didn't know, only that I couldn't stay stationary, because otherwise I was going to drive myself crazy.

The phone dinged again.

hes kept me chained up in the same room for months

I paused suddenly, realizing I had no idea where I was headed—except that I did, didn't I? I'd been heading toward the kitchen. Toward the fridge. Toward the unopened bottle of wine that sat next to the milk and orange juice.

I wanted to ask a question but wasn't sure how to word it. Not while communicating like this. Not while I already knew deep down we had limited time.

Instead, I typed: What does he look like?

tall
dark hair
dark eyes
strong
he hurts me mom

I could feel my legs wanting to give up. To let me fall right there in the middle of the hallway.

But I shook my head, shouted, "No!" and kept moving so that I now paced around the living room.

Call the police right now!

Another ten seconds or so of silence, and then my phone dinged.

cant
he did something to the phone
i can only watch videos and play games
he only lets me have it when im being a good girl
i didnt even think this was going to work
mom help me

"I'm trying," I whispered, but the problem was I had no idea what to do. They didn't teach this sort of thing in parenting classes. Or maybe they did—I never took parenting classes, only learned the old-fashioned way, as my mother had done before me and her mother before her. Trial and error. See what worked, see what didn't work, and try not to screw things up.

I closed my eyes again, took another deep breath, and then typed:

When did he take you? Where did he take you?

Those gray dots again, and then the phone dinged.

i cant remember
its been so long
mom im sorry i said i hated living with you
i didnt mean it
i was upset
i miss you so much
please help

I typed: I'm calling the police right now.
The reply was almost instantaneous.

no
he wears a badge
he is the police

And then that was it. I texted several more times, asking what kind of badge, what kind of uniform, but there was never any reply. I stared at the screen, needing to see those gray dots again, some kind of proof that my daughter was still there.

Instead, my mind had filled with terrible images.

The man who'd abducted my daughter realizing what she was doing and tearing into whatever room he'd locked her in and prying the phone from her desperate fingers and smashing it on the floor.

The man grabbing her by the hair and dragging her out of the room to do God knows what with her.

That very well may have been the final communication I'd ever have with my daughter, and I hadn't even told her that I loved her.

That was somehow the worst part.

When I realized Bronwyn wasn't going to answer again, I nearly dialed 911. But that last line kept repeating itself in my mind. If I closed my eyes, I could still see it, buzzing like a neon bar sign.

he is the police

I highly doubted whoever had taken my daughter was a police officer in town. It had been almost a year—Bronwyn could have ended up anywhere, taken by any police officer across the country.

So if I didn't call the police, then who?

That's when I realized Joe was the only person who could help me right now. The only person who might know what to do next.

I almost called him then, at five o'clock in the morning, but I wasn't sure just how the conversation would go. I could tell him what happened, but would he believe me? I was still feeling a bit hungover. He might hear a slur in my words. Would assume I was drunk again.

I needed to clean up first. Needed to take a fast shower. Gargle half a bottle of mouthwash. Then drive straight to Joe's.

And so that was what I did, which is why I'm here now, in Joe's home office, with Police Chief Tony Parsons.

I'm the only one sitting. Emma has brought me a mug of coffee, but my hands are trembling so much I'm afraid to take a sip in case I spill it.

Joe's desk is a mess of papers. In one corner of the room is a pile of yard signs, just like the one outside. COLVIN FOR CONGRESS in white letters with a blue background. Simple and direct. To the point. Just like Mayor Colvin himself.

Tony is off duty today. He's dressed in jeans and boots and a flannel shirt. It looks as though he was about to go hunting before Joe called and told him he needed to come to the house immediately.

Joe did most of the talking, though there wasn't much to say. Most of what needed to be said was on my phone. Which Tony has been poring over the past several minutes in silence. Scrolling down the chain of text messages, then scrolling back up to review them again.

Finally, he sets the phone on the edge of Joe's desk and takes a step back, crosses his arms, and stares down at the floor.

For a moment, there is a heavy silence. Then Tony clears his throat and shakes his head.

"Good Lord," he whispers.

Joe picks up the phone, scrolls back through the messages he has already read through a dozen times.

"What are our options?" he says.

Tony stares down at the carpet, thinking it over. When he finally looks up, there is sorrow in his eyes.

"Honestly, I have no idea. Your daughter could be anywhere. And if the bastard that took her is a cop . . ." He pauses, shaking his head. "We're gonna have to keep this in-house. Keep our cards very close to our chest. Bring in people we can trust one hundred percent."

"You don't trust your men one hundred percent?" I ask.

He actually looks offended by the question.

"Of course I do. But this is obviously very sensitive. Too many cooks in the kitchen and all that. This guy could be a county away. A state away. Who knows? I'm worried if we do a full court press, it will alert him to the fact that we now know your daughter's been abducted. You said you called her, right?"

"I did. It went to voicemail."

"It's an iPhone. Isn't there a way iPhone users can track their phones?"

"I tried that too. Nothing came up. Remember, Bronwyn said that this psycho did something to her phone. Maybe he made it so it can't be tracked."

"Christ." Tony rubs a hand over his face. "Okay. There's a guy I want to contact. He's a Fed. I think he'll know how to handle a situation like this."

Joe is nodding, liking this idea, but then he says, "What if the guy who took our daughter *is* a Fed?"

This makes Tony pause. Clearly the idea hadn't crossed his mind. I have to admit it hadn't crossed my mind either.

"Fair enough," Tony says finally. "This guy may be a Fed. Or he may be a state trooper. Or he may be from any one of several law enforcement agencies around the state or the country. Who knows how long it was after Bronwyn ran away—"

"Stop saying that." My voice is tight. "This guy abducted her. She said he's had her for a long time. He probably took her from the start."

"Either way, Jess. There's just too much we don't know. Not yet. But we will. I promise you that. You too, Joe. But the only way we can make this work is to bring in someone a bit higher up than me. I honestly think that's the only way we'll be able to save your daughter."

"Maybe not just our daughter," I hear myself whisper. I feel both of their eyes on me while I stare down at the screen. At those awful words that snapped me awake this morning.

i think he's going to kill me

"Maybe our grandchild too," I say, lifting my eyes to Joe. My voice so quiet and hoarse it can hardly be considered a voice at all. Then, to Tony, as if it needs explanation: "Bronwyn's baby."

8

Jessica

Two Days after the Pep Rally

Danny Scarola, one of the assistant managers at Shepherd's Market, called me early Sunday morning.

"Ms. Moore? Sorry to call you so early, but I had a message here that you wanted me to reach out to you."

I'd barely slept the night before, having drowned myself in a couple of bottles of wine after work. Joe had told me to call in, have my assistant manager oversee everything, but I'd said I needed the distraction, something else to focus my mind on, though I'd been a mess most of the evening, cursing myself for going back to Steven's apartment Friday night when I should have just gone home. Even if I had arrived home after Bronwyn had already left, at least then I might have noticed she'd packed her things sooner. Maybe I could have notified Joe hours earlier, and he could have called Tony, and . . . well, *something*.

"Yes," I managed, my head pounding that all-too-familiar beat. I was still in bed, my head against the pillow, the phone against my ear, hazy sunlight streaming in through the blinds.

"It's my understanding you called yesterday asking about Wyn." He paused. "I heard about what happened at the pep rally. A real shame, that. She's such a talented girl."

"Thanks, Danny. That's very kind of you."

I'd called yesterday and spoken to one of the other assistant managers but hadn't gotten much help. So I'd later called back and asked customer service to leave a message for Danny, who Bronwyn had once told me was the only *nice* manager the store had.

"Sure thing," Danny said, and then paused again. "So how is Wyn doing, anyway? I haven't seen her since Friday night."

This was enough to snap me fully awake.

Bolting upright in bed so quickly it caused my headache to scream, I said, "You saw her Friday night?"

"Yes, ma'am. She came in around ten o'clock or so, right before we closed."

"Did you speak to her?"

"No, I did not. I saw her from a distance. She was in and out."

"Do you know where she went when she stopped in?"

"The break room, I believe. Is there something wrong, Ms. Moore? Did something happen to Wyn?"

I closed my eyes, not sure how to proceed. Yesterday Joe and I had spent several hours calling all over, asking friends from Bronwyn's school if they'd seen her, with no luck whatsoever. Steven Clark must have caught wind of what had happened, because he'd texted me and even called, but I'd been ignoring him since.

"It looks like she ran away," I said. "We're trying to see if anybody might know where she may have gone. We've already reached out to everybody at the high school and was hoping to hear from somebody at work."

"Oh dear. Well, all the kids who work here go to the high school, so if you've already spoken to them, there's no use talking to them again.

But we have some older folks who work here, and I'm happy to ask around for you."

"I'd appreciate that, Danny. Also, I had another question."

"Go ahead."

"Bronwyn's father and I accessed her checking account. She appears to have made quite a few large transactions at Shepherd's."

There was a beat of silence on Danny's end, and then he said, "How much are we talking in each transaction?"

"Most of them were just over one hundred dollars or so. A few over two hundred."

"Ah, yes, I see what she did. Sounds like she got cash back. You know, instead of going to an ATM and having to pay a fee, she just buys a pack of gum or whatever and gets a hundred dollars back in cash. It happens all the time."

I closed my eyes again, released a breath. So that meshed with the theory that my daughter had run away. That she'd clearly been planning it for some time. She was a smart kid: she would have known that her debit card transactions could be traced, so she had cleared out her account.

"Ms. Moore, are you still there?"

"Yes, Danny. Thank you for all your help."

"Sure thing. And I'm happy to ask around for you, but something did just occur to me."

"What's that?"

"Well, it might help to see what's in her locker here at work. She's got a combination lock on it, but we have cutters to help us with that kind of thing."

I was at the store an hour later, after hastily showering and brushing my teeth and gargling Crest mouthwash. My hair was a mess, and I wasn't wearing any makeup, but I didn't care.

Danny led me past the employee restrooms into the break room, which was empty except for one lone employee sitting hunched at one of the tables, sipping a small Styrofoam cup of coffee and reading today's newspaper.

Danny all but ignored the woman as he hefted the cutters—which were much bigger than I'd imagined, like they were the Jaws of Life—and snapped the hefty Master Lock. He set the cutters aside, gingerly pieced apart the two broken pieces of the lock, and started to open the locker himself before he paused and glanced back at me.

"Suppose I should let you do the honors."

He stepped aside with a quaint bow of his head, and I stepped forward, my entire being buzzing with anticipation. I wasn't sure what I was expecting to find—there couldn't possibly be anything of importance in here, though at least it was something, and right now something was better than nothing.

At first, all I saw was an apron hanging on a hook. A blue apron, in much need of a wash, which my daughter wore when she worked the cash register.

The top shelf of the locker had only a few items. A pack of peanut butter crackers. A bottle of spring water. A few loose dollar bills, probably saved to buy a hot dog from the deli when she was on break.

That was all.

I had started to shut the locker door when Danny, who stood several inches taller than me, pointed at the top shelf.

"What's that in the back?"

That's when I rose up on my tiptoes and peered deeper into the locker. The bright lights in the break room ceiling were angled in a way that cast the item in shadow.

I reached inside, hesitantly, because even in shadow I could tell what it was, and I feared that the moment I touched the thing it would become real, would become reality, would somehow change everything moving forward.

I even closed my eyes, hoping that the item wasn't real, that it was just a figment of my imagination, an added shadow. But when my finger touched what was there, that flimsy hope shriveled up into a husk.

I opened my eyes, and pulled out the item.

Danny's sudden inhalation almost made me jump.

"Oh my goodness," he whispered.

Yes, I thought. Oh my goodness.

The item was a pregnancy test.

And it was positive.

9

Wyn

Day of the Pep Rally

She took a detour on the way to school.

Instead of heading down the highway clogged with traffic—kids her age racing to get a good parking spot at school or adults heading to and from work—she turned off at Hemlock Road and took the back way into the heart of town.

Wyn had lived in Bowden her entire life. She'd visited other places, of course—had gone to New York City with her mother three times over the years, had gone to the Inner Harbor in Baltimore, had gone to the Butterfly Pavilion at the National Museum of Natural History when she was just a girl, right before her parents split—but most of her time had been spent in this sad little town.

Well, that wasn't fair. Bowden wasn't a sad little town. At least, not anymore. Two decades ago, when the factory had closed and so many people had lost their jobs, yes, but over the past several years Mayor Colvin had done his best to help revitalize the town.

Bowden was still just a rural speck on the landscape of the state, but it was a homey speck, and Wyn realized she would miss it.

What are you talking about? the Taylor voice said. *You can always come back and visit.*

True, she could always come back and visit, but the question was, Would anyone besides her parents even want her to?

She knew a few people would be happy after they learned the truth, but she imagined overall the majority would be pissed. Not enough to drive her out of town—this wasn't a Shirley Jackson story—but enough that she might become a pariah.

Wyn knew what she wanted to do with her life. She knew what she was, more than anything: a singer-songwriter. Yes, it was true—she did still suffer from stage fright, had even had a handful of panic attacks when she'd pushed things too far, but she knew she would get over that eventually, that she would *have* to get over it if she wanted to make even the tiniest dent in the industry, and so that's why she'd decided today would be her last day in Bowden.

She still wasn't quite sure where she would end up. The country was vast, as were her options. But she didn't have that much money—she'd been withdrawing a hundred dollars here and there from work before every shift, stuffing the wrinkled twenties in her pocket and then later transferring them to an envelope she kept under her mattress—and so she didn't want to go anyplace that would be too expensive.

Which ruled out New York and Los Angeles and Nashville, at least right away.

Or . . . did it?

She'd heard stories of people going to those places with hardly a dollar to their name and still managing to make it work. All they'd needed was hard work and persistence and dedication to their craft.

And luck, the fake Taylor said. *Don't forget luck.*

Yes, of course. Wyn wasn't about to forget luck. It was certainly important, no question there, but she also knew that most times you had to make your own luck.

This was what she was thinking as she drove down Main Street, passing by the dry cleaner's and the Laundromat and the flower shop and Jo's Diner and Holderman's Hardware and all the places she'd passed by her entire life, though now she drank it all in as if for the very last time.

Because it would be.

When she spotted Little Angels Daycare up ahead, she quickly averted her eyes, trying not to think about all the babies and toddlers inside. Because when she thought about babies and toddlers, she thought about how they changed your life forever—sometimes for good, sometimes for bad—and how sometimes that meant giving up on your dreams.

Over the past few years Wyn had sometimes wondered if she was a mistake. She'd never felt courageous enough to bring it up with her parents, though she figured if she were going to ask either one of her parents, it would be her dad.

She knew her parents loved her very much and that they would do anything for her, but they'd had her before they were married, and even after she was born they hadn't gotten married. Not that they *needed* to get married—Wyn had friends whose parents had never officially tied the knot—but she often wondered what might have happened had her parents waited until they married to have her.

She sometimes wondered what her parents would be like now had she never been born. Had her mother one day taken a pregnancy test but found that it was negative.

Thinking of pregnancy tests, Wyn realized her fingers had started to squeeze the steering wheel, her breathing beginning to increase.

Okay, okay. Good thoughts.

Good thoughts for Wyn always began with butterflies. Even as a little girl she'd been fascinated by them. The fact that they had four wings. The fact that their brightly colored wings had unique patterns made up of tiny scales. The fact that some scientists believed there were between fifteen thousand and twenty thousand different species of butterfly in the world.

She'd learned everything she could about butterflies. Had even memorized the many different kinds. So when she'd pestered her parents enough so that they broke down and took her to the Butterfly Pavilion in Washington, DC, she could easily name all the butterflies that fluttered around them.

Like the postman butterfly or the emperor swallowtail butterfly or the zebra mosaic butterfly or the paper kite butterfly.

She remembered pointing out the different ones as they walked through the pavilion, feeling a strange sort of pride in the fact that she knew something her parents did not. But neither her mom nor dad seemed to care, both of them too preoccupied with whatever they were arguing about that day. Despite all that, Wyn wouldn't let it deter her from enjoying the exhibit and reveling in all the beauty.

And while she'd loved butterflies, she knew she couldn't have one as a pet, and so she had also been begging her parents to get a dog. For a while, it seemed like they had actually considered it, had even taken her to Wayward Animal Rescue to browse all the dogs in their kennels, and Wyn had wanted to take each and every one home, but in the end her parents said it wasn't the right time.

Not long after that, her dad had moved out of the house, went to stay with her grandparents for a while until he got his own apartment and then started dating Emma.

Wyn liked her stepmom, for the most part. She'd never had any problems with Emma, and Emma was always nice to her. Wyn had even tried to convince Emma to adopt a dog from the shelter, but Emma had claimed she was allergic, so Wyn hadn't bothered pushing it.

When she became old enough to volunteer, Wyn had gone to Wayward Animal Rescue every weekend. She knew the job entailed more than just playing with the cats and dogs. She fed them, walked them, cleaned their kennels. She didn't have a favorite of the bunch; she loved them all, and it broke her heart when some cats or dogs would go weeks and months and even years without finding a home.

There was one dog in particular, a mutt named Uno, who had been at the rescue for almost two years. He was maybe three, four years old. He'd been clearly abused as a puppy. He needed to be in a home where there were no other dogs to compete with and no children.

He'd been adopted previously but the couple had brought him back after a week, saying they didn't think he was a right fit. It was explained to them that sometimes it takes a while for a dog to adjust, but the couple didn't want to bother.

Uno had looked so confused. He didn't understand what was happening. He'd gone back into his kennel, his ears down, and curled up in the corner, looking so hopeless.

Wyn had wanted nothing more than to adopt him herself. She'd even talked to her mom about it, and it was clear her mom had considered it before pointing out Uno would be alone most of the time, what with her mom working practically ten hours a day and Wyn going to school and then work, and then what would happen once Wyn graduated and went to college? (At that time, Wyn had been on board with the idea of college.)

Now that wouldn't be fair to the dog, her mom had said, would it?

Part of Wyn hadn't cared; she just wanted to bring Uno home, show him that there was life outside the rescue. But she knew her mom was right. And so Wyn had made it her goal to get Uno adopted.

In the end, it had taken almost three months. Wyn had started a social media campaign, taking pictures of Uno in super-adorable poses that she would upload to the rescue's Facebook and Twitter accounts. One of them had him sitting at a table, a cake in front of him, a bib tied around his neck. Uno's eyes were big at the knowledge this was a treat for him. Wyn had added the caption: UNO LOVES CAKE, BUT HE'D LOVE HAVING A HOME EVEN MORE!

She'd done a few other photos, stressing that he was sweet and lovable but that he'd had a hard life, and so it was best he not be in a home with children.

The posts went viral. The rescue received several calls about Uno, and some people had even dropped in to see him, but despite a few people saying they'd like to adopt him, nobody ever filled out an application.

Those were times Wyn had cried herself to sleep at night. She hated to think about all the animals in the world who didn't have homes. The ones who became so accustomed to their kennels or crates that being outside or around people scared them.

But finally a young couple did adopt Uno. They'd driven up from Lanton. Wyn had been there the day he left. She'd crouched down, scratched him behind his ears, and said, "You're going to do great, Uno. You're a good boy."

And Uno had leaned forward and licked her on the chin.

After that, Wyn never went back to the shelter. By that point, several other kids her age were volunteering, so she knew Wayward Animal Rescue had all the help it needed. But it had pained her seeing all those animals locked in their kennels—it had physically drained her—and by then she'd started concentrating more on her music, knew that she couldn't have any distractions.

Still, she often wondered how Uno was doing. She hoped he had found the right family. She hoped he was happy.

Now, feeling her eyes start to tear up, Wyn steered around the bend near the northern end of town and then pressed down on the gas. Bowden High was two miles away, and she was in danger of missing the first bell.

Even though she planned never to set foot in the school after today, she still didn't want to be late.

There were just over five hundred kids in her high school, about 150 in her class. Many of the juniors and seniors drove secondhand

and thirdhand cars and pickups, and a majority had already filled the parking lot by the time she arrived.

Wyn found a spot near the far corner of the parking lot. She hefted her gray canvas backpack—a gift from her father at the start of freshman year, her initials monogrammed in white on the exterior pocket—onto her shoulders and grabbed her guitar case and hurriedly weaved through the parking lot toward the entrance doors.

Some kids were still outside, milling near the doors. A few stood in a circle but were on their phones, each with their heads bent and their thumbs tapping their screens. A few others were actually playing with a rainbow-color Hacky Sack, bouncing it off their knees and thighs and shoes, laughing and cajoling each other the longer the Hacky Sack didn't touch the ground.

Principal Webber and Coach Hatfield stood off near the entrance doors, Webber with a coffee cup in hand, Hatfield with a shiny can of Red Bull, watching the stragglers and announcing the time every minute.

Five minutes until first bell. Wyn had made it on time.

She was vectoring straight for the entrance doors when somebody called her name.

"Wyn!"

Pausing midstride, she swiveled her head to watch Catherine Colvin detach herself from the Hacky Sack group and hustle over to her. One of the guys had knocked the Hacky Sack toward Catherine right when she'd made her departure, and nobody was able to grab it in time. Audible groans issued from everyone, and someone barked, "What the fuck, Cat?"

Principal Webber said, "Language!" Then, after taking a sip of his coffee, he glanced at his watch and announced: "First bell in three minutes."

The warning didn't persuade the Hacky Sackers or the cell phone–tapping statues to head inside.

It didn't seem to persuade Catherine, either, as she strode right up to Wyn with a bright smile.

"What's with the guitar?"

Catherine was popular enough to hear all the juicy gossip as soon as it hit, so Wyn was surprised she hadn't heard about the planned pep rally performance. Still, Wyn didn't feel like getting into it with her right now, so she chinned at the entrance doors and said, "Running late."

Catherine didn't slow a beat, saying, "Sure, me too," and she walked with Wyn as they headed past Principal Webber and Coach Hatfield into the school.

As soon as they were inside, Catherine said, "Did you see my brother this morning?"

Wyn faltered a step, surprised. When she looked at Catherine, the junior grinned and shrugged.

"He never gets up early if he doesn't have to. Is always hitting his snooze like a half dozen times. But this morning he was up before any of us. Even my dad, and my dad's always up early. I don't know why, but I thought maybe he went to see you."

Wyn had known Catherine practically as long as she'd known Aaron. Wyn had watched her grow up through the years, from a spunky little girl to an attractive teenager. Unlike her brother, who was a year older, Catherine was confident and outgoing. Boys were always flirting with her, and her current boyfriend was on the football team.

Hesitating again, still not sure what to say, Wyn blurted, "We're not together anymore."

Catherine's delicately trimmed eyebrows knitted, and she offered up a lopsided grin.

"Yeah, I know, but that wasn't my question."

Wyn didn't want to get into it with Catherine. She'd always liked the girl, who had always been cool to her, especially when Aaron and

Wyn had started dating, but Catherine didn't need to know about Wyn's visit to Fox Lane that morning and how Aaron had shown up uninvited.

"I have to go," she said, and continued up the hallway, squeezing into the crush of students before Catherine could say anything else.

The bell would ring in the next minute and Wyn knew she wasn't going to make her homeroom class in time. But that was okay—her homeroom teacher was Miss Weaver, and Miss Weaver wasn't too strict if students happened to trickle in a few minutes late.

Up ahead, Mr. Murphy stood outside his classroom. He was the new teacher, fresh out of college, tall and slim with a warm smile and dark hair and dimples in his cheeks. He wore khakis and a blue dress shirt with the sleeves rolled up to his elbows, his tie partly loosened.

Because Mr. Murphy was only maybe five years older than the seniors, he interacted with them almost as buddies, bumping fists with the guys and laughing with the girls as he welcomed them into his classroom.

"Hey, Wyn!" Mr. Murphy called to her as she passed him in the hallway, and she merely smiled at him in response, continuing on to Mr. Parker's room.

Mr. Parker taught math. He didn't have a homeroom class, which meant Wyn wasn't surprised to find only Mr. Parker inside when she opened the door.

Mr. Parker was in his thirties, a big guy with a bald head and a full beard. The kids adored him—he was hilarious and somehow made math fun—and Wyn had come to view him as a friend after being in his class last year, often staying after school to talk music and books and movies and just about everything.

"Can I leave this in here for now?" she asked, hefting the guitar case.

Mr. Parker turned away from his computer to squint at her.

"Good morning to you too."

The first bell rang then, loud and shrill.

Mr. Parker said, "Guess you're late, huh?"

Usually Wyn liked talking to Mr. Parker. But today she felt too anxious and just wanted to get to homeroom so that she could get her day started, because the sooner she could get the day started, the sooner the pep rally would arrive, and then the rest of her life.

"Can I?" she said again.

"Of course," Mr. Parker said, and then frowned. "Why not just leave it in your car?"

"I'd rather keep it in a teacher's room."

Because she didn't trust her guitar to be safe in her car. The guitar was the most precious thing she owned: a Gibson G-45 Studio Acoustic-Electric that her mom and dad had gotten her for Christmas two years ago after she'd begged them and begged them and begged them. And she knew there were idiots out there—the trolls who posted those vicious comments on her social media, for instance—who would love to take her guitar and hide it just for fun.

At least if it were locked in a teacher's room, like Mr. Parker's, she would feel better.

Mr. Parker stood from his chair, pulling his keys from his pocket as he gestured her over to the closet in the corner of his room.

As he neared her, though, he paused to study her face.

"Nervous about later today?"

In a manner of speaking, absolutely, but she wasn't sure how to vocalize it. Typically she had no problems expressing her feelings to Mr. Parker. He made her feel comfortable, made her feel safe. But today was different for some reason. She couldn't let anyone in, not even her favorite teacher, for fear that somehow she'd lose her nerve and not go through with what she had planned.

When she didn't answer, Mr. Parker squared to her, only a foot or two away.

"Seriously, Wyn, are you okay? You look . . . off."

"I'm fine," she said, and pivoted to the closet to wait for him to unlock it.

Because the closet was cluttered with school supplies, the space was tight, but still she managed to secure the guitar case against the wall.

"I'll come back right before the pep rally to get this if that's okay?"

Mr. Parker stared at her. He knew she was keeping something from him, but it was clear he wasn't going to pry.

"Sure thing, Wyn." He quietly closed the closet door, dropped the keys into his pants pocket. "I guess I'll see you later today, then. You take care."

Forcing a smile, she headed out into the empty hallway and hurried to her homeroom.

10

Jessica

Now

Joe had gone to Bowden High with Stuart Colvin, and they each had gone to separate colleges, but then later both moved back to where they'd grown up, like two magnets forever fated to connect.

Stuart was never much into politics, at least from what Joe had once told me. But after having moved back to Bowden, there was a pothole on the street just outside Stuart's apartment, one that seemed to grow larger by the day, though it wasn't yet too deep and so most people either swerved around it or drove over it without any problems.

But late one night, when Stuart was driving home after having maybe a beer or two too many, his car's front tire passed right over the pothole. And maybe it was because the tire was worn, or maybe it was because the pothole had finally gotten just deep enough—or, who knows, maybe it was destiny—but whatever the case, the tire popped.

On the surface, a flat tire isn't a life-changing event, but it was for Stuart Colvin.

Climbing out of his car, a bit unsteady on his feet, Stuart had crouched down next to the tire and muttered a curse under his breath.

Then he popped up, his shoulders loose, like a man ready to enter the boxing ring, and he approached the pothole a few feet away, his hands clenching into fists.

"You piece of shit," he said to the pothole. "You want to fuck with me? Then I'm going to fuck with you."

At least, this was how Joe once relayed the events, so it's not clear just how accurate any of it was, but I do know that Stuart had made several complaints to the town council. And while he'd gotten some promises, they'd been empty promises, and when election time came around, Stuart decided to get on the town council himself, if for no other reason than to fix that damned pothole.

By then, the pothole had grown even bigger and deeper. The town had sent out somebody to fill it with gravel, but it'd been a sorry attempt, and soon the pothole began to grow again.

Stuart hadn't expected to win a seat on the town council, so it was a shock when the election results came in.

By that time, he'd started dating Rachel, the new pediatrician in town, whom he would eventually marry. Joe was Stuart's best man; I was one of Rachel's bridesmaids.

Stuart's stint on the town council gave him the politics bug, and he soon realized his ambitions were much bigger than sitting on the council. So after a couple of years, he decided to run for mayor and talked Joe into helping him campaign.

Joe admitted to me more than once he didn't think Stuart had a chance. That's why Joe continued to work at the Wonderwall while he helped Stuart canvass the town on the weekends and everything else that went into campaigning to become a town's mayor.

It wasn't until election night, once all the votes had been tallied, that Stuart was shocked yet again.

Joe was too.

Because Stuart had promised him a position in the township administration if he were to become mayor.

Joe had almost declined, knowing that the Wonderwall still wasn't quite in a place where I had full control, but I encouraged him to take the job. I told him I could manage running the Wonderwall on my own. I told him everything would be fine.

Sometimes I wonder how things would have turned out had I asked Joe to stay at the bar. There's a chance he may not have listened to me, but there's a good chance he would have stayed, which meant he probably wouldn't have met Emma and started spending so much time with her down at the municipal building, which meant he wouldn't have started seeing me less and less, and the space between us wouldn't have started to expand more and more, like Stuart's pothole.

For a while, after arriving home after one of the many stressful nights at work and downing a bottle of wine, I'd wonder if Bronwyn wouldn't have run away had Joe and I stayed together.

Maybe, I'd think as I sat on the couch and flipped through the channels, the glow of the TV bouncing around the dark living room, if Joe and I had actually gotten married, then things would have been a whole lot different.

I don't know why, but this is what I'm thinking as we pull into the Colvins' driveway. I'm staring ahead through the windshield, lost in these thoughts, when Joe hits the brakes a little too hard and the car rocks forward and I blink and suddenly remember where I am and what we're doing.

Joe cuts the engine, slips the key from the ignition, glances at me. The same worry that bloomed on his face when he first read the text messages is still there.

"How are you holding up?"

I glance past him at the house. A sturdy two-story colonial. White siding and blue trim. An American flag hanging off the porch.

The lawn is well manicured, just like Joe's. And just like in Joe's lawn, a Colvin for Congress sign is planted in the grass. Not a couple, but just one. Rachel Colvin isn't one to allow tackiness inside or outside her home.

"I'm fine," I say. "Let's just get this over with."

It's like déjà vu: the same conversation from a year ago, when Joe and I had come over to this house. Only we'd come here for an entirely different purpose.

Joe opens his mouth to say something, but that's when Tony appears and taps his knuckles on the window.

Joe actually jumps, turning to glance up at Tony, who's parked his truck behind us in the driveway.

By then, the front door has opened and Stuart stands there, in jeans and a polo shirt. Even from this distance I can see the concern on his face.

Joe had texted him that we were coming over because it was an emergency—he didn't want to tell Stuart what this was about, not by text or by phone, because he knew there would be too many questions.

Tony offers a wave, then hurries around the car and opens my door. Then, before I know it, we're hurrying over the brick walkway and up the porch steps and through the front door, the house smelling of vanilla and chocolate chip cookies.

"So what is it?" Stuart says, his green eyes bright with alarm. "Tell me what's going on."

Joe holds out his hand to me, and for a crazy instant I think he wants to dance. But it's just because the pressure has started to get to me, everything pushing in from all corners, and before I realize it, tears have sprung to my eyes and I start sobbing.

"Goodness," Stuart says, stepping forward and pulling me into an embrace. It's his immediate reaction to seeing somebody distraught in front of him, and it's that empathy that has made him into the successful politician he is today. "What is it, Jess? What's wrong?"

But I can't tell him what's wrong. My voice won't work, no matter how many times I try to speak.

Just then Rachel appears down the hallway, an oven mitt on her left hand. At first she isn't sure what to say, and then she says, "Bring her in here," and then I feel hands on my arms, leading me down the hallway, and Rachel scoots out one of the chairs at the table and I'm gingerly lowered down on it.

The smell of chocolate chip cookies is even stronger. Of course it is—there's a tray of them cooling on the counter.

People ask questions and other people answer, but I can't make out their words. It's like I'm underwater and my ears are plugged and all I hear is a muffle.

Then somebody tugs at my hand, and I realize that it's Joe and that he's trying to extract the iPhone from my ironclad grip.

"It's okay, Jess," he says, and somehow his voice manages to make it through the muffle. "I'll bring it right back."

At first, I don't want to let go—what if our daughter texts in the next minute and I'm not there to see it immediately? But then my fingers start to loosen, enough so that Joe plucks the phone away, and he starts to turn toward Stuart but then turns back, holds the phone out to me.

"I need you to unlock it."

Nodding distantly, I press my thumb half-heartedly against the sensor at the bottom of the phone.

The screen opens up, which is enough for Joe. He gestures down the hallway, and he and Tony and Stuart head back toward Stuart's office.

Only Stuart turns back at the last second, hurries over to me, places his warm hand on my shoulder.

"Do you need something to drink, Jess?"

Yeah, I think. *How about a shot of bourbon?*

It's a ridiculous thought because it's barely midmorning and I never even drink bourbon anyway, and part of me wants to burst out laughing, while another part wants to burst out with more tears.

"I'll look after her," Rachel says to her husband.

Stuart lingers a moment, his hand still on my shoulder, and then he nods and disappears up the hallway. I hear him asking what's going on, and I hear Joe start to answer, but then their voices dissipate as the door closes.

The soft scrape of four wooden legs on a linoleum floor, and then Rachel sits down beside me, leaning forward and placing a hand on my arm.

"Jess? What is it, hon? What's wrong?"

I look at her, suddenly unable to speak, imagining instead all the terrible things that might happen to my daughter today—all the terrible things that have happened since the day she was taken—and that's when Rachel grabs a napkin from the holder on the table, reaches out and wipes the tears running down my cheeks.

Footsteps sound behind me, coming up the basement steps. It's Catherine, and she stops dead as soon as she sees me, her pretty face full of confusion before it flips over to concern.

"Ms. Moore? Are you okay?"

"Everything's fine, Cat," Rachel says. "Give us a couple minutes, okay?"

It's clear Catherine doesn't want to leave. She's inherited the same empathy from her father and wants to help in any way she can, but after a moment she says, "Actually, I was about ready to head over to Lucy's to help her with a project. Is that okay, Mom?"

For a moment I find myself lifting my head, opening my mouth to respond. But she's not talking to me—*of course* she's not talking to me—and I quickly look back down at my hands while Rachel tells her daughter that's fine, and Catherine hurries away.

When she's gone and it's just the two of us and the clock ticking on the wall, Rachel hands me a fresh napkin and then tilts her head at the counter.

"Want a cookie? I made them for the church bake sale later today, but it'll be okay if a handful of them go missing. Push comes to shove,

I have to make another batch, which is fine by me. I've been wanting an excuse to gorge myself silly anyway."

It takes a bit, but I manage a smile.

"Thanks, but I'm okay."

"Are you sure? Not to toot my own horn, but they're pretty tasty."

I wipe at my eyes, though by now I'm pretty sure the tears have stopped.

"I'm sure," I say. Then, because I don't feel like getting into it with Rachel right now—I'll start crying again if I do—I shift my gaze toward where Catherine was standing a minute ago. "She's been doing great at the Wonderwall. All the customers love her."

Rachel's smile is so bright I almost have to squint.

"The girl certainly takes after her father." Then the smile dims a bit, and she says, "I probably shouldn't be telling you this, but I was worried when you hired her. It's her first job, you know."

"Why were you worried?"

"Well, I remember what it was like back when I worked as a waitress in high school. Customers can sometimes be so rude. And Cat . . . she can be sassy at times."

Smiling, I ask, "How's Aaron?"

The instant the question slips through my lips, I'm sure I've made a mistake. That it'll remind Rachel of what happened a year ago. The tense confrontation in this very kitchen. The accusation I leveled at her son. Even though Rachel and I have seen each other a handful of times since then. Even though, as far as I can tell, everything is fine between us.

The smile reappears, glowing even brighter.

"Aaron's doing great! Basic training took a lot out of him, but he says he's enjoying himself. It's helped him build his confidence too."

Then the smile dims again, and Rachel says, "I'd be lying if I said I wasn't disappointed when he told us last year he didn't want to go to college after all and instead planned on signing up for the army. I'd also be lying if I said I haven't been nervous every day since. A lot of young men go into the military and they come out just fine. But others . . ."

She pauses, shakes her head.

"I'm sure it'll be fine. Aaron's a good boy. He'll make a great soldier. Plus—and this is just the cynical part of me, after being a mayor's wife all these years—it's going to go over great with the voters. Have you seen the latest polling? Stuart's up four points."

I'm not sure what to say, because the last thing I want to talk about right now is her husband's standing in the polls, but it's also a nice distraction, something to keep away those awful images of what might right now be happening to my daughter.

"He'll win," I say, because I can't think of anything else. And because Stuart is the kind of person who never seems to lose. Who is always in the right place at the right time.

Rachel leans back, shrugs. She glances around the kitchen, as if she'll never see it again, and I realize what she's thinking.

"You won't have to move to Washington," I say. "Not if you don't want to."

"Oh, I know. But with Aaron in the military and Cat going to college next year, this house is going to be very empty when Stuart's in Washington. To be honest with you, I'm split—one half of me wants to stay here and keep working with my patients; the other half wants to take an early retirement so I can go with him. We have the extra money to rent a place. We'll need to keep the house, of course, because we have to maintain an address in the district, but . . ."

She shrugs again, offers up a half smile, and then her eyes narrow again when she remembers how I first entered the house.

"Tell me, Jess. What's going on? Why did Joe need your phone?"

Before I can answer—or not answer, which was most likely going to be the case—Joe steps soundlessly into the kitchen.

"Jess, can you follow me?"

Rachel helps me up from the chair, and I follow Joe down the hallway to Stuart's office.

Tony's standing in the corner, his phone squeezed in a fist, and the moment I step inside Stuart pulls me into another embrace and whispers that it's okay, that everything is okay and that we'll find Bronwyn.

I want to start crying again, but I force it down and only nod at him, again not able to form words.

Joe says, "I told Stuart I need to leave the campaign. At least until we get Wyn back. I'll be too distracted otherwise to help, and besides—"

Stuart adds the rest.

"Besides, the campaign doesn't matter right now. Jess, Joe and Tony told me about the circumstances, and I just . . . I don't know what to say. I'm so sorry. But we're going to figure something out, okay? Even if *I* have to step aside from the campaign for a time, just as long as you and Joe have all the help you need."

I find myself shaking my head, wanting to tell him no, that he doesn't need to do that, but before I can, Tony's phone buzzes in his hand.

He glances down at a text message, then flicks his eyes up to us.

"My friend in the FBI? He said he's leaving the field office in Philly now. He'll be here in two and a half hours."

11

JESSICA

Two Days after the Pep Rally

Joe stared down at the pregnancy test on the kitchen table. He had yet to touch it. Had yet to look away since the moment I placed it down in front of him.

For several seconds there was complete silence, and then I said, "Joe."

He blinked. Tilted his face so that it was pointed in my direction. Opened his mouth but said nothing. Wet his lips and tried again.

"Where . . . where did you say you found this?"

His face had taken on an uncharacteristic pallor, his eyes glistening in the soft glow of the overhead lamp. He was staring down at the pregnancy test again, laser focused on the white-and-pink item, and his mouth was slightly open, as though he wanted to say something again but still couldn't.

"Joe," I repeated, this time with much more force, and when he blinked again and looked at me, it was clear he'd snapped himself out of whatever trance he'd been stuck in.

"Her locker at work," he murmured, answering his own question. Then, his brow furrowing: "Why would she keep it at work?"

I pushed away from the counter I'd been leaning against, started pacing back and forth in the small kitchen area. This was a place Joe and Bronwyn and I had shared breakfasts and lunches and dinners. It hadn't always been good times, but we'd been together, and there had always been the unspoken agreement that we would be together in one way or another forever.

"I don't know," I said, my voice tight. "It makes no sense to me. Maybe she was afraid I'd find it, so she took it with her to work. Maybe she *took* the test while she was at work. Then again . . ."

He looked up at me, hesitant. "What?"

"I checked what pregnancy tests they sell at the store, and this isn't one of them. As you can see, it's digital. I looked it up online. The idea is it'll show positive for a couple of months, so that"—I paused suddenly, had to swallow—"so that women can share it with their boyfriends or husbands or whoever."

This last part seemed to flick a switch inside Joe's head, and his eyes widened just a bit.

"Aaron?"

I looked away. Found myself staring at Bronwyn's regular spot at the kitchen table. Pictured her as a little girl, sitting on her booster seat, leaning forward as she spooned Cheerios from her bowl to her mouth, drops of milk splatting the table and my daughter giggling when Joe or I warned her to be careful.

He closed his eyes, issued a heavy sigh. "Do we know how long ago they broke up?"

"I think it was a week or two after Taylor's accident."

Joe raked his fingers through his hair, rubbed the back of his neck as he stared down at the pregnancy test.

"Christ," he said.

"Joe, you know what we need to do next."

He looked up at me then, his eyes guarded. "We've known that kid almost his entire life. We're friends with the family."

"*You're* friends with the family."

"You know what I mean. Plus . . ."

I finished the thought for him: "Stuart is your boss."

Joe shook his head slowly. "I can't believe this."

"We need to go over there right now."

He snapped his face up at me. "Where?"

"You know where. I'm not messing around here, Joe. Not with Bronwyn missing. Maybe Aaron isn't the father, but maybe he knows something he isn't telling anyone. We need to talk to him as soon as possible."

"But—"

"Do it, Joe. Make the call."

Like Joe, Aaron stared down at the pregnancy test on the kitchen table. Only this table was in his own house in his own kitchen, Joe and I sitting on one side, Stuart and Rachel on the other, with Aaron sitting at the head.

Five seconds or so after I'd laid the test down in front of him, Aaron said, "What is *that*?"

His voice echoed in the kitchen, his eyes wide and his face paling much the same way Joe's had when he first saw the test and understood its significance, and then he paused and cleared his throat.

"I mean, I know what it is. But, like, why are you showing it to me? Do you . . . do you think I'm the—"

But he cut himself off. Shifted his gaze back down at the pregnancy test. His hands, I noticed, were shaking.

Rachel and Stuart hadn't spoken this entire time. Rachel was leaning forward, her elbows on the table, her face in her hands.

"Is it true?" she asked quietly.

Aaron looked at his mom. "Is *what* true?"

She lifted her face, her eyes red but tearless.

"Did you get Wyn pregnant?"

Before Aaron could answer, footsteps hurried up the basement stairs and the door opened, and there stood Catherine, looking bewildered.

"What's going on?"

She glanced around the kitchen, quickly scanning each person's face for an answer, and then her gaze settled on the pregnancy test.

"Holy crap," she said, her eyes widening.

Stuart said, "Cat, go to your room."

"But—"

Her mother said it louder and with much more authority: "Go to your room!"

Catherine stomped out of the room without another word, and then Rachel focused again on her son.

"Well?"

Aaron was slumped in his seat, staring down again at the pregnancy test in front of him. It looked like he wanted to reach out and touch it but was worried it might bite him.

"I didn't . . . I didn't know she was pregnant. I swear to God. I mean, she never told me, but . . ."

There was a heavy silence, and the fridge behind us kicked on, and then Aaron wiped at his eyes, which had started to tear up.

"We loved each other. I mean, I loved Wyn. I even told her so. But she . . . she had a hard time saying it back, and even when she did, I don't think she really meant it. But, like, we did . . . *it* . . . you know. But only once. And when we did, we were safe. But I . . . I think maybe the first time hurt her. I mean, she never wanted to do it again after that, no matter how many times I . . ."

His voice trailed off, and it looked like he might start sobbing, and I don't know what got into me right then—maybe the desperation of a mother who's just found out her missing daughter is pregnant—but I nearly lost it.

"Aaron, if Wyn didn't want to have sex, why did you keep pressuring her?"

From the corner of my eye I could see Rachel turning her face to look at me. Only she wasn't looking so much as glaring. I could feel the sudden anger radiating from her across the table.

Aaron wiped once more at his eyes.

"I . . . I didn't *pressure* her. I just wanted to fool around, but—"

"But you said it yourself: you knew she didn't want to."

"What? No. I mean . . . yeah, she never wanted to do it, but—"

I cut him off again, my voice now tight and tremulous.

"Why did my daughter break up with you, Aaron? Did you force yourself on her?"

"You bitch!" Rachel shouted.

She shot to her feet, her chair tipping straight over, clattering against the floor. She started to circle the table, her one hand clenched into a fist, and I realized I'd stood up, too, that I was facing her, ready to fight her because there was nothing else I could think to do.

But in an instant Joe and Stuart inserted themselves between us, their backs practically touching as each tried to steer his significant—or in Joe's case his once significant—other to a safe corner.

And all that time Aaron stayed slumped in his chair, openly sobbing, and I saw the panic in Joe's face, the what-the-fuck-have-you-done look flash through his eyes, and that was when Stuart's normally calm and measured voice echoed in the kitchen.

"I think you both should leave now."

After two o'clock in the morning I finally started to drift off to sleep. I'd had a bottle of wine, had considered opening a second bottle before deciding it was time for bed.

Joe had updated Tony and the other cops about the pregnancy test, which would at least give them more context about why Bronwyn had run away. They could keep an eye out for pregnancy centers or even abortion clinics or wherever a seventeen-year-old pregnant girl might end up.

So far, the police hadn't had any luck. Joe told me he'd posted about our daughter on social media, and that while a lot of people had shared the notice and offered their thoughts and prayers, so far nobody had come back with any reliable information.

I hadn't gone into the Wonderwall, and I wasn't sure when I would return. Tomorrow I would contact Bronwyn's friends again, her classmates, her coworkers, anyone who might know anything. Maybe a few days of thinking might jog some of their memories.

I lay in bed, a warm tipsiness floating through me, and eventually drifted off.

I had no dreams. At least, no dreams I remember. I just remember that I was floating in darkness when I heard a noise, a soft, almost indistinct thump, and opened my eyes.

I stared up at the ceiling, my heart thudding fast at the realization that the noise hadn't been in any dream.

Somebody was in the house.

12

Wyn

Day of the Pep Rally

First period was a slog—Mrs. Deighton's Advanced Algebra—and Wyn did her best to keep herself focused on something other than the pep rally.

She was seated near the back, simply the stroke of luck from a random seating chart, giving her a good angle of the entire class.

Especially Summer Green, sitting near the front. Because it was a game day, she wore her cheerleading uniform, the skirt a bit too short, showcasing her lean and nicely tanned legs, her chestnut hair in a simple french braid.

Every time Mrs. Deighton turned to the SMART Board to review a new equation, Summer inconspicuously uncovered her cell phone on her desk and tapped out a quick text message.

The text could have been for anybody (Autumn Porter or somebody else on the squad, maybe Summer's current boyfriend), but a second or two later Monika Stevens—who wasn't a cheerleader but was popular nonetheless—glanced down at her own phone, hidden from Mrs. Deighton by her propped-up textbook. Monika read the text, tapped her phone several times, and then a few seconds later Summer glanced down at the reply.

Wyn didn't think too much of it until near the end of class, when Summer must have sent something hilarious—a meme, perhaps, or a funny GIF—because Monika nearly burst out laughing but managed to stop herself just in time with a heavy snort.

But still it was enough to have drawn Mrs. Deighton's attention. She was middle aged and had fair skin and dark-red hair. She'd made a deal at the beginning of the semester that as long as everybody paid attention to most of the lesson, she'd allow five minutes at the end of class for everyone to get out their phones and check social media or play a game or whatever.

Brow furrowed, she scanned the classroom for a moment and then said, "Ms. Stevens, how would you solve the current equation?"

If Wyn were in a regular math class, she maybe would have felt some satisfaction that Monika would be embarrassed by not knowing the answer. But this was Advanced Algebra, and all Monika needed to do was take one glance at the current equation on the SMART Board and she answered without any hesitation.

"Very good," Mrs. Deighton said, and she stared at Monika for just a moment longer to remind her that it wasn't the last five minutes of class yet before turning back to the board.

Summer glanced back at Monika and rolled her eyes.

A couple of seconds later, Monika glanced back at Wyn—and Wyn felt her heart skip a beat at the grin on the girl's face.

They'd been texting about her.

Wyn clenched her jaw. There was no telling if the texts really were about her. And even if they were, so what? Summer and the rest of the crew were dumb bitches, and whatever they thought about her or said about her behind her back shouldn't matter.

But it did, despite how much she tried to tell herself otherwise.

Wyn suddenly had an intuition, and as quietly and as stealthily as she could, she extracted her phone from her backpack. It was still ten minutes before the end of class, but Wyn couldn't wait. Besides, she was near the back of the class, and if she positioned her phone behind the boy in front of her, Mrs. Deighton wouldn't notice a thing.

Just as she'd suspected, she had a new notification on her YouTube channel. A new comment on her most recent video. Feeling her stomach tighten, she tapped on the notification to see the comment.

> Guys I did it! I found the absolutely worst singer in the world! I played this song for my dog and he started howling!

As insults went, it wasn't very clever, though Wyn didn't expect much from the likes of Summer Green. Of course, there was no way to tell if the comment did in fact come from Summer—it appeared to be from another troll account, posted five minutes ago—but Wyn deleted it anyway.

Wyn often wondered why she allowed comments on her videos. Sometimes she received a nice comment, and that always helped lift her spirits, made her think that maybe she wasn't wasting her time after all. But those comments were too few and far between, and nasty ones like the comment she'd just deleted slithered in, making her doubt herself even more.

Nothing to doubt, babe, said the voice of Taylor-who-wasn't-really-Taylor. *You're one of the most talented people I know. Or did know before I ran into that tree.*

This last part wasn't something the Taylor voice would typically say. Maybe it was because Wyn had visited Fox Lane earlier that morning, the accident site still fresh in her memory. The scent of the trees so strong she could still smell them now.

The YouTube app was still open, and she saw a brand-new notification pop up.

Her stomach tightening again, Wyn tapped it to find another comment on the same video from a new troll account. This one was a bit more to the point.

Worst voice I've ever heard. She should do the world a favor and kill herself.

Wyn felt a tic of warmth crawling up her neck into her face. Her eyes still on the phone, she was very much aware of the other students around her, of Mrs. Deighton working through yet another equation. And she was very much aware of Summer and Monika nearby, no doubt sneaking glances at her.

She wasn't going to give them the benefit of showing emotion. Not today. Not with everything she had planned. They were petty mean girls who would eventually get theirs in the end—wasn't that how karma worked?—but even so, Wyn wasn't going to give them the satisfaction of knowing they'd rattled her.

She tapped the screen harder than was necessary to delete the comment, and then she was about to return the phone to her backpack when Mrs. Deighton's voice startled her.

"Bronwyn?"

Wyn froze, her fingers tight around her iPhone, and then her eyes shifted up toward the teacher at the front of the room.

Mrs. Deighton said, "How would you solve this equation?"

Wyn liked algebra. She typically had no problem breezing through the work. But now, for some reason, her mind suddenly wasn't working, like a sprocket in her brain had loosened and fallen off.

Uh-oh, said the Taylor voice. *Brain fart.*

Mrs. Deighton decided not to drag things out. After five painful seconds of silence, she said, "Okay, then. Can anybody else solve the equation?"

Wyn opened her mouth, wanting to answer the question, wanting to prove that the most recent YouTube comment hadn't shaken her. But the equation on the SMART Board looked foreign, a hodgepodge of numbers and symbols she knew made sense on some academic level, but which now looked to be the mathematical equivalent of a Jackson Pollock painting.

Summer's hand shot up, her bright-blue fingernails waving to catch Mrs. Deighton's eye.

"Yes, Summer, please go ahead."

Sitting at attention in her seat, her spine ramrod straight and her shoulders pushed back, one lean leg crossed over the other, Summer solved the equation in a matter of seconds.

"Thank you, Summer," Mrs. Deighton said. "That is correct." Then she glanced at her watch, said, "I believe we have time for one more equation," and turned back to the SMART Board.

Almost at once Summer turned as well, shifting seamlessly in her desk, her gaze drilling through the students behind her straight to Wyn.

The smile had slipped off Summer's perfectly formed face, and a darkness had entered her eyes, one filled with hatred and spite and loathing.

She mouthed two words at Wyn, two words that were silent and yet echoed loudly in her head.

Do it.

13

Jessica

Now

Special Agent Edward Donovan arrives at my house in a black sedan. He wears a gray suit with a red-striped tie, dark-brown shoes, and dark-brown belt. He looks to be in his midfifties, solidly built, his head resting on his neck like an anvil, his salt-and-pepper hair shaped into a crewcut.

Tony thanks him for coming and then introduces him to Joe and me. The agent flashes his badge, shakes our hands, and then jumps right to it.

"Tony told me your daughter ran away last year."

Joe says, "That's right."

The agent's eyes shifting to me: "And he said your daughter texted you last night."

I nod, suddenly unable to speak.

He gestures at the phone squeezed tightly in my hand. "May I see that please?"

I nod again, start to hand it to him, but then remember I need to unlock it first. Once I've done so, I open to Bronwyn's text messages and pass him the phone.

He stares down at the phone, then glances around the room at the couch and easy chair.

"Would you mind if we moved into the kitchen? I'd like to take notes."

He's brought along a yellow legal pad. I nod a third time, manage to say, "Yes, of course," and then soon we're all in the kitchen, Agent Donovan sitting at the head of the table, Tony beside him, with me across from the agent.

Joe leans against the counter, his arms crossed, his face tight with worry. He's had the same expression for the past several hours, and I'm immediately reminded that after Bronwyn went missing last year, Joe had admitted he hadn't seen her in a week or two, and how the realization had dawned on him he might never see her again.

As Agent Donovan reviews the text messages, I glance at the refrigerator. Its quiet hum is a siren's song: two bottles of wine currently chilling inside, waiting to be opened.

"Would you like something to drink?"

I ask the question without even thinking, automatically seeking an excuse to pour myself a glass, but of course the agent merely lifts his eyes and shakes his head with a murmur of "no thank you" before returning to the text messages.

"How about some coffee?" I ask, now directing my focus on Tony and Joe.

Both men decline but I need something to drink, even if it is caffeinated sludge. So I push back my chair and turn to the Keurig on the counter, pop in a pod, and then wait as it fills my mug with hazelnut coffee.

When I turn back around, it's clear Agent Donovan has finished reading the text chain. He's now jotting down notes, the cap of his BIC pen flicking back and forth like the tail of a frenzied lion. When my phone's screen starts to dim, he taps it to keep the phone awake and then eventually sets the pen aside and glances up at me.

"Ms. Moore, would you be willing to allow me to take possession of this phone?"

I'm holding the mug in front of my face, softly blowing on it. My eyes never once leave his.

"Absolutely not."

He nods. "I figured as much but needed to ask."

I set the mug on the counter, suddenly no longer interested in coffee. I cross my arms over my chest, hug my elbows.

"The moment my daughter reaches back out, I need to know. I need to be the one who responds."

"Completely understandable."

Joe redistributes his weight from one leg to another. The shift is almost imperceptible, entirely silent, but the subtle action doesn't go unnoticed. Our daughter texted me, not him. It's simply a fact. And I'll be damned if some FBI agent takes my phone away from me for even a minute, because in that minute Bronwyn might text again.

Tony clears his throat. "Eddie, as you can see, we're kind of in a bind here. I explained as much as I could on the phone, but now that you've seen these messages for yourself . . . What do you think?"

The iPhone's screen starts to dim again, wanting to go back to sleep. Agent Donovan taps it again, almost absently. He scrolls through the text message chain once more, slowly, taking his time, and then he leans away and takes a heavy breath.

The mere sound causes something deep inside me to shrivel.

"I'm not going to sugarcoat things," the agent says, addressing Joe and me. "It's not fair to either of you. Your daughter has been missing for almost a year. She was ruled a runaway. And most likely that was the case. It happens all the time, I'm sorry to say. It's my understanding she left in her car. There's a chance her car might not have taken her very far.

The car may have broken down. Somebody may have stopped alongside the road to help her, somebody who was no good Samaritan, and—"

"Our daughter was abducted by a cop."

The words breeze through my lips like steam. I'm a teakettle, about ready to blow my top. My arms are still folded over my chest, chewed fingernails pressing into my elbows.

"Our daughter," I say again, in case he didn't hear me the first time, "was abducted by a *cop*."

Agent Donovan stares back at me, his expression grave. "Yes, ma'am, I understand that's what your daughter said in her text messages. But the unsub might not even be involved in law enforcement."

This comment throws me for a second, almost like I hadn't heard him correctly. But of course I had. I'm just shocked it hadn't crossed my mind.

Joe asks, "What's an *unsub*?"

"Apologies," the agent says. "*Unsub* is FBI shorthand for *unknown subject*. In this case, I'm referring to the man who took your daughter. Now, he may have been law enforcement at one time. Or he may be somebody who simply purchased a badge off of eBay. There are people out there who impersonate officers all the time."

I know where he's heading with this—at least, I think I do—and I shake my head quickly.

"No," I say.

His left eyebrow notches up just a bit. "I'm sorry?"

"I understand people impersonate law enforcement all the time, but we can't take that chance."

"What chance?"

"By putting it out to the state police, to the FBI, whoever. Because even if there's a chance this sick bastard might be impersonating a cop, he might actually *be* a cop."

"She's right," Tony says. "It's a risk we can't take right now."

Joe shifts again from his place leaning against the counter. "Isn't there a way to track her location?"

My phone has since fallen back to sleep, the screen dark. It needs my passcode or thumbprint to be opened again. But that doesn't stop Agent Donovan from tapping it absently as he shakes his head.

"I'm afraid not. With a call, maybe, but not a text message. In fact, there's a chance we might have a hard time even tracing a call."

I lurch forward, as if flung away by the counter. "How is that possible? Don't you work for the FBI? Don't you people deal with stuff like this all the time?"

Agent Donovan stares back at me, his face a mask of patience. "Ms. Moore, the FBI employs some of the most brilliant minds in the country, but this isn't some TV show. I can have one of our techs examine the phone, but determining your daughter's location is almost impossible. We have to assume the unsub is smart."

"He's not that smart," I say, a trace of pride in my voice. "Bronwyn said he fixed her phone so that she couldn't call or send text messages, but she managed to do it anyway."

"There's no doubt in my mind that your daughter is a bright and resourceful young woman. She obviously did manage to alter her phone to the point where she sent you those text messages. Speaking of which, this is how your daughter typically communicates via text, with all lowercase and no punctuation?"

I nod distantly, remembering all the times my daughter texted me throughout the years. Usually simple messages of whether she'd be home late or a request for me to pick something up from the store, though she also had a habit of randomly sending me funny animal videos. There were even times when I was having a stressful day at work and I texted her asking for a video to cheer me up, and within a minute my phone would ding with the link to a YouTube clip and a note saying *love you mom*.

Tony clears his throat again, says, "Eddie, I just realized I forgot to tell you something important."

"What's that?"

"Wyn may very well have a baby with her."

Alarm enters the FBI agent's eyes. He looks at Joe and me.

"Explain," he says.

Joe fills him in because he probably thinks I can't handle it right now, and he's probably right. It doesn't take long. Joe covers the basics, and then Agent Donovan is quiet for a long time before issuing another heavy sigh.

"So we don't know for certain your daughter did in fact have the baby."

Tears sting my eyes, and I wipe them away as quickly as I can. I start to shake my head, but it's Joe who answers.

"No, we don't."

"Still," the agent says, "we should move forward with the idea that the baby is with your daughter. In fact, Ms. Moore, the next time she reaches out, I'd like you to try to bring it up. Along with a few other things I want to go over since you won't allow me to take possession of the phone."

Tony says, "Do you have a game plan in mind yet?"

Agent Donovan nods. "I do, in fact. As soon as I leave here, I'll give my ASAC a call and update him on the situation."

The man pronounces it *A-sack*, and Joe repeats it as a question.

"ASAC?"

"Assistant special agent in charge of the field office. He'll understand the significance of what's happened and how we need to keep this quiet. He'll also know the best course of action at trying to figure out a way to track down your daughter. Is that okay with you, Ms. Moore?"

Wiping again at my eyes, I nod.

"Very good. Now, while I'm gone, there are a few things I'd like you to keep in mind for if and when your daughter texts you again."

"If," I say, my voice rising on that single syllable. "What do you mean, *if*?"

The agent stares back at me, his eyes dull and flat, but still I know what he's about to say even before he says it, and it terrifies me.

"We have to move forward with a few assumptions, Ms. Moore. We also have to move forward with the little information we currently have. Your daughter said herself she thought the person who abducted her was going to kill her. And I'm sorry to have to say this, but it's possible that may have already occurred."

14

Jessica

Three Days after the Pep Rally

I didn't move. Didn't breathe. Just lay there in my bed, a living statue, staring up at the dark ceiling and listening for any sound.

Maybe I was imagining things. Maybe my already overstressed mind was feeding me this paranoia because it was desperate and didn't know what else to do.

After a minute passed in silence, I released a breath. Tried to untangle the nerves that had become so tightly wrapped around me.

Then, somewhere in the house, I heard the tiniest noise.

The soft but persistent sigh of a floorboard creaking.

I almost shot up in bed but managed to stop myself, managed to keep myself steady.

Any sudden movement and the bedsprings would make noise.

The bedsprings made noise and the person in the house would be alerted to the fact I was awake, and then . . . what?

Maybe it's Bronwyn.

The simple thought sent a bolt of hope through me, arrowing me to my core. I even opened my mouth, meaning to shout my daughter's name, but then just as quickly another thought crossed my mind—*maybe it's a burglar*—and my lips glued themselves shut.

Again I didn't move. Didn't breathe. Just listened.

Silence.

Heavy, deep, penetrating silence.

I was conscious of my iPhone only inches away from me, charging on the bedside table.

All I needed to do was dial 911, and then . . . what would I say? Surely it wasn't unreasonable for a single woman of my age to call for the police when she suspected somebody has broken into her house. The worst that could happen was they would show up and find that nobody had broken in, that the whole thing was just my imagination after all.

No, the worst that could happen is the person who just broke in is a murderer who will slice you up with his knife.

Okay, that settled it.

Moving as quietly as I could so that the bedsprings wouldn't make any noise, I groped for the phone on the bedside table. After pressing my thumb to the sensor to unlock the screen, I went to dial 911 but then paused. The emergency dispatcher may ask me a dozen questions, and I didn't have time to run through all of them, not if I wanted to stay quiet and not alert the intruder.

My focus shifted to the time at the top of the screen—3:17 a.m.—and I realized there was only one person to call at this time of night.

Joe's phone was always on in case of official emergencies. This wasn't a municipality emergency, no, but at least I knew Joe would answer if I called, and if I told him the basics, he would make sure to take care of the rest.

After two rings, Joe answered, his voice gravelly with sleep.

"Jess?"

"There's somebody in the house."

My voice was so faint I worried he might not have heard me. For a moment it seemed that way, the silence on his end so stark we may as well have been disconnected, and then his voice suddenly lost its sleepiness.

"Stay put and don't make any noise. I'll call the police right now."

He clicked off, and then I just lay there at an awkward angle, my left shoulder digging into the bed, the phone to my ear.

Out beyond the closed bedroom door, that heavy silence.

Knowing that Joe was now in control—at least in terms of calling for help—made me feel a little better.

Maybe it's Bronwyn.

The thought fluttered through my mind again, but I knew it couldn't be true. If my daughter did decide to come back home in the middle of the night, she wouldn't be so quiet. She might leave her things in the bedroom, but then she would come to see me. Tell me that she was sorry. That she was scared because of the baby but that she didn't want to run any longer.

Before I knew it, both my feet were on the floor, my toes digging into the carpet. Only a couple of paces from the bed to the door, and I made it there in no time, my hand on the knob, my other hand gripping the iPhone.

My forehead was almost pressed against the door as I drew in a deep breath, and when my phone issued its soft ding—*Damn it, Jess, why didn't you turn it to vibrate?*—I glanced down at it for only an instant, saw the message from Joe that the police were on their way, and then thought, *Screw it,* and opened the door.

"I know you're there!" My voice boomed through the quiet house, echoing off the walls. "The police are on their way!"

No answer. Not that I'd expected one.

I didn't own a gun. Didn't own a steel baseball bat conveniently leaning against the wall nearby. There was the fire poker, though that was down the hallway and in the living room. Which wasn't too far, at least not in the larger scheme of things.

Except the intruder could be hiding in the living room right this moment. Gripping said fire poker.

I started down the hallway, slowly. The light switch hung on the wall nearby, which I could flip to flood the house with light. The only downside would be momentary blindness, though that went both ways. I'd be blind, but so would the intruder.

For now, my eyes had adjusted to the dark. I could make out the familiar shapes of the kitchen table and couch.

Another slow step.

Another.

I passed by Bronwyn's room—hadn't the door been closed when I went to bed?—and then moved deeper into the house.

The living room was only a few feet away. The poker stood upright in its iron tray next to the fireplace right around the corner. I could reach it in seconds.

Assuming the intruder wasn't right around the same corner.

"Do yourself a favor and leave right now before the police get here."

Again no answer.

I woke my phone from sleep, hovered my thumb over the button I'd need to trigger the flashlight. Any sudden movement in my direction, I'd slam my thumb on the button and blind the intruder. It would only last a second or two, but that should be enough time to scramble past the person and make it to the front door. I could run down the road and not once look back over my shoulder until the police reached me.

Another slow step.

Another.

And then, all at once, I sprinted into the living room. Squeezing past the easy chair and reaching for the fireplace. My fingers grasped the poker as my thumb hit the flashlight button, and light bloomed from the phone.

I stood there then, the poker raised above my head, the phone illuminating the room.

Which appeared to be empty.

No intruder in sight.

That was when I heard two cars pull into the driveway. A pair of heated engines idling, red lights strobing through the curtains.

Lowering the poker but keeping it in hand, I sprinted for the front door. I had the crazy thought I should be thankful I didn't sleep in the nude as I tore open the door and raced outside in sweatpants and a T-shirt, my bare feet slapping against the cold stone walkway.

Two officers were already out of the cars, Kenny Gorman and James Healy. At the sight of me, they placed their hands on their pistols and hurried over.

"Are you all right?" James said.

"Inside," I managed to say, between breaths. "I think somebody's still inside."

"I'll go around back," Kenny said, and headed toward the side of the house.

James told me to stay put and that he would be right back. Then he proceeded up the walkway, a flashlight in hand, and entered through the open front door.

The lights came on inside the house, one room after another, and then a minute later James appeared in the doorway.

"If someone was inside, they're gone now."

A couple of seconds later, Kenny hustled around the other side of the house, shaking his head.

"Nobody out back."

So it was just my imagination after all. Embarrassing, what with two cops standing in my front yard with their cars still flashing their roof lights, but so be it.

"I'm sorry," I said.

"Nothing to be sorry about," James said. "Let me walk you through the house. Kenny, Joe asked us to give him an update. Mind giving him a call?"

Kenny nodded and extracted his phone from his pocket while I followed James into a house that suddenly didn't feel like home anymore.

James said, "I checked every door and window but didn't see any signs of forced entry. I also checked every room, every closet, even the basement. I didn't find anyone, but if you'd like, I'll walk with you through the house so you can be sure."

I wanted to thank him for all the trouble, tell him it wasn't needed, but still part of me wasn't convinced. I'd been so certain that I'd heard a noise. That I'd felt a presence. Somebody had been in my house. I was sure of it.

I moved from room to room, checking the closets, the bathroom, the basement. Even Bronwyn's room. Because now every single light in the house was lit, it didn't take long.

Officer Healy was right: nobody was there.

"I'm sorry," I said again, though this time it was less out of shame and more out of anger. That I did in fact look foolish. That I'd wasted not only their time but my own.

Kenny said, "Not a problem, Ms. Moore. That's why we're here."

"Would either of you like something to drink before you go? Some water, coffee, a soda?"

Both men politely declined.

"Well," I said, once again a tangle of nerves, "I could sure use something to drink."

I was thinking about the bottle of wine in the fridge. The second bottle I'd decided not to open before going to bed. I pulled open the fridge door, already tasting the wine in the back of my throat, but then froze.

The bottle of wine was gone.

15

Wyn

Day of the Pep Rally

The next two classes went by without a hitch: Advanced Biology and AP History.

Wyn sat in her seat in each class, staring up front at each teacher, but she wasn't really paying attention. She kept thinking about the recent comment on her video, what it had told her to do. And how Summer Green had mouthed at her to do it.

What a bitch.

But Wyn wasn't surprised. The Seasons and their minions had never liked her. The truth was Wyn had never much cared for them. She didn't *dislike* Autumn and Summer and the others so much as she had simply become indifferent to them, ever since middle school when they had corralled Taylor into their group.

Taylor had joined them, but she hadn't stopped being friends with Wyn. Far from it. They had talked on the phone or chatted online almost every night, hung out together on the weekends, though of course Bowden being Bowden, there wasn't much to do.

Wyn had fond memories of the two of them in fifth grade, riding their bikes down the back roads, standing up on their pedals as they coasted down a hill, their long hair blowing in the breeze along with the streamers on their handlebars, Taylor hooting and shouting, *I feel like I'm flying!*

Or the times they'd gone down to the creek and stuffed their rolled-up socks in their sneakers so they could tramp through the cool water, laughing as they splashed each other and sent minnows scattering.

Or when they'd gotten older and one of their parents had dropped them off at the movie theater, expecting them to watch some PG-13 flick, only they'd sneaked into the R-rated horror movie instead. The usher taking the tickets had known exactly what they were up to, but he'd purposely looked the other way, and they'd sat in the back, sharing a large tub of popcorn, and every time the monster showed up on screen, Taylor would scream and grab Wyn's hand and squeeze it tight.

When Taylor said she wanted to try out to become a cheerleader, Wyn had encouraged her, though internally Wyn had rolled her eyes. But if that's what her best friend wanted to do, she wasn't going to dissuade her.

Likewise, when Wyn had discovered her passion for music, Taylor had always been there to encourage her.

Taylor herself had loved to sing, but she was always off-key, even on the times Wyn tried to coach her. But Taylor never seemed to care, always singing along to the radio while they were driving in her car, and because she knew she didn't have a great singing voice, sometimes she'd sing even louder just for the hell of it.

By eighth grade, Wyn had already decided she wanted to be a musician. If need be, she would go to college and major in music. Do whatever it took for her to reach her goal.

It was Taylor who pointed out that many artists never even bother with college. That they pack their things and head to the city. Whether it be New York or Nashville or Los Angeles—or, well, *any* city seemed like a major city when you grew up in a town as small as Bowden—it was there a struggling artist truly understood what it meant to struggle.

And that, in their struggle, great art is formed.

To make great art, one must first suffer.

Or something like that.

Except up until then Wyn hadn't really suffered for her art, not really. It was only in tenth grade when they'd had tryouts for *America's Got Talent* down in Philadelphia that Wyn realized just how difficult reaching her goal would be.

Taylor hadn't been able to go with her but she'd called later that night, asking how everything went—she'd texted throughout the day, but Wyn hadn't responded—and it was then that Wyn, lying on her bed with her bedroom door locked and the lights turned off, told her just how humiliating it had been.

"Oh my God," Taylor said. "What happened?"

For the longest time Wyn wasn't able to put it into words. Then she said, "I just . . . froze up. I got up there in front of a producer, and I started strumming my guitar, and . . . and I felt this tightness in my chest I'd never felt before. And my hands and fingers started to feel numb, and I suddenly had this crazy thought that I was going to die."

That had been her first panic attack, and it had left a mark. It was like a living nightmare: standing up there in front of a stranger, her mom waiting in the wings, as Wyn worried she might collapse right there onstage.

Taylor had offered up words of encouragement, trying to downplay what had happened, and for the first time Wyn realized something.

"Taylor? You would tell me if I sucked, wouldn't you?"

Taylor hadn't even hesitated.

"Of course I would," she said. "But you don't suck. You're amazing."

And it was her friend's confidence in her that helped Wyn understand she couldn't give up. Though the next year, when tryouts for *America's Got Talent* came around again, Wyn had come up with excuse after excuse why she wasn't able to go this time, and it had been Taylor who had called her out.

"You want to make a career out of this, don't you?"

"I do."

"Then stop being a chickenshit and make it happen."

Taylor had even planned to go down with Wyn and her mom, to cheer her on, but at the last minute Wyn claimed she was sick—and she'd even forced herself to throw up so that her retching sounded real enough from the bathroom when she saw no other way of getting out of it.

After she'd come out of the bathroom, her mom had looked sympathetic, though Taylor had seen straight through her. She'd shaken her head, her face full of disappointment, and that made things even worse.

By then Taylor had been dating Sean Heller for over a year. Things had started to get serious. At Taylor's urging, Wyn had started dating Aaron Colvin, though she wouldn't have called things serious. At least not the way Aaron might.

Sean had graduated that June. He would attend Penn State in the fall with a full scholarship. Despite going to college while Taylor was still in high school, Sean had promised not to break up with her because, according to Taylor, they were in love.

Which was why Wyn had refused to tell her what Sean had done to her one night.

Later, Wyn would wonder if maybe things would have turned out differently had she opened up to Taylor.

In many ways, Wyn blamed herself for Taylor's death.

That was the reason she was going to perform at the pep rally. In front of the entire high school. Over five hundred kids and teachers, many of whom she had known for years.

Sean Heller would be in attendance. After all, it was homecoming weekend.

Wyn was going to make sure this was a homecoming nobody would ever forget.

Then, because Wyn knew to cross a bridge before you burned it, she would do the only thing left for her to do.

Disappear.

16

Jessica

Now

"You should go home."

"I can stay."

"Joe, I mean it."

It's almost 11:00 p.m., and so far no further text messages from Bronwyn. I've since tried sending a few myself, but like the countless times before, the messages never showed that they were delivered.

We're in the living room, Joe and I, and the TV is on in the corner, but it's muted. A rerun of *Shark Tank* graces the screen, and Joe sits on the couch, his feet up on the coffee table, just as he did years ago when we'd first moved in. He has his laptop open, the soft glow from the screen reflected off his reading glasses, and he is responding to emails and other work he may have missed today. It's Saturday, but the job of a town administrator and zoning officer—not to mention US Congress campaign manager—is never-ending.

I lean forward on the easy chair, rap my knuckles on the coffee table to get his attention.

"Your ignoring me is giving me flashbacks of the tail end of our relationship."

I say it with some attitude but then grin when I see the smile start to light on his face. Joe taps the keyboard for another ten seconds or so, then closes the laptop and sets it on the couch beside him.

"I'm not leaving," he says.

"You always were stubborn."

"I've always thought of it more as tenacious. By the way, when was the last time you heard from Suzanne Walker?"

"It was a few months back, but don't change the subject. Emma and the kids need you at home."

"The kids aren't babies anymore, Jess. And they're pretty well behaved. Emma is just fine."

It's true—Emma did seem fine earlier tonight when she stopped by the house to drop off a bag for Joe as well as food. She'd picked up a large pepperoni and some other greasy snacks from Mama's Pizza. The kids were with her, and we all ate at the kitchen table as though we were one big happy family. But it had mostly been in awkward silence, because while the kids know me, they don't know me that well, and Emma was aware of what was going on but didn't want to ask any pointed questions in front of the kids, and so it was mostly vapid small talk that eventually fizzled out.

But before she and the kids left, Emma had taken me aside and whispered, *He hardly gets any sleep as it is, and this whole thing isn't going to help matters. Please keep an eye on him, okay?*

"There's nowhere for you to sleep," I remind him.

Joe holds his hands out over the couch, says, "Of course there is." Then he grins. "Come to think of it, this might be the first time I've ever slept on this couch."

He's trying to lighten the mood, trying to make me feel better, but it's practically impossible. Tony has since reached out, saying he heard back from Special Agent Donovan, who would be back tomorrow. Tony made it clear the FBI agent wasn't able to spend too much time on this but that he wants to help in any way he can.

It's at least something, though it doesn't feel like much at all. It hasn't even been twenty-four hours since my daughter's first text message came through, and already I've started to feel hopeless about the entire thing.

Special Agent Donovan's words certainly hit me hard. A solid right hook across my mental jaw. It was staggering to think that Bronwyn—and possibly my grandchild—had been abducted, and yet it was even more staggering to accept the reality that at this moment my daughter and her baby might already be dead.

Joe notices the worry on my face, and he knows exactly what I'm thinking because he's no doubt thinking the same thing.

"Everything's going to be okay, Jess."

I've been staring off into space, I realize. Seeing Bronwyn and the baby without really seeing them. Imagining the monster who took them stepping into a dark room as he caught my daughter texting me.

Blinking the terrible image away, I look at Joe.

"You don't know that."

He forces a smile. "But I do."

"How?"

"Because," he says, his voice soft, "I can't imagine a world where this doesn't work out. Where"—he pauses, swallowing—"where we lose our daughter."

And grandchild, I almost add but don't. The baby is certainly implied. It's something we'd discussed after Tony and the FBI agent left and before Emma arrived with the kids. We don't even know for a fact Bronwyn actually had the baby, but if she *did*, then that means . . .

"I'm proud of you," Joe says, and his words have a strange effect on me, almost cause me to lose my breath.

"For what?"

"So far you've been handling this pretty well."

"Are you kidding? I nearly had a breakdown at your house this morning."

"I don't mean that. I mean . . ." He points at the plastic bottle of Diet Coke on the coffee table. "You haven't had a drink all night."

My eyes shift down to the soda, and now I find it's my turn to swallow. Am I that transparent? Joe always was able to read me so well, and the years apart—at least the years apart from living under the same roof—haven't changed that.

"If you need a glass of wine," Joe says, "go right ahead."

Need. Not *want*. Part of me thinks I should find it insulting he would phrase it like that, but another part knows it's true. I may not be a raging alcoholic—at least, not anymore—but I certainly find myself drinking more and more some nights.

I find that my jaw is tight when I answer.

"I'm fine."

Joe stares at me for a beat, and then nods, says, "Okay, sounds good," because he knows this isn't a battle he wants to wade into right now, not when he's stuck in enemy territory.

A lengthy silence ensues. *Shark Tank* has since gone to commercial break—the usual ShamWow and South Beach Diet and Clegg & Hawthorne ads—and now a new set of entrepreneurs are onscreen. These two I recognize, and I remember their pitch. I'm pretty sure they get a deal.

"Joe, if I ask you a question, will you be honest with me?"

He tilts his face in my direction, his expression filled with worry. "I guess that depends. What's the question?"

"Are you sick?"

His expression deepens into a frown. "What do you mean?"

"It looks like you've lost thirty pounds since the last time I saw you. Maybe more. You would tell me if you had cancer or something, right?"

The guarded look in his eyes softens. Joe knows just how much my mother's death shook me. How I felt abandoned—first by my father when he took off, then by my mother when she passed.

There were times during our relationship when I would scrutinize every bump or spot on either of our bodies, no matter how minuscule. One time I noticed a freckle on Joe's back I hadn't remembered seeing before, and I sent him straight to the dermatologist. Joe balked at first, telling me I was overreacting, but that made things even worse. A few months prior, I had found what felt like a lump while in the shower, and I'd gone to the doctor, already fearing the worst. Bronwyn had been four at the time, and I had already envisioned a future where she relived the same fate I had, and one tearful night I had begged Joe not to leave if it turned out to be cancer, that he made sure our daughter had at least one parent to take care of her.

In the end the lump turned out to be just a cyst, and eventually it had gone away. But that didn't ease my paranoia that one of these days the same type of cancer that had taken my mother's life would take mine too.

Joe takes off his reading glasses and sets them aside, rubs at his face.

"No, Jess, I don't have cancer. But I have been working out almost every day. Emma bought me a rowing machine two years ago for my birthday. A real nice NordicTrack. Most mornings I'll get up early and go down to the basement and row my heart out."

He's smiling now, patting his flat stomach, but I just stare back at him, not buying it. A moment passes, and then the smile fades and Joe sighs.

"Yeah, okay. I am exercising, but also the past year's been really stressful. First Wyn disappears, and then Stuart decides to run for Congress, and working for the township and Stuart's campaign at the same time . . . I think maybe I've bitten off more than I can chew. My appetite is pretty much nonexistent these days. There are even times

Emma has to force me to eat something. Plus . . . well, this doesn't help either."

He pulls something slim and several inches long out of his pocket. At first I can't make it out—is it a pen?—but then all at once I realize what it is: an electronic cigarette.

"You're kidding me," I say. "Since when did you start smoking?"

"I used to, back in high school. Not sure if I ever told you that. But when I started college, I wanted a fresh start, so I stopped cold turkey. By the time we met, I'd gotten past it and didn't miss it at all. But now, with everything going on . . ."

He grins and puts the cigarette to his mouth. The LED tip glows briefly as he inhales.

"Hey," I tell him. "No smoking in my house."

"It's not smoking," he says, breathing out a tiny cloud. "It's vaping."

"Well, whatever you want to call it. What does Emma think?"

Joe offers up an embarrassed grimace and says, "She doesn't think anything, because she doesn't know, and I'd like to keep it that way if that's all right with you."

Great. Now Joe and I are keeping secrets from his wife.

"Whatever. Your secret is safe with me. But I'm serious, though. You don't need to stay."

"And I'm serious too. I am going to stay. As long as it takes. Hopefully she texts you back tonight."

My stomach does a flip at the thought. Not just a leisurely one, either, but an Olympic gymnastics kind of flip.

As much as I want Bronwyn to text again, part of me hopes to never learn the more awful things that have happened to our daughter in the past year. It's not like we didn't try our best to find her, but surely we could have done more, and if we had done more, then maybe our daughter wouldn't have been taken.

"Do you know what I've been thinking all day?" I ask quietly.

"What's that?"

"When we took Bronwyn down to Washington, DC, that one summer to the Butterfly Pavilion. And how she—"

"Went missing," Joe finishes. His expression is solemn at first, and then he smiles. "But at least we found her right away."

"It was at least five minutes, but it felt like hours. And the whole time, I just . . . I knew that if we didn't find her—if she was somehow gone for good—my life as I knew it would be over. That I forever would be defined as the woman who lost her child. I didn't think I could live with myself."

"Again," Joe says, inhaling once again from his e-cig before setting it aside, "we found her almost right away. She wasn't in any real danger."

I can't believe how flippant his attitude is right now, but I suppose he's right: we *had* found our daughter almost right away. We had just seen the exhibit and were leaving the National Museum of Natural History. There were people everywhere—mostly tourists being dropped off by the busload along Constitution Avenue—and Joe and I had been arguing about one thing or another, and the next thing I knew we were out on the National Mall and I looked back and realized our daughter was gone.

At that moment I'd never felt more panicked in my entire life. Joe had still been arguing his case—I can't even remember what that particular argument was about—and I had to grab his arm and spin him around and point at the empty space where our daughter should have been.

We immediately split up, calling out our daughter's name, pushing past people who didn't move out of our way fast enough. One minute became two, two minutes became three, three minutes became four, and I was about ready to find the nearest police officer when I spotted her near a tree. She'd wandered away because she thought she'd seen a butterfly, she told me, but I had been so thrilled to find her I hadn't cared and just wrapped her in a near-suffocating hug.

To change the subject—because I need to focus on something else, anything else—I say, "So Colvin for Congress, huh?"

His smile clicks over to proud.

"Yeah," he says. "Every day that passes it looks more and more likely."

"And if he wins—"

"*When* he wins."

"Okay. *When* he wins, what does that mean for you?"

Joe's quiet for several seconds, and that smile gives way to something else that I can't ascertain, but it's enough to give me the answer.

"You're going to move to Washington too."

"Yeah," he says quietly. Then: "Well, no, not entirely. I'll get an apartment down there somewhere, but we're going to stay here in town. The school is good, and Emma has her work, and . . . I mean, we can't just pick up and leave like that. At least not right away. That's not the plan."

There's something in his tone I almost don't catch. Maybe if I'd had one or two glasses of wine, I would have missed it, but since I haven't, I ask, "What's the plan?"

His smile now beams. Just like the day Bronwyn was born and Joe held her for the first time. You could have powered a small city with the level of wattage radiating from his smile.

"Ideally, two terms in Congress before we run for Senate. A term there, maybe two if need be, and then . . ."

The lighting in the living room isn't the best, but still I see the sparkle in his eyes.

"You're joking," I say.

The sparkle fades, and he looks properly insulted.

"You don't think Stuart would make a great president?"

I open my mouth but then shut it, not sure what to say. This conversation has veered off the course I'd expected. Then the answer comes to me, and I shrug.

"Sure, I guess. I mean, he's been a great mayor. I'm sure he'll make a fine congressman. But president of the United States? That's . . . ambitious."

"Well, Stuart's always been an ambitious guy. He's always been smart too. And dedicated. And sincere. I think it's the sincerity that attracts people to him. They're used to politicians—especially Washington politicians—being all stuck up and fake. That's not Stuart. He's pure. His whole life is about helping people. I've already worked out how it's going to happen. From day one in office, he's not going to take money from any lobbyists or corporations. He—"

"All right, all right. I get the picture. Now I think it's time for bed."

From having been with Joe for as long as we had been together, I know cutting him off like that is the only way to stop him once he gets going. Joe knows this, too, and he nods and tells me that he'll be here when I wake up.

I grab my phone off the coffee table, tell him good night, and start toward my bedroom.

I pass Bronwyn's room and pause briefly. The door is partly ajar, left open from when Joe had looked inside earlier today. The hallway light filters in on a room that has mostly been untouched this entire year.

I continue on to my bedroom.

I consider undressing and putting on sweats and a T-shirt but instead simply crawl into bed with my clothes on. This way if and when Bronwyn texts, I'll be ready to go at a moment's notice.

I connect the iPhone to the charging cable, set it on the bedside table. Then I lie down and stare up at the dark ceiling as the realization hits me that it's now been twenty hours without even a sip of wine.

Not a major accomplishment, no, but at least it's something.

It takes a while before I eventually drift off to sleep, certain that at any moment the phone will issue its soft ding as a new text message arrives.

But it's three days later before Bronwyn texts again.

17

JESSICA

Three Days after the Pep Rally

Joe peered into the refrigerator, the profile of his face aglow in soft light, and after several seconds he stepped back and shut the door and turned to Officers Healy and Gorman.

"Thank you both for coming out tonight. Sorry to have wasted your time."

I was standing on the other side of the kitchen, leaning against the counter, my arms crossed. Joe had shown up only five minutes after I'd realized the wine bottle was gone, and he wore jeans and a sweatshirt, obviously thrown on in a hurry before grabbing his keys and running out the door.

Before either officer could reply, I spoke in a low, deliberate tone with just a hint of a quiver.

"Somebody was in the house."

Joe didn't even bother glancing back at me. He took a few paces over to the two black plastic bins used for trash and recyclables. Both were lidded, and he casually opened the recyclables lid before dropping it back in place and clearing his throat.

"Thank you again, guys. It's much appreciated."

"Anytime," James Healy said. "That's what we're here for."

Both men somehow managed to tell me good night and avoid looking at me at the same time. It was actually impressive. I stayed where I was, leaning against the counter, while Joe showed them out the front door, and when he returned, his face shadowed in exhaustion, I finally felt the nails digging into my palms.

"Somebody," I said, my tone this time slow and enunciated, "was in the house."

Joe ignored me. He crossed over to the recyclables bin, lifted the lid again.

"How much wine do you go through a night?"

"Joe."

"There are seven in here, Jess. Seven empty bottles."

"Joe, listen to me."

Dropping the lid, he turned back to me, his face tight. "How much did you drink tonight?"

When I didn't answer, Joe shifted his posture. Just a bit. Straightening his back, tilting his chin up.

"I know this is stressful, Jess—I'm stressed myself—but you need better coping skills than drinking yourself numb."

"Fuck you."

His face still tight, he took a step forward, and I said, "There!"

He paused, frozen in place.

"Didn't you hear that?" I said. "That slight sigh from the floorboards? That's *exactly* what I heard tonight."

My words were frenzied, almost a blabber. I'd come off the counter and approached Joe, feeling a new wind, that doubt I'd momentarily had suddenly blown away. I practically pushed Joe aside so I could stand where he'd stepped, and I pressed my weight down on the spot a couple of times before I produced the same sighing noise.

"There!" I shouted, nearly delirious now. "That's what I heard! Call James and Kenny back. Let them hear it too."

Joe just stood there, staring back at me. His face impassive, his eyes flat.

"I'm not drunk," I whispered. "And I'm not crazy."

Joe didn't bother disputing this. Not even a passing attempt. He simply pulled his phone from his pocket to check the screen, issued a yawn.

"I should head home."

"Joe."

"If you'd like, I'll walk the house with you before I go. I know James already did, but let's at least make sure every window and door is locked."

"You don't have to believe me, Joe. That's fine. But the truth is somebody was in the house. Somebody took that last bottle of wine. Those are facts."

Joe stared back at me, silent. It was clear he didn't know how to respond.

I wanted to say it again—*I'm not crazy*—but I felt voicing it twice might somehow incriminate me. A sane person might tell others they weren't crazy only once, but more than once?

Jesus Christ, maybe I was losing it.

Joe said, "I miss her, too, Jess. I hope she comes home soon. But until then, both of us need to keep our shit together."

I said nothing and watched Joe as he started toward the front door, and then something occurred to me.

"Any word from Tony?"

Joe's broad shoulders dropped. He slowly turned back around.

"No," he said softly. "At least, no news. They checked the ATM camera at the bank but had no luck. They've asked around town, but nobody has come forward with seeing where Wyn may have gone that night."

"What about the state police?"

"They've been on the lookout, too, but I think Tony was right—Wyn's a seventeen-year-old girl who's clearly a runaway. She isn't a priority. It's not like they're canvassing the state. Hell, at this point, she's probably not even in the state anymore. She could be on the other side of the country."

I felt tears starting to sting my eyes, and I wiped them away, quickly, not wanting Joe to see me cry.

"I don't know why she wouldn't tell me about the baby."

Now it was Joe's turn to stay silent. He stared back at me for a long moment, and then finally cleared his throat.

"Maybe she was embarrassed. Or scared. Or . . . hell, any number of things. I meant to tell you, by the way: I've shared the news of Wyn on social media. Emma has too. It's gotten a lot of shares, has really gotten out there, but so far nobody has come back with any solid leads."

"What about Stuart?"

Again, that slight tightening in Joe's face.

"What about him?" he said.

"Is there anything he can do? Stuart's known Bronwyn most of her life. There's a chance the baby's even—"

Joe cut me off.

"After what you tried to pull at the Colvins' yesterday, do you honestly expect Stuart to go out of his way to help us?"

"What are you talking about?"

"You essentially accused his son of raping our daughter."

"No I didn't. I mean, okay, I may have overreacted a bit, but—"

"Jess, you have to understand something about Stuart. His whole worldview is filtered through a political lens. His son getting a girl knocked up out of wedlock? Nowadays that's barely a scandal. But his son sexually assaulting a girl and getting her pregnant? Even if it's not true, the mere allegation could ruin his career."

I closed my eyes, released a breath.

"You're right," I said. "I'm sorry. I'll apologize to Stuart and Emma and Aaron in the morning if that will help things."

"Honestly, Jess, at this point it's probably best you keep your distance for right now. But to answer your previous question, Stuart's already shared news of Wyn's running away on his personal social media. So has Rachel. So has everyone we know. I wish there was something more that can be done, but I hate to say right now we're in a holding pattern. We have to wait for Wyn to reach out to us. Or to come home. Or something."

"I'm not giving up."

"Christ," Joe said. "Do you think *I'm* giving up?"

"I'm not sure what you're doing."

"I'm praying. Every day. I'm making phone calls. Every day. I've even created a business account on Facebook to boost my posts about Wyn so that even more people will see it, and I made a website so that people can leave tips. What the hell have you been doing besides drinking yourself silly?"

When we were together, Joe and I almost never fought. We bickered, we sniped at one another, but we never got into loud arguments. A friend had once observed that maybe that was why things hadn't worked out between us. A stable, healthy relationship consisted of those times when the couple has a rage-filled argument. Screaming and shouting with maybe a TV remote or phone thrown at the wall. It wasn't healthy to suppress all that anger and frustration; it needed to come out, and if it didn't, the relationship suffered.

I wasn't sure if that was true—if Joe and I would have lasted had we had more full-out arguments—but it was beside the point. When I got angry, I never started screaming and yelling. I became quiet. Too quiet. A volcano pushing all its hot magma and lava and whatever else deep down to its core.

I said, as calmly as I could, "I want you to leave."

Joe had clearly realized his mistake. It was written across his face, the sudden guilt.

"Jess—"

"Right now."

Joe knew better than to argue. He left without a word, pulling the door closed behind him.

The next day I went into work.

It didn't go well.

I couldn't concentrate, and it didn't help that most of the staff had heard about my daughter running away, or if they hadn't heard about it, they'd heard about what happened at the pep rally or even watched one of the videos online.

I'd checked that morning and found the views for the most popular video were up to over ten thousand. An hour later, it was almost eleven thousand. A few hours after that, fifteen thousand.

It had indeed gone viral, and I feared that meant Bronwyn might never come home.

When it became clear I was too distracted—and that several of the guests for lunch had heard about Wyn, some even going so far as to offer me their condolences as I drifted through the dining room—my assistant manager suggested I go home.

I didn't want to—it felt like an acknowledgment of failure, both as a boss and as a mother—but in the end I relented.

Halfway home, I remembered I didn't have any wine. I almost started toward the liquor store—my car drifting into the turning lane as if on its own—but I kept thinking about what Joe had said and how those two officers had done their best to avoid looking me in the eye, because there I was, a hysterical woman who'd maybe had too much to drink before bed and was hearing noises in the night.

No, I decided, I wasn't going to continue that cycle. I didn't *need* to drink. I wasn't my father's daughter.

Of course, that meant when I did arrive home, I had nothing to do.

I hadn't gotten much sleep the night before, so I decided to try to take a nap.

It was as I was headed down the hallway toward my room that I glanced at my daughter's bedroom door.

The door was closed, as it almost always was, but hadn't I seen it partly ajar when I was creeping down the hallway in the dark last night?

Maybe, maybe not. It had been dark, after all. And I had believed somebody was in the house.

No, stop that. Somebody was *in the house.*

I gripped the knob, waited a beat, and then opened the door.

Bronwyn's room looked no different than it had the last time I'd looked in. I'd gone through it the other day, after she'd disappeared. The police had too. I hadn't found anything, at least not anything that helped determine where my daughter may have gone, and neither had the police.

Still . . . it wouldn't hurt to search it one more time, would it?

I stepped into the room, my fingers flexing in and out of fists. I told myself it was just because I was anxious to get this done. Not because I needed a drink.

I almost didn't find the note. It was hidden pretty well in her desk. In the top drawer, stuffed in that underneath portion in the back. I could have sworn I'd already looked there the other day, but there it was.

It was a piece of ruled worksheet paper, folded several times.

I felt a strange mix of dread and excitement rush through me as I unfolded the note. Whatever was written here, it could mean everything.

Then my eyes lighted on the words, and I felt a tightness in my chest.

Wyn,
I miss you. Please call me.
CM

A number was included with the note, a local number I didn't recognize.

Who the hell was CM?

I racked my brain. Tried to think of all Bronwyn's friends. A few had first names that started with C, a few had last names that started with M, but none that were CM.

The bedsprings of my daughter's bed sighed as I sat on the edge. I had my phone out and started to dial the number but paused. Decided to google the number first instead.

No luck. Nothing came up.

It took longer to dial the numbers than I anticipated, that feeling of dread now bubbling in the pit of my stomach.

I tapped the green phone icon with my thumb, closed my eyes, and placed the phone to my ear.

It didn't even ring. Went straight to voicemail.

"Hey, it's Chad. Leave me a message."

I disconnected before the beep. Then just sat there, staring down at the phone.

Chad wasn't the name of any of Bronwyn's friends, at least that I could think of. But the voice . . . something about it sounded familiar, though I couldn't tell why. It sounded young, but not like a teenager. It sounded like an adult.

And then it hit me—practically sucker punched me in the stomach.

Chad.

Chad Murphy.

My daughter's social studies teacher.

18

Wyn

Day of the Pep Rally

Fourth period didn't go by any quicker than the first three.

She was in Mr. Murphy's social studies, the class right before lunch, and Wyn spent much of that time wondering where she would sit in the cafeteria. She had the weird feeling Autumn and Summer and the other cheerleaders were going to do something to her.

Wyn didn't know how she knew this, exactly, only that it was a gut feeling, and in her seventeen years of life Wyn had learned to trust her gut.

She could just skip it, of course—get a pass for the library or claim she wasn't feeling well and see the nurse—but Wyn didn't like the idea of surrender. Not with the pep rally only two hours away. Surrendering now might be the thing that caused her to wimp out, and she refused to wimp out.

Then, before she knew it—hunched over her textbook, barely listening to Mr. Murphy as he babbled on in his way-too-friendly baritone—the bell rang, and like that, everybody scrambled for the door.

"Wyn, can I see you for a minute?"

She was almost to the door, her canvas backpack strapped to her shoulders, her textbook hugged tightly against her chest, when Mr. Murphy's words cut through the din of sneakers and heels and boots already stampeding through the hallway.

There were a few other students behind her, waiting to follow her out, and Wyn stepped aside to let them pass by before turning to Mr. Murphy.

He stood there with his hands in his pockets, his shirtsleeves rolled up, tie loosened around his neck in that perpetual Jim Halpert look. He smiled at her, then quickly crossed over to the door to shut it before lowering his voice.

"Is everything okay? It didn't look like you were paying attention most of class."

"I'm fine," Wyn said. She should already be in the cafeteria, securing a table and making sure she didn't look weak.

She started for the door, but Mr. Murphy stepped in front of her. His hands were out of his pockets now, his arms crossed over his chest.

"I'm worried about you, Wyn." His voice was soft, almost tender. "I know you were close to Taylor, and it's a damned shame what happened to her. Ever since her accident, you've been . . . distant."

The second bell rang, meaning she was late for lunch.

"Hey," Mr. Murphy said, shifting slightly on his feet, and Wyn suddenly had the sense that he wanted to reach out and touch her arm or her shoulder or maybe even her chin, and this feeling somehow transferred itself to Mr. Murphy, whose face suddenly went blank, like he'd been caught.

"I should go," Wyn managed, and Mr. Murphy nodded quickly, stepping back and clearing his throat.

"Of course. Did you want me to write you a pass?"

"No thanks."

Wyn had her hand on the doorknob but paused. Something had occurred to her, a revelation that almost knocked her sideways, and she turned just slightly enough to see the young teacher from the corner of her eye.

"Onyx Butterfly?"

There was a pause, maybe an extra second or two where Mr. Murphy attempted to process what Wyn had just said, and she felt her stomach tighten at the possibility that he would smile, chuckle, do *something* to acknowledge the fact that he had indeed been communicating with her all this time.

But Mr. Murphy, after that extra second or two of what Wyn realized was confused silence, said, "Huh?"

"Nothing," Wyn said, pushing open the door. "See you later."

By then the hallway was deserted, a ghost town or, well, a ghost hallway. Students were either in the cafeteria or class, and Wyn hurried down the hallway, wanting to make sure she made an appearance, that she showed the Seasons—and herself—that she wasn't afraid.

She turned the corner and stopped short.

Coming her way were Autumn Porter and Summer Green, as well as Monika Stevens and Skylar Jennings.

They moved side by side, the four of them, Autumn and Summer in the middle, Monika and Skylar flanking them.

As soon as they saw Wyn, they slowed to a stop.

They just stood there then, staring at Wyn.

Wyn stared back at them.

She thought about Taylor, and how Taylor had always told her not to overthink things, to not worry about what anyone thought of her, especially the Seasons, and before Wyn knew it she was in motion, angling toward one side of the hallway to bypass the girls.

None of them moved or even made a sound until Wyn had almost reached them, and that was when all four girls, as if controlled by the same puppeteer, moved to the side to block her path.

Autumn said, "Where do you think you're going?"

There was more than the obvious challenge in her tone. Her blue eyes practically shone like a hungry predator's, a slight smile riding her glossed lips.

Wyn still had her textbook hugged to her chest, which she felt made her look weak, defensive, so she slowly lowered it to her side.

She wasn't going to say anything, she decided. Engaging with these four—or at least Autumn, who had crowned herself the queen bee once news of Taylor's death had spread throughout town—wasn't worth her time. They wanted to rattle her for whatever reason, and the only way to fight back was to show that she wouldn't, that she *couldn't*, be rattled.

When Wyn didn't respond, a touch of anger flickered through Autumn's eyes.

"We heard you're performing at the pep rally."

Wyn didn't answer.

Summer took over, maybe sensing her friend's rising impatience.

"Are you sure that's such a good idea? We heard about what happened at the *America's Got Talent* tryouts. You really want to embarrass yourself like that again?"

It was hard—damn near impossible—but Wyn managed to keep her face blank. Every fiber in her body wanted to scream, wanted to shout, wanted to take her textbook and throw it. But she couldn't do that—she *wouldn't* do that—and so she just stood there, staring back at them. Doing her best to look bored.

Summer smiled, her face as radiant as a black hole sun.

"Taylor told us all about it. How you choked. Would be a real shame for that to happen again, wouldn't it?"

Again, Wyn did everything she could not to react. She was almost positive Taylor hadn't said anything to the girls—Taylor wasn't the only one Wyn had confided in, which had been stupid of her, for sure—but still, the mere idea that her best friend in the world had betrayed her confidence . . .

"We've been wondering," Autumn said, "why you would even want to perform at the pep rally in the first place. You could have performed at the special assembly for Taylor last month, but you didn't. Instead, you want to perform at the pep rally. I even heard you asked to perform at the homecoming game tonight but that they couldn't fit you in. Tell me, Bronwyn"—and the way she said Wyn's proper name dripped with so much disgust it was a wonder the head cheerleader didn't spit after she uttered the word—"why do you so badly want to perform at the pep rally?"

As Autumn asked this, she pushed a strand of hair away from her face. A simple gesture, one so common and natural it barely warranted Wyn's notice, except that in doing so Autumn briefly exposed the inside of her wrist, and the small tattoo nestled there.

A black butterfly.

Wyn's heart seized. She felt her eyes start to widen, but she told herself she couldn't react, that she couldn't let Autumn or any of the girls see her surprise.

Autumn said, "It wouldn't happen to be because Sean will be there, would it?"

She knew she should continue with her silence—there seemed to be power in that, though now her silence was mostly due to shock—but still she couldn't help herself.

"Do the rest of the girls know the truth, Autumn?"

Autumn's eyes narrowed, her jaw tightening, but she said nothing. Wyn shifted her gaze to the others.

"Do you?"

Nobody answered.

Wyn smiled, said, "Well, if you stick around, maybe you'll find out."

And before she lost her nerve, she pushed through the chain of girls, hard enough to nearly fling Skylar into the lockers. Wyn didn't bother looking back, though she worried that one of them—Autumn, most likely—would come at her from behind. So she listened past the blood thundering in her ears for the sudden squeaking of sneakers rushing at her, and when she didn't hear anything, she turned the corner and picked up her pace.

Wyn slowed only when she noticed that Mr. Parker's door was slightly ajar.

Sensing that something wasn't right, she hurried forward and opened the door.

Wyn expected to see Mr. Parker behind his desk, maybe eating a sandwich while he graded papers, but his chair was empty.

The entire room was empty.

Like the main classroom door, the closet door was slightly ajar.

Now feeling her heart in her throat, Wyn rushed over to the door and swung it open.

And stared at the empty spot where her guitar case had stood earlier that morning.

19

Jessica

Now

Sunday afternoon.

Special Agent Edward Donovan has returned to the house, along with Joe and Tony Parsons.

Carter Redcross is here too. Tony stated that he felt it would be good to include another officer, especially one who had been involved in the search from the beginning. Tony said that until further notice, he wanted an officer with me at all times so that the moment Bronwyn texts again, there will be someone there to immediately contact the troops.

So after the Keurig machine dutifully makes coffee, we sit around the living room and try to come up with a game plan.

It's Agent Donovan's idea to write out a list of questions to ask Bronwyn once she again makes contact.

While he told us yesterday there's a chance our daughter is dead, he is at least moving forward with the premise that Bronwyn is still alive, and I appreciate that.

He scribbles on the legal pad as he speaks.

"First, ask her if she knows where she is. The state, town, whatever."

"I already—"

"Ask again. Directly. We might not have much time, just like before. Next, ask her to describe where she's being kept. The walls, the floor, the ceiling, everything."

The tip of his pen scratches quietly against the legal pad.

"Third, ask her to describe the unsub. Whether or not he's given her his name. What he looks like. What he smells like. What he typically wears."

I sit on the couch, a coffee mug held tightly in both hands, my knee bouncing with anticipation. My iPhone is on the coffee table, still and quiet.

"Now," Agent Donovan says, "once your daughter does make contact, it's important you hook your phone up to this computer ASAP."

He's brought a laptop along with him, as well as several different cords. He powers on the laptop. He notes that there's already an LTE card inside, so it's connected to the internet.

"See this icon here on the desktop? As soon as you plug in the phone, click on the icon to launch the program. At the same time, somebody needs to contact me. I have a tech who will anticipate my call, day or night. He'll remotely access the laptop and do his best to track your daughter's location."

"I thought it wasn't possible to track her location if she's not on a cellular network," Joe says.

"She probably isn't on a cellular network. Most likely, your daughter managed to get on Wi-Fi somewhere. We hope to determine the Wi-Fi location. We determine the IP address, we have ourselves a starting point."

"That's it?" Joe says. "It's just that easy?"

"Well, we also need to assume the unsub might be using a VPN."

"What's a VPN?"

"Virtual private network."

We all stare at him, silent.

Agent Donovan turns to me, says, "You have internet here in the house, correct?"

I tell him that I do.

"Right. So when you go to a website or send an email, it originates from an IP address. That's *your* address, and it tracks right back to you. People who know what they're doing can manage to use that IP address to determine your actual location. That's our hope here. But if the Wi-Fi network is using a VPN, that means their location will be masked. The server could be in California, or Canada, or Croatia. They could be right next door, but the IP address puts them on the other side of the world."

"Christ," Joe murmurs, his eyes closed as he rubs his temples.

"How will we know if they're using a . . . What did you call it?" I ask.

"VPN. And we'll know almost immediately. Once we determine the IP address, we can verify it. If the unsub is using a VPN, that just means the tech will need to do a lot more legwork on his end. It's not the end of the world."

I feel the stirrings of hope deep down in my gut.

"And if there isn't a VPN?"

Agent Donovan offers up a small smile.

"If that's the case," he says, "then we shouldn't have much of a problem at all. We'll be able to determine your daughter's location in a matter of seconds."

Except for the rest of the day there is no contact from Bronwyn.

Not the next day either.

It's Tuesday before she reaches out. Almost eleven o'clock at night.

Only Carter Redcross is at the house. He's had several cups of coffee and has gotten little sleep, his eyes bloodshot, his face shadowed by stubble.

We're in the living room, the TV on, the volume so low it might as well be muted, when the iPhone on the coffee table issues its soft ding.

—

And like that, everything goes into motion.

Carter, perched on one corner of the couch, his head back, his eyes half-closed, bolts upright. He almost knocks his mug of cold coffee off the table but manages to catch it at the last second, then whips his face in my direction as I lean forward from the easy chair.

My pulse has ticked up, so much so that I can feel it reverberating throughout my body. This may just be Joe, checking in before bed, or maybe Tony, checking in too, but somehow I know that it's not either of them, that it's my daughter.

mom are you there

I nearly cry out at the sight of the four words. Then I glance up at Carter, who's watching me like a hawk. He already has his own phone in hand to contact everyone if it's indeed my daughter.

I nod at him.

Carter starts tapping at his phone, then puts the phone to his ear as he stands and heads to the kitchen. That's where the laptop is set up with all its different cords.

The iPhone dings again.

mom please answer

I snatch up the phone and start to type a reply, but just like before my thumbs are shaking, and I pause to focus, to take a breath.

I'm here.

In the kitchen, I hear Carter speaking urgently into his phone.

"Yes, I just started the laptop, and we're going to connect it to the phone now. I've also already alerted Chief Parsons and Mr. Hayden, who said he'll be here as soon as he can."

I know I should get up, hurry into the kitchen to connect the phone, but I can't move. Instead, I stare down at the first question on the single piece of legal paper that Special Agent Donovan left behind Sunday afternoon.

Do you know where you are? The state? The town?

I start to type but become distracted by the three dots on my daughter's side of the screen. She's typing something to me, and I want to see what that is before I do anything else. For all I know, she might be cut off before I have a chance to make it to the kitchen.

i dont think i have much time left

Panic spreads through my body like spilled gasoline. What does this mean? That she doesn't have much time left to text me, or that she doesn't have much time left in general?

Carter has returned to the living room. He clears his throat, impatient.

More dots, and after a few more seconds the phone dings.

mom i need to tell you something

I'm aware that Carter has taken a few steps closer, his own phone still to his ear. He's angled himself so that he can see the iPhone screen.

"Ms. Moore," he whispers, "we need to connect your phone."

Nodding, I start to stand—leaning forward, ready to push off with my legs—when the phone dings three times, all in rapid succession, and I glance down at the screen and practically lose my balance.

i was pregnant
that was why i left
i was so scared and didnt know what else to do

I stare down at the screen, not sure how to respond. Despair is a struck match, tossed down on the panic that's currently circulating throughout my body.

Before I can type anything—sitting there on the easy chair, stunned silent, tears already welling in my eyes—the phone dings again.

i lost him right after daddy abducted me

Part of me wants to drop the phone. Put my hands to my face and wail.

But another part knows time is limited, and that there is time later for wailing.

Now I need to stay focused. In control.

Because while Carter Redcross is here physically, as far as I'm concerned, it's only Bronwyn and me.

I type: I'm so sorry. Honey, where are you? Are you okay?

Impatience radiates off Carter Redcross.

"Now," he says.

The dots again. They're hypnotic. I know I should get up, hurry into the kitchen so we can connect the phone to the laptop, but I can't look away from the dots. I can't even move.

The iPhone dings again.

im just so sad

Carter's impatience finally gets the better of him. He mutters, "Screw this," and snatches the phone from my hands.

I shout at him but he's already moving, racing ahead of me into the kitchen, using his shoulder to pin his own phone to his ear as he connects one of the cords to the iPhone.

"Okay," he says into his phone, "we're connected."

On the kitchen table, the iPhone dings.

I hurry over and push Carter aside and sink into one of the kitchen chairs, snatch the phone back up.

daddy says it was my fault the baby died

That Molotov cocktail of panic and despair hasn't quite destroyed me yet, but this nearly does.

More tears filling my eyes, I type out a hurried reply.

Do you remember where you were when daddy abducted you?
no
Do you know his real name?
no i dont
he makes me call him daddy
and says im his good little girl

Revulsion overpowers the panic and despair. I feel like I'm going to be sick. Might throw up right here at the kitchen table, all over Agent Donovan's fancy laptop.

Focus, Jess.

I type: What does daddy look like?

It sickens me to keep using the name, but I feel I have no choice.

More dots.

ive never seen his face
he always wears a mask
but his eyes are brown
i think hes white

I glance over at Carter, who still has the phone to his ear.

"Well?" I ask him.

He repeats the question into the phone, listens a beat, and then shakes his head.

"They need more time."

Then Carter realizes we've left the list of questions in the living room. The phone still to his ear, he runs into the living room and then returns and slaps the paper down in front of me.

"Stick to the script."

Gritting my teeth, I type: Before you said he was a police officer. How do you know for sure?

The dots again.

he showed me his badge

Carter, reading over my shoulder now, says, "Ask her to describe the badge."

I ignore his hot breath on my ear and type back a reply.

Can you describe the badge?
it was so long ago i think it was silver
Do you remember what was on it? Any words or symbols?
i cant remember
it was so long ago
im sorry mom

Carter, stepping away to check the laptop screen, says into his phone, "Status?"

He's silent for another beat, listening, and then shakes his head at me. "They still need more time."

I type: Can you describe where you're being kept?

At first nothing on the screen. Not even the dots. Almost a minute goes by, and dread starts to form in the pit of my stomach.

"Shit," Carter whispers, now standing beside me again. Then into the phone: "Have you made a connection yet?"

That's when the iPhone dings again.

i think hes coming

i have to go

he will kill me if he knows what ive done

mom i love you

tell dad i love him

I type back a reply—I love you too—but unlike the rest of the messages, this one doesn't go through. Which means her phone must be off again.

Carter still has his phone to his ear. It's clear he's listening to someone speaking, and then he issues a heavy sigh, shakes his head at me.

That's when we hear the screech of tires as a car pulls into the driveway.

Seconds later Joe bursts inside. His eyes are wide, and he's breathing so heavily it looks like he might have a heart attack.

"What happened?"

20

Jessica

Four Days after the Pep Rally

Nicole Mitchell was several years younger than me, petite with sharp cheekbones and strawberry-blonde hair just like her daughter's.

She was a woman marred by tragedy—first her husband, then her daughter—and she tried to put on a brave face, but you could tell how much she was hurting underneath the surface.

"I'm thinking about moving," she said, taking a sip of her tea.

We were in her kitchen, just the two of us, sitting at the table that was now too big for a woman who lived by herself.

I had known Nicole for nearly two decades—our daughters had gone to preschool together—but we had never been close. I was always too busy working, too focused on managing the Wonderwall to socialize.

Now, sitting across from Nicole, I wasn't thirsty but took a sip of my tea, set the cup back down on the saucer.

"Where are you thinking of moving to?"

Nicole sat forward in her chair, stirring her tea. The last time I'd seen her was at Taylor's funeral. She'd put on that brave face then, just as she had when her husband had died. But the problem with brave faces is that they don't last forever; eventually they fade, and the pain and fear beneath peek through.

"California, maybe. My sister lives out there with her husband and kids. She told me there's a spare room I can use for as long as I'd like. I . . . I don't want to interrupt their lives, but I'm not sure just how much longer I can stay here. It's not like I need all this space anyway."

She lifted her eyes to the ceiling, to the rest of the house. A two-story colonial with four bedrooms certainly wasn't the ideal space for a widow who had recently lost her only child.

"She wanted to be a social worker. Taylor, I mean. When Peter got sick, the social workers at the hospital really helped us through. They were such great supports. Taylor told me about a month or so after Peter passed that that was what she wanted to do. She wanted to help people like that. People like . . . us."

Nicole was staring down at her teacup as she spoke, a distant smile on her lips. Even after her death, Taylor still made her mother proud.

"So," Nicole said suddenly, clearly wanting to change the subject, "still no word from Wyn?"

"I'm afraid not."

Nicole leaned forward to take my hand, gave it a soft squeeze.

"I can't even begin to imagine what you're going through. What happened to Taylor was awful, but at least there was closure in a way. This . . . I'm so sorry."

"Thank you," I said, forcing my own smile. "You were a good mother to Taylor. To be honest, I was always jealous of you."

"Me? You were the one raising a daughter while running your own business. I was in awe."

"That's kind of you to say, but I don't think I was ever a good mother. At least, not as good as I should have been."

"Don't put yourself down, Jess. Being a mother is hard. There's no textbook you study. And there's certainly no test you eventually take that determines whether you passed or failed."

I wasn't sure that was quite true, but I didn't want to argue the point.

"When I saw you that first day of preschool," I said, "I felt bad for you. I remember telling Joe I couldn't imagine raising a kid right out of high school. But you . . . you somehow made it look so easy. Like you were a pro."

"Believe me," Nicole said, "I had no idea what I was doing. But I . . . I did my best."

Even though I still wasn't thirsty, I took another sip of my tea and quietly cleared my throat.

"Did you know my mother was a teacher? She taught middle school science. I remember some nights she would sit at the kitchen table grading papers for hours. It didn't look fun to me at all, but my mom never complained. In fact, I think she loved it. No—I *know* she loved it. But . . . she loved me even more. No matter how many papers she had to grade, she always put me first. That was something I always remembered, and what I tried to do with Bronwyn. That no matter how busy I got, no matter how exhausted I might become, I always put her first."

I was staring down at my teacup now.

"I never really knew just how great a teacher my mom was. She didn't teach at my school, so it wasn't like I ever heard other kids talk about her. But then at her funeral, so many of her past students showed up. And when there was time for people to say something about my mother, it was like an endless line of these kids I'd never known standing up one after another to say how my mom had helped them in some way."

Nicole leaned forward again, gave my hand another soft squeeze. "Your mom sounded amazing."

"Oh, she was. She's the reason I studied to become a teacher in college. I thought maybe I had it in me too, like being a great teacher was hereditary or something. And while I did okay, I just . . . it wasn't for me. The kids drove me nuts. I could barely control them on a good day. Part of me wondered whether or not I even liked kids. If, well, I eventually had my own, would I even like them? Would I be halfway as good a mother as my own mom?"

Nicole still had my hand in hers. She gave it another squeeze as she leaned back.

"If you're thinking Wyn ran away because of you, just stop that right now."

"But we had an argument last week. It was really bad. Maybe—"

"Stop it, Jess. You'll drive yourself crazy. Heck, Taylor and I had arguments all the time. Especially when it came to Sean. I didn't want her making the same mistake I made."

"What mistake?"

"What do you think? Becoming pregnant so young. But she promised me they were always being safe, and . . . well, after her accident, I'd gotten back the autopsy report from Chief Parsons. Part of me was worried that she'd been pregnant, but the only thing in the report was that she had alcohol in her system."

There was a silence then. Nicole wiped at the tears starting to well up in her eyes. I stared down at my tea, not sure how to continue, and then just said it.

"Bronwyn's pregnant."

Nicole's eyes went wide. "How do you know?"

"Danny Scarola let me get into her locker at work. There was a pregnancy test inside. It was positive."

"Oh my God. Do you know who—"

I shook my head.

"No. I thought maybe Aaron Colvin, but he denied it, said that they'd only had sex once and that they'd used a condom. And then . . . well, let me ask you a question. Do you still have the poster board from the school assembly?"

"Of course. It's up in Taylor's room. Why do you ask?"

I slipped the note from my pocket, unfolded it, and placed it on the table. Pushed it toward her so that she could read the handwriting.

Nicole said, "What is this?"

I told her about searching my daughter's room a second time. About finding this note. About calling the number and hearing the voicemail prompt.

"Chad Murphy?" Nicole said, incredulous. "I can't imagine it's him. He . . ." But then she glanced down at the note again, her eyebrows knitting together, and said, "Wait here."

She went upstairs and then returned a minute later. Somebody at school had taken a photo of Taylor and blown it up to the size of a poster. It was a lovely photograph, Taylor smiling brightly at the camera and looking as beautiful as ever.

All over the poster board, the high school staff had written messages and signed their names. I remembered seeing it at the assembly the school had hosted. Parents had been encouraged to attend, so of course I'd made sure to be there.

Now, standing at the table holding the poster board, Nicole pointed at the bottom-left corner.

Chad Murphy's note—*One of the brightest and the best. You will be missed, T*—was there in black ink, his signature underneath.

I held up the note beside it.

The *M* on the note was more of a scribble; it looked close but wasn't exact.

The *C*, however, looked very much the same, both on the poster board and the note.

The slope of the *Ls* matched even more.

"Well?" Nicole asked.

Feeling my stomach drop, I nodded at her.

"Thank you."

A second after the final bell rang that Tuesday afternoon, an army of students poured through the doors. Some hopped on buses, while others climbed into their cars and pickup trucks and SUVs.

Teachers started to trickle out of the school as well, headed for their vehicles in the employee lot.

I was parked near the far corner, my car facing the baseball field. In the rearview mirror, I watched each teacher as they came out the side exit, ready to head home.

As soon as I spotted Chad Murphy, I dialed his number on my phone.

I used *67 so the number would come up blocked. I didn't want him calling me back. I'd gotten lucky yesterday when it went straight to voicemail; if my number had in fact ended up on his incoming call log, fortunately he hadn't bothered to call me back.

Chad was walking with another teacher. She was young and pretty, and her name escaped me. Chad must have said something funny, because she let loose a flirtatious laugh, even went so far as to touch his arm, and that was when Chad's cell phone started vibrating in his pocket.

He paused and pulled out the phone. Frowned down at the screen. He saw it was a blocked number, so he debated whether or not to answer it, and then decided to dismiss the call.

Again, I heard his voicemail prompt.

"Hey, it's Chad. Leave me a message."

I disconnected, then dialed again.

Chad had slipped the phone back into his pocket, shaking his head at the pretty teacher, and then he once again felt the phone start to vibrate.

Again with a frown, he pulled out the phone, stared at the screen, and this time decided to give it a try.

My phone stopped ringing as he put his own phone to his ear.

In the rearview mirror, I watched him mouth the single word a half second before I heard it on my end.

"Hello?"

I terminated the call, released a heavy breath.

"Gotcha," I whispered.

—

The conference room next to the school office was pin-drop silent.

Joe and I sat on one side of the conference table, Chad Murphy and Principal Webber across from us.

It was early Wednesday morning and Chad had been cheerful at first, joking about how he hadn't been called down to the principal's office like this in years, but then once Principal Webber placed the note in front of him, his smile started to fade.

"What is this supposed to be?" he asked.

"You tell us, Chad," Principal Webber said. "Isn't that your phone number?"

Staring down at the note again, his frown deepened.

"It is, yeah. But—"

"Ms. Moore found this note in her daughter's desk drawer at home."

Chad stared at him as though not quite comprehending the words. Then, suddenly, they hit the right nerve, and his eyes widened.

"Wait. Hold up. Do you think *I* wrote this?"

"That is your number, isn't it?"

"It is, but—"

"And from what I can tell, that also looks like your handwriting."

While I'd heard "trapped like a cornered animal" used to describe people before, I'd never actually seen it with my own eyes.

"I don't know what's going on here," Chad said, his tone panicked, "but I didn't write this note."

Principal Webber let out a disappointed sigh.

"I mean it!" Chad practically shouted. "That's my number, yes, and that looks like my handwriting. I'll admit that, but *I didn't write it.* And I especially didn't give this or anything to Wyn!"

He was directing his focus across the table. Pleading with us to believe him. Now he no longer looked like a cornered animal; he looked like an animal that knows it's next up to be euthanized.

"Look," Chad said, "I liked Wyn a lot. She was a cool kid. She *is* a cool kid. I don't know where she's gone, but I've never had any contact with her outside of school, and I've never once given her or *any* student my cell phone number."

He was looking at Principal Webber now, pleading with the man who had the power to destroy his career. I almost felt sorry for him. But I felt even sorrier for my daughter, wherever she might now be, and I steeled myself as I glared across the table.

I said, "How many other students have you had inappropriate relationships with?"

"Christ!" Chad said, throwing up his hands. "Inappropriate relationships? Are you kidding me?"

Principal Webber said, "Chad, calm down. We're simply trying to get to the bottom of where Wyn may have gone."

"No, screw that. You bring me in here and accuse me of this BS without giving me any heads-up? Where's my fucking union rep?"

Principal Webber cleared his throat, said in his deep, low voice, "Chad, watch your mouth."

"You want to talk about inappropriate relationships?" Chad knew he was on his last leg, and he wanted to find anything that might save him. "Why don't you bring Bryan Parker in here. He and Wyn were always talking. Even after school, I'd sometimes see her in his classroom. *That's* who you should be talking to right now. Not me."

21

Wyn

Day of the Pep Rally

Gone.

There was just no other way to describe it.

Her guitar had been there only hours ago—she had placed it in there herself—but now it was gone!

Her breathing had started to increase, bit by bit. She didn't know how long it had been going on—probably when she'd first spied the butterfly on the inside of Autumn Porter's wrist—but she felt it now, that tightness in her chest, that feeling like she was losing all her oxygen.

A hand touched her shoulder, and she would have screamed if she'd had any breath at all. But as it was, all she could do was spin around to find Mr. Parker standing behind her, having just entered the room, his eyes full of concern.

"Wyn?"

She didn't answer—couldn't answer—but it didn't matter anyway, because Mr. Parker realized what was happening and dashed past her toward his desk. He opened the bottom drawer and pulled out a brown lunch bag, dumping the contents—sandwich, Goldfish crackers, an orange—onto his desk and then hustled back and handed the now-empty bag to her.

"Here, here, take this. Breathe into it. Come on, Wyn. Breathe into it."

She did as he instructed, taking the bag and putting it to her mouth and breathing in and breathing out, breathing in and breathing out.

"There you go," Mr. Parker said, leading her to one of the desks in the front and helping her sit down.

He watched her, still worried, before crossing over to close the classroom door and then returning to sit down next to her.

The closet door was still ajar, and Wyn was sitting at the perfect angle to see that nothing—at least not her guitar—was inside.

"Where is it?"

"Hmm?" Mr. Parker said, frowning at her. Then, tracing her gaze with his own: "Oh, don't worry about that. It's safe. I put it in my car."

"Why?"

Mr. Parker rolled his eyes, shaking his head.

"Wasn't as much room in there as I'd thought there was. First period, I opened the door to grab something and the guitar nearly fell out on the floor. Some of the kids in class actually gasped, like I'd just caught a baby or something. And that's when I noticed a few of your . . . well, *friends* watching me."

Mr. Parker was very well aware of the animus between Wyn and some of the cheerleaders. He wasn't blind.

"They knew exactly whose guitar it was. When I came back from the teachers' lounge during third period, one of them was standing in the doorway as the lookout. She ducked out of the way, and seconds later three of them hurried out of the room and headed in the other direction. I had a hunch they were trying to get into the closet, so to be safe I decided to take your guitar and put it in the trunk of my car."

Wyn's breathing had slowed back to normal, and her heart no longer felt like it was going to burst out of her chest, but that didn't mean she was feeling better.

Far from it.

Mr. Parker said, "Are you going to tell me now?"

She blinked, tearing her gaze away from the closet for the first time. "Tell you what?"

"What you plan to do at the pep rally. I know you, Wyn. I know you're up to something."

He grinned when he said this, and normally she would have smiled, but now she just shook her head and spoke quietly.

"I know what I'm doing."

"You might be able to play your guitar and sing on those videos you post on YouTube and Twitter, but in front of a crowd as big as the pep rally it's going to be different. Are you sure you're up for this?"

The mention of Twitter made her pause. For the past several minutes she'd been trying to reckon with the idea that Autumn Porter was Onyx Butterfly. That Wyn had been opening herself up to the biggest bully in the school these past two months. It wouldn't be surprising. Autumn was the most manipulative person Wyn knew, and secretly befriending her on social media just to piece together intimate details about Wyn that could later be used against her seemed right in Autumn's wheelhouse.

But now that Wyn's panic attack had started to subside, she began to wonder if maybe she'd been seeing things. She had definitely seen the tattoo—that was for sure—but was it a butterfly? It had happened so fast, and Wyn had already been on edge, that maybe her already overstressed mind had overlaid an image of something else.

So now she was forced to wonder: Could it be Mr. Parker instead? Wyn didn't think that was possible, because they were already so close that there was no reason for Mr. Parker to play games like this. But still . . .

"Onyx Butterfly," she said, and then, as with Mr. Murphy, she watched the frown spread across his face.

"You mean your song?"

"Never mind."

She wanted to get up, back onto her feet, start to move because she had to do *something* to keep her mind occupied, but when she started to shift in her seat, Mr. Parker reached out and gently placed his hand on her arm.

"Hey," he said, his voice soft, "tell me what's wrong."

She wanted to; she really did. Now with Taylor gone, Mr. Parker was probably the closest friend she had. He knew more about her than pretty much anybody else in the world, even her parents, and if everything went according to plan, Wyn knew that she would miss Mr. Parker more than any other teacher in the school.

The desire to tell him everything was almost too tempting, because she realized part of her wanted to be talked out of it.

That was a traitorous part too consumed with its own self-preservation. It was the part of her that worried about everything, that was continually second-guessing all her decisions, always coming up with worst-case scenarios.

Wyn knew that if she was going to do this—if she was to expose the school, the *world*, to the truth about Sean Heller and what had happened to Taylor—then she needed to ignore that traitorous part, no matter how much it was trying to save her.

Mr. Parker's hand was still on her arm. It felt good there. Felt right.

Maybe she should tell him what she was planning, after all. Let him be her sounding board instead of that part of her that sometimes spoke in Taylor's voice.

Instead, she whispered, "Thank you."

He sat back, that warm comfort of his hand on her arm disappearing, and gave her a lopsided smile.

"For what?"

She stood up from the desk. Feeling steady now on her feet. Feeling like she wasn't going to have another panic attack.

Mr. Parker stood up too. He didn't say anything, just watched her, waiting for her to answer.

She stepped close and opened her arms, and after a stunned moment, he hugged her back.

"For everything," she whispered.

22

Jessica

Now

It's early Wednesday morning, not even ten hours since Bronwyn's last contact, and everyone is at the house again.

Joe, Tony Parsons, and I are squeezed around the kitchen table to see Special Agent Edward Donovan on the iPad screen. Joe has brought the tablet along and set it up so that the agent can speak to us via Skype.

Carter Redcross stands by the fridge, his arms crossed, leaning against the counter, while James Healy—who arrived with Tony—leans against the counter on the other side of the kitchen, by the sink.

"I'm going to be honest with you," Agent Donovan says, looking out at us from the iPad. "I've never handled a situation quite like this before. No agent that I know of has. I've already updated my ASAC. I've even had him review the screenshots of the most recent text messages. We thought our tech would be able to determine a location, but unfortunately he just didn't have enough time to establish a proper trace."

Carter makes a noise, a kind of snort, and mumbles something under his breath as he shakes his head.

I turn in my seat to glare at him. "What the fuck did you just say?"

"Jess," Joe says, touching my arm, but I shake him off.

"No, I want to know what he said."

Carter looks as if he's using every last ounce of willpower left to not roll his eyes.

"I didn't say anything," he tells me.

Joe clears his throat loudly, trying to get us back on track.

"You did what you could, Agent Donovan. The only question now is what more can be done, if anything."

"We think we might have a plan, though it's too premature to discuss right now. But I need you to understand that this is top priority for us. We're doing everything we can to locate your daughter. It's just . . . well, right now we don't have much to go on."

"We understand," Joe says. "And it's much appreciated. But . . . what can Jess and I do in the meantime?"

"That's something else that came up during my conversation. As of right now we don't know whether or not the unsub is truly law enforcement. We don't even know whether he's in the state or somewhere across the country. He might not even be aware of who you are. But on the other hand, he might know exactly who the two of you are. He might even be watching you."

I'm still fuming about what Carter may or may not have said—part of me knowing that I could have reacted faster last night, that maybe an extra couple of seconds might have been all it took to establish a trace—but this last bit by Agent Donovan catches my ear and nearly makes me shout.

"*Watching* us?"

"Maybe not physically, but he might be monitoring social media, the news around this area, that sort of thing. Again, Ms. Moore, we don't know whether or not that's the case, but we don't want to take any chances. It probably doesn't help that there's been more activity than usual at your house the past couple days, which was one of the reasons I decided not to come up today. It's my understanding that Tony would like to keep an officer with you at all times moving forward, and in that case it's important the shadow be as inconspicuous as possible."

Agent Donovan falls silent. He looks down briefly, and sighs.

"I wish I had better news. But I want both of you to know that we're not giving up. I have a meeting scheduled for later today, and I hope to bring back a new plan to you soon. Until then, Tony has my number."

After we say our goodbyes, Joe closes the tablet. For a moment, there's silence while we all take in what we just heard, and then Tony clears his throat.

"Carter, thank you for everything the past few days. Now I want you to head home and get some rest."

Carter nods and heads for the door, ignoring me as I track him with my eyes.

After Carter leaves, Tony says, "I'm going to have James stay here for the time being."

"No need," I say.

"Jess, I know it's an inconvenience, but we need somebody close in case—"

"You heard what Agent Donovan said. This psycho could be *watching* us right now."

"She's right," James says. "I can find a place to park down the road, and when Ms. Moore needs to go anywhere, I'll tail her at a discreet distance."

"That's fine," Tony says. "But, Jess, the moment your daughter makes contact again, you need to let me know ASAP so I can call Eddie."

Since Tony isn't in uniform, I ask, "Are you working today?"

"No. Carol's personal care aide called in sick, and the agency doesn't have anyone else to cover it, so I need to stay home with her today. I probably shouldn't even be here now, but I wanted to make an appearance."

"We appreciate it, Tony," Joe says, and leads Tony and James to the door.

As soon as it's just the two of us, Joe turns back to me, his face pinched.

"I told you she was pregnant," I whisper, and Joe holds me as I cry.

Joe doesn't want to leave. He feels guilty not being here last night when Bronwyn texted. Not that it would have changed anything.

I tell him he needs to head home. He has a wife and two children to take care of. Plus, Stuart needs him back on the campaign.

Eventually Joe agrees, though he says he'll stop by later tonight to check in. At the very least, he'll call.

After he's gone and I have the house to myself, I take a long shower. It's longer than usual because I cry half the time, feeling so weak and vulnerable and helpless but knowing that I'm not nearly as weak or vulnerable or helpless as my daughter is right now, wherever she is, and that makes me cry even harder.

When I leave the house, I spot James parked down the road, just as he promised. He watches me pass as I speed by, and then just before I draw out of sight, he pulls out to follow me.

He follows me at a distance all the way to Shepherd's Market.

I park near the entrance, but James backs his car into a space near the rear corner of the parking lot.

Inside, I grab a cart and gather the essentials.

I spot Danny Scarola helping out in the deli, and he notices me and gives me a nod of acknowledgment, but that's it. I've seen him countless times over the past year. For a while, he'd seek me out, ask if there was any word from Bronwyn, but after a few months it became clear what the answer would be, so he stopped asking.

I turn the corner into the snack aisle and stop short.

Sean Heller is standing at the far end, grabbing a bag of potato chips and placing it into his cart filled with several other snacks.

His injury from a year ago has left him with a slight limp. He's gained a lot of weight during that time. No longer is he the tall, lean star quarterback destined for greatness.

Sean starts to push his cart toward me, and for an instant our eyes connect.

I remember that evening, almost a year ago, when he came into the Wonderwall with his parents. A month or so after Bronwyn had gone missing. When Sean Heller was still riding high and everything looked like it was coming up roses.

Based on his expression, Sean remembers this too. He stares at me for another moment, and then wheels around and pushes his cart out of the aisle toward the registers.

James is still in the same spot when I exit the store.

I load the groceries into my car and head out of the parking lot, James trailing behind me, but I don't head home.

Instead, I head to Tony's.

Tony Parsons lives in a farmhouse about a half mile off Timber Road. It sits on about ten acres of land, much of it woods. From what I was once told, the farmhouse had been handed down through the generations, from Parsons male to Parsons male, though it didn't seem as though any of Tony's kids were interested in taking it over someday.

The farmhouse itself has stone siding with white trim. A large wraparound porch that sports several wooden rocking chairs and a swing hanging by two chains from the ceiling.

Just behind the farmhouse is the barn. It's not a large barn, and it's certainly seen better days, the siding weathered, the roof in not-so-great shape.

Tony steps out of the barn as I ease to a stop.

He frowns, wiping his hands on a rag, and then glances past me at James as he comes up the long drive in my wake.

"Jess?" Tony says, as I step out of the car.

"I don't want Carter Redcross involved in this anymore."

Tony checks to make sure James hasn't gotten out of his car. He sighs and nods.

"Yes, I heard him mumble something this morning too. You have to understand, Jess, Carter hasn't gotten much sleep these past couple of days. None of us have."

"I just don't feel comfortable including him in this anymore. I know I can be difficult at times, and maybe I was a bit slow to react last night, but this is my daughter we're talking about here, Tony. I don't want whatever little spat Carter and I may have had to interfere with things."

"I understand your concern, Jess. This is a stressful situation. I can't even begin to imagine what you and Joe are going through. If you don't want Carter involved anymore, I respect that. The problem is, I'm not sure who I have to replace him with."

"You don't have to replace him with anyone. I don't need a babysitter."

"They're not *babysitting* you, Jess. They're there for support."

"Well, I don't need them."

"I know you don't, Jess. But *I* need them. Say the next time your daughter texts you again, she tells you where she is, or gives you more information to let us know how to track her down. I want somebody there who can react immediately. Somebody who . . . well, who isn't as emotionally invested as you and Joe, if that makes sense."

It does. Of course it does. And I realize that no matter how much I might protest, Tony isn't going to let up. Part of him feels responsible for what's happened to my daughter. That had Tony done more a year ago, maybe Bronwyn wouldn't be in the situation she's in right now.

I think part of Tony feels that way because that's exactly how I feel.

Despite the fact it's the first week in October, the sky is clear and the sun is bright. The trees around Tony's property have already started to turn, just like the trees all around Bowden.

I glance up toward the farmhouse and ask, "How's Carol?"

"She has her good days and bad days, but recently more bad days than good. That's why she's supposed to have her personal care aide with her until I get home. Normally there aren't any issues, except for today. But the truth is I'm not sure just how much longer it'll be before I won't have any choice but to put her in a nursing home."

I remember when Tony and Carol would come into the Wonderwall for dinner almost every week before her illness grew worse, how kind and gentle Carol could be, how loving she was to Tony. Carol always joked with the waitstaff, and whenever I happened to be nearby, she'd call me over and take my hand in hers as she asked how Bronwyn was doing.

"She used to have so many friends," Tony says quietly. "Used to be involved in so many social activities at church. The grandkids used to visit all the time. But they get nervous around her now, just aren't sure how to act. One day Carol might know all their names, remember their birthdays, and then the next time it'll be like she doesn't even recognize them. It scares them. And so I'd hoped putting in the pool would help make the grandkids want to come visit more often, but . . ."

From where I'm standing, I have a good view of Tony's backyard and the in-ground pool he had put in last year. It looks to be a pretty decent size, and it's covered now for the season.

"They didn't like the pool?"

"Yes and no. It was a good incentive to get them to come out here. I'd told my son that we'd put in a pool specifically for the grandkids, and back in July they came out. And it was nice at first, what with Carol having one of her good days. But then Billy slipped while getting out of the pool and cracked his skull right open."

"Christ."

"Yeah, it was bad. I didn't think the bleeding would ever stop. And he was just lying there howling, and my son and his wife were trying to keep him calm, and we thought maybe we might be able to get him in the car and take him to the hospital, but instead we needed to call for an ambulance. And you know just how far out we are. It felt like it took that ambulance forever to show up. But . . . well, Billy got stitched up, and he's fine now, but they haven't visited since. Can't say I blame them."

Tony stares off at the covered pool for a long moment, and then he sighs again.

"You don't want Carter Redcross involved anymore, that's fine. There's somebody else I have in mind—somebody who I think would do a real good job—but . . . well, I'm not sure you're gonna like it."

23

Jessica

Five Days after the Pep Rally

Bryan Parker sat in the same spot Chad Murphy had sat in less than a half hour ago, and like Chad, Bryan immediately sensed the tension.

"What's going on?" he asked.

"We'd just like to get some clarification on a few things, Bryan," Principal Webber said. "Regarding Wyn Hayden."

The man didn't appear at all nervous after hearing my daughter's name. If anything, he looked concerned.

"Any word from her yet?"

Chad, I suddenly realized, hadn't even bothered asking for an update. I wasn't sure whether that made him more or less suspicious. I still wasn't convinced he hadn't slipped my daughter the note. He could take a polygraph test and pass it, and I would still think he was lying.

Otherwise, how did the note—written in Chad's own hand and including his cell phone number—end up in Bronwyn's bedroom, hidden in her desk?

Chad maintained that he'd never written it, let alone given it to my daughter, though he did acknowledge the handwriting looked like his own.

He had a girlfriend, he said, who lived and worked one town over. When he wasn't at school, he was always with her.

When he'd announced this, I'd thought about him with the pretty teacher and how she'd laughed and touched his arm, and not once had he made it clear that he wasn't interested.

I'd almost brought it up too, had almost blurted out that I'd seen Chad with the pretty teacher, but I'd left out my visit to the high school yesterday from what I'd told Joe—and then later Principal Webber, when we came to the school this morning—because already I had the feeling that Joe thought I was losing it.

"How close would you say you are with Bronwyn Hayden?" Principal Webber asked.

Bryan shrugged. "We get along pretty well."

"We've heard reports that she's often in your classroom after school."

"She's come to my classroom, yes. So have a lot of students. What's going on here?" He looked around the room again, this time doing his best not to put too much focus on either Joe or myself. "Is Wyn still missing?"

Principal Webber cleared his throat. "Did you see Wyn last Friday?"

Another glance around the room, cautiously this time, as though he knew he was now under some kind of suspicion. He nodded.

"She'd brought her guitar to school that morning. She asked if she could leave it with me in my room. I guess she was afraid some of the kids might try to break into her car if they knew it was there. I put it in my closet, but then later I suspected some of the students were trying to get into the closet, so I went and put it in my own car. Say what you will about these kids, but they know better than to mess with a teacher's car. Anyway, I retrieved the guitar right before the pep rally and gave it to Wyn. And then . . . well, you know what happened."

Joe asked, "Why was she afraid some of the kids might try to break into her car?"

Bryan stared across the table at Joe, a thoughtful frown on his face. "She never told you, did she?"

When Joe and I didn't answer—because it was clear the question was aimed at both of us, Bronwyn's parents—Bryan sighed and shook his head.

"I'd say the majority of the school likes Wyn just fine. She gets along with practically everybody. Except some of the cheerleaders. They . . . well, they hate her."

"I still don't get it," Joe said. "Why do they hate her? Just because she was friends with Taylor?"

"Because she isn't one of them."

I spoke so quietly I didn't even hear myself at first. I was only half-aware of Joe turning to look at me, and then I realized it was me who had spoken and found myself continuing.

"She isn't the same kind of popular as the rest of them. Wyn and Taylor were close. They were best friends. That . . . that isn't the normal chain in high school. It doesn't make sense. So they hate her."

Silence. Almost that pin-drop silence from an hour earlier with Chad Murphy.

Bryan said, "I'm not sure what you think is going on between Wyn and me, but I can assure you nothing is. I've always liked her. She's a bright kid. Very talented. I get along with a lot of my students. Some of them come to my room between classes or after school to talk about whatever. Wyn liked to talk to me about music. She knew in college I used to play the piano. Still do, but not nearly as well as I used to."

He paused a beat, looking around the room once again, before his gaze settled on me.

"I don't know where Wyn's gone, but every day I pray that she's safe and that she'll be back soon. Otherwise, I don't know what more I can tell you."

Later that day around four o'clock, feeling exhausted and defeated, I'd already gone through a bottle of wine when there was a knock at the door.

It was Aaron Colvin.

He wore his Bowden Badgers hoodie and the gray Phillies cap Bronwyn had gotten him last year.

"Aaron? What are you doing here?"

I'm sure I sounded surprised to see him, especially after our encounter in his kitchen only days ago.

Aaron said, "I'm sorry to stop by like this, Ms. Moore . . ."

His voice trailed off, and in that pause, my stomach clenched. Whatever had brought Aaron here, it wasn't good.

"Do you want to come inside?"

He glanced down at his sneakers, seemed to think about it for a moment, then nodded.

Once he was inside, he just stood there, looking around the living room like he'd never seen it before, when in reality he'd been inside this house dozens of times.

"So what can I do for you, Aaron?"

He continued to look around the living room, and it hit me a second later that it was so he didn't have to look me in the eye.

He said, "About the other day . . ."

His voice trailed off again, so I decided to fill the silence.

"Yes, about that. I'm sorry about what happened. I never meant to accuse you of—"

"No, I get that, and it's cool. I mean, I'm worried about Wyn too. But about what you'd asked me, you know, the pregnancy test and everything . . ."

I gave him a few seconds, and when he didn't say anything further, I said, "Yes?"

"I just . . . like I said, we'd only done it once, and when we did, we were safe. And I hate to think that maybe I'd pressured her to do it again, like you said."

"Again, Aaron, I didn't mean to—"

"I know, but it's just been bothering me. When Wyn broke up with me, she didn't really give a reason. And somehow that made it even worse. Like I said before, I loved her. Still do love her. And then one day she tells me that she doesn't love me anymore and that's that. It . . . it wrecked me, if I'm being honest. Totally messed me up, all that constant wondering what I'd done wrong. And then you came to the house with that pregnancy test, and I . . . well, I've been wondering now if she'd been seeing someone else at the same time."

I just stared back at Aaron, silent. I wasn't sure how to respond. I thought again about sitting across from Chad Murphy this morning. He claimed he'd never had any contact with Bronwyn outside of school, and that he'd never given her or any student his cell phone number. He had seemed sincere, had sounded convincing, but maybe it was all a lie.

Still, I couldn't bring it up with Aaron. Not now. Not until I had more evidence besides a note that Chad promised he had never written.

"I'm not sure what to say, Aaron. If you're asking if Wyn had ever hinted about anything like that, the answer is no."

Aaron nodded slowly.

"I get that. I do. And I just . . . Like I said, I'm worried about Wyn. After what happened at the pep rally, and then later at Autumn Porter's house, I just—"

"Wait," I said. "What happened at Autumn Porter's house?"

Aaron paused and looked at me now. There was worry in his eyes, as though he'd been caught doing something he shouldn't have been doing.

"Aaron," I said evenly, "tell me what happened."

He swallowed before glancing back down at his sneakers, and then sighed.

"It was later that Friday night, after the game. Autumn was throwing a party at her house."

"And Bronwyn was there?"

"Yeah, but she wasn't there long."

"Why not?"

"Because . . ."

"Aaron, please. You can tell me."

Aaron swallowed again. He stared at me for a beat before taking off his cap and running his fingers through his hair.

"I get why everybody loves him. He's the star quarterback. Everybody's hero. Did you know some people think he's going to make it to the NFL someday? I mean, he puts on a good show, acts like he's a real stand-up guy, but the truth is he can be such an asshole."

I took a step forward, wanting to reach out and shake Aaron so that he'd focus and tell me what I wanted to know. Instead I spoke quietly, hoping the gentle approach would work.

"Are you talking about Sean Heller?"

Aaron looked up at me sharply then, as if surprised I had figured it out, though who else could he possibly be talking about?

I took another step forward, and this time I did reach out, though I gently laid a hand on his shoulder.

"What about Sean Heller, Aaron? What did he do?"

When you've had a bottle of wine, it's usually best not to get behind the wheel of your car, but if you do, it's most certainly not a great idea to drive straight to the police chief's house.

But that's exactly what I did as soon as Aaron left.

I broke every speed limit on the drive over, and then tore up the half-mile drive to the farmhouse and hit the brakes a bit too hard. This caught Tony's attention, and he stepped outside even before I cut the engine.

He came down the steps, wearing jeans and a flannel shirt, his work boots clomping over the flagstones.

"Jessica?"

I started toward him, purposefully, my shoulders back and my chin high, but then all at once I felt unsteady on my feet. I worried Tony would smell the wine on my breath even though I'd chewed gum on the drive over, and I had the crazy thought that he would make me perform a sobriety test right here in his driveway.

"Jess, what's wrong?"

He was only a few feet away now, his expression filled with worry.

I asked, "Why didn't you tell me about Sean Heller?"

For an instant, it looked like he had no idea what I was talking about, and then he said, "Why don't you come inside."

"No. Tell me now. Why did nobody say anything about Sean Heller? Does Joe know?"

Tony stared at me, his expression now neutral. He looked like he was trying to figure out the best way to answer before he finally decided to just go for it.

"He does, yes."

The betrayal felt like a sword to my stomach, slicing me in half.

"Why didn't anyone tell me?"

"Because, Jess, there was nothing to tell."

"It's my understanding Wyn was at Autumn Porter's house Friday night."

"Yes, that's right."

"And that she had some kind of argument with Sean Heller."

"That's our understanding too."

I stared at him, completely perplexed by his indifference.

"Well," I said, and my voice was trembling, almost to the breaking point, "isn't that something I should have been told about?"

Again, that neutral expression.

"Jess, as I said, there was nothing to tell. Yes, we were informed Wyn was at Autumn Porter's house that night, and that she had some kind of disagreement with Sean Heller. James Healy interviewed several of the kids who were at the party, as well as Sean himself, though Sean wouldn't go into much of what the argument was about except that it had something to do with Taylor Mitchell. After that . . . well, everybody said Wyn left the party, and they hadn't seen or heard from her since."

"Why didn't you tell me?"

"We considered it. I spoke to Joe at length about it, but we decided in the end not to trouble you."

"*Trouble* me?"

"Jess, this entire situation has been stressful for everyone involved, especially you. A case in point is the other night when you thought somebody was in your house."

"Somebody *was* in my house."

I almost shouted it, feeling like I was about to blow, but I knew right then that was the last thing I needed to do.

Stay calm, Jess. Focus.

Tony offered up a half-hearted smile.

"I know it's tough, Jess. I can't imagine what all you're going through. But I want you to understand that my officers—as well as the state police—are doing everything we can to find your daughter."

"Not everything," I said, almost spat.

"Fair enough. As I noted the first time we spoke about this, our hands are tied in some respects. Right now . . . well, it still looks like Wyn ran away. We're keeping an eye out, but we can't justify extra man-hours when right now it doesn't look like any crime's been committed."

"You're covering for him, aren't you?"

"Who?"

"Sean Heller. He's Bowden's golden boy, right? The person who will put the town on the map again. That's why you kept it quiet."

Now Tony gave me a look of pure pity. "No, Jess. Nobody's covering for Sean Heller. It's just that, as I've said, nothing happened. They had an argument, that's all."

"But maybe the reason she ran away was *because* of that argument."

Tony said nothing. He just stared back at me.

So that I wouldn't have to face Tony's pitying expression, I glanced around the property. The large field and the trees and then the barn.

"What's that?" I asked, and took a few steps to edge past Tony.

Behind the barn was a piece of construction equipment. Large and yellow and caked with dirt. If I hadn't been standing where I was, I never would have seen it.

"What?" Tony said. Then: "Oh, that? It's a backhoe. Martin Jarrett brought it over for me."

"What's it for?"

Tony pointed at the empty backyard directly behind the house.

"We're putting in a pool."

When Tony noticed my frown, he shrugged.

"Carol hasn't gotten any better, and at this point, it doesn't look like she ever will. We love when the grandkids visit, but . . . this farmhouse isn't their favorite place in the world."

I saw it now, and it broke my heart.

"So you want to bribe them," I said with a smile.

Tony chuckled. "Well, not in so many words, but yes, we want to make this a fun place for them to visit. A more positive experience for them, you might say. Carter Redcross actually suggested it to me. He pointed out that it'll increase the property value once I sell. This place has been in my family for generations, but once Carol . . . Well, let's just say eventually I'll no longer need all this land."

We were quiet then, staring at the empty backyard. Suddenly, all the fight in me had gone out like a single flame in a windstorm.

"Please keep me in the loop moving forward."

"Of course," Tony said. "Can I ask how you heard about it in the first place?"

"Let's just say a little bird told me."

Tony smiled, and then gestured up at the house.

"Would you like to come inside and say hello to Carol? I can't guarantee she'll remember you, but I'm sure she'll love the company."

24

Wyn

Day of the Pep Rally

Sean Heller hadn't always been a star.

In middle school, he had tried out for sports—football, basketball, baseball—but either he didn't make the cut or he rode the bench.

The fact was, Sean had been chunky most of his young life, and he had gotten bullied in elementary and middle school because of it. It wasn't until the eighth grade that Sean started laying off the junk food, started running a couple of miles after school every day, and spent extra time in the gym at school.

When freshman year came around, he tried out for football and—to the surprise of many—made the team.

As it turned out, Sean had been practicing all summer, strengthening his throwing arm, and while he didn't play much that first year, by sophomore year he had become the second-string quarterback, and by junior year he was the starting quarterback and managed to get the team to the state finals, a place Bowden High hadn't been to in decades. While they hadn't won the championship that year, his senior year Sean was able to turn them into state champions—as well as setting a national passing record, solidifying Sean Heller's name in Bowden history and securing him several scholarship opportunities. In the end, Sean had decided to go to Penn State because that was where his dad had gone and Sean loved the team.

Wyn had never had any issues with Sean. In fact, back in middle school, she'd been paired with him during a drama elective, and they had gotten along well. He had been sweet and funny and Wyn had liked talking to him, and Taylor had told her she should hang out with him, like go to the movies or something. But Wyn had said she was too shy, so Taylor had said she would talk to some of Sean's friends to see if Sean liked Wyn, and Wyn had begged Taylor not to do that, and Taylor, because Taylor was Wyn's best friend, had given her a wink and said, *Sure, okay, if that's what you really want.*

Such was the life of a thirteen-year-old girl.

But because of that experience in middle school, Wyn had always gotten along with Sean, saying hi to him in the hallways if they passed each other, but their friendship never went any further than that.

Until the time came when Taylor started dating Sean, and Taylor—who wasn't about to ignore all her friends, especially her close friends, just because she was dating a boy—made sure that Wyn was still included in her life, like when groups went to the movies or the bowling alley or even parties at one kid's house or another.

And Sean was always nice to her, even bringing up how they'd both been in that drama elective back in middle school. Wyn had never gotten the sense he was just putting on a show—she honestly believed Sean was a good guy who had managed to become a star, not one of those guys you hear about who ends up falling in love with himself once he starts to become popular—and after a couple of months it became clear that Taylor's relationship with Sean was becoming serious, and after a year it had become clear to everyone that they were perfect together. Then Sean had won the championship and had accepted the scholarship to Penn State, and he and Taylor had discussed how they weren't going to break up even though Sean was going to college and Taylor had one more year left before she graduated.

He's my soul mate, Taylor had once told Wyn, and Wyn had laughed because for a second she thought Taylor was kidding—like, who actually said stuff like that?—but it quickly became clear Taylor wasn't kidding, that she was serious and that Wyn's laughter had pissed her off, and it had taken almost a week before Taylor had returned any of Wyn's text messages.

It was those times—when Taylor's undying love for Sean Heller made her immune to facts or reason—that Wyn knew better than to talk to her about some of the rumors floating around the school.

How at parties when Taylor was absent, Sean would get drunk and hook up with someone, usually a cheerleader on Taylor's own squad. Though the few times Wyn knew that Taylor had confronted Sean about it (the rumors often being bandied about on social media), Sean had flatly denied such a thing occurred, telling Taylor that he loved her and only her. Eventually Taylor would forgive him and they would go about how they always did—the two of them holding hands as they'd traverse the hallways between classes, cuddling in the cafeteria during lunch—and then a few weeks later there'd be another party and those rumors would start again, about how Sean had gotten a blow job from one girl or another, and then the fighting would start again, only to end once Sean publicly declared his love for Taylor as being his one and only and his—sigh—soul mate.

Wyn had known better than to start trouble. Not if she wanted to remain in Taylor's good graces. Because while Wyn and Taylor had been friends longer than Taylor had even known Sean, Taylor was at a place where her love for Sean was more important than her friendship with her best friend. That was something Wyn didn't want to sacrifice, even when she knew it would be wise for her friend to open her eyes to the truth.

Sean Heller could act like a nice guy, be all funny and sweet, but other times—usually when he was fueled by alcohol—he became a real dick.

Was that somebody Taylor really wanted to be with?

Wyn certainly didn't think so, but she knew her place. Even after the incident with Sean, just weeks before Taylor died.

Wyn had been out at a party, and she hadn't been drinking because she didn't like to drink, even when some of the kids made fun of her. Taylor had asked Wyn to take her and Sean home because both of them were wasted, and Wyn had agreed, because when Taylor asked her to do something, Wyn always did it.

She drove Taylor home first, because Taylor's house was the closest, and then Sean had jumped into the passenger seat, and for the next minute or so they didn't speak at all, until suddenly Wyn felt Sean's hand on her leg.

Wyn hadn't told Taylor what happened after that, because she knew Taylor would never believe her. Taylor always wanted to think the best of her boyfriend, even when she probably knew it was a lie.

If Wyn had to name one fault in her friend, it was that weakness she couldn't stand.

Taylor had always been smarter than that, Wyn thought. She'd always been stronger.

But Wyn knew that sometimes love made people do crazy things. Especially when it came to how they interacted with other people. Even more so, especially how it affected others.

Sometimes Wyn wondered what might have happened had she told Taylor the truth. If that would have changed anything. If two weeks later, Taylor wouldn't have smashed her car into the tree near the bend on Fox Lane.

She thought about that now—what had haunted her all this time—as the bell rang. Usually students would head to whatever elective class they'd signed up for, but today was Homecoming Friday, which meant the entire high school would now head to the gymnasium for the pep rally.

And which meant that very soon Wyn was going to stand up onstage in front of all her peers—not to mention the faculty—and do something that terrified her.

Stop it, the Taylor voice said. *You can do this, babe. You got this.*

Yes, she thought, she did have this. And that was what kept her going, that resolve, and maybe it was because she was so focused on this that she didn't notice some of the squeals at first, like preteen girls at a boy-band concert. But then she realized that everybody was crowding around Taylor's locker, their phones out and held high to take photos and video, and that was when she saw why.

Sean Heller was standing there. He was wearing jeans and his Penn State jacket, and he had a single red rose in his hand.

From her angle several lockers away, Wyn watched as Sean touched his index and middle fingers to his lips, then reached out and pressed those fingers against Taylor's locker.

Then Sean bent down and placed the rose on the floor in front of her locker, stepped back, and whispered, "I miss you so much, baby."

A few *Awwws* sounded out around the hallway, nearly echoing against the tile walls, and Wyn realized her jaw was clenched. But it wasn't until Sean turned, offering up a sad smile to everybody watching, that he spotted her.

They stared at each other for several seconds, and then Wyn turned away and pushed through the crowd.

She was worried if she stayed any longer, she might scream.

25

Jessica

Now

The last time I saw Kenny Gorman, he had just thrown up on the hardwood floor and was being escorted out of the bar by James Healy.

He'd been a wreck, his eyes bloodshot and his mouth curled up in a drunken sneer, completely out of place in the Wonderwall.

Now he looks much better. His hair combed neatly to the side. His eyes bright and aware. His face freshly shaven.

He isn't wearing his uniform but instead a pair of khakis and a polo shirt, and he stands in my kitchen, his eyes lowered, as he makes his apology.

"I was out of line. There's no excuse for my behavior. Especially for . . . well, making a mess of your place."

"That's all right, Kenny. Water under the bridge."

"I said some pretty awful things too. At least, from what I can remember. I said some awful things to you and some other people at the bar, didn't I?"

I merely smile. Fact is, I owe Kenny an apology as well for what I said to him, but I'm not sure this is the time or place. Especially now that Kenny has admitted he doesn't remember much of what happened that night.

"Again, Kenny, it's all right. Sometimes people drink too much."

"It's just my mom . . ." Kenny stares down at his shoes, shakes his head. "It can be a lot to take care of her sometimes. When I'm not working, I take care of her, and when I'm not taking care of her, I'm working, so it's nice to get out of the trailer every once in a while, and then . . ."

He lets it trail there, and I remember what he'd said Friday night, about being stood up. Apparently he'd corresponded with somebody online, made plans to meet up at the Wonderwall, and then the girl was a no-show.

Or maybe she wasn't. Maybe she had shown up, seen Kenny in action, and then decided to bail.

If I were in that girl's shoes and had come in and seen Kenny acting a fool, I would have left too.

"Honestly, Kenny, it's fine."

He looks up at me, surprised. "I'm not banned?"

"No, Kenny, you're not banned."

Tony Parsons, who has been standing off to the side in the kitchen this entire time, claps his hands together just once.

"Excellent," he says. "I see we've let bygones be bygones. So do you think you'll be okay with Kenny shadowing you from now on, Jess?"

"I don't see why not."

"Very good. Now, I need to head back to the office. I'm going to give Eddie a call on the way, see if he and his supervisor have come up with another game plan. You're heading to work now, Jess?"

"That's right."

I notice the hesitant expression on Kenny's face, and smile.

"Don't worry, Kenny. Like I said, you're still welcome there. But just do me one favor."

"What's that?"

"Try not to throw up on the floor again."

"May I see your phone, Ms. Moore?"

Special Agent Donovan holds out his hand, hesitant, understanding how my iPhone has become a lifeline to me, and giving it up for even a couple of seconds could be traumatizing.

It's Friday morning and we're squeezed into my office at the Wonderwall—Joe and Tony and Kenny and the FBI agent. The thought is that if the person who abducted my daughter is surveilling Joe and me, it's better to meet up in public places like this.

After some hesitation, I unlock the screen and give Agent Donovan the phone. He consults his legal pad as he types something into the phone, and then hands it back to me. The whole thing takes less than a minute.

"What did you do?"

He points at the phone, says, "See that there in the Notes app? I inputted what's called a short link. Just copy and paste it into the message next time your daughter texts you."

"What does it do?"

"It'll determine your daughter's location."

Joe makes an irritated sigh and says, "You said that last time."

"Yes, well, this is a bit different. When your daughter clicks on the link, it will access a website that will immediately determine her location. Even if the Wi-Fi your daughter is using has a VPN, it will cut through all of that. Trust me—we had some of our best techs come up with this. Right now, it's the only thing we've got to go on."

I start to smile, suddenly flooded with hope, but then just as quickly I remember to keep myself in check. Because what's unspoken is the possibility that Bronwyn may never reach out again. That her abductor either found the phone and destroyed it or . . . something worse.

Every night I've cried over the horror my daughter has been forced to experience, that I had a grandchild I'll never meet, a baby my daughter didn't have long to know. The crying starts as sad but soon turns angry, and I tell myself if I ever come face-to-face with the monster who took my daughter, I will kill him.

It's not something I've ever thought myself capable of, but motherly rage does something strange to a person.

There isn't much more Agent Donovan can add. The important thing is the link. The agent even has me practice copying and pasting it into a text message, and I feel like a fool, like somebody who doesn't know what she's doing, but I do appreciate that this man is trying to help.

After that, they all start to leave.

Joe hesitates, and it's clear he wants to tell me something, so I ask him what it is.

He tells me that Congressman Thomas has agreed to a debate. It's scheduled for next Tuesday night, at the library one county over. The congressman wants to downplay the debate, but Stuart is hoping to get it televised.

"Wow," I say. "That doesn't seem like much notice for you guys."

"Oh, we'll be fine. Stuart's been practicing for a debate with Thomas for the past several months. But I just . . . I want you to understand the debate and the campaign and everything else are all secondary for me right now. My main focus is Wyn, but right now there isn't much we have to go on, and besides, Stuart really needs my help with—"

"It's fine, Joe."

He hesitates again, like he can't find the right words. Then he says, "Maybe you should come to the debate. It might be a good distraction."

I have no intention of going to the debate, but I'm exhausted and just want this conversation to end, so I tell Joe what he wants to hear.

"Sure," I say. "Maybe I will."

It's Saturday afternoon and I'm in my office with Catherine Colvin.

I let her sit at my desk as she works at the computer. She has access to the Wonderwall's social media accounts on her phone—something I'd been leery of giving her, since she's just a seventeen-year-old kid, but so far she's done a fantastic job.

Now she's telling me about Facebook ads and how we're able to target them not just to individuals in town but to individuals outside of town as well.

The idea, she says, is not merely to keep business where it is (she actually uses the word *plateau*) but to increase business exponentially.

Catherine says she's learned about this strategy in one of her high school classes and has been doing her own research, and that it's worth a try.

The worst that can happen is we lose some money, she says, and I almost laugh because it's not her money to lose, though I do see the value in it.

I remember back when Joe and I opened the Wonderwall and we had printed a thousand flyers to distribute around town, plus splurged on a billboard ad that may or may not have done anything to help bring in customers.

It's crazy how technology has changed in the past two decades. Practically everybody has a smartphone, and practically everybody uses social media, so why not advertise to them on the one device they're sure to never be without?

"Should I launch this?" Catherine asks, circling the cursor around the ad she whipped up in no time. It's a rather artistic photo of the bar's interior and announces our weekend drink specials. "We can start it at just ten dollars a day. I can monitor the CPC if you'd like."

"What's CPC again?"

"It means cost per click. You know, what you're charged every time somebody clicks on the ad."

She smiles up at me, her eyes bright, and I think about sitting in her kitchen just a week ago with Rachel Colvin, and how when Catherine had asked if it was okay for her to go to her friend's house to help her with a project, I had almost answered. I hadn't thought much of it at the time—it was only hours after having been woken by that first text message, and I had been distraught, completely panicked—but now I look at this girl in a whole new light, and I wonder whether I would have hired Catherine had Bronwyn not disappeared. If maybe I had been looking to fill the void of a daughter figure in my life so badly that when Catherine had stopped in asking if there were any open positions, I hired her on the spot.

Thinking of Bronwyn, I feel my eyes starting to tear up and have to turn away.

"Ms. Moore, are you okay?"

I wipe at my eyes with the back of my hand, force a smile.

"Again, Catherine, call me Jessica."

"Well, Jessica, are you okay?"

"I'm fine. And the ad looks great. Go ahead and launch it."

Catherine does just as there's a knock at my office door. Pushing away from the chair, she says, "I'll get it," and walks over to open the door.

Kenny Gorman peeks in, sees that I'm not alone, and quickly says, "Oh, I'm sorry. I didn't mean to bother you."

"No bother at all, Kenny. Catherine was just leaving."

Kenny steps back so that Catherine can squeeze past, and then he steps inside, closing the door behind him.

As I reclaim the chair behind my desk, I ask, "So what can I do for you, Kenny?"

"Oh, nothing. Just . . . I wanted to get away from out front. One of your bartenders has been giving me the stink eye for the past hour."

"Young, good-looking guy with great hair?"

"That's the one."

"Nick Jennings. You might want to apologize to him too. Last time you were in here you almost took a swing at him."

Kenny groans as he holds a hand to his face, then sinks down onto the couch.

"I'm such an asshole," he murmurs.

"We can all be assholes at times, Kenny. In fact, I think I may have said something mean to you that night too. I'm sorry about that."

"Did you? I gotta say, I don't quite remember if you did, but no worries. This is a really nice place, by the way. You and Mr. Hayden built it together?"

"Well, we didn't build it—we bought it cheap as an empty building—but yes, we founded the bar."

"Is that what you always wanted to do? Like, growing up as a little girl, you wanted to have your own business?"

"No. Growing up I wanted to be a Supreme Court justice."

Kenny's eyes go wide.

"Really?" he says. "Why's that?"

"I was in middle school when Ruth Bader Ginsburg was sworn in as a justice on the Supreme Court. I remember being excited because Ruth is my middle name, and for some reason I thought it was just so cool. And when I read more about her, it was inspiring. For a while there, I actually thought about becoming a lawyer, but . . . well, sometimes dreams are just dreams. They're not meant to ever come true."

I don't mention that my mother's untimely death also played a factor. My ambitions shifted from becoming a lawyer to becoming a teacher, just as she had been. Only it turned out becoming a teacher wasn't in the cards either, and after moving to Bowden and finding this empty building and securing a small business loan, I never looked back.

"Sometimes dreams are just dreams," Kenny echoes thoughtfully, and shakes his head. "Damned if that's not the truest statement I ever heard."

"Why? What was your dream as a kid?"

He thinks about it for a moment and then makes a face and shakes his head and says, "Nah, I better not say. It's embarrassing."

"Why is it embarrassing?"

"Because it's . . . embarrassing. A silly kid dream kind of thing."

"I told you mine, Kenny, so it's only fair you tell me yours."

He looks away from my grin, stares up at the ceiling, and then issues a heavy sigh.

"Okay, fine. But don't say I didn't warn you how stupid this was."

I motion for Kenny to continue.

"Well," he says, still not looking at me, "I wanted to be an astronaut."

"Why is that silly or embarrassing or stupid?"

"Well, I mean, look at me. Do I look like the kind of guy who'd be an astronaut?"

"To be honest with you, Kenny, I don't think astronauts have a specific look."

"Yeah, well, when I think back on it, it was pretty silly. But then I soon got interested in football, and I started playing and got really good, and there was talk about me going to college, kind of like how Sean Heller did, though I was nowhere near as good as him, but then . . ."

He trails off, shrugs, says, "But then I went and got drunk one night and screwed everything up. Climbed up onto the roof to do a handstand, and . . . well, no more football for me. Though, if I'm being truthful, I think part of me was glad I had that accident. Because I was scared, you know? Sure, in high school I was a good football player, but would I be any good in college? If anything, I'd be that little fish in the ocean, or however you put it."

I smile but say nothing. It's clear that Kenny is working through something on his own, and I don't want to interrupt him.

"Anyway," he says, "my parents were always supportive of me. Back then, my dad was still alive and working at the factory and making a good salary. We were living in an actual house, so I had my own bedroom, and when I was around ten or eleven, I told my folks one day I wanted to be an astronaut, and they didn't laugh at me or treat me like I was dumb. I mean, they told me not many people manage to make it to space, but they still encouraged me in their own way. In fact, they even got me these glow-in-the-dark stars. You know how your daughter has butterflies on the walls in her room? My parents did something just like that, only with those stars. On the walls, on the ceiling, everywhere. So when you turned off the lights at night, you—"

A knock at my office door cuts Kenny off.

"Come in," I say loudly.

The door opens and Catherine pokes her head in. "Um, Ms. Moore?"

"What is it, Catherine?"

"There's a Suzanne Walker out at the bar. She says that she needs to speak to you, and that she's not leaving until she does."

26

Jessica

Two Weeks after the Pep Rally

If it weren't for Joe putting out those calls for help on social media, I would never have met Suzanne Walker.

Joe had posted on his personal Facebook page that our daughter had run away and asked for people to help spread the word. A good number of people had—about two dozen or so, which to me seemed like a lot—but it wasn't until Mayor Colvin also shared the news that things took off.

Soon hundreds of people shared the notice about Bronwyn. Joe was inundated with messages and emails, many expressing their condolences, while a few others offered what I'm sure they thought were helpful tips, all of which we passed on to law enforcement.

Unfortunately, nothing ever came of those tips, though somebody in Ohio claimed to have seen Bronwyn's car, which resulted in Tony getting in touch with the highway patrol out there, and a trooper did what he could to try to track down any leads, but in the end, nothing came of it.

The news media got involved too, of course. I'd given Joe the go-ahead to speak to the reporters, and a few articles appeared in local outlets, but nothing seemed to go beyond that.

Of the emails that had come in, only a few didn't come across as . . . well, batshit nuts.

One of those was Suzanne Walker's.

Her email was simply a short note saying she'd read about our daughter and how she could relate, as her own daughter had disappeared the year before. Suzanne said she lived in Maryland, where she worked as a dental hygienist, and she even provided her phone number.

This happens more often than we like to think, Suzanne had written. *Unfortunately, it is hard to connect with others in your position. I learned that the hard way. It is not like there are support groups nearby that you can attend. So that is why I am happy to speak to either of you if you would like. Feel free to call or text anytime.*

Joe had forwarded on the email, encouraging me to reach out. He noted that while we were both Bronwyn's parents, his current situation was much different from my own. Joe at least had Emma and Amanda and Trent.

At that point, two weeks had passed since Bronwyn had gone missing. I'd already started planning my extracurricular activities, the ones I purposely kept from Joe and Tony.

I did appreciate Suzanne's email, though. It was thoughtful.

It also turned out that Joe had received a lot of other messages he'd kept from me on purpose, though when I'd pressed and he finally relented and showed them to me, I understood the reason why.

People can be so cruel. Especially strangers on the internet.

While there were those who wanted to help, there were even more who wanted to ridicule our daughter. They'd seen what had happened at the pep rally—some of the videos online had view counts as high as one hundred thousand—and all they wanted to do was demean the most important person in my life.

Some said Bronwyn had obviously run away because she was embarrassed, and she deserved to be.

Others made more insidious claims, pointing the finger at us for killing her.

More than one person admonished Joe and me for having never married, and that had Bronwyn grown up in a nuclear household with parents who had a healthy relationship and attended church every week, the thought to run away never would have crossed her mind.

A few others even went so far as to suggest that Bronwyn had not only run away out of shame, but that she had no doubt also killed herself.

And some of these messages were practically *gleeful*.

Which is why I think I finally responded to Suzanne Walker's email.

By then, it had been in my inbox for over a week. I felt weird texting or calling her, even though she had encouraged it, so I sent her a quick email thanking her for her thoughtful note.

She responded a few hours later, asking if there had been any news regarding Bronwyn.

I told her that unfortunately there hadn't been any news so far. I considered going into more detail—I was sitting at my desk at work, my fingers hovering over the keyboard as I debated whether or not to say more—but decided in the end this woman didn't need to know everything that had happened so far. She had her own life, and she was simply being nice, and there was no reason to bring her into this.

The next day, I received a follow-up email. Suzanne detailed some of what had happened to her daughter, Amber. That she had been sixteen years old. That Amber had played the violin when she was younger, though in high school she had stopped altogether and instead joined the drama club.

Amber, Suzanne said, had wanted to be an actor one day. Nothing too grand—she hadn't had ambitions of going to Hollywood or

Broadway, but just doing local theater. Apparently she had even planned to apply to an acting school. It had been her dream.

Then one day she'd disappeared.

It has now been over a year, and still I have no idea what has become of her, Suzanne wrote.

Because Suzanne had opened up to me, I felt it only fair that I return the favor. I told her how Bronwyn had loved butterflies when she was a girl. How she'd been sad to hear that people collected them, because she believed the butterflies had been killed just so they could be put in those glass cases. When it was explained to her that most times the butterflies were already dead, she still hadn't liked it, equating it to someone putting a dead person in a glass case to display at home.

I admitted that even at such a young age, my daughter had been very insightful, and it had delighted me to no end.

I mentioned how Bronwyn had started playing guitar, first only for fun before she had started taking it much more seriously, teaching herself from watching videos online, and how she had even started writing music and wanted to make that her career.

I sent the email, feeling even more hollow inside, and in the quiet of my office, I cried yet again.

Every day, the sinking feeling that Bronwyn wasn't going to return home became more and more of a reality. I found myself drinking even more at night, going through two, sometimes three, bottles of wine, though never four because I'd determined that four bottles of wine was just *too* much and so would not let myself cross that line.

Then one day Suzanne emailed saying she would be in Harrisburg for a conference, and she knew Bowden was about an hour away and would I be open to meeting for dinner or maybe a drink?

I almost said no. Part of me was scared. It was silly. I didn't have many close friends, especially none that had ever been in my situation, and here was a woman who was very similar to me, and I was afraid to meet her.

We agreed on a midway point, a cozy bar that I knew served American fare, and when we finally met, Suzanne pulled me into a hug and whispered, "I know, Jessica. I know."

She was a bit taller than me, and she had long brown hair and a thin face with a pretty smile.

We took a table at the back of the bar and decided on a pitcher of beer, and Suzanne told me how boring the conference had been so far and asked about my job, and I realized I had never told her about the Wonderwall.

"Hold up," Suzanne said. "Are you telling me you own a *bar*, and we came to this crappy place?"

Her voice was a bit louder than she probably intended, catching the notice of some of the employees, and we both sniggered into our beers.

We talked about our daughters, which I had expected, and then we talked about our daughters' fathers, which I hadn't.

Suzanne told me how Amber's dad had died. He was a fireman who had risked his life trying to save a family in an apartment fire. The stairs had collapsed on him and he had fallen down three flights, breaking his neck on impact.

This had happened when Amber was five years old, and Suzanne had been wrecked. She had fallen into a deep depression, started taking pills, but eventually got herself together and hadn't taken any since.

For my part, I admitted that while Joe and I had never married, we still had a decent relationship even after he had married someone else.

Suzanne took a sip of her beer and glanced around the bar, shaking her head.

"Sometimes I see these happy couples, and I want to go up to them and warn them that it doesn't last. That while they're happy now, something is bound to happen where one of them gets angry at the other, and then both of them will be miserable, so they might as well just save themselves the time and heartache and end the relationship now."

Then she stared off into the distance, and the smile on her lips faded.

"Then again, Mike and I were a good couple. We fought sometimes, sure, but we were never unhappy. Though . . . sometimes I wonder what might have happened if Mike hadn't died. If he were still alive, would . . . would we still be together?"

She looked at me then, waiting for an answer, almost begging for one, and I didn't have the heart to tell her probably not.

After a moment Suzanne shrugged and looked back out at the couples.

"It's so silly, the stuff that makes us fall in love. It was our third date, and we had walked by this homeless man, and Mike had given him twenty bucks. I thought, hey, he's just trying to impress me, but the truth was, I could tell he wasn't, that had I not been there he would have given the homeless man the same amount of money. That's what made me fall in love with him. Like I said, it's silly."

"It's not silly."

"No?"

"Not at all. Do you know how I fell in love with Joe? When he told me about how he'd killed a deer."

Alarm flickered in Suzanne's eyes.

"He killed a deer?"

"Yes. But . . . well, not like how you think."

And so I told her about how growing up in Pennsylvania deer hunting is pretty much a rite of passage for young men. And so Joe, just twelve years old, had ventured into the woods at the crack of dawn, following his father through the trees, both of them wearing hunting gear and bright-orange vests.

They'd set up near some trees and waited nearly two hours before a deer appeared.

An eight-point buck, Joe had told me, and he knew how excited his father had been, no doubt wanting to take the shot himself. But they were there for Joe, so his father silently gestured at the deer, and Joe had settled himself behind the rifle, his eye to the sight, watching the deer as it slowly walked through the woods. He had lain there, watching the buck, his breathing shallow, trying to remember everything his father had taught him—how to track the deer, when to squeeze the trigger—and then, just as the buck was in the best position possible, with his finger on the trigger, moments away from ending its life . . . Joe leaned away from the sight and shook his head at his father.

"Joe said he'd never seen his father more disappointed in his entire life. He said that he'd expected his dad to yell at him, to swear, but his dad had just shaken his head in disgust and said they might as well leave."

And it was as they were driving back out of the woods, the pickup truck's tires digging in the mud, his father quietly stewing beside him, that a deer had bolted out of the trees right in front of them.

His father slammed on the brakes, but it was too late: there was a heavy thud, and the windshield in front of them was now cracked down the middle.

As his father tore open his door and got out to inspect the damage, Joe stared out the fractured windshield at the deer lying just off the muddy roadway. This one was a female. Maybe three, four years old. The pickup had hit her with enough force that she couldn't get back onto her feet, no matter how much she tried. He saw that the deer was in agony, and before he knew it, Joe had stepped out of the pickup truck.

He went to the back, grabbed his rifle, and then approached the deer.

His father didn't say anything. He just watched as Joe stepped up to the injured deer—the deer that was beyond saving—and aimed at the deer's head and squeezed the trigger.

"Joe was just a boy at the time. Not even thirteen years old. And here he was feeling empathy toward this random creature. He said that he saw it was in pain, and he wanted to end that pain. To him, he wasn't killing the deer. He was simply putting it out of its misery."

Now I was staring out at the couples, not really seeing them. They were lost in a haze, their movements as slight as shadows. Slowly, I shook my head.

"My father lacked empathy. He walked out on my mom and me when my mom got sick with cancer. I never saw him again. He was a true bastard. I think what made me fall in love with Joe was the simple fact he was the exact opposite of my father. I thought that's what I needed in my life to be happy. But I guess I didn't really love him. I think what I loved was the idea of him, if that makes sense. Either way . . . well, sometimes things just don't work out."

Suzanne offered up a sad smile and raised her glass. "Hear, hear."

I tapped my glass against hers, and we drank.

Then later, before we left, she asked if there were any updates regarding Bronwyn. She knew there wouldn't be any—if there were, I would have already shared them—but still she felt the need to ask.

"Nothing," I said. "As far as I can tell, the police are doing everything they can, but it doesn't seem like a lot. In fact, I've been thinking about hiring a private investigator."

I saw a flash of hesitation cross her face, and asked, "You don't think it's a good idea?"

She shrugged. "Honestly, not really. I actually hired one myself a while back. Like you, I was frustrated with the police, because it didn't seem like they were getting anywhere. And, well, the PI didn't have any luck. And it cost me a lot of money. Like, a *lot* of money. More than I could afford."

"I'm sorry to hear that," I said, taking one last sip of my beer. "Maybe you're right. Maybe I should just let the police keep doing what they're doing."

"Hey," Suzanne said, no doubt noting my frustration as she leaned forward to once more take my hand in hers. "We have to have faith, right? We have to remember God is in control. He's looking over our daughters as we speak. And when he's ready, he'll send them back to us."

27
Wyn
Day of the Pep Rally

She followed Mr. Parker out the rear exit door to the employee parking lot and his car, where he opened the trunk and pulled out her guitar case. He started to hand it to her but paused, looking at her closely now.

"Are you sure you want to do this?"

Silent, Wyn held out her hand.

Mr. Parker stood there for a moment, watching her, and then handed over the guitar case.

Their fingers touched during the handoff, just for an instant, and Wyn suddenly considered telling him everything. Not only what she had planned for the pep rally, but all of it.

Because the truth was, she was scared. And not just because of her stage fright—she was certainly worried about that—but at the possibility she'd fail.

That after all the time she'd spent writing her song—working endlessly on each lyric, on each note, practicing for hours on end in her bedroom late at night while her mom was asleep across the hall—it would make no difference in the end. Her song would fall on deaf ears. Nobody would care what she had to say about Taylor, about Sean Heller, about herself. She'd have no reason to leave, no reason to drop out of school to pursue her dream, and instead would forever be stuck in Bowden, a penance for having failed her best friend.

"Thank you," Wyn said quietly, and shifted her gaze so she wouldn't have to look him in the eye.

A minute later they were back in the school and she was headed down the hallway, her pace twice as fast as Mr. Parker's; then she turned the corner and saw the gymnasium up ahead and the straggling students as they entered through the open doors.

Music pulsed out into the hallway—"Stronger" by Kanye West—and she heard some of the students clapping and shouting, so she knew Autumn and Summer and all the rest of the cheerleaders were already doing their thing, pumping up the crowd, getting everybody excited.

Principal Webber was still in the hallway, monitoring the stragglers to make sure nobody tried to cut, and when he spotted her, he waved her over.

"Wyn, why don't you come this way?"

He led her down the hallway toward another door that led them into the corridor with the locker rooms. This area was already busy with movement, the entire football team huddled around in their jeans and sneakers and jerseys.

For a second she thought the team was huddled around Coach Hatfield, giving the guys some words of encouragement. But it was Sean Heller who was in the center, telling some kind of story or joke, because everybody looked super focused and then they started laughing and clapping.

Principal Webber tapped her shoulder and told her to wait here until her name was called, and then he pushed through the door into the gymnasium, and soon she heard his voice booming through the speakers.

"All right, folks, take a seat."

Wyn gravitated toward the corner of the corridor, as far away from the football team as possible. She noted that Coach Hatfield and the assistant coaches were here too, standing on the other side of the huddle.

She wanted to get out her guitar, tune it one last time, but she didn't want to draw attention to herself, so she just stood there in the corner, the guitar case at her side, and waited.

After what felt like forever, Principal Webber's voice boomed through the speakers in the gymnasium again.

"All right, folks. Are you ready to welcome your favorite team?"

The gymnasium exploded with applause, and several students started stomping on the bleachers.

"First, welcome Coach Hatfield!"

The coach hustled out through the doors, followed by the assistant coaches, and soon the microphone was passed off to Coach Hatfield, his thunderous voice now roaring through the speakers.

"What's up, Bowden High?"

More cheering. More stomping.

Coach Hatfield started talking about this year's team, about the games they'd won so far and how they were going to beat the Hartford Hawks tonight. Then he began announcing the starters, and one by one the players ran out into the gymnasium to even more applause.

To distract herself, Wyn pulled her phone from her pocket, checked her messages.

Nothing new from Onyx Butterfly. But the message from earlier that morning—what may or may not have been sent by Autumn Porter—made her smile.

Good luck today! I know you're going to kill it ☺

She slipped the phone back into her pocket, glanced around the corridor again. Half of the football team had already entered the gymnasium. She figured Sean Heller had also gone out at some point, because he wasn't with the rest of the team anymore.

She laid the case down and opened the lid to take out her guitar, strap it over her shoulders.

Soon the last of the football players were called out into the gym, and suddenly Wyn was alone.

"So you're gonna sing one of your little songs, huh?"

Sean Heller's voice nearly made her cry out. She whirled around to find him stepping out of the boys' locker room.

He edged up next to her, glanced through the narrow window looking out at the crowd.

"They told me you wanted to do a tribute to Taylor. Said it would be good for me to introduce you, what with you being Taylor's best friend and me being her boyfriend."

Sean turned his face just slightly to look at her from the corner of his eye.

"Tell me, Wyn, why does a girl with stage fright want to perform a song in front of so many people?"

Out in the gymnasium, Bobby Johnson—this year's quarterback—was telling everyone how they were going to win the state title, just like they did last year. He was eating the microphone but the crowd didn't seem to care, cheering at his every word.

"Everybody needs to hear what you did."

The words were so soft that Wyn wasn't even sure she'd spoken them at first. But they were loud enough for Sean to hear. He spun toward her, took a step closer. She knew he was trying to use his height to intimidate her, and she wasn't going to back away.

"And what did I do, Wyn?"

Her hand unconsciously touched her belly as she glared up at him.

"You know exactly what you did."

He stared at her, his handsome face all glare, and then he offered up a grin.

"Nobody will believe you. It's your word against mine. And, no offense, but you think anybody out there gives a shit what you have to say?"

"I have the pregnancy test."

"Doesn't mean a thing."

"And I saw you that night. The night Taylor died."

The grin faded, and Sean said, "Bullshit."

"Is it? I guess we'll see, won't we?"

He moved faster than she'd anticipated, nearly stepping into her, pushing her back against the wall. His one hand pressed flat against the painted brick by her head, his other hand pointing a finger right at her face.

"Are you fucking threatening me?"

Suddenly the hand pointing at her moved. She flinched, expecting him to hit her, but then she realized what he was doing just as quickly as he had started. Shifting away from her, grabbing the neck of the guitar, and twisting the tuning pegs on the headstock.

First one peg, then another, both so fast there was no way she could have stopped him even if she tried.

Then, before she knew it, he'd pulled two of the strings loose, stepped away, and said, "Whoops."

Out in the gymnasium, Coach Hatfield had the microphone again. *"And now, the man of the hour—the guy who took us to the finals last year and helped us win it all—Bowden High's very own Sean Heller!"*

It felt like the gym was about to fall down, the cheering and stomping was so intense, and Sean turned and hurried out through the door, waving to everyone as he hustled over to Coach Hatfield and took the microphone.

"Thank you, thank you, thank you! But I wouldn't be here today without the help of Coach Hatfield and all my teammates and the greatest student body in the world!"

Incredibly, the noise that erupted from the crowd was even louder.

Wyn felt like a dead butterfly stuck behind glass, that tightness once again having materialized in her chest.

Settle, settle, settle, she thought, and the voice was maybe Taylor's and it was maybe her own; it was impossible to say, only that it was helping bit by bit.

Out in the gymnasium, Sean continued.

"I've been very fortunate—there's no question about that. I've worked hard, but I've been lucky too. And I never would have been able to accomplish any of this without the support of my number one: Taylor Mitchell. She blessed me every day we were together, and she will always be part of my heart."

Applause followed this, but it was a quieter applause, somber and respectful.

The tightness in Wyn's chest was starting to loosen. In the next few moments Sean would call her name, and she would be expected to go out there, but she needed to restring her guitar before that happened.

"Earlier I spoke to Coach Hatfield and the boys in the locker room, and the entire team has chosen to dedicate this game to Taylor's memory. Give it up for Taylor, everyone!"

Wyn ignored the renewed cheers and stomping and focused on the first string, working it through the tuning peg and then tightening it until the string grew taut.

"Now I'd like to bring out one of Taylor's best friends. Wyn Hayden has written a song to celebrate Taylor's life, and she's going to come out and sing it for us all. Let's give it up for Wyn!"

This came right as she tightened the second string. Both of them were taut but the guitar would still need to be tuned, and there was just no way she could do that with the roaring crowd out in the gymnasium—where she needed to be right now.

Wyn stared ahead at the door leading into the gym, then glanced over at the doors leading into the hallway.

She remembered the second half of Onyx Butterfly's message, sans smiley-face emoji.

I know you're going to kill it

Taking a deep breath, Wyn opened the gymnasium door.

28

Jessica

Now

"You haven't been returning my text messages. You haven't been returning my calls. And with the fact that it's coming up on the one-year anniversary of when your daughter ran away, I just . . . well, I know how tough it can be, which was why I decided to get into my car and drive all the way up here."

We're sitting at a table in the back of the bar, Suzanne and I, a tall pitcher of beer between us. I never drink while I'm working (well, at least not anymore), but I've consciously clocked out for the day because I knew I had no choice but to meet with Suzanne.

Mostly because this is my fault. I lied to Joe the other night when he asked if I'd heard from Suzanne recently. She had been texting and calling, and I'd been avoiding her because I didn't want to be roped into another get-together like this, where we'd sit across from one another and talk about our missing daughters and act like after all this time they would just one day suddenly appear on our doorsteps.

"I get it," she says, taking a sip of her beer. "It's been two years now since Amber went missing, and some days all I want to do is stay home and cry. It's the . . . the *not knowing* that drives you crazy. Nobody was there for me that first year, and I told myself I wasn't going to let the same thing happen to you."

I smile at her because there's nothing else I can do. I spot Kenny at the bar across the room, nursing a Coke. He's playing on his phone but watching us from the corner of his eye.

"But seriously, Jessica. How are you holding up? You can be honest with me."

Can I? Can I tell her how I've recently learned a psycho has abducted my daughter and kept her God knows where? Can I tell her how I've recently learned my daughter gave birth to a baby boy who has since died?

I know the answer is yes, that I can probably tell Suzanne anything and she would understand, or at least do her best to try to place herself in my position, but it's already a heavy burden that's mine and mine alone.

"Some days are harder than others," I say.

She watches me, waiting for more, and when none is forthcoming, she nods.

"Yes, of course." She leans back, looks around the bar. "This place is impressive, by the way. The photos on the website don't do it justice."

Maybe I'll put Catherine in charge of updating the website next.

"When did you check out our website?"

"Pretty much right after we met and you told me you owned a bar. I mean, how often do you meet somebody who actually owns a bar? I had to see it for myself. And then, when I couldn't get hold of you, I figured the only way to track you down was to come here. Just my luck you were working today."

Yes, just her luck. Had she come a few days sooner, I wouldn't have been here. Because I would have been sequestered at home, along with

Joe and Tony and maybe another police officer, waiting for the moment Bronwyn texted me back.

Thinking of this, my hand unconsciously touches my iPhone. It's sitting facedown on the tabletop, just a few inches from my beer.

"I sound like a stalker, don't I? Jeez. I don't know what to say. I was just . . . I was getting nervous. Worried that . . ."

But she doesn't say the rest. She doesn't have to. Already the unspoken words have flitted through my mind, the sudden knowledge that this woman—one of the only friends I have, and I barely know her—thought maybe I was at risk of taking my own life.

It happens, of course. People become so despondent, so depressed, that they can't think of doing anything else. They've lost purpose. They've lost the desire to live. For them, they feel like they have no other choice.

The thought, I realize, has never once crossed my mind. Though I do wonder if maybe it should have. If a normal parent in a situation like this would miss their child so much they couldn't bear to keep living.

"No," I say, and force another smile. "I'm doing okay."

Suzanne places a hand to her chest, as though a great weight has been lifted off.

"Thank God for that. But then . . . it leads me to wonder why you've ghosted me."

"Ghosted you?"

"It's what the kids say. At least, I'm pretty sure it is. I've heard them say it on TV."

"To be honest, I don't have a good reason for not returning your texts or calls. I've just been busy."

At that moment, my phone issues its soft ding. Even under the music sifting through the bar, it sounds as loud as a gunshot.

My reaction is almost Pavlovian. A mixture of excitement and dread flashes through me. Suzanne notices, and frowns with concern.

"Are you okay?"

Stay calm, stay calm, stay calm, I think, and reach for the phone. My hand, I realize, is trembling. Suzanne notices this too, and she shifts uncomfortably in her seat.

"Seriously, Jessica, what's wrong?"

The phone issues another soft ding, and it's almost enough to cause me to jump.

Already I'm running through what I need to do next: go to the Notes app, copy the link Agent Donovan put there, and paste it into the text message. Hope like crazy Bronwyn, wherever she is, clicks the link. Then I'll signal to Kenny, who will call Tony, who will call Agent Donovan, and fingers crossed the FBI can follow through on their end.

In the next couple of minutes, there's a very good chance I'll know exactly where my daughter is.

But when I turn the phone over and glimpse the two messages, my heart sinks.

Is everything OK?

Kenny said some woman came to see you at the bar.

I close my eyes, take a deep breath. Then I open my eyes again and reply to Joe that everything is fine and that I'm meeting with Suzanne Walker.

The phone dings a third time.

OK. Just checking in. Keep me posted if anything changes.

"Jessica," Suzanne says firmly, "is everything all right?"

I set the phone aside, facedown again, and glance up at Suzanne.

"I found him."

The concern in Suzanne's eyes shifts to confusion.

"You found who?"

"My father."

For a second, it's as if the words don't register. I can't blame her. The last time I spoke about my father was when we met almost a year ago.

Then, bit by bit, understanding lights in her eyes.

"Holy crap," she says. "When was this?"

"Back in August. I . . . Well, it's going to sound silly, but I hadn't seen any butterflies all summer. Usually a few floated through our backyard because of the flower beds. And when I realized I hadn't seen any butterflies, I thought maybe it was a sign. That, I don't know, if I were to see a butterfly, it would be like Bronwyn was sending me a message that everything was okay."

"That doesn't sound silly."

I stare down at my beer, shaking my head slowly.

"I went to parks. Went to places you were apt to find butterflies. I'd stay there for hours, and I couldn't spot a single one. It started to drive me crazy. Like I had maybe just imagined butterflies existed. I even googled them, and of course they exist, and I knew that I could go somewhere, a zoo or something, and see butterflies there, but it just wouldn't be the same."

"And"—Suzanne pauses, not sure how to continue—"and that's how you ended up finding your father?"

"After you and I met last year, it was clear the trail had gone cold. Hell, there wasn't much of a trail to begin with. And, well, I know you said it wasn't worth it for you, but I went ahead and hired a private investigator."

"What happened?"

"Not much. The first one didn't pan out, so I hired a second one."

"And neither of them had any luck."

"No, they didn't. But the second one was very good at his job. He knew his stuff. He was expensive, but he was worth it. And so when it became clear that he couldn't find my daughter, I tasked him with finding my father."

"And he found him."

"Yes."

"Where?"

"Arizona. I guess after my father walked out on me and my mother, he headed west. Did odd jobs here and there. It took the investigator a couple of months to track down certain leads, but then he managed to determine where my father had ended up. In a small town an hour or so from the Mexican border. He had been married and divorced twice. Had another kid, a son, though the investigator told me it didn't look like he was in contact with my dad."

"That's impressive. What did you do?"

"I didn't do anything at first. I wasn't really sure what to do with the information now that I had it. But then I flew out there."

"You *what*?"

I nod, thinking about the rental I drove from the airport to the town my father had ended up in, how the car had reeked of cigarette smoke. About how the investigator had told me where my father lived, the apartment he rented by himself. I had parked in the lot just outside the complex, a dingy place with bars over the windows and trash overflowing the dumpsters. I sat in the car for hours, watching the apartment, trying to build up the nerve to get out and go knock on the door.

And then the apartment door opened, and my father shuffled out. Even though he was much older than when I last saw him, I recognized him at once. He was stoop shouldered and harried. He took his time as he came down the steps and then trudged up one block after another to a local bar.

I followed him on foot, and I slipped into the bar right after him. I watched as he climbed up onto a stool near the end of the bar and ordered a drink. It was a run-down bar, rather shady. I took a table across the room and ordered a beer.

I sat at the table and watched my father drink alone. Hunched over his beer, staring up at the TVs over the bar, he was there for nearly three hours before he paid his tab, and when he did, he had to count out the crumpled dollar bills as well as the scattered change from his pocket.

He didn't leave a tip.

I followed him back to his apartment and then watched him lumber up the stairs to his room. Halfway up the steps, it looked like he was in pain, and he gripped the railing tightly as he struggled.

I waited until his apartment door closed, and then I got into the rental and drove back to the airport.

"Nothing came of it," I say. "It turned out he was just a sad old man. His life was pathetic."

"You didn't speak to him?"

I shake my head. "I wanted to. I wanted to confront him. I wanted to tell him what a bastard he was. I wanted him to see what kind of woman I'd become. And I . . . I wanted to ask him how he did it."

"Did what?"

"Disappear. It's something I've been wondering lately. How to disappear. How one day you decide you don't want to be where you are anymore, and just leave. I mean, I suppose sometimes it happens on the spur of the moment, but most times it has to be something people have thought a lot about, right? My mind doesn't work that way, I guess. For better or worse, I'm content with my life. But people like my father, he must have been looking for an out for a while, and he used my mom's cancer as the excuse."

I shrug, take a sip of my beer.

"And that's why I didn't bother confronting him. He didn't deserve any of that. What he deserved, I realized, was to be forgotten."

"Wow," Suzanne says, and she looks stunned. "I can't believe you did that. That must have cost a fortune, and it didn't lead to anything."

"But it did lead to something. Even if I didn't say anything to him, I still found my father. I proved that nobody just disappears. That my dad may have walked out on us, may have vanished, but he was still out there, somewhere. I decided that if I could find my father, even with the help of a private investigator, it meant I could also find Bronwyn. That she wouldn't always stay disappeared. That . . . that maybe I would even see a butterfly again."

Suddenly my thoughts are no longer on the broken man my father had become, but instead on the horror my daughter has been suffering. Trapped in a dark, scary place. Used and abused by a madman.

It's enough to make me squeeze my glass so hard I'm afraid it might shatter.

"I know it's frustrating," Suzanne says quietly, noting my expression. "Lord, do I know it's frustrating. But you can't lose hope. Some days it's tough, and you feel like giving up, but you can't."

She leans forward, reaches across the table, and squeezes my hand.

"We have to keep that hope alive. Our daughters are still out there. One of these days they're going to come home. One of these days we're going to see them again."

29

Jessica

Four Weeks after the Pep Rally

During the second week of November, Joe came into the Wonderwall on his lunch break. Sometimes I'd procure a table in the back and do work there while I ate lunch so I wouldn't feel so constrained by my office. I was at this table, my laptop open, picking at a crab cake sandwich on a brioche roll, when Joe strode over and slid into the other side of the booth.

"You hired a private investigator?"

I took a bite of my crab cake sandwich, set it back down on the plate. I chewed for a bit, watching him, and then I swallowed the food and wiped my mouth with a cloth napkin.

"What does it matter to you?"

"Our daughter, for starters. Don't you think I would give anything to find her?"

This wasn't quite the answer I'd been expecting. I stared across the table, studying him.

"How did you find out, anyway?"

"How do you think? The investigator reached out to the police department. Tony reached out to me. He feels a little insulted."

"Yeah, well, I feel a little insulted by being kept out of the loop."

"Is this about Sean Heller? Jess, I apologized for that. Remember, at the time, you were—"

I cut him off, because I didn't want to get into it.

"Is there something else I can help you with?"

"There is, in fact. How much is he charging?"

"It doesn't matter."

"Of course it matters. I want to help pay at least half."

When I told him the rate, he thought about it for a moment and nodded.

"Sounds reasonable. Forward me the invoice once it comes in." He paused then, glanced around the dining room. "Business seems to be going well."

"You know it is. You're still a silent partner."

He shrugged as he looked around the room again. I wondered if he remembered how it had looked when we'd first walked into the space. Cold and grimy with spiderwebs everywhere. We'd purchased the building for just a couple thousand dollars because nobody thought anybody could make anything of it.

"How has everything else been going?" he asked.

"What do you mean?"

"Are you sleeping better at night?"

Meaning, was I waking up in the middle of the night with delusions that somebody had broken into the house?

"I've been okay, Joe."

"And the drinking—"

"Is none of your business."

He lifted his hands in surrender. "Fair enough. But the other reason I wanted to stop in was because Stuart and I have been talking, and . . . we'd like you to come to Thanksgiving at Stuart's this year."

Thanksgiving was less than two weeks away. Several years back, Joe and Stuart had started hosting the dinner at their houses, switching back and forth every other year. Our daughter had always gone, and while I'd always been invited, I always declined, opting to work instead.

"Thanks, but I have to work."

"Come on, Jess. You don't *have* to work. We just thought . . . it would be good for you to be around family."

Family? I wanted to say. *What family? My only family has run away, and I've got nobody left.*

"I'll think about it," I said.

Joe forced a smile and then glanced at his phone after it vibrated on the table.

"I have to head back to the office. Just please keep me updated on the investigator. I'll pay whatever to get Wyn back."

I watched him as he slid out of the booth and headed toward the front door, relieved he hadn't asked me what else I'd been doing.

I hadn't told him about my extracurricular activities, and right now I had no intention to—unless I found something useful.

How do you follow two people at the same time?

You can't. Maybe if you had the equipment and time and money, you could make it work, but I was just one person, and I had a full-time job that often required fifty hours of my time per week.

I started with Chad Murphy. Principal Webber had promised to do an internal review, though it was unclear what that meant. The school couldn't fire Chad just because a note that looked like it was written by him was found in my daughter's room, though it was damning.

I followed him home after school one day. I tried to stay far enough back so I wouldn't be noticed but not too far back that I would lose him.

Chad lived in an apartment complex near the end of town, down near the strip mall. There was a twenty-four-hour gym in the strip mall, and the gym was all windows, so when he went there I could stay in the parking lot and watch him as he worked out. Cardio on the elliptical, then some free weights. He often wore his earbuds to listen to music or whatever, and sometimes he took them out to talk to people, some of them young women about his age, though none of it appeared too flirtatious.

When Chad wasn't at the gym, he was at his apartment. And when he wasn't at his apartment, he was at his girlfriend's place.

It took me two weeks before I managed to follow him there. She lived outside of town, in an apartment complex much like his own.

One night he picked her up and they went to a bar for a couple of hours before heading back to her apartment. Chad spent the night, or at least I assumed he did, because after an hour I gave up and headed home.

Bryan Parker lived in a ranch house toward the southern end of town. Because it was a small neighborhood, it was harder to spy on him. With Chad, I could park in the apartment-complex lot along with dozens of other cars, but in Bryan's neighborhood my car would be easily noticed, especially with somebody sitting inside it.

Bryan, from what I could tell, didn't have a girlfriend. At least, he didn't drive out of town every other night to see someone the way Chad Murphy did. Bryan went to the same gym as Chad—the only one in Bowden—and there were a few times when Bryan and Chad were there at the same time, though besides nods of acknowledgment they never really interacted, from what I could tell.

Bryan went to Shepherd's to buy groceries. He picked up food at the deli or the Chinese restaurant. Once he stopped in at Holderman's Hardware for whatever he needed to fix around the house.

After a few weeks of my amateur sleuthing, I decided to focus on Bryan Parker. A note from Chad Murphy may have ended up in my daughter's room, but he didn't appear to have any contact with Bronwyn. He was rarely home, so it wasn't like he was hiding her in his apartment—though if he was, he was doing one hell of a job of acting like there wasn't anybody there. The same with his girlfriend, who usually stayed the night once or twice during the week.

I considered asking the private investigator to help me with the surveillance. I'd told him about Chad Murphy's note, and he'd offered to dig into Chad's past, but now that Joe was getting updates as well, I was hesitant. Besides, it didn't seem like the investigator was having much luck on his end anyway, and I was already starting to consider the idea of replacing him with somebody new, though I wasn't going to tell Joe about the second investigator.

Still, if I did ask the investigator for help, what would I tell him? That I simply had a weird feeling about Bryan Parker? That while I'd sat there with him in the conference room at school, I knew he was lying about something but just couldn't put my finger on what it was?

I couldn't quite rationalize my obsession with him other than that without following him, I felt useless, as though I wasn't doing everything I could to find my daughter. At the very least, I might discover what Bryan was hiding, if anything.

So I started following him more often. He rarely left Bowden. When he wasn't at school, he mostly spent his time at home. It got to the point that I went to his house during the day. I parked across the street and approached his house, making sure he didn't have any cameras near the front door or around the overall structure that might alert him at school that he had a visitor. I rang the doorbell, just to see what would happen, but there was no movement inside, not even a barking dog.

I walked around to the backyard, ignoring the houses around me, trying to make it look like I belonged. Most of his windows were covered by shades but a few were partly open, and I peered inside, purposely not touching the glass for fear I might leave a fingerprint behind.

If Bronwyn was hiding inside, she wasn't making it easy for me to see her.

Or maybe she's not hiding. Maybe she's chained up in the basement. Maybe there's tape over her mouth and she's screaming out to you right this second.

The thought came out of nowhere, the kind of thing I'd been trying to keep at bay all this time. It was a mother's worst nightmare—the idea that my daughter hadn't run away but had been abducted instead—and I shivered at the images flashing through my mind.

It was enough for me to try the back door. But of course it was locked. So were the windows.

I felt like I'd overstayed my welcome, conscious now of the houses around me, and I drove away quickly, as though I'd just robbed the place.

"Come on, Bronwyn," I whispered, my fingers kneading the steering wheel. "Where are you?"

Then that Friday (two days after Joe had come into the Wonderwall to invite me to Thanksgiving), Bryan Parker left school and went home. Four hours later he came back out of the house—now wearing dark jeans and a sweater—and got into his car.

I figured he was going out on a date. Or meeting friends. From what I could tell, he didn't have any friends in town, not like Chad Murphy did. I was curious where he was headed.

Bryan got on the highway and headed south. I stayed behind him, a few car lengths back. Bryan was doing five over the speed limit, so I set the cruise control and waited to see where he would take me.

We ended up in Harrisburg, down near the capitol building. Bryan parked along the street. I parked a block over and managed to catch up to him as he headed down the block.

Tall row houses lined both sides of the street. Trees towered over the sidewalk, obscuring the streetlamps and casting shadows everywhere.

It was Friday night, and by now it was getting late. We were near downtown, where the bars and restaurants were located. I figured that was where he was headed.

I turned the corner at the next block and stopped short.

Bryan was gone.

Hurrying forward, I looked across the street, up the block, behind me.

He was nowhere in sight.

The street was quiet. I thought about continuing down the block, seeing if I might spot him outside one of the bars, but then I wondered just what the hell I thought I was doing. This had been a waste of time. All of it—following Bryan, following Chad Murphy, hiring the private investigator.

I was ready to head back to my car when I heard sudden movement behind me in the dark, and a strong hand grabbed my shoulder.

30

Wyn

Day of the Pep Rally

The gymnasium had gone quiet. Not completely quiet—she was aware of murmurs throughout, some whispering, some giggling, and there was a smattering of polite applause—but compared to the uproarious cheering and stomping from seconds ago, it was a Zen garden.

The bleachers were packed. She spotted Mr. Parker near the back, and in that half second or so when their eyes connected, he gave her a slight nod.

A stage had been set up near the front of the gym. A small riser, only a few feet off the floor. It was where Coach Hatfield had stood to announce the team, and where Sean Heller was standing now, waiting for her as she slowly made her way forward.

The lights started to dim throughout the gymnasium. Some kids from the AV club had quickly set up a video projector that would show photos and video of Taylor during Wyn's song. It was the same looped video that had played during the assembly last month. Principal Webber had suggested it because he thought it would help to have a visual aid.

The last couple of lights went off as she reached the stage, but many of the students used their phones to light up the gym, so it wasn't completely dark. Several wires stretched across the stage for the lights and the video projector, and she was so focused on the microphone stand she almost tripped right over them.

Sean reacted instantly, his athletic ability pushing him forward in the blink of an eye to gently take Wyn's arm to hold her steady.

"Are you okay?" he asked, so soft and sweet it made her want to scream, because she heard a few *Awwws* emitting from the crowd, people who saw the image Sean Heller wanted to project and not the monster that he truly was.

Wyn knew she couldn't give in to her base instinct—to violently shake him off, push him away—so she merely nodded with a smile and continued on to the microphone.

Sean had drifted back to the crowd of football players lingering near the side. He stayed front and center, though, so that everybody could see him while images of Taylor played on the white screen set up behind Wyn.

She spotted the cheerleaders near the front too. All of them in their tight uniforms and perky ponytails and toned legs. The Seasons were standing side by side, their faces expressionless. Only, wait, no—was Autumn suppressing a smirk?

Forget it, the Taylor voice said. *Forget all of them, Wyn. You've got this.*

But do I?

Yes.

I don't think I do.

You do, Wyn. I believe in you.

She was faintly aware that the soft murmuring and whispering had started to gain in pitch. The crowd was getting restless. They'd come to enjoy the pep rally and would now be bummed out by images of a dead girl while her best friend sang some song.

How many seconds had passed since she'd stepped on the stage? Five? Ten? Thirty? It felt like a full minute, and in this dull silence that minute felt like an hour, and she wondered when she was going to get the cue to start when she suddenly realized there was no cue and that the montage would begin as soon as she started.

The only problem was her guitar wasn't in tune. She forced a smile at the crowd as she started tightening the pegs, then strumming the guitar to tune it. Only this caused one of the AV kids to think that she'd started and so the montage began, first a picture of Taylor taken sometime last year, a stunning photo of her with her hair down and her smile bright, and Wyn cleared her throat and spoke into the microphone.

"Actually, sorry, I'm not ready yet."

Her mouth was a bit too close to the microphone, causing some feedback, and the AV kid quickly stilled the montage as a quiet bout of nervous laughter rippled across the gym.

What are you doing? The guitar doesn't need to sound perfect. Just sing!

Shut up. I know what I'm doing.

Do you?

Again she forced a smile, ignoring her subconscious, wanting everyone to know this was just part of the show. Her gaze skipped to Autumn, who was most certainly suppressing a smirk, and then she glanced over at the football team and saw Sean Heller giving her an encouraging smile and nod.

What an asshole.

But no, she couldn't let him get to her. Couldn't let Autumn and Summer and all the rest of the cheerleaders get to her either. She couldn't—

That tightness again, building in her chest.

No, not now.

Sing through it, she thought, and started strumming the guitar. It didn't sound right, not like it should, but for the setting it was fine. The main thing would be her voice, her lyrics, the truth about Sean Heller. The guitar was merely a prop.

The AV kid waited to make sure this was really it, and then he released the montage from its hold.

Wyn knew the pictures would cycle through, and as much as she wanted to see them, she needed to focus on the crowd in front of her. Except, no, that was wrong. She needed to focus on the song. Act like the crowd wasn't even there. Just like she had tried to do when she auditioned for *America's Got Talent* right before she'd had her panic attack.

Don't think of that. Just think of the song.

She was trying, she really was, but that tightness in her chest grew stronger, and as she worked through the chords, she realized she'd missed her cue, so she started through the chords again, and still that tightness grew even more, and when the cue came to start singing she opened her mouth but had no voice, no breath whatsoever, and she suddenly became very attuned to the entire gymnasium, to every single murmur and whisper and giggle, to the fact that not just one or two or three cameras were recording her right now, but a dozen cameras, two dozen cameras, three dozen, and she cycled through the chords again, telling herself that she could do this, that she *needed* to do this, but when the cue came back around and she tried to sing the first note, the noise that came from her mouth was like a croak, the kind of sound a mummy in a horror movie makes, and a renewed bout of nervous laughter rippled through the crowd, a bit stronger this time, only maybe that was in her head—she couldn't really tell—all she knew for certain was the tightness in her chest was getting stronger—those invisible fingers squeezing tighter and tighter—and those images of Taylor kept flipping through on the screen, one after another, and the murmuring and whispering was getting even louder, almost as loud as the laughter, and before she knew it she'd spun away from the microphone to make her retreat.

Later, she would wonder what truly went wrong—that she'd turned away in haste, focused only on the locker-room door, or that the tightness in her chest was so severe she could barely breathe, or that the murmuring and whispering and laughter were so loud in her head it almost drowned out the blood screaming in her ears—but whatever it was, she completely forgot about the wires lying across the stage.

Until the toe of her foot got snagged, and she lost her balance.

Sean Heller wasn't nearby to help catch her this time. Nobody was. She fell forward, right off the stage, and her sneaker caught one of the riser steps but couldn't find enough purchase to save her. If anything, it helped propel her forward even faster, and before she knew it she was falling toward the gymnasium floor, and like any person who falls forward, she raised her hands to try to catch herself.

But she wasn't fast enough—and instead of her hands, her guitar broke her fall.

It was like getting kicked in the chest. She landed right on the guitar—her precious Gibson, one of the most valuable things she owned—and she knew at once that she had destroyed it, that pieces of it were going to be left behind.

Because a second later she was struggling to her feet, the broken guitar hanging off the strap over her shoulder, and the gymnasium was growing louder and louder now with noise, that soft ripple of laughter becoming a tsunami, and as she bolted forward it was all she heard, that laughter, and like a wave it chased her out into the locker-room corridor and down the hallway and all the way to the parking lot.

31

Jessica

Now

The dishwasher's name is Dennis.

He's young, having just turned nineteen a few months ago, and he still has traces of acne scars on his face from when he was a kid.

He sits slumped in the chair in front of my desk, looking worried, while my assistant manager stands off to the side, her arms crossed.

"I'm sorry," he says quietly. "I'll stop—I promise."

Dennis has been harassing some of the girls at work. Nothing too extreme, from what I'm told, but sometimes he'll stand a bit too close to someone or send messages via text or social media repeatedly, even when he's asked to stop.

"You understand what *no* means, don't you, Dennis?"

He nods quickly, swallowing. "Yes."

"So when somebody tells you no or to stop doing something, what should you do?"

"I should stop doing that thing."

His eyes shift back and forth between my assistant manager and me. We've already established how we would play this. She's the good cop; I'm the bad cop.

"Okay, Dennis, so if you know what *no* means, why did you keep messaging some of the girls here at work even when you were asked to stop?"

He looks down, shrugging, and mumbles, "I dunno."

"If it were up to me, you would already be fired. But the woman standing over there—she says you're a good kid who means well. She wants to give you a second chance."

Dennis swallows again, his eyes still shifting back and forth between us.

"I'm sorry. I'll be better. I promise you, I will."

A few minutes later Dennis has left my office, and it's just my assistant manager and me. She waits until the door closes before she releases a sigh.

"You better know what you're doing," I say.

"I do. Like I said, he's a good kid. Has had a hard life. I'm confident he'll turn it around."

"I hope you're right. Otherwise, the next time he steps out of line, he's done."

She nods in agreement as she starts for the door but then pauses.

"Can I ask you something?"

"Of course."

"Why has Kenny Gorman been hanging around this place so much the last couple of days?"

"My guess is he likes the ambiance."

She makes a face. "Come on, Jess. Kenny Gorman has never stepped foot in the Wonderwall since it opened, and then the other night he comes in here and creates a scene, the kind that gets somebody banned, and now he's been in here four straight days. He shows up when you show up, he leaves when you leave. So, please, don't treat me like an idiot. What's going on?"

"I can't tell you," I say. "At least, not right now."

She stands there for a moment, watching me, before she shrugs, says, "Okay," and leaves.

Suddenly I'm alone. I typically like the quiet of my office. It feels safe. Welcoming. But after five minutes of trying to get work done, I'm too wired to keep sitting any longer. I grab my iPhone and empty soda glass and head out through the restaurant toward the bar.

It's Tuesday evening, almost eight o'clock, and the place is pretty calm. All the TVs have been flipped over to the local congressional debate. Stuart Colvin stands up onstage along with Congressman Thomas, each positioned behind lecterns.

I step up next to Kenny at the bar, who's watching one of the TVs.

"How's he doing?" I ask.

Kenny says, "The mayor's doing pretty good. Definitely holding his own."

On the TV, Stuart looks across the small stage and asks, "Tell me, Congressman, does the name Krystal Rogers mean anything to you?"

"This is absurd," Congressman Thomas says to the audience. "I came here tonight to debate policy, not to be lectured by a man who's lived off a trust fund his entire adult life."

Stuart allows a small smile as he says, "It's true. My grandparents were very well off and left me a trust fund when they passed away, a trust fund that I used to help pay for college and which I used when I started a career in public office. As you well know, Congressman, Bowden isn't large enough to pay its mayor a full-time salary. I've used the trust fund to support myself and my family while I focused one hundred percent on revitalizing our town. But now to get back to my original question, does the name Krystal Rogers mean anything to you? It should. She's one of your constituents who has been asking for your help for the past two years."

Nick Jennings finishes up with a customer and makes his way down the bar.

I place the empty glass on the bartop and say, “Fill ’er up, barkeep.”

Grinning, Nick dumps the melted ice and soon sets a fresh glass of Diet Coke down in front of me.

“I’m kind of surprised you didn’t want to go tonight,” Kenny says, tilting his chin up at the TV.

“Politics isn’t really my thing,” I say. “Besides, look how swamped we are in here.”

The bar, of course, is far from swamped. An older guy nearby gets the joke and chuckles. I toss him a wink as I grab my soda and start back toward my office. I get only a few paces before my cell phone vibrates in my other hand.

I glance down at the screen—and a second later, the glass slips through my fingers, shattering on the hardwood floor.

mom

That single word is like a blade to the heart.

The phone vibrates again.

ive never seen him so angry

I’m briefly aware of people around me. My assistant manager hurrying over to see what’s wrong. Kenny stepping close, asking if everything is okay, and then spotting the two new text messages.

“Come on,” he says, taking my arm.

He leads me out of the bar through the restaurant and down the hallway to my office. My assistant manager tries to follow, and Kenny tells her everything is okay, that he’s got this.

Then we’re in my office and I realize I’m still watching the screen, waiting for those dancing dots.

“The link,” Kenny says, nearly shouts, and I nod and close out the window and open the Notes app, copy the link, and then return to

Bronwyn's text messages. I paste the link and send it, and then type so fast it's like my thumbs are working of their own volition.

Click the link, Bronwyn. Click it now!

I watch the screen, waiting for those dancing dots, waiting for *anything,* and after several gut-wrenching seconds when nothing happens, I glance up at Kenny.

He has his cell phone to his ear, his eyes on mine. He's called Tony Parsons, who will now be calling Special Agent Donovan.

Kenny says, "Okay, Chief," and puts down the phone, then glances around the office and motions at the couch against the wall.

"Maybe you should sit down."

I shake my head, staring again at the screen. Those dancing dots have started up again, and then the phone vibrates once more.

i clicked the link what is it

I type back: Why is he angry?

Several long seconds of no reply, and then the phone vibrates.

he says im a bad girl

mom

hes coming back in

Kenny's own phone vibrates. He places the phone to his ear, says something quietly. After several seconds, he nods at me.

Suddenly, my legs don't work anymore. I start to fall. Kenny springs forward, holds me steady, and directs me to the couch.

"Where?" I manage to ask, and Kenny answers simply.

"Three hours away."

32

Jessica

Four Weeks after the Pep Rally

"Why are you following me?"

Bryan Parker let go of my shoulder but didn't step back. He was so close I could smell his cologne, a strong woodsy scent.

I swallowed, trying to find my voice, and managed, "Where is my daughter?"

"I don't know."

"You're hiding something. I could tell when Principal Webber brought you into the conference room."

The man's phone was in his left hand. The screen lit up with an incoming text message.

"Who is that?" I said, my tone automatically ticking up a notch. "Is that Bronwyn?"

I leaned forward to see the screen, but Bryan tilted the phone away from me. He stared at the screen for a moment, his expression pensive, and then he typed a response and shoved the phone into his jeans pocket.

"Do you want to get some coffee?"

"What?"

"Coffee," he said. "There's a coffee shop around the corner."

I just stared at him, not sure how to respond. I had imagined several different scenarios as to how this might go, all of which weren't great, but this was certainly not one of them.

When Bryan saw that I wasn't going to answer, he sighed.

"Look, I don't know where your daughter went. She never told me. But I do want to tell you a story. I . . . I think it might help give you a better understanding of who she is."

We sat at a table near the door. The coffee wasn't very good, but it was hot and I wrapped my hand around my mug to keep warm because suddenly I felt cold and hollow.

I didn't know what Bryan Parker planned to tell me, but I already didn't like it.

"Where did you grow up?" he asked finally.

The simple question threw me.

"A small town outside of Pittsburgh. Why?"

He grinned. "Pittsburgh, huh? You a Steelers fan?"

"What's this all about?"

Bryan took a sip of his coffee, cleared his throat as he set the mug back down.

"I grew up outside of Philly. It was a nice area. My parents made good money, and we lived in a nice big house, and I went to an excellent school."

"That's great," I said, not bothering to hide my impatience. "And your point is?"

"Growing up I never had many friends. I was always big and slow, so I didn't play sports. Mostly I played video games. But I did have a few friends, and one of those friends I considered my best friend. His name was Matthew. He was much more popular than me—his older brother was the star on the school's basketball team, and that gave him extra clout—but he let me hang out with him anyway, and . . . well, looking back at it now, I understand the reason why. I was his verbal punching bag. He was always putting me down, making me the butt of jokes. But like I said, he was popular and I wasn't, so I just went along because it beat sitting in my basement by myself playing video games."

Bryan sighed, staring down at his coffee.

"Anyway, eventually Matthew stopped giving me a hard time. I guess maybe he'd gotten bored or something. But he still let me hang out with him. I was like his sidekick. Matthew being popular made me semipopular by default. He would let me tag along to parties, though I think it was mostly so that I could drive him home after he'd had way too much. He was a nasty drunk. Would start fights just for the hell of it."

"I'm sorry, but I still don't understand what this has to do with my daughter."

"I'm getting to that," Bryan said. "You see, our senior year there was this new kid who showed up at school. He was skinny and wore glasses, and I didn't think much of him except that something about him pissed off Matthew. He hated the kid. Just flat out hated him. When they'd pass by in the hallways, he'd shoulder-check the new kid into the lockers. Or in the cafeteria, he'd smack the kid's tray out of his hands. Just typical bullying stuff, and because Matthew's parents were so well regarded—you know, because they had a lot of money—he usually got away with messing with the kid at school. He'd get a stern talking-to by the principal, but nothing more ever came of it. I thought eventually he would get tired of picking on the kid, but after a couple of weeks it just kept going. In fact, it got to the point I finally asked him why he hated the kid so much."

"What did he say?"

"He said the kid was gay, but . . . well, he called him a name I'm sure you can imagine, as if that explained everything, and when I think about it now, it did explain everything, at least for Matthew. I didn't even know why he thought this, or where he'd heard it from, but somehow he just knew, or at least thought he did. And after hearing him say this, I started paying closer attention to the kid. To the way he walked. The way he talked. None of it looked any different to me than any of the other guys, and when I told Matthew this, he got all quiet before he said to me, *No, there's a difference. I'm telling you, he's a* . . . And, well, he used that word again."

Bryan shook his head.

"One time the kid showed up at one of the parties we were at, and Matthew, who had already had too much to drink, lost his temper. He went right up to the kid and knocked him down. When the kid tried to stand back up, he knocked him down again. Got to the point people had to hold Matthew back and tell the kid to leave before things got worse."

I now saw where he was going with this and said, "But things did get worse."

"They did, yes. Not that night. It was a few weeks later. I'd come down with a stomach virus, so I hadn't gone to the party that night. But I heard about what happened later. How the new kid showed up there. And, well, I guess the kid had had enough, because when Matthew started messing with him, the new kid tried to fight back. Matthew, well, he started beating on him, and he didn't stop. I guess they were outside, and not many people were around to try to stop Matthew even if they wanted to. So Matthew, he just kept beating on the kid until it got to the point where the kid's face . . . It was awful. The kid was in the hospital for over a week. He'd needed reconstructive surgery to try to fix his face. Charges were pressed, as you can imagine, but Matthew's parents hired some high-priced lawyers, and in the end he only got probation. As for the kid, his parents sued, and Matthew's parents managed to settle the case outside of court."

There was a silence then as Bryan stared back down at his coffee, and I wasn't sure what to say, so I simply said, "I'm sorry."

"Teenagers do stupid stuff. There's no excusing what Matthew did. But . . . I always wondered."

"Wondered what?"

"Why he hated that kid so much. If maybe Matthew . . . maybe he saw something in the kid that he saw in himself. Something that terrified him. Something that caused him to want to nearly kill the kid."

Bryan fell silent again, his gaze focused on the street outside, not wanting to look me in the eye.

"I don't understand what that story has to do with my daughter."

He looked at me again, and there was a haunting in his eyes I hadn't expected to see.

"In college, I finally stopped lying to myself about who I was. It was difficult to do that growing up around my friends, especially around Matthew. But once I was away from them, I could finally accept the truth. It suddenly made sense to me why I didn't like kissing any of the girls I hooked up with at parties. Why . . . why in high school I found myself thinking about Matthew's brother so much I would have dreams about him. Part of me thought it was just because he had been so popular, but in college I realized that wasn't the case. And that if Matthew knew who I truly was, he wouldn't have been friends with me at all. In fact, he might have put me in the hospital just like that kid."

I stared at Bryan Parker for a long moment, unable to speak. Then, little by little, I found my voice.

"Are you saying that my daughter . . ."

"Some kids realize who they are right away. They accept it. They let other people know. Others . . . others like me, we kid ourselves into believing it's not true. We worry that we won't be accepted, either by our family or our friends or just everybody in general."

"But Bronwyn . . . she dated Aaron Colvin for almost a year. She had other boyfriends."

And she's pregnant, I thought but didn't add.

Bryan said, "I was heading to see a guy tonight. Most of the guys I see are in this area. Keep in mind Bowden is a small, rural town. It's become progressive in some ways over the past couple of years, but it's still pretty conservative. As you can imagine, most parents in town wouldn't like to know that one of their kids' teachers is gay."

"Bronwyn would have told me if she was gay. She would have told her father. We wouldn't have judged her. We would have accepted her just as she was."

"Maybe it wasn't you or her father she was worried about," Bryan said. "Look, it's not like she ever told me any of this. But I've been in her place. The high school has an LGBTQ club, and some of the students are very open, but others aren't. They just aren't ready to come out yet, either to themselves or anyone else. And with Wyn . . . I think there was a reason we gravitated toward each other. Why she felt comfortable talking to me. I can't say for certain; it's just a feeling I had."

Bryan pulled out his wallet, extracted a ten-dollar bill, and placed it on the table.

"Now, Ms. Moore, if there isn't anything else I can help you with, I've left my date waiting too long. I told him I had to take care of something and he said he understood, but you know how guys can be. Hopefully he's still there."

33

Wyn

Day of the Pep Rally

She was driving faster than she ever had in her life, the Escort's already overburdened engine doing its best to comply with her desired speed as her foot stayed planted on the gas pedal and the speedometer kept ticking up and up—seventy, seventy-five, eighty—and then she heard the voice in her head, the one that sounded like Taylor, and the voice said, *You don't want to end up like me, do you?*

That practically broke her. Almost sent her right over the edge—literally.

There was a bend in the road and she nearly lost control of the wheel, slamming on the brakes.

Fortunately, the other side of the bend was an empty field, the line of trees a good two hundred yards away, and when the car skidded to a halt just off the road, she was in no danger of hitting anything.

Christ, just what the hell was she thinking? She was upset, yes—that was understandable under the circumstances—but it was no excuse to act reckless, no excuse at all, and besides, she was smarter than that, wasn't she? All those parties where she'd refused alcohol, refused weed, refused anything that might alter her brain just a bit, because she was terrified to end up like her mother and grandfather.

She'd been a little girl when she'd asked about her grandparents, maybe eight or nine years old, and her mom had been hesitant at first, not sure how to explain to Wyn why she had grandparents on her daddy's side but not her mommy's side, and then her mom had finally told her the truth.

Her grandmother, she said, had died from cancer.

Her grandfather, well, he was a drunk who they should be thankful was no longer in their lives.

Years later Wyn would see echoes of her grandfather's alcoholism in her mother, who would sometimes pass out on the couch late at night and who one time nearly crashed the car into a house. Wyn had been little then and only remembered bits and pieces, but it was mostly the fallout—the loud arguments between her parents, the threat that Wyn would go live with her dad full-time—that stayed with her. And much later, when she'd researched alcoholism and learned it could be genetic, Wyn was terrified to think that she might suffer the same fate.

The downside to her abstinence, of course, was the teasing. But nobody had ever given her too hard of a time. Not with Taylor on her side.

Wyn wasn't sure at what point her love for Taylor as a friend had morphed into . . . something more. It had been in the past year or so; she was sure of that. While Wyn had always thought her friend was beautiful, she'd begun noticing it in a whole new way. While she'd always thought about Taylor, it had been harmless, just one friend thinking about another, but then she'd realized what she was doing wasn't thinking so much as longing, and it had scared her. Not because she might be gay—she wasn't afraid of that—but simply the idea that her being gay might cause her to lose Taylor as a friend.

It was a silly worry, she knew. Taylor wasn't like that. She was gentle and sweet and welcoming of everyone.

But despite the assurance Taylor might not think any less of her, Wyn still knew the truth would dramatically change their relationship, and she'd begun to realize that the only consistent thing she had in life was her friendship with Taylor. There were the guys she dated off and on, because Taylor dated guys, and so Wyn knew she was expected to date them too, and then there were the friends she'd had throughout middle school and high school, but none of them were *close* friends, not like Taylor.

Of course, then Taylor started dating Sean Heller and it was clear that Sean wasn't just another guy, that this was serious. Which was why Wyn finally gave in to Taylor's suggestion to go out with Aaron Colvin, who had always had a crush on Wyn. And so Wyn had started talking to Aaron more and more, giving him the signals she knew a straight girl would give, and then pretty soon they were going steady, just like Taylor and Sean. And while Wyn played it up that she was happy with this arrangement, part of her had felt like she was trapped in a box inside her chest, right next to her heart, screaming so loud she worried others might hear.

She realized now that had been part of her hesitancy to perform at the pep rally—not just the accusation leveled at Sean Heller, but the truth about herself. Because anybody paying even the slightest bit of attention would understand the song wasn't just about Taylor, but also about Wyn. And that the love the girl in the song—Wyn—felt for her friend wasn't totally platonic.

Wyn hadn't been able to come out to her friend, so she had planned to do this instead: come out to the entire school while also accusing her best friend's boyfriend of having a hand in her death.

A pickup truck speeding around the bend honked at her, making her jump.

The Escort's engine was still running, making its usual heavy ticking noise. How long had she been sitting here, lost in her thoughts?

Her phone was down in the footwell of the passenger side. She'd tossed it on the seat when she had gotten into the car, throwing the remains of her guitar in the back seat, and when she'd slammed on the brakes the phone had shot down onto the floor.

She placed the car in park and then undid her seat belt—thank God she'd remembered to put that on in her haste, at least—and leaned down to grab the phone.

Two missed calls, both from Aaron. He'd even texted.

Are you alright? Please call me.

A few other messages had come in from some of her friends. They all offered up notes similar to the one Aaron had sent. Feeling sorry for her. Telling her to reach out.

Without really thinking, she opened Twitter. She didn't realize she'd been holding her breath until she saw that Onyx Butterfly had sent her a message.

> I'm so sorry that happened. Ignore the videos. Everything will be fine.

Wyn's blood suddenly went cold.

Videos? What videos?

She logged on to Facebook and was immediately bombarded with notifications. A few kids from the school had tagged her in their videos. She knew exactly what the videos would show but still had to check just to be sure.

There were three up so far, all from different angles. One angle was to her left from where she'd been onstage. The other angle was to her right. Another was directly ahead.

Each video already had a ton of likes and comments. She was tempted to read what people were saying but instead logged out as fast as she could.

She felt the oncoming tightness in her chest again, those invisible fingers starting to squeeze.

Focus, focus, focus, she thought, and did everything she could to slow her breathing.

After a minute, it seemed to help.

Then, because she knew she might as well get it over with, she returned to Twitter.

A few more people had tagged her in videos and photos. A few were the same kids from Facebook, but there were others.

It hadn't even been a half hour yet and already some of the videos were getting a bunch of retweets and likes.

A direct-message notification popped up. She tapped over and saw a new message from Onyx Butterfly.

> If you need to talk to someone don't hesitate to reach out.

This was new. Wyn had suggested having direct contact with Onyx Butterfly in the past, either by phone or in person, and Onyx Butterfly had either ignored the suggestion or shot it down, saying it wasn't time yet. Apparently Wyn embarrassing herself in front of the entire high school—and having that event start to go viral on social media—was the time to make verbal contact at last.

But Wyn needed more than just a voice right now. She needed to see Onyx Butterfly with her own eyes. Needed a physical shoulder to cry on.

She started to type a response—can we meet—but then quickly deleted it. She stared down at the phone, but all she saw was the smirk on Autumn Porter's face back at the pep rally. Autumn Porter, who may or may not have a butterfly tattooed on the inside of her wrist.

Wyn typed: autumn you bitch is that you

She hit the arrow to send and then waited. Thirty seconds. A minute.

The more time that passed, the more convinced Wyn became that it really was Autumn Porter. She was already thinking about all the things she'd told Onyx Butterfly, all the personal details Autumn now knew, and wondered just how much damage she had done to herself.

That was when her phone vibrated with an incoming DM.

???

Wyn stared at the reply. Wasn't sure how to take it. Maybe she'd been jumping to conclusions after all. Autumn might be sneaky and duplicitous, but did she have the patience for such a drawn-out and elaborate scheme?

Drawing in a slow breath, she decided to ask her original question.

can we meet

Another thirty seconds passed. A full minute. Wyn suddenly realizing that whatever connection she may have had here she'd messed up because she'd let Autumn Porter get inside her head.

But then the phone vibrated again, and Onyx Butterfly's response was enough to bring calm back to her heart.

Yes.

34

Jessica

Now

It's just past eleven o'clock by the time we arrive at Black Creek State Park.

The park sits about an hour outside of Pittsburgh, and I've been told it boasts just over two thousand acres of woodland; there are some state park buildings, a few cabins, but no permanent residences. The park closed hours ago, but a police car is stationed at the entrance, an officer with a grim face waving us through.

Kenny steers us past the officer, Joe following in his car. He was contacted right after we got confirmation that this was where Bronwyn's signal had originated from. He'd rushed out of the debate, eventually managing to catch up with us on the highway.

A mile down a dark weaving road brings us to several parked cars. Tony is leaning against one of the cars, a flashlight in hand.

Tony orders Kenny to stay with the cars and then leads Joe and me down the lane, telling us to stay to one side. He notes that Agent Donovan and a handful of field agents had flown in via helicopter and have since started investigating the crime scene.

"Have you found anything?" Joe asks, his voice unsteady.

I haven't spoken at all in the past two hours. Not since we received word that Bronwyn wasn't at this location; the state police troopers first on scene had searched the area and found an abandoned cabin in the middle of the woods—an *empty* abandoned cabin. The moment I heard the news, something inside of me shattered. I barely have a voice, let alone the desire to speak.

I suppose this is what actual hopelessness feels like.

Tony shines his flashlight at tire tracks on the lane. He says based on the tread size, it appears to be from an SUV or pickup truck.

At the cabin, battery-powered spotlights have been set up on tripods to brighten the area. Part of the cabin's roof is sunken, and most of the windows are broken or missing.

An FBI agent is standing over one of the tire tracks. He's young, with a familiar face, but it's dark and my daughter is gone again and I can't think straight, so maybe it's not that familiar after all. He looks up at us briefly as we walk past and then continues taking pictures of the tire tracks with the large camera hanging around his neck. With every shutter of the lens, the area explodes as if from a lightning strike.

Agent Donovan is waiting in the doorway to the cabin. He's wearing latex gloves. As we approach, he speaks in a calm, measured tone.

"It appears he kept her down in the root cellar."

Joe leans forward slightly to look inside the cabin.

"Where?"

"There's an entrance around back."

"Can we see?"

The agent shakes his head. "This is still an active crime scene. Honestly, you shouldn't even be here. But as it is, there isn't much to see anyway. Part of the base of the cellar is stone. Our unsub appears to have drilled in steel rings, which he ran a chain through. We believe that was where he secured your daughter. The ring and chain are still down there."

"Tony texted me that you found other items."

"We did."

Agent Donovan turns and disappears into the cabin and reappears a few seconds later holding a large plastic bag.

"Do either of you recognize this?"

Joe sucks in a breath. "That's Wyn's backpack. Jess, that's her bag, isn't it?"

Behind us, the night explodes with another lightning strike.

This area, I suddenly realize, is entirely quiet. All wildlife must have been spooked away. It's like we're on a soundstage and they haven't added the nature sounds yet. Is that how it is in the middle of the night? Was this how it was for my daughter, for all those nights she was chained right near the place I'm now standing?

When it's clear I'm not going to answer, Joe asks, "What else is there?"

Agent Donovan hesitates. He just stands there, holding the large bag out to us like an offering.

"Come on." Joe squeezes the words out through clenched teeth. "What is it?"

The FBI agent holds the bag for another moment—and yes, it is Bronwyn's backpack, gray canvas with her initials monogrammed on the exterior pocket—and then gently sets it down on the floor of the cabin, clears his throat.

"Obviously there's no Wi-Fi out here. Depending on your provider, you might not even get a signal. So we believe the unsub must have turned on his phone's hot spot when he came out here. Your daughter mentioned how she was able to use her phone for games and videos. We believe she managed to get onto the hot spot Wi-Fi, and that was when she managed to contact you, Ms. Moore."

I blink. Look up at him numbly.

"We're back in the pickle we were before," Agent Donovan says. "We can tell by the tire tracks that your daughter's abductor drives an SUV or pickup truck. We could put out an APB for the entire state, but truth be told, we don't know what specific vehicle we're looking for, and besides, we still need to proceed with the idea the unsub might be part of law enforcement. We put anything out over the wire, he'll know immediately."

"And that's not all," Tony says quietly, and his voice makes me jump.

"What's not all?" I ask. It's the first time I've spoken since we arrived, and my voice is surprisingly steady.

Tony glances at Agent Donovan, clearly not wanting to speak the rest, so the FBI agent continues the thought.

"What Chief Parsons is saying is that we no longer have the opportunity we had before."

Somehow, in a snap, that hollowness has dissipated. A warmness has started to stir in my chest, filling me with heat.

Agent Donovan opens his mouth to say more, but I don't give him the opportunity. I push past Tony and Joe and round the cabin to the root cellar.

It looks to have been dug into the side of a hill. The door is already open. Bright light shines out from inside, no doubt from another one of those tripod spotlights.

Voices shout at me to stop, to not go down there, but I go down anyway.

The root cellar is dank and smells like old earth. The space isn't very large; no more than twelve-by-twelve feet, the ceiling only about six feet high.

Another FBI agent is busy taking pictures. He's hunched slightly due to the low ceiling and turns to gawk at me.

I barely note his surprise.

I stare past him at the dirty mattress on the ground and the large ring that's been screwed into the wall.

I stare at the heavy chain lying abandoned on the damp earth floor.

And I stare down at what's left of my daughter's iPhone. It's been smashed apart. Like it was stomped on by a malicious boot. The glass pieces scattered across the ground, sparking from the harsh glow of the spotlight like stars in a void.

35

Jessica

Six Weeks after the Pep Rally

Catherine Colvin answered the front door. She was dressed in nice jeans and a blouse and a long cardigan, and when she saw me, her face lit up and she said, "Happy Thanksgiving, Ms. Moore!"

"Thank you, Catherine. Happy Thanksgiving to you."

She took the pumpkin pie from my hands and then stepped aside for me to enter. She pointed to the closet where I could hang my coat and then took the pie to the kitchen.

Even from the hallway, I could smell the turkey and stuffing and potatoes. I hadn't eaten all day, and my stomach growled its impatience.

Stuart stepped out of the living room to say hello and give me a hug.

"Great to see you, Jess. I'm so glad you were able to make it."

"Thank you for inviting me."

"Of course. You're always welcome."

He directed me to the living room, where football was on the TV. He introduced me to his dad, who was hunkered down on the recliner and offered up a half-hearted hello. Amanda and Trent were on the floor, each playing with a tablet. Joe's dad sat in another recliner, his head tipped back, lightly snoring.

Aaron was there, too, slumped on the sofa. He raised his hand, nodded a hello. I smiled in return. The day he came to the house and told me about Sean Heller had been the last time we'd seen each other. He'd made me promise not to tell anyone, not even Joe, because he didn't want to get in any trouble, and I had honored that promise.

Joe appeared and hugged me and mentioned that Emma was in the kitchen with Rachel and Joe's mom. I nodded and drifted in that direction.

"A shame, really," Rachel was saying.

Stepping into the kitchen, I asked, "What's a shame?"

Everyone looked up with smiles and said hello. Then Emma answered.

"Sean Heller. About what happened to him at the game last week."

"What happened?" I said, though I already knew.

"Broke his leg in last Saturday's game. It's a bad break. There's a chance he might never fully recover."

"Terrible," Rachel said. She picked up my store-bought pie and transferred it from one counter to another. "Everybody thought he had such a bright future."

I thought about how Sean had come into the Wonderwall the other weekend with his folks for dinner. And when he had, the whole place had burst into applause like it was a surprise party and Sean was the special guest. Only it hadn't been a party; just everyone was thrilled to see the hometown hero.

I'd watched him all night. He looked so smug. Laughing with his parents, even taking selfies with the people bold enough to approach their table.

At one point he went back to the restrooms. I caught him as he was coming out of the men's room. I told him I knew about the party that Friday night. That he'd gotten into an argument with my daughter.

Before, he'd been strutting around like the cock of the walk, but the moment I called him out, it was like he'd become a frightened child.

At first he tried to deny anything had happened, but then he admitted they had argued. That it was about Taylor. Bronwyn accused Sean of cheating on Taylor, which Sean said was a total lie, and eventually she'd left. Sean promised he hadn't seen her since.

"Anyway," Rachel said, checking the timer on the stove before she turned to me. "How are you doing, Jess? Joe says there hasn't been any word from Wyn."

I shook my head. I remembered how we'd left things in this kitchen two months ago, and it had been bothering me ever since.

"No," I said. "Not yet. By the way, Rachel, about the last time I was here—"

She cut me off, wiping her hands on her apron.

"Don't worry about it. Seriously. I can't even imagine the stress you'd been going through. It's water under the bridge."

She was letting me off too easy, but I wasn't about to argue.

Soon the turkey and mashed potatoes and stuffing and green bean casserole and all the rest were ready, and everybody gathered in the dining room.

Aaron ended up sitting across from me. I remembered how devastated he said he'd been when Bronwyn broke up with him, how she hadn't given him an actual reason why. Now I knew the reason, but I didn't feel it was my place to share it with Aaron.

Once everyone was situated, Stuart stood at the head of the table and said a quick prayer. He included Bronwyn in the prayer, saying he hoped she was safe and healthy and would return soon. Then, once he said amen, Stuart told me that before we started eating it was tradition to go around and say one thing that you were thankful for.

"In fact, I'll go first," he said. "I'm thankful every day to be blessed with a beautiful wife and two beautiful children, not to mention the greatest job in the world."

"Such a politician," Stuart's father muttered, and everyone laughed.

Around the table they went, each person offering up thanks, until it came to me, and I froze.

Five seconds of silence ticked by. Then ten seconds.

"It's okay, Jess," Stuart said. "We can skip you."

"No," I said. "I can go."

"Are you sure?"

I nodded. Thinking of what to say. Wondering what I possibly could be thankful for now that my daughter was gone and I had nobody else in the world.

"Umm," I said quietly. Then: "No, never mind. Pass."

I spent the rest of the meal thinking about how this had been a mistake. How I should have just stayed home. And how when I got home later that night I would go straight to the unopened bottle of wine in the fridge.

That, I realized, was what I was thankful for: cheap wine and the ability to drink myself numb.

36

Wyn

Day of the Pep Rally

She'd backed her car into a spot near the rear corner of the park so she could sit behind the steering wheel and watch people coming and going.

It was almost four thirty now, and the park was mostly deserted. An older man walked his dog along the trail. A woman had brought her two children to the playground, and she sat on one of the benches looking at her phone while her kids climbed on the contraptions.

This was where Onyx Butterfly had chosen to meet Wyn.

Be there at 4:30, the message had said, and now it was 4:32.

Maybe Onyx Butterfly wasn't as punctual as Wyn. Maybe Onyx Butterfly had run into traffic. Maybe—

Onyx Butterfly is standing you up, the Taylor voice said. *Have you considered that?*

She glanced down at the phone in her hand. Debated whether to check Twitter and TikTok and Facebook and wherever else the kids from her school had posted their videos. The last time she'd looked, one of the videos had already hit over one thousand views.

No. She wasn't going to torture herself like that. She already had a plan. She probably would have already done it by now if it hadn't been for—

Her heart dropped when she spotted the red Civic pulling into the park.

"No," she whispered. Then, her voice growing louder: "No, no, no, no, no!"

How had she been so stupid? So naive?

Wyn reached for the ignition, meaning to turn on the car and drive straight out of there, head home to grab her things so she could get on the road, when Aaron Colvin slid to a halt. He'd parked at an angle that boxed her in, and unless she wanted to tear up some of the park's freshly mowed grass, she wasn't going to be able to leave unless she caused damage to both of their vehicles.

Aaron stepped out of his car and squinted at her over the roof. Wyn glared back at him, feeling so betrayed she couldn't even move. Then, before she knew it, she'd flung open her door.

"Are you shitting me, Aaron?"

His face froze. "What are you talking about?"

When she didn't answer him, he circled the front of his car, slowly, cautiously, and then began to advance toward her but paused the moment she raised a hand.

"Don't," she said. "I can't fucking believe this."

He took off the gray Phillies cap she'd bought him and ran his fingers through his hair.

"I know. I'm sorry. It's all over the internet. I wish I could take those videos down for you—I can't even begin to imagine how you must feel—but it'll be okay."

She stared at him then, understanding there was some kind of disconnect.

"Aaron, be honest with me. Are you Onyx Butterfly?"

"What? You asked me that this morning. I have no idea what you're talking about."

"Then why are you here?"

"I've been looking everywhere for you. I texted and I called, but you didn't answer me, and I was worried, so . . ."

He paused, his brow furrowing as he studied her. "Who were you expecting, Wyn?"

She glanced past him, toward the rest of the park. That older man still walking his dog. The woman still looking at her phone while her kids scrambled all over the playground. Traffic on the main road, moving back and forth, but no cars turning into the park.

"Hey," Aaron said softly, taking a step toward her. "It'll be okay. Everyone will forget about what happened in a couple of days."

She felt her jaw tighten, her eyes starting to water.

"It was awful, Aaron. Everybody was laughing at me. No one is ever going to forget what happened."

"What? Nobody was laughing at you. I mean, there were a few assholes, yeah, but mostly everyone was stunned silent. Everyone's really worried about you, Wyn."

She looked away from him, not sure what to say. It had all happened so fast, and her panic attack had been getting worse, that maybe her imagination had fed her the worst-possible scenario.

Still, that didn't matter. Even if everybody in the gymnasium hadn't been laughing at her, it didn't change what she needed to do next.

Aaron took another step toward her.

"Is it true what Sean Heller said?"

Every muscle fiber in her body went tense.

"What did he say?"

"That"—Aaron wet his lips, cleared his throat—"that you had a thing for him. That you came on to him one night after a party. That you drove him home and that you—"

"Absolutely not."

"Sean said that you wanted to break up Taylor and him so you could go out with him. Is that . . . is that why we broke up?"

"Listen to me, Aaron. Sean Heller is full of shit."

"But he said—"

"He's a liar, Aaron, and you know it."

Aaron just stared back at her, his face tense and his bottom lip trembling. She wanted to say something to help defuse the situation, but she kept glancing past him, searching for any sign of Onyx Butterfly.

"Wyn, I . . . I miss you."

He was on the verge of tears, and she didn't know what to do. She'd always felt terrible being with him. He was the kind of boy any girl would love to be with, though it would need to be a girl who wasn't already in love with her best friend.

It hadn't been fair to Aaron, not one bit, and the longer she'd drawn it out, the more massive the guilt became.

And then Taylor died, and Wyn realized she no longer had to pretend, at least with Aaron, and that was why she had broken up with him, never giving him a reason why, nothing that might provide him with closure, which was an even shittier thing for her to do.

"I'm sorry, Aaron. Honestly, I wish . . . I wish things could have been different. But it's over."

He nodded quickly, fighting back the tears.

"I don't even know what to think anymore," Aaron said quietly. "Sean told me all that stuff, and how you . . ."

But he shook his head, wiped at his eyes.

Wyn asked, "Sean said how I what?"

"Huh? Oh. He said that you . . . I forget. Something about how you had something of his. He sounded pissed."

The pregnancy test. There was no other thing it could be.

"Did he say what this something was?"

"No, but he told me whatever it was, it was bullshit. That you were setting him up. Because . . . well, you know."

"Because of what?"

"Because . . . you're obsessed with him."

"I'm not obsessed with Sean Heller, Aaron. If you don't believe anything else, believe that."

Only . . . that wasn't really true, was it? In a way, she was obsessed with Sean Heller. Just not in the way Sean was telling people.

"Go home, Aaron."

He just stared back at her. A kaleidoscope of emotions passed over his face. But then he nodded, wiped at his eyes, and turned away. He was back in his car within seconds, the engine revving loudly, and sped out of the park.

Wyn waited until Aaron's car was back on the main road, his engine fading, and then she lifted the phone in her hand.

She opened Twitter, expecting a message from Onyx Butterfly.

Nothing.

She typed: where are you

Wyn waited for a response.

She waited five minutes. She waited ten. She waited a half hour.

Feeling more alone than she'd ever felt in her entire life.

37

Jessica

Now

"Well?" Joe says.

Tony lowers the phone from his ear, sets it gingerly on Joe's desk. It's Wednesday morning, 10:00 a.m., and we're in Joe's home office again, just like when this all started: Joe behind his desk, Tony and I in the chairs facing it, all those Colvin for Congress signs stacked around the room like this is a warehouse.

"Eddie says right now there's not much we can do. They're still analyzing the tire tracks. After we left last night, a team came in to take samples. The same with the boot prints—they found some of those too."

"Shit," Joe says quietly. Then, louder: "Shit!"

"I know. It's not ideal. But right now . . ." Tony pauses, turns to look at me. "How are you holding up, Jess?"

I'm sitting in the chair, staring ahead but not seeing anything. A couple of seconds tick by before I realize Tony is speaking to me.

I blink, look at him, and say, "I haven't gotten a single minute of sleep since Monday night, and, oh yeah, my daughter is still missing and probably in more danger than she's ever been in her entire life. How do you think I'm holding up?"

Before Tony can answer—though based on his expression it's clear answering me is the very last thing he wants to do—Joe leans forward and clears his throat.

"Jess, you should try to get some rest. Emma can set you up in the guest room if you'd like."

"I'm fine."

"Come on, Jess, don't—"

"Why didn't they shut down the state?"

Tony frowns. "Say that again?"

"Shut down the state. Or at the very least the county, once they realized Bronwyn was no longer at the cabin."

"And do what, Jess?" Joe says. "Logistically, it would have been impossible."

"Why?"

"Well, for starters, we still don't know what vehicle they were in—and there's no telling just how fast they may have abandoned that vehicle for another."

"Then the police could have stopped every car. Gone door to door. Searched every—"

"Jess, that's enough!"

Joe's staring at me hard, having just used his stern father voice, as though I'm one of his kids and not the woman who gave birth to his first child.

Then his eyes soften, and he sighs.

"Look, I'm just as frustrated by this as you are. Believe me. But the simple fact is the police—not to mention the FBI—don't have the resources to do what you're asking."

"She could be anywhere by now, Joe."

"I know. I know, and it drives me crazy, but—"

"Let's contact the news. Local, national, whatever. Let's tell them about Bronwyn. How she's been abducted by—"

"By who, Jess? Tell me—who? See, that's the problem. We have no idea who this guy is. All we know is that he may or may not be in law enforcement. And if he is in law enforcement, then that makes this even more difficult. If we take this to the media and they start running it everywhere, it might provoke him. If he feels like he's being backed into a corner, he might . . ."

But Joe can't bring himself to say the rest. He stares back at me, his eyes bloodshot, and shakes his head.

"I'm sorry, Jess, but right now the only thing we can do—the only thing besides wait—is pray."

Later, Tony drops me off at home, and I try to sleep, but all I do is lie there and stare up at the ceiling. My mind is going a mile a minute, and eventually I shower and dress and head in to the Wonderwall.

My assistant manager is surprised to see me, especially after what happened last night—my dropping the glass in the bar and then soon after rushing out of the Wonderwall with Kenny Gorman. She asks if everything is okay, and it takes everything in me not to burst out crying. I simply nod and tell her everything is fine and then head back to my office and close the door.

I feel like I need to talk to somebody. Somebody beyond Joe and Tony and Kenny.

I think about calling Suzanne Walker, but what am I going to tell her? Besides the obvious, there isn't much to tell. No real news to share except the fact my daughter is still alive but being held captive by a madman.

But is she still alive?

I close my eyes and try not to scream out my frustrations, and the next thing I know a knock at the door wakes me.

I lift my head and stare around the room, at first not sure where I am. Then my eyes fall on the clock on the wall near the door—it's almost five o'clock—and I realize I've been asleep for nearly four hours.

My mouth tastes sour. A small puddle of drool sits squarely on my desktop, right next to the keyboard. I grab a tissue to clean it up as I call for whoever it is to come in.

Catherine Colvin pokes her head inside. She's dressed for work, dark slacks and white blouse, and her honey-blonde hair is neatly pulled back in a tight ponytail.

"Ms. Moore? They told me you had come in today, and I wanted to see how you were doing."

I use another tissue to wipe at my mouth, hoping to rid any traces of dried drool.

"I'm fine, Catherine, thank you."

"It's just . . . I was at the debate last night. I saw Mr. Hayden run out halfway through, and when I asked my dad what had happened, he didn't want to talk about it. And then I heard about how you had run out of here last night, too, and I just . . . are you sure you're okay? It looks like you're about to cry."

It looks that way because I am about to cry. I can't help it. Seeing Catherine here in my office, now the same age as Bronwyn was when she disappeared, is just too much to take, and before I know it tears spill from my eyes.

Catherine doesn't hesitate; she quickly closes my office door and hurries over to the desk, grabbing several bunches of tissues and offering them to me as she places a hand on my shoulder.

But somehow I don't cry. I manage to hold in most of the tears, and soon my eyes are dry and I force a smile at Catherine.

"Thank you," I say quietly.

She continues to look at me, her pretty face painted with worry. "Ms. Moore, are you sure you're okay?"

"I'm fine, Catherine. Honestly."

She doesn't buy it, but she knows better than to keep pressing. She turns to leave and only pauses when I say her name again.

"Catherine, you know a lot about social media, right?"

She smiles at this. "Well, I'm a teenager, so yeah. Why?"

"How do you make something go viral?"

"Viral?"

"Yes," I say. "How does something—how does anything—go viral on social media?"

Catherine thinks about it for a moment and then shrugs.

"Hard to say. You can't just *make* something go viral. I mean, companies try all the time, but most people don't like being force-fed stuff. If anything, they hold it against those companies. The main thing, I guess, is authenticity. Why? Are you thinking maybe we can make the Wonderwall go viral?"

No, I'm not thinking about business at all. I'm thinking about the man who abducted my daughter—Agent Donovan's unsub—and how he's severed the only communication I had with her.

He and Bronwyn could be anywhere—halfway across the country by now—and there is absolutely nothing that I can do about it.

Only . . . is that true?

When I'd brought up taking this to the news media, Joe had pointed out how that might provoke our daughter's abductor. That if he feels like he's being backed into a corner, he might panic, and in his panic, he might kill Bronwyn.

The only problem is this psycho might kill Bronwyn regardless, so what good is sitting by and waiting for it to happen?

Maybe, I think, this guy needs to be backed into a corner.

And if anyone is going to be the one who does it, it's me.

It's ten o'clock by the time I get home.

I kick off my heels and go into the kitchen and open the fridge. Two bottles of wine are there. One hasn't been opened yet. The other has just enough for a single glass.

I pull out this bottle and turn to grab a glass but then think, *Screw it,* and start toward my bedroom, taking a swig as I go.

There's some lightness in my step. That weight that's been pressing down on me hasn't come back since after Catherine Colvin left my office, and especially not since I posted the video.

I've turned off my phone because of all the calls and text messages. They've been coming in nonstop. Relentless. Stupid to have given out my personal number, but whose number was I supposed to give? As soon as I realized most of them were crank calls or messages from trolls, I turned off the phone. I'll sort through them tomorrow once I've had a decent night's rest.

I pause outside Bronwyn's room. I open the door and take a step inside. I don't bother flicking on the light switch and instead let the hallway light stream in, my shadow eclipsing nearly the entire room.

I take another swig from the bottle, and whisper, "I hope I did the right thing, baby. I hope that did the trick and we find you soon."

I start to turn out of the room when I hear a banging coming from the front door. Then, suddenly, the door opens and Joe's voice booms through the house.

"Jess! Where the hell are you?"

I pause, the bottle to my lips. The last thing I want now is for Joe to catch me drinking—I don't need to see that look in his eyes, even if this is my goddamned house—and before I know it I hop over to Bronwyn's desk and set the bottle down behind it and then turn around and step into the hallway.

I watch Joe marching toward me and say, "Can I help you with something, Sunshine?"

His face is flushed. His hands are shaking.

"Are you insane?"

"I guess that depends on who you ask."

"Tony and I told you not to take this to the news media."

"And I followed your advice. I didn't take anything to the news media."

"You posted a video to the internet. The whole thing's gone viral."

"Tell me about it."

"This is serious, Jess."

"No shit, Joe. I got tired of waiting around and doing nothing."

His shoulders drop, and he looks at the carpet, shakes his head. "This could get her killed."

"Or it could save her life."

"You have no idea what you've done."

"Oh, I think I know exactly what I've done. And it's more than you've done this entire time. Now get the hell out of my house."

His eyes are flat, his expression blank. He just stares at me for another few seconds before turning and storming out the front door.

I wait to hear his car leaving the driveway before turning back to Bronwyn's room.

But no—what I need now, I decide as I head toward the kitchen, is a whole fucking bottle.

The video is just under two minutes long.

I sat at my desk, staring at the little camera at the top of my laptop screen, having wiped all my tears away but not touching up my makeup or hair.

"My name is Jessica Moore. My daughter, Bronwyn Hayden, disappeared almost a year ago. In fact, it was October sixteenth when she disappeared. Her father, Joe Hayden, made a website to receive tips, and the local police and state police kept an eye out, and I even hired private investigators, but nothing ever came of any of it. It was determined that my daughter was a runaway, and everybody seemed to decide they would just wait for her to come back.

"Well, she never came back. And the reason is that my daughter was abducted. I do not know where or when she was abducted. But I do know that my daughter was pregnant when she was taken. She did not have the baby, however; it was a stillborn. Over the past week and a half, my daughter managed to text me that information and more in bits and pieces.

"She claims the man who abducted her and has kept her captive all this time is in law enforcement. I cannot say what law enforcement he works for, but the fact he is in law enforcement has made it difficult so far for the authorities to do a proper investigation.

"Just last night we were able to determine where my daughter has been held. She was chained in the root cellar of an abandoned cabin in the middle of Black Creek State Park. By the time the authorities arrived, my daughter and her abductor were gone. What was left behind were the remains of her cell phone, which she had been using to contact me.

"So I am making this video in the hope of finding my daughter. If you know anything—if you even suspect something—please contact the police or the FBI or even me directly. I will include those numbers in the space below this video. My daughter's life is on the line. Thank you."

In my dream, I approach the cabin in the woods. Joe and Tony are not with me.

I am alone.

Except . . . no, that's not right.

As I walk down the heavily wooded lane, the large branches of the trees swaying ominously above my head, I can see the young FBI agent taking pictures of the tire tracks. He holds the large camera around his neck as he focuses on something on the ground. It's only as I near that he glances up at me, and once again I see his familiar face, though I'm not sure where I've seen it before.

I continue toward the cabin, walking past the FBI agent.

Agent Donovan stands in the doorway, waiting for me. He holds a small plastic bag in his left hand. His right hand is behind him, and I know that he is gripping another plastic bag.

In the small plastic bag is a pacifier.

What's in the other bag? I ask, though because this is a dream my words make no sound, at least not to my dream ears.

He stares back at me with empty eye sockets, and says, Your grandson.

It's then that I struggle up out of the dream—the nightmare, it's a nightmare—and I lie still for a minute, staring up at the ceiling, trying to slow my breathing.

The bedroom is dark. Faint moonlight filters in through the closed curtains.

My head is pounding with a hangover. The empty wine bottle sits on the bedside table, along with my iPhone.

I reach over and pick up the phone and remove the charging cord. I have over two hundred missed calls. Fifty-seven voicemails. Nearly one hundred text messages. Almost three hundred emails.

What the hell was I thinking giving out my private number?

Only, no, now is not the time to worry about that. Not after the dream—the nightmare—I just had.

The young FBI agent's face. I realize now why it looked so familiar.

I check the time on the phone. It's just past 3:00 a.m. I got maybe four hours of sleep, depending on when I dropped off.

I consider using my phone for what I need to check, but instead I crawl out of bed, realizing that I'm still wearing my clothes.

I flick on the lamp in the corner of the living room and sit down at the computer. It takes almost a minute before it's up and running, and then I click open the web browser and bring up YouTube.

I type in "clegg & hawthorne tv commercial" and hit Enter. I hold my breath, certain that what I'm looking for won't come up.

It's the first search result.

I click on the video, my jaw tight. It's the same commercial I've seen countless times. It's always on TV, always mingled between portions of *Shark Tank* or the local news.

A man sits at his kitchen table, going over bill after bill. His shoulders are slumped. He has a hand to his forehead as his wide eyes take in the amounts written on the bills. Finally he looks up at the camera and says, "How am I supposed to pay all of this debt when I just got laid off?"

I pause the video right before it flips to one of the lawyers from Clegg & Hawthorne telling people to call if they need help.

I realize that I've been holding my breath, and I slowly let it out. The man's face was visible on screen for only a few seconds, but seeing it every once in a while over the course of weeks and months, that face had become burned into the back of my brain. That's why the young FBI agent's face had looked so familiar.

Because it's the same face.

Maybe it's just coincidence. Maybe this was filmed before the man became an FBI agent. Or maybe it was filmed while he was an agent— Are agents allowed to have part-time jobs? Can they moonlight on the side in low-key small-market TV commercials?

Before I can decide what to do with this information—and I'm still trying to process what it all means—there's a knock at the front door.

I'm on my feet at once, worried that it's some kook who's used my number to track me down. It wouldn't be too difficult to find my address online. Not if they know my full name and the town I live in.

Another knock at the door, now heavy and loud, and this time it's accompanied by a voice I haven't heard in almost a year.

"Ms. Moore? I know you're in there. I need to talk to you."

I should call the police. Or at the very least I should call Tony. But my interest has been piqued so much so that I find myself stepping past the coffee table and crossing over to the front door.

Sean Heller stands on the front stoop. He looks beaten down and hollow eyed. His hair a mess. His clothes all out of sorts.

Mostly, though, he looks drunk.

He spots me through the tiny window in the door, and those hollow eyes widen.

"Ms. Moore? Please, I need to talk to you about Wyn."

Blame it on the fact I've been searching for my daughter for a year. Blame it on the fact my head is still pounding from all the wine. Blame it on the fact I just uncovered a curious wrinkle about the TV commercial and the young FBI agent. Whatever the case, I shouldn't bother with this kid—I should call Joe—but still I can't help myself.

"What do you know about my daughter?"

He glances over his shoulder at the dark, empty road. Then glances back at me.

"I know where she is."

I have the door unlocked and open before I even know what I'm doing. I'm not sure if I'm ready to invite Sean inside or step outside to talk to him, but I stop dead as soon as I see the gun in his hand, held down low at his side.

"I'm sorry, Ms. Moore, but I really need you to do as I say. And I'd rather you don't make this any harder than it has to be."

38

Jessica

Ten Months after the Pep Rally

Late August. The sky cloudless and the sun bright and the temperature higher than it should have been.

It was almost too quiet on the back patio. I sat on one of the chairs and stared out at the lawn and listened to the occasional car pass by out front on the road and some squirrels climbing the trees.

I lifted the wineglass off the table, took a sip. I could barely taste the wine—something that had begun to happen all too frequently—and so I took another sip, and then another.

I still hadn't seen a butterfly, even after all these months.

I'd thought finding my father would do the trick. That it would somehow set everything into motion. One event triggers another event triggers another event, like some cosmic Rube Goldberg machine.

None of it made sense. Not my daughter running away. Or the pregnancy test. Or the note I found in her desk from Chad Murphy.

The only thing that made an inkling of sense was what Bryan Parker had told me, and which I still hadn't yet told Joe. Maybe I never would.

I started to take another sip of wine and realized the glass was empty.

I almost got up to head inside to pour another glass, but I was afraid that would be the moment a butterfly would appear. My sign from the universe that my daughter was still out there.

So I stayed on the patio and stared out at the backyard.

Waiting.

39

Wyn

Day of the Pep Rally

She opened her eyes to darkness.

Only . . . it wasn't complete darkness. Some light was coming in through the curtains near her desk. Not a lot of light, but some.

It was nighttime.

How long had she been sleeping?

Her phone was still in her jeans pocket. She wiggled it out and turned it on, dreading to see how many more text messages and voicemails she'd have. Turned out there were quite a bit, but not nearly as many as before she'd powered off the phone.

The clock on her phone told her it was almost 9:30 p.m.

She'd been asleep for nearly four hours.

Wyn glanced over at her closet. She'd packed most of her clothes last night, cramming her shirts and pants and underwear into two large garbage bags. The plan had been to retrieve the bags right after the pep rally, along with her laptop and her piano keyboard and anything else she wanted to take with her. She'd hit the road, ignoring the inevitable calls and text messages from her parents once they realized she was gone;

part of her knew that hearing her mom's voice might break her resolve, force her to turn the car around. She planned to wait a few days before contacting her parents and telling them that she loved them and missed them but that this was for the best. She would tell them that she was safe and would invite them to come visit once she was working and had a proper apartment and was getting closer and closer to her dream.

But now . . . now she no longer had the excuse of needing to run away. She'd failed Taylor, and her punishment would be to stay in this godforsaken town for the rest of her life.

Her hands trembling, she checked her social media. She still had a barrage of notifications from those jerks who had tagged her in the videos. Now there were over five thousand views.

When she opened Twitter—having saved it for last, worried there would still be no communication from Onyx Butterfly even though she'd sent several more messages after coming home from the park and then promptly crying herself to sleep—two direct messages were waiting for her.

> I'm sorry I flaked out.
> But why was he there with you?

The *he* was Aaron, of course. Meaning that whoever Onyx Butterfly was, they'd come to the park to meet with her, but Aaron had gotten there first. And because Aaron had gotten there first, they'd decided not to show themselves.

For the first time all day, a spark of hope flared inside Wyn.

She typed: he just showed up

For about a minute or so there was no reply, not even those dancing dots. Then all at once a response came through, one that made her frown.

> Are you getting back together with him?
> no
> Do you still have feelings for him?

Wyn stared at the screen, not sure how to answer. This conversation had suddenly veered off course from wherever she'd expected it to go.

She typed again: no

Another brief pause, this one lasting almost thirty seconds, and then the next question that came through caused her pulse to quicken.

Why not?

Christ, how had she not seen this coming? Obviously this was Aaron. After all, hadn't Onyx Butterfly first contacted her *after* she had broken up with him? Hadn't Onyx Butterfly shown genuine interest in her, just like Aaron had done? Of course Aaron would play stupid if she asked him if he were Onyx Butterfly, because he'd want to string her along, get it to the point where it was Onyx Butterfly who would ask that ultimate question of why Wyn had broken up with him.

Wyn closed out Twitter and opened her messages. She ignored all the texts that had come in and opened Aaron's. The last time he'd texted her was after she'd left the high school, right before he showed up at the park.

She typed: youre an asshole

She wasn't sure if he would respond, but his reply came almost instantaneously.

What are you talking about?
why did you lie to me

This time he asked the same question, only in all caps and with several more question marks.

WHAT ARE YOU TALKING ABOUT???

Wyn wasn't sure if she was surprised by his denial. If he'd denied it before, wouldn't he deny it again? Except . . . hadn't he gotten the answer he was looking for? If so, then there was no reason for him to play these games.

Her phone buzzed with another message from Aaron.

Sean keeps talking shit about you.

i dont care

I know. But he keeps saying how you have something of his.

He's super pissed.

Staring down at her phone, she wasn't convinced Sean wanted the pregnancy test so much that he was pissed at the idea Wyn had kept it. Sean had been right: the positive test didn't prove anything, but it still rankled Sean, and that was at least something.

Because Wyn hadn't been lying to Sean when she told him she'd seen him the night Taylor died.

He'd passed her on the back road. And while it had been dark and she'd glimpsed his face for only a second, she knew it was him.

Wyn typed: where is the party tonight

She wasn't sure if Aaron would tell her, especially not after calling him an asshole, but after a minute he responded.

Autumn's house.

Autumn's house. Of course. Wyn had always suspected Sean was messing around with Autumn behind Taylor's back.

Wyn hadn't been able to confront Sean at the pep rally as she'd planned, but that didn't mean she couldn't get a second chance.

The more people at the party, the better.

40

Jessica

Now

"I was never really confident, you know? Growing up, I was as bad as Aaron—shy, I mean. Could never build up the nerve to talk to girls. I mean, I was friends with them, but that was it."

Sean Heller sits in the passenger seat of his car, shifted so his back is to the door. This way it makes it easier for him to aim his gun at me.

"At the next stop sign, make a left."

I slow as we reach the intersection. I have my seat belt on. Sean doesn't. If I swerve off the road going fast enough and hit a tree, it'll send Sean into the windshield. At the very least, it'll knock him off his seat. Of course, that doesn't mean he might not get off a shot in the process.

Then again, Sean said he knows where Bronwyn is. He may be drunk, may smell like the floor of the Wonderwall after a Saturday night, but that doesn't mean he's not telling the truth. There has to be a reason he showed up at my door in the middle of the night. With a gun.

"Where are we going?"

"I told you, don't ask any questions. We'll get there soon enough."

"To Bronwyn?"

Sean just stares at me for a couple of seconds, then shifts in the seat and clears his throat.

"Wyn was always nice to me, you know. She was always nice to everybody. She wasn't even in my grade, but whenever I'd see her in middle school, she would always say hi and wave. The way I was then . . . it felt good to be liked."

Wherever we're going, it's not toward town. It seems Sean is purposely directing me along secondary roads. This time of night, there's no traffic. All the houses we pass are dark.

"In eighth grade, I started trying out for sports. I knew my dad was disappointed that I didn't have any real interest up until then. Like, what boy my age doesn't want to play sports? The fact is I was scared. Thought I would suck. And I *did* suck. But the few times I played football, I really enjoyed it. So I started focusing on that. And then in high school, Coach Hatfield started talking about my 'arm talent,' started working with me, and the more I played and won, the more my confidence grew, and then . . ."

Sean reaches into the back of the car, grabs a can of Old Milwaukee. He sets the gun on his lap while he opens it, and for a moment—one single instant—I consider lunging for the gun. But then Sean grabs it again and lifts the beer to his lips.

"Randy, the assistant coach, he was the one who started talking Penn State. I was just a sophomore. Like, who in their right mind puts that into a kid's head—into everyone's head? The pressure started to build, but I kept working hard, and we kept winning all those games, and then went to the state championship, and then . . . um, hey, up here make a right."

I slow for the stop sign, automatically turn on the blinker even though there's no other driver in sight.

When I don't move forward, Sean says, "I said make a right."

"Sean?"

A beat of silence. "What?"

"Are you going to kill me?"

"What? No. I just . . . I took my dad's gun, okay? I knew I'd need you to come with me, and I knew you weren't just gonna do it on your own."

"So if I got out of this car right now, you'd let me go?"

He stares at me, his eyes hooded in the dark.

"You want to leave, go right ahead. But then you'll never know where Wyn is."

"Do you honestly know where my daughter is?"

He takes another swig of the beer, wipes his mouth with the back of his hand.

"I do."

"Where?"

"I'm taking you to her."

"But . . . how do you know?"

"Christ, just drive and you'll see. I'm trying to tell you."

"Why were you outside my house tonight?"

"Why do you think? That video you posted. Now drive!"

I pull out onto the road, my foot heavy on the gas pedal.

Sean watches me for a while, the gun in one hand, the can of beer in the other, and then he clears his throat again. He's been aching to tell his story to someone, obviously.

"For a shy kid, getting all this attention all of a sudden, especially from girls . . . like, I knew it was because I was so good at football, that I was popular, but I didn't care. I'd go to parties and I'd get drunk and I'd hook up with so many different girls. But then . . . then I started dating Taylor, and it got serious, and everybody saw us as like the king and queen of the school, which is so lame, but that's how it felt, and she told me that she loved me, and I told her that I loved her, but the entire time I was still messing around on her, even with some of her friends."

I think about the pregnancy test, and I think about how Bronwyn had that heated argument with Sean the night she ran away, and I ask, "Did you and my daughter—"

"What? No. No way. I mean . . . yes, there was that one night."

My fingers white around the steering wheel. A tremor in my voice. "What night?"

"After some party, she drove me and Taylor home. Wyn, you know she never drank or anything, right? We always teased her about it, called her Little Miss Goody Two-shoes. Anyway, after Wyn dropped Taylor off, it felt weird to sit in the back by myself, so I got up front with her. And then like halfway to my house, I reached over and—"

"Christ, Sean."

"I didn't do anything! I mean, not like what you think. She told me not to touch her, and I did as she said, but then she got to my house and stopped the car, and I just . . . I tried to kiss her, that's all. She pulled away and told me she'd tell Taylor, said while Taylor would always forgive me for messing around with other girls, she'd never forgive me if she knew I'd just tried to hook up with her best friend. And I got angry—*real* angry—and I told her she better not say a word, or I would destroy her entire life, and then . . ."

We've come to another intersection. It's a four-way stop. No headlights are coming in any direction. Ours are the only lights, shining into the darkness ahead.

Feeling like I could squeeze the steering wheel to dust, I say, "What did you do to my daughter, Sean?"

"I told you, I didn't do anything. I swear to God. Now, keep going straight."

As I put the car in motion once again, I ask, "What does my video have to do with anything?"

Sean takes another swig of his beer, shakes his head as he stares out his window.

"You know, I had to drop out of Penn State. When it got obvious I wasn't going back to the team—not after the hit I took—I felt so embarrassed that I just stopped going to classes. Like, everything had been set: They built me all up—ESPN, the internet, everybody. We were winning, and I was going to the NFL. And then, *bam*: I get blown up, blown up for good, and it wasn't even like it was the first time I got sacked. By then we'd played almost an entire season, and I knew how to take a hit, and then . . . well, it was over. All of it. After that, it felt like everybody was laughing at me. I guess I got depressed. Got really low. Decided to stay home and work for my dad."

He shakes his big, ignorant, self-pitying head, and I do everything I can to keep my voice steady as I say, "My video, Sean. Why did it make you come to my house tonight with a gun?"

"Because of what you said. About Wyn. About her being pregnant."

"What about it?"

"Wyn was never pregnant," Sean says. "Taylor was."

41

Sean

Two Months before the Pep Rally

She's pregnant.

Standing in the locker room—the expansive locker room in the Lasch Building, his new favorite place in the world, which glowed Nittany blue when the lights were dimmed and had those sweet in-facility barber chairs where he'd already gotten a cut just last week—he stared at the words on his phone for nearly a minute before he realized he'd stopped breathing.

Sean gulped in air and dropped his phone, all in the same motion. It was enough to catch the attention of a junior linebacker standing nearby. He turned at the sound of the OtterBox-cased phone smacking against the floor, then glanced up at Sean.

"Dude, you okay?"

Sean nodded numbly, staring down at the phone. One minute earlier and he would have been on his way to practice, not in this locker room with a bunch of the other guys, many of whom he knew were jealous of him even though they acted all cool to his face. Now here he was, the superstar freshman who hadn't even played in a game yet, and he was acting like a scared chickenshit.

The phone had fallen screen up, so Autumn's next text message stared back up at him.

R u there???

"Seriously, dude, what's wrong?"

"Nothing," Sean mumbled as he grabbed the phone off the floor and hurried toward the bathroom.

He locked himself in the farthest stall, as if he could hide what was happening from the rest of his teammates, and then drew in another deep breath before replying to Autumn.

I'm here.
How do you know she's pregnant?

He watched the dancing dots for a second before the phone vibrated.

She told me!
I thought u said u were being safe ☹

Sean swallowed, not sure how to respond. At first, Autumn had been just another booty call, someone who wouldn't hesitate to suck his dick if he looked at her right, but after the past couple of months things had gotten serious, almost as serious as things were between him and Taylor, and Autumn had even flirted with saying those three dreaded words, the ones that Taylor had said to him and which he'd said back because he knew it was the right thing to do even though it made him sick inside to say it, feeling like a pansy.

Did he care for Taylor? Absolutely. Did he love her? Sure, why not. But was he *in love* with her? Sean certainly didn't think so, and he figured he was the best judge of that, though there were times he'd admit that he really wasn't a great judge, because half the time he was wasted and hooking up with anything that had tits.

His phone vibrated with another text.

Answer me lover!

Lover. That was what Autumn had started calling him, her way of being cute—no *babe* or *darling* for Autumn Porter, no way—and he had just started going with the flow, letting her call him whatever she wanted as long as she kept letting him do whatever he wanted to her.

But now there was this. This . . . this news that had literally taken his breath away, and what the fuck was he supposed to do now?

He typed: I'm here. Where are you?

Home. She just came over to tell me the news.

He started typing out a response—Does she want to keep it?—and then deleted the text, typed again.

Does anyone else know?

Autumn: I bet Wyn knows.

Sean bit his lip, thinking and pondering and calculating, but all that he saw when he closed his eyes was a baby, a motherfucking baby, and he felt like smashing his phone so hard even the OtterBox wouldn't protect it.

The phone vibrated again.

Do u love me?

That was a loaded question, especially coming from a girl like Autumn. He knew she felt she deserved to be head cheerleader, not Taylor, and while Autumn and Taylor had been friends for years and looked like such great girlfriends on the outside, Sean had never known just how much Autumn truly despised Taylor behind her back. And so when a girl like Autumn asks if you love her, during a time like this when you just learned that your girlfriend—your steady girlfriend, the one you take home to meet your parents—is pregnant, a smart man knows just what to say.

Of course.

Those dancing dots again, and then Autumn replied: Come to my house tonite. 9 o'clock. I have an idea.

She wouldn't tell him much more, even when he pressed. She only said that her parents were away and that he shouldn't drive his car.

Borrow somebody else's. Be discreet!

She finished off with a heart emoji and then sent him a selfie. Her standing in front of the first-floor bathroom sink, pursing those big red lips. It hit him a second later that she must have excused herself to the bathroom so she could text Sean without Taylor knowing.

Sean stared down at his phone. Why hadn't Taylor texted or called him yet?

Because, you dummy, she wants to tell you in person.

Sure, that made sense. Unless maybe Taylor didn't want to keep the baby. At least there was that hope.

Somebody banged on the stall door with enough force that it nearly knocked it off the hinges.

"Heller! What are you doing in there!"

Sean cleared his throat, flushed the toilet, his mind racing a hundred yards a second as he opened the stall door.

"Sorry, Coach. I'm not feeling so good."

His QB coach stared at him. "How's that?"

"My stomach. I think it was something I ate."

The interrogation lasted much longer than Sean would have liked, but finally he was given the green light to head back to his dorm. The last thing his coach said to him was that the first game was next week, and it would be a shame if Sean let down his team by being too sick to play.

By then, it was almost five o'clock. It would take about two hours to get to Bowden, so he knew he had more than enough time to find a different vehicle, but from whom?

In the end, Sean managed to score a ride from a kid in his dorm. He came up with some bullshit story about how there was a family emergency and his car had been acting up and he was afraid to drive it too far. He told the kid he'd fill the tank when he got back and promised he would be careful not to wreck it. He even threw in two tickets to the opening game to sweeten the deal.

On the way Autumn texted him periodic updates, and each one managed to deflate his heart more and more.

Taylor was scared but ecstatic.

She wanted to keep the baby.

She planned to tell Sean later this weekend when she drove up to surprise him.

Autumn said Taylor hadn't told anyone besides her and Wyn, and that she'd sworn Wyn to secrecy and that Taylor had begged Autumn not to tell anyone else, either, at least not until Taylor made it official by telling Sean, and as each text came in Sean found himself sweating more and more, his foot heavy on the gas pedal, and when a state trooper's lights strobed behind him on the highway, he cheered and shook his fist as soon as he realized the trooper had targeted another car going about as fast as him.

And then he had made it to Bowden, driving those familiar back roads as he waited for Autumn's signal, and at just after nine o'clock he received the text letting him know to come on over and to park in the garage so that nobody would see the car. Which struck Sean as odd, because the house sat far enough back from the main road that nobody would see this car or any car, but he'd begun to understand it was never wise to question Autumn Porter, not when she was scheming. So he did as he was told, making sure nobody saw him pull into her driveway, and after he'd parked in the garage and made it inside—pausing a beat on the porch to take a breath, steady his nerves—he found Taylor practically comatose on the sofa.

"What the fuck did you do?"

He'd seen Taylor wasted before, but never this far gone. She could barely open her eyes, let alone curl her lips into a smile when she heard his voice.

Autumn stepped up next to him, kissed him full on the mouth, tongue and everything, and then she leaned back and gave him her lethal smile and said, "Protecting our future, lover. Now, go pick her up and take her outside. I already have everything set up in the car."

42

Jessica

Now

"Pull over up there."

"Where?"

"There! There!"

We're on Hidden Valley Road, one of those tree-lined roads without a house in sight, and I'm doing the speed limit, which is forty-five miles per hour, and so I practically need to slam on the brakes to stop the car fast enough.

Centrifugal force kicks in and Sean, who still isn't wearing his seat belt, almost falls straight into the dash. He manages to catch himself, but only because he drops his beer, which fizzes all over the floor mat. He doesn't let go of the gun and points it at me as he shouts, "What the fuck was that?"

"You said to pull over, so I pulled over."

"Christ," Sean says, looking down at the spilled beer. Some of it's gotten on his jeans and is already starting to soak through. He motions with the gun at the barrier farther ahead. "Go down there."

"Go down where?"

"Don't you see the sign?"

"You mean the sign that tells people it's no longer a roadway?"

Right after Taylor Mitchell died, the town finally decided to shut down Fox Lane. They put up road-closed barriers on both ends. Then, about two months later, they put up permanent barriers, designating the once-dangerous road a hiking trail.

What little gravel on the roadway that was once there is now mostly gone. Nature has started to take over, the bushes and trees having reclaimed some of the space.

The barrier stretches across the entire roadway.

Sean says, "You can squeeze through."

"What are you talking about?"

"I want you to drive past that."

"Why?"

"Just do it, okay?"

Clenching my teeth, I twist the steering wheel slightly and take the car off the road and onto the grass. It's bumpy here, the car's suspension not well equipped to handle even the slightest bit of rough terrain, and I'm suddenly worried that a hard enough bump might cause Sean to pull the trigger.

Then, after several long seconds, we make it past the barrier and onto the roadway that's no longer a roadway.

"Okay, now what?"

He gestures at the Old Milwaukee–splattered windshield with the gun.

"Drive."

I do as he says, though I don't let the speedometer go up any higher than ten miles per hour. I flick on the high beams and illuminate the canopy of trees. This time of year, most of the leaves have fallen and blanketed the roadway.

"You know what they used to call this road, right?" Sean says.

"I've lived in this town for almost twenty years. Of course I know what they used to call it."

"Fast Lane," Sean says thoughtfully. "Such a stupid thing to call it, right? Our parents would tell us not to drive too fast down Fox Lane, and we'd say, *Okay, sure, Mom and Dad, whatever you say,* and then we'd come down here and jam the gas as hard as we could. It's a surprise nobody ever killed themselves until—"

He cuts himself off, as if suddenly remembering who did in fact die on this road. I've never driven on it personally—there was never any reason to—but I did see pictures of the crash. Some of them had been in the newspaper. Nothing too graphic. Just shots of the scene, both mourning the loss of a promising young woman and reminding people not to drink and drive.

"I didn't know what she had planned," Sean says. He's slumped in his seat now, staring forward. The gun sits on his knee, pointed at the door. "I mean, I knew she had something planned, but I didn't . . . I didn't know just how bad it was gonna be."

My foot instinctively touches the brake, and I bring the car to a complete stop.

"What are you talking about, Sean?"

"Taylor. What . . . what we did to her."

"Who is *we*?"

"Autumn."

"Autumn Porter?"

He's still staring ahead, seeing something beyond the reach of the headlights.

"She lives on the other side of those woods, you know. Or, well, lived. She's at college now. Her folks still own the house, but they travel all over the place. I never understood why they keep it. That's a lot of land. Has to cost a lot to keep it going, right?"

"Sean, what did you and Autumn do?"

"Autumn said it was for the best. That having the responsibility of a child would ruin my future. She said . . . she said that we needed to do it to protect me. To protect us."

His voice has become a whisper, and he's still staring forward, lost in thought.

"I mean . . . I think I can finally admit I was always sorta scared of Autumn. She had this nasty streak about her. Sometimes I found it sexy, and other times . . . other times it scared the shit out of me."

"Sean, what did you and Autumn do to Taylor?"

He blinks and glances at me, and he looks so alone, so scared, so sad.

"Autumn had managed to get her drunk before I got there. I guess she'd crushed some sleeping pills into her lemonade, and then started mixing it with vodka or whatever once Taylor got to the point where she couldn't tell what she was drinking anymore. When I got to the house, Taylor was out of it."

I don't speak. I wait for him to continue.

"Autumn had me pick her up and take her out to the car. At the time I . . . I was just working on autopilot, you know? I wasn't even thinking. But when I got outside and saw Autumn had her hair up in a baseball cap and was wearing those latex gloves, I stopped. I asked her, What the hell are you doing? She told me to put Taylor in the back seat."

He goes silent then, his eyes starting to water, and I nudge him along.

"Then what happened?"

"We . . . we drove Taylor's car down to Fox Lane, at the other entrance. It was about a half mile from Autumn's house. It was late enough that no cars were around. We drove down Fox Lane a bit, and that's when Autumn stopped the car and told me to get Taylor out and put her behind the wheel. Again, I was working on autopilot and did everything Autumn told me to do. I thought we were just going to leave

Taylor there in the car, passed out. But that wasn't at all what Autumn had planned."

"Go on, Sean. What did Autumn have planned?"

"She'd also brought along bungee cords. She hooked them to the steering wheel and the side doors tight enough so it would keep the wheel from turning. And then we put Taylor behind the wheel. And Autumn leaned down and spoke so sweetly to Taylor, like they were the best of friends, telling her that there was an emergency at home, that her mom had called and was in trouble and Taylor needed to drive as fast as she could. And Taylor . . . she was out of it, right, and the entire time I wasn't sure if she knew I was even there, but then she looked up at me, and she sorta smiled and said, *Sean, there's something I need to tell you*, and that was when Autumn pushed me away and told Taylor that she needed to go, needed to save her mom. She closed the door and we stood back, and at first nothing happened; the car just stayed there, and that was when Autumn remembered it was still in park, so she opened the door again and leaned in and put it in drive, and the car started coasting and Autumn ran alongside it, encouraging Taylor to drive to drive to drive, and suddenly the engine revved and the car just bolted forward and I watched it all happen, just stood there and watched as Taylor's car rocketed away from us and then . . ."

He pauses, his face now streaked with tears, and I whisper, "Jesus Christ."

Sean says, "I guess the idea was for her to get into an accident. Like, that's what Autumn told me. That Taylor had said she was a month or two along, and that if Taylor was in an accident, a really bad accident, it might cause her to lose the baby. And I was like . . . yeah, okay, let's do that. That makes sense. But usually when a car hits something straight on, the airbags pop, right? Well, the airbags in Taylor's car didn't go off. Apparently they were defective. And so Taylor, she went straight through the windshield and hit that tree."

Sean wipes at his eyes with the back of his hand, shakes his head, and nervously starts tapping the gun on his knee.

"I wanted to call an ambulance. I had my phone out and started dialing. But Autumn stopped me. She reminded me that *we* had done that to Taylor, her and me. That if we called for an ambulance, called for the police, then we would both go to jail. And there would go my career."

The gun keeps tapping on his knee: tap tap tap tap.

"We hurried over to the car. We had to get rid of the bungee cords, you know? And Taylor, she was just lying there on the ground, all bent and broken. And I . . . I started crying. I felt like such a baby. I got my phone out again to call 911, and Autumn had to take my phone away from me. She slapped me hard and told me to act like a man. And then . . . then we went back to Autumn's house. There was a trail through the woods connecting Fox Lane to her house. We didn't say anything to each other the rest of the way. Not even when I got into that car I'd borrowed and headed back to State College. I tried taking back roads to avoid people, but still I passed a few cars. One of them . . . one of them was Wyn's."

"What did you do to my daughter, Sean?"

"I didn't do anything. I swear. But I guess she was coming home late from work. We both ended up at a four-way stop at the same time. I had the right of way, so I pulled out into the intersection, and as soon as I did, I glanced over and . . . I knew it was her. And I was pretty sure she recognized me. I mean, I *know* she recognized me, because she said so later that homecoming weekend."

"This was at Autumn's house, later that night after the game."

"Yes."

"The same night my daughter went missing."

Sean's face tenses up. He squeezes his eyes shut so hard it's as though he'll never open them again. I eye the gun still tapping on his knee, debate whether I can grab it in time. But before I can even move, Sean speaks again, and his words cause my blood to go cold.

"I'm so sorry for what happened."

I can't tell if he's referring to what happened to Taylor or . . . something else. Either way, I don't like it.

"Autumn said I can't tell anybody about what happened. That we would both go to jail. And it was our secret, right? We were together then, boyfriend and girlfriend. We were going to stay together forever. But then . . . then I broke my leg and my football career was over, just like that. And Autumn . . . she broke up with me. Didn't even wait a day or two. Sent me a text that she hoped my leg got better and that if I knew what was good for me, I'll keep my mouth shut about that night. That was it. That was the very last thing I heard from her."

"Sean"—I try to keep my voice steady despite the fact my entire body is trembling like a tuning fork that's just been struck—"focus. Tell me about Bronwyn."

His eyes are still closed, and more tears squeeze through the clenched lids. The gun on his knee keeps tapping, but I ignore it as I grab his arm and shake him.

"What happened to my daughter?"

43

Wyn

Day of the Pep Rally

The last time Wyn had been at Autumn Porter's house was over the summer, at one of Autumn's famous parties. That was also the night Sean Heller had tried to kiss her when she drove him home.

Two weeks later, Taylor learned she was pregnant, and then later that night, she was dead.

Wyn still remembered that day, just at the start of the school year, how Taylor had come over to her house so that she could take the pregnancy test. Taylor was scared but excited, and when the result came up positive, she'd actually cried tears of pure happiness. Seriously—Wyn had never seen someone so happy before, though Taylor had acknowledged the hard part would be sharing the news with Sean.

As before, Wyn had bitten her tongue, wanting to tell Taylor so many different things. She could have told Taylor about what happened the night she'd driven Sean home, or how Sean was most definitely cheating on her, but Wyn also knew that it wouldn't matter. Taylor loved Sean, no matter what he did, no matter who he was, and now that she was pregnant, she wasn't going to let anything stop her happiness.

Before Taylor had left, she'd asked Wyn to take care of the pregnancy test. The last thing she needed, she said, was for her mom to find it. Taylor's mom had had her when she was in high school, and she knew her mom was going to be absolutely livid once she learned the news, though she believed that eventually her mom would come around. But Taylor definitely didn't want her mom to find the test before Taylor had a chance to tell her, so Wyn had promised to dispose of the test for her, as any good friend would do.

Only . . . she hadn't.

Wyn had *planned* to, yes, and she had almost followed through with that plan, but because Taylor had stayed over at the house longer than anticipated, Wyn had been running late for work, and as soon as she'd parked her car, she'd rushed inside, straight to the break room, the pregnancy test still in her bag. During her shift she decided she would toss it in one of the trash cans in the break room, but then after she'd clocked out, there had been so many people around that she suddenly felt too self-conscious, worried they might spot the test and think it was hers, and so she'd slipped it from her bag and shoved it to the far corner of her locker, intending to dispose of it later.

Of course, later that night on her way home from work she'd seen who she could have sworn was Sean Heller driving through an intersection, though the car wasn't Sean's, and so she had just assumed it had been someone who looked like him.

And then she learned the next morning that Taylor had died, and Wyn didn't know what to do with the pregnancy test, so she kept it there in her locker, where it had stayed all this time, even tonight after she'd hurried into the store, so focused on getting back at Sean Heller, thinking that the pregnancy test would be proof of his wrongdoing—which was what, exactly, Wyn couldn't say—but when she'd opened the locker and reached inside, she realized that, no, she didn't want to play this wild card quite yet, not tonight, and so she left the test where it was, secured her locker, and hurried back out of the store.

And now here she was driving up the long drive to Autumn Porter's house, cars and pickup trucks everywhere, their windshields glinting in the moonlight, and she parked her car off to the side, stared ahead at the wall of trees in front of her, and took a deep, silent breath.

In her head, the Taylor voice spoke up for the last time.

Nothing to worry about, babe. You got this. Now go show them who's boss.

There were about fifty people in the house, at least from what Wyn could see, most of them football players and cheerleaders and their boyfriends and girlfriends and other popular kids from school.

Almost immediately everyone took note of her. Not just a random girl at the party or the best friend of the late Taylor Mitchell but *that girl* from the pep rally. There were smirks and laughter and people turning away to gesture to their friends, and Wyn's fight or flight was starting to lean toward the latter, telling her she should leave now before things got even worse.

But she was equipped with her iPhone and what she had recorded on it before leaving the house, her other wild card should she feel the need to play it, and so she pushed on.

The music was loud and thumping and kids were everywhere, dancing and laughing and drinking, celebrating the school's victory. The football players were stoked, and the cheerleaders were excited, and Wyn had begun to wonder if Aaron hadn't told her the truth after all—if maybe Sean Heller had gone to another party—when she heard a familiar voice shout so loud it nearly shook the house.

"There she is! The star of the pep rally!"

Some people laughed, and she steeled herself as she turned toward the sound of that voice.

The crowd parted just a bit, enough for her to see Sean Heller standing in the living room, Autumn Porter right next to him in a tight skirt and heels, a manicured hand on his arm.

And there was Aaron, too, still wearing his Phillies cap, suddenly looking sheepish, embarrassed both for her and for himself because they had once dated and so were inextricably linked.

Again, that urge to flee spiked through her, but she tamped it down, feeling her nails digging into her palms as she marched forward, right at Sean.

"You're a fucking liar."

The volume of the music was suddenly lowered, and at once it seemed that everybody had quieted to watch the show.

Sean made a face, a plastic Solo cup in his hand. "How's that now?"

"I never had a thing for you."

He took a sip from the cup, nodding.

"Uh-huh, sure. Keep telling yourself that, superstar. Shit, I think by now you're more famous than me. I should be jealous."

Another bout of laughter rippled through the crowd, grating at her nerves.

"Don't worry," Wyn said, her gaze steady with his. "Once everybody finds out who you truly are, you're going to be more famous than Tom Brady."

Sean's grin froze, and his eyes darkened.

"Careful now. You don't want to go shooting your mouth off when you don't know what you're talking about."

"I know exactly what I'm talking about. Taylor—"

Sean cut her off, his voice loud enough for everyone in the house to hear.

"Was your best friend. Yeah, yeah, we all know. But what I don't think everyone knows is the truth about *you*."

"What are you talking about?"

"Oh, come on. We're all friends here. You can finally tell us the truth."

Somehow, someway, Sean had managed to flip the script. Wyn wasn't even sure how he'd done it. She had been so focused on what she wanted to do—what she *needed* to do—that this last part caught her completely by surprise.

"Taylor knew, by the way," Sean said. "She joked about it. She told me about how she'd suspected it for a while, but that you hadn't said anything to her, and so she wasn't going to say anything until you were ready, and then she was going to stop being your friend."

So far, Aaron had maintained that sheepish demeanor, still looking embarrassed, but now he stood up a bit straighter, a scowl spreading across his face.

"What are you talking about, Sean?"

"She's a lesbian!" Sean said gleefully. "She wanted to get with Taylor! Except, well, you never had a chance, did you, superstar?"

Sean paused then, his grin so big it nearly split his face, and then he turned to Aaron.

"Oh shit, dude. My bad. You didn't know, did you?"

Aaron's expression in that moment was of complete shock. He looked gutted, too, but that wasn't all Wyn saw in his face.

Now there was anger. Betrayal. Rage.

Sean leaned in, just close enough for Wyn to take a swing at him, but she couldn't find the strength to do anything but just stand there.

He whispered, "You come at the king, you best not miss."

Then he leaned back, that grin spread across his face again, and he downed the rest of his beer before his voice once again boomed through the house.

"Uh-oh! Looks like she choked again!"

Laughter rippled through the crowd, rambunctious and cruel, and Autumn laughed, too, throwing her head back as she reached out to run her fingers through Sean's hair, and it was in that moment where her wrist was exposed that Wyn saw she had been wrong after all.

The tattoo wasn't of a butterfly, but a bird.

Autumn, feeling Wyn's gaze on her, made a face and said, "Ugh, stop undressing me with your eyes!"

That was it, then. Whatever fire she'd had in her had suddenly been extinguished. In its place were those dreaded invisible fingers, squeezing her chest.

No, she thought. *Not here. Not now.*

This was the last place she wanted to have a panic attack, the very last, and instead of going right back at Sean and Autumn and everyone else as she wanted, she turned away to make a retreat.

She tried to push past a few people to get to the front, but they wouldn't budge, and still that tightness was getting worse, making it hard to breathe, and she looked all around the room for an escape and saw a hole she could push through, toward the back of the house, and that was where she headed, pushing someone aside as they tried to step in her way, hands to their throat as they pantomimed choking, and then she was breezing down a hallway with no one ahead of her and she had no idea where she was even going until she spotted the bathroom door.

It was right near the kitchen door, which would let her out into the backyard, but along with that tightness was a churning in the pit of her stomach, and she feared she might throw up and didn't want to throw up all over Autumn's house, no matter how much she might hate the girl's guts.

Wyn staggered into the bathroom, closing the door behind her, and fell to her knees in front of the toilet.

Nothing came out—she hadn't eaten all day—but she stayed hunched over the toilet for about a minute, until she realized her breathing had slowed back to normal.

She took some toilet paper off the roll, wiped her mouth, flushed it, and started to stand back up.

And that was when the bathroom door behind her opened, and somebody stepped inside.

44

Jessica

Now

"You know, when I look back at it, I was such an asshole. Not just for what I'd done to Wyn that night—that was pretty bad, no doubt—but in general. I mean, I used to be that shy kid, right? I tried to be nice to everybody. And . . . hey, does the name Summer Green mean anything to you? She was a cheerleader, just like Taylor and Autumn. And after Taylor . . . after she, well, you know, I guess Autumn made it her mission to really hammer home the point about just how much she and the rest of the cheerleaders hated Wyn. Those girls, they were so mean to her. And, well, after my accident, after Autumn had broken up with me, Summer reached out on Facebook. She said she'd only been at college for like two months, but already she was regretting just how mean she'd been to Wyn. She said that she had like . . . I don't know, fallen under Autumn's spell or something. She said she couldn't believe it had been that toxic, and she felt really bad and was happy to hear me and Autumn weren't together anymore, because, and these were her words, *That girl is one hundred percent evil.*"

Sean tilts his face slightly to look at me. I've since turned off the headlights, have left only the running lights on, but still there's enough light to see the dried tears lining his cheeks.

"What happened after?" I ask quietly, my voice just as hollow as my soul feels right now.

"After what?"

"After you whispered what you did to my daughter."

"You come at the king, you best not miss." A small smile forms on his lips, and Sean shakes his head. "That's from *The Wire*, you know. You ever watch that show?"

"Sean, do me a favor."

"What?"

"Fucking focus and tell me what happened after my daughter left the party."

The small smile disappears, and Sean stares down at his lap again. The gun has stopped tapping on his knee. It just sits there, the barrel pointed in my direction, but that doesn't seem to be from any active thought on Sean's end.

Finally he says, "Pretty soon, someone turned the music back up, and everybody started partying again. I could tell Aaron was pissed. Obviously he didn't know . . . you know, the truth about Wyn. I was pretty close with him, and I'd wanted to tell him before, but Taylor had sworn me to secrecy. I'd told Wyn that Taylor had made fun of her for being gay, but that wasn't true. Taylor . . . she cared so much for Wyn. In fact, Taylor had said she worried that by not coming out, Wyn might be . . . I don't know, causing herself too much stress or something. Taylor said she wanted to figure out a way to talk to Wyn about it, to try to help her out, though she said she knew it had to be Wyn's decision if and when she ever did want to come out. Taylor . . . Christ, she was just the best person in the world."

Once again we have gotten off topic. Only I guess we still are on topic, in a way. Sean is talking, being open and honest with me about the night Bronwyn disappeared, only we haven't gotten to the part yet about how she disappeared.

But it's coming, and the closer we get there, the more hesitant I am to hear the truth.

"Anyway, Aaron ended up heading outside to get a smoke. I decided to follow him. I knew he wanted to be alone, but I wanted to talk to him because I felt like I'd betrayed him in some way. But again, I was still pissed, and I wanted to hurt Wyn even more. Not like physically or anything, but just . . . I'd seen how much it hurt her, what I said to her about Taylor. And . . . I mean, I know this is going to sound awful, but I wanted to do it again. I wanted to keep hitting her right where it hurt."

"Why?"

Sean jerks his head up at the sudden anger in my voice. One simple word spoken with such intensity it almost makes the kid jump.

"I . . . I'm not sure. I think it was because Wyn was probably the only other person who knew about Taylor being pregnant. And, you know, that she happened to see me the night Taylor died. Like, she *knew* I was in town, even though I'd later told everyone I had been up in State College. She knew I had lied but couldn't prove it."

"So you wanted to hurt her."

Again, rising anger laces each word, enough so that Sean has started to look worried. Even in the dark I see a shadow of fear cross his face.

"I did, yeah. It's no excuse. I know that, but I just . . . I was pissed. And I had adrenaline pumping through my veins. I was *hyped.* And so I followed Aaron out to the porch, and he lit up a cigarette and started going off about Wyn. Like how he'd been in love with her, how she had even told him that she loved him, and that she'd been lying to him all that time. And I was just standing there, listening to him, wanting to make sure he didn't feel like a complete tool. And then . . . that's when I spotted Wyn."

"Where was she?"

"She was coming from around the back of the house. She was headed for her car. She looked even more upset than when I'd seen her inside."

"Sean, be honest with me."

A slight pause. "Okay."

"Did you kill my daughter?"

"No. God, absolutely not."

"You killed Taylor."

"I—" He pauses. "That was an accident."

This makes me rub my eyes with my fingers, start to laugh.

"You've got to be kidding me."

"Look, I'm trying to tell you what happened. I'm not . . . I'm not making excuses. I'm just laying everything out."

"Okay, fine. You're laying everything out. You're outside with Aaron, and you suddenly saw my daughter. Then what happened?"

45
Wyn
Day of the Pep Rally

She pushed out of the bathroom and then through the kitchen door, the brisk night air cooling the tears on her face, and then she was rounding the house and headed straight for her car, wanting to get away from this place more than she'd ever wanted to get away from anything in her entire life.

"Hey! Superstar, where do you think you're going?"

The voice made her stop at once, though she didn't look over. She'd thought her opportunity to confront Sean Heller had passed, but here the gods had granted her one last chance, and she knew she couldn't pass it up.

Drawing in a deep breath, she slowly turned to see him up on the porch. But he wasn't alone.

Aaron was standing up there, too, smoking a cigarette.

She said, "Aaron, I am so sorry. I—"

"Fuck you."

And he flicked his cigarette over the railing, right in her direction, though it fell several feet away and smoldered in the grass.

Sean Heller made a face and let loose a loud laugh. "Somebody sure is angry!"

Aaron turned away. It looked like he wanted to say something to Sean, something combative, but Aaron had never been the type of guy to stand up to those like Sean Heller. His shoulders dropped a bit, and he started toward the front door but then suddenly turned back around.

He lifted the Phillies cap off his head, shook it at her.

"You want to know why I've kept wearing this? Because of you, Wyn. Because you gave it to me. And, I don't know, I guess part of me thought that if I kept wearing it, you'd remember all the good times we had. But I guess even those good times were all a fucking lie."

He chucked the cap at her, and it sailed much farther than the cigarette butt but still landed a few feet shy of where she stood. Still, Wyn found herself stepping forward and crouching to pick up the hat.

"Aaron, please—"

But he turned away again, and this time went straight inside the house.

Leaving only Wyn and Sean.

Wyn said, "Does he know the truth?"

"What truth?"

"How you killed Taylor. You and Autumn."

That easy grin on Sean's face started to slide off, and his eyes went flat.

"You don't know what you're talking about."

"I told you—I saw you that night. You were in somebody else's car. You were coming from this place, if I had to guess. Taylor must have come here to tell Autumn the news, and Autumn had contacted you—I always suspected you were cheating with her behind Taylor's back—and somehow she managed to get her drunk. Then the two of you somehow managed to get her behind the wheel of her car down on Fox Lane and—"

"You. Don't. Know. What. You're. Talking. About."

"I might not know all the details, but I'm pretty close, aren't I? The thing is, Sean, that song I'd planned to perform today at the pep rally? It wasn't so much about Taylor, but you. About what kind of monster you are. About how you had something to do with Taylor's death."

"You're crazy."

"Maybe. But before I came here tonight, I recorded myself singing that song. Those videos right now of me face-planting all over social media? Those view counts will be nothing compared to when I upload the song."

She held up her phone then, having snaked it from her pocket with her free hand. She lifted the phone above her head, like it was some kind of talisman. Like she might upload the video right then and there.

Sean was off the porch a second later. He didn't bother going down the three steps but jumped straight over them—an error on his part, because he immediately slipped on the grass, lost his balance, and fell to the ground.

Granting Wyn a few precious seconds to make her escape.

Her iPhone in one hand, Aaron's Phillies cap in the other, she darted for her car.

Sean Heller may have been drinking tonight, but he was still fast. And he was livid. There was no telling what he might do to Wyn if he caught her.

So she ran as fast as she could. She worried that she might drop the phone and pushed it into her pocket, pried her car keys out of her other pocket.

When she finally reached the Escort, she dropped Aaron's hat so she could focus on unlocking the car, and against her better judgment she risked a glance over her shoulder.

Sean was back on his feet and heading toward her. He would reach her in a matter of seconds.

And it was that knowledge—that sudden awful knowledge—that caused her to fumble the keys. They dropped into the grass. She paused and looked down, but it was too dark to see them, at least where she was standing, and then she looked up again and saw that Sean was only a couple of yards away, and so Wyn did the only thing left for her to do.

She turned and ran.

Straight for the woods.

Where she would go once she reached the trees, she didn't know; all she knew was that she couldn't let Sean get within even inches of her.

And so she ran.

And ran.

And ran some more.

And when she reached the trees, she saw there was an opening, like the entrance to a trail, and she went straight for it.

It was dark in the woods, much too dark, and there was a chance that she might trip or fall at any moment. Twist her ankle, say, or tumble into a tree. But the same might happen to Sean, and Wyn thought that Sean wouldn't want to take the chance of hurting himself midway through his first college season.

She was banking on the idea he would give up.

But when she risked another glance over her shoulder, she saw that wasn't the case at all. He was still back there. A bit farther than before—he was taking his time, moving carefully—but he was still coming after her.

The trail was narrow and bumpy, with roots and rocks sticking up from the ground.

Wyn nearly tripped a dozen times but managed to keep herself upright, sometimes using a nearby tree to regain her balance, sometimes simply pinwheeling her arms until she recalibrated. She knew that this trail must lead somewhere, and that somewhere would most likely be Fox Lane, and she knew that at least the roadway would be more open, which might benefit her, but which would most likely benefit Sean even more.

A minute ticked by, and she knew she was almost to Fox Lane because she saw headlights coming down the road through the trees. This somehow gave her extra momentum, helped increase her speed, and she sprinted down the rugged incline, shouting for help at the oncoming car.

In an instant, Wyn was aware of two things.

First, Fox Lane was closed to traffic, so it made no sense why there was now a car speeding in her direction.

Second, the overworked, ticking engine sounded familiar. Way too familiar. It didn't make sense to Wyn, not at first, but then a moment later she understood the reason why.

It was *her* car.

And as that second realization dawned on her, she had just squeezed through the last couple of trees, and like déjà vu the top of her sneaker snagged something on the ground, only this time it wasn't a wire but another root, and before she knew it gravity sent her flying forward.

Straight into the oncoming headlights.

46

Jessica

Now

"No," I say softly, my voice having lost its intensity. Then: *"No! No! No! NO!"*

I smack the wheel once, twice, three times, and then I grab the wheel and start shaking it with so much force that it's a wonder I don't tear it off the steering column.

I'm an active volcano, and all my suppressed anger and rage over the past year—all that emotional hot magma and lava and whatever else I'd pushed down deep to the core—has finally erupted.

It feels like my soul has just been ripped out of my body, like every cell is screaming out in pain and frustration.

My daughter is dead—*has* been dead this entire time—and I'm once again that teenage girl who lost her mother and father in a matter of weeks: alone and hopeless in a world hell-bent on destroying me next.

But no. I won't let that happen. I *can't* let that happen.

Because Bronwyn didn't deserve what happened to her, and she definitely doesn't deserve her mother giving up on her.

Not now.

Not ever.

Sean says, "I . . . I'm so sorry."

I turn to him. He still has the gun on his knee, but I ignore it as I lean forward and slap him across the face.

"You knew. You knew, and you said *nothing*."

Sean stares back at me, stunned, his eyes wide with fear and regret.

"All this time, you could have said something. For the past year all I've done was search for my daughter—every single second of the day she was all I thought about—and you could have told me how she—"

I stop, realizing that I've gotten ahead of myself. Already filling in blanks that might not exist.

"Did the impact kill her?"

"No, not really."

"What the fuck does that mean?"

He squeezes his eyes shut, says, "I don't know."

"You don't *know*?"

"I was scared, okay? It wasn't like what we did to Taylor. I mean, in a way, it kinda was, but at least Autumn was there with me. I realized then it was Autumn who kept me going that night with Taylor. I couldn't have done anything like that on my own. It made me sick. Made me feel so guilty. But I had to keep acting like nothing happened."

"Sean?"

"Yeah."

"Do me a favor and stop with your fucking pity party."

He doesn't speak. Doesn't make a sound.

I lean back and stare out the window into the darkness.

"Who was driving?"

No answer.

I glance at him. "Well?"

Sean still doesn't speak, but I see the answer on his face, and the simple truth shakes me to my core.

"It was Aaron Colvin, wasn't it?"

He nods slowly, wipes at his face with the back of his hand.

"You should have seen how pissed he was at the party. It was like Wyn had literally stabbed him in the back."

"Did he get out of the car?"

"Not while I was there. I mean, I guess he started to—the door opened for like half a second and the dome light came on, and I saw that Phillies hat he always wore, the one Wyn had gotten him. But then he shut the door and just sat there in the car. In *Wyn's* car. Christ, he hit her with her own goddamned car. After that night, I never spoke to him again. And Aaron, he stayed far away from me."

I think about the day Aaron Colvin came to the house, the day Joe and I had gone to the school because of the note I'd found in Bronwyn's desk. Even then Aaron was wearing his Phillies cap. And he'd played it all innocent, as though he didn't know where my daughter had gone and was so worried, and then he'd brought up Sean Heller, because of course he wanted to point the finger at someone else.

"That's why he went into the army," I say quietly, more to myself than to Sean. "Rachel said he'd decided last year not to go to college after all, and so he signed up for the army. He wanted to disappear. Go to the other side of the world to get away."

The gun on Sean's knee has started tapping again.

"You remember that night at the Wonderwall last year, when you came at me right outside the restrooms? You'd asked me what happened that night, and I told you about how it was just a little disagreement, and I . . . I could tell by your face you didn't believe me. All that time I'd managed to BS people right to their faces and they always believed me, but you hadn't—you'd somehow seen right through me, even if you couldn't quite figure out the truth—and it . . . it really fucked me up, started messing with my head."

"Are you seriously trying to blame me for what happened to your leg?"

"What? No, not like that. But I just . . . it started eating away at me. It was all I thought about. Even during that game, my last game, I couldn't focus—I thought I'd be able to, but, I don't know, the lights in the stadium were extra bright and everything was so loud and I just . . . you're trained to protect yourself when you get hit. It's drilled into your head. But for whatever reason, I didn't that night. All that time I spent in the hospital, I thought about calling you and telling you the truth. Even about what happened to Taylor. What Summer had told me, about how she was sorry, too, made me think it might be a good idea. But then I'd remember what Autumn texted me, how I needed to stay quiet, and I just . . ."

"Sean?"

"Yeah."

"I don't give a shit about Autumn Porter or anybody else right now. How much longer did you stay and not help my daughter?"

Sean flinches at the question, as if worried I'll slap him again.

"I don't know," he says quietly. "I just stayed where I was, and I could hear the car's engine still on—I knew it was Wyn's car because it was making that ticking noise—and I . . . I could hear her breathing. It was sorta shallow, you know? Like she'd busted her lungs or something. Maybe five minutes passed. Maybe ten. I only left when I saw another car coming down the road."

"What other car?"

Sean stares out the windshield again, seeing something beyond the darkness.

"He's always been cool to me, you know? One time he pulled me over for speeding and let me go with a warning, even though I'd been doing like twenty over the limit. He said that he'd played football in high school and knew what it was like to have such a promising future, only he had screwed his up, and he made me promise not to screw up mine too. And . . . and I broke that promise. I screwed up everything."

I think I know who he's talking about, but I need to hear him say the name out loud. To place one of the last puzzle pieces on the board that will finally permit me to accept the truth I've wanted to reject for the past half hour.

"Sean"—my voice calm now, quiet and measured—"was the other car you saw that night a police cruiser?"

He nods slowly, still not looking at me.

"Who was driving, Sean?"

And his face shifts in my direction, only a little, so that I can see the stark emptiness in his eyes.

"Officer Gorman."

47

Kenny

Almost One Year after the Pep Rally

James made him sit in the back, like he was a common thug, and when Kenny tried to protest James told him it was because he didn't want him throwing up in the front seat.

"I ain't gonna throw up," Kenny said, slumped in the back, staring out the window as James pulled out of the Wonderwall's parking lot.

"Yeah, sure, tell that to the bar floor back there," James mumbled, then eyed him in the rearview mirror. "Seriously, Kenny, what the hell were you thinking? The Wonderwall of all places?"

"That's where she told me to meet her."

"Who?"

"Dunno," Kenny said, his words still slurring. "Some bitch I met on the dating app."

"Christ on a cracker, Kenny. The Wonderwall's the last place you should be in your condition."

"My *condition*?" He snorted a laugh. "I had a couple beers, that's all."

Again James eyed him in the rearview mirror as he made a turn through an intersection.

"I've known you a long time, Kenny, and I've seen you drunk before. This right here? You're shit-faced."

James waited for Kenny to say something, to maybe apologize, and when Kenny just glowered out the window at the passing town, he sighed.

"You remember the rules, don't you? Rule number one: stay far away from Jessica Moore."

Kenny rolled his eyes and then pressed his hand to his mouth, afraid he might throw up again.

James noticed and said, "Want me to pull over?"

"No, keep driving. I'm fine. And I don't give a shit about Jessica Moore. She don't scare me."

"That's not the point, and you know it."

They drove for the next minute or two in silence.

Kenny said, "You ever think about that night?"

James didn't answer him at first, just kept driving across town to Little Texas, where Kenny lived with his mom. Double-wide trailer, which was actually kinda nice and gave them both their own space. And it also allowed Kenny to save money, because he knew one of these days he wouldn't be able to take care of his mom anymore and so he'd have to set her up someplace, a home that didn't treat its old folks like shit.

Kenny rolled his head on the seat, tearing his gaze away from the rolling scenery to focus on the back of James's head.

"Well?"

James said, "Sometimes, yeah."

"You ever feel guilty?"

A beat of silence. "Sometimes."

"Interesting," Kenny said. "Me, I haven't felt one bit of guilt since it happened. You think . . . you think that means something's broken in me?"

He was thinking about his old man, how his old man had had something wrong with his head near the end of his life, and when

Kenny, just a teenager at the time, had asked his mom about it, she'd stubbed out one of her pack-a-day cigarettes as she shook her head and murmured, *I can't tell what's wrong with the man, only that there's somethin' broken in him.*

James regarded him again in the rearview mirror, and now all that Kenny saw in his eyes was pity.

"Hard to say, Kenny. I suppose all of us are broken in our own way. Some of us are just more broken than others."

Ten minutes later James had dropped off Kenny at home, telling him that someone would pick him up tomorrow to take him to get his truck. James looked like he wanted to say something else but then just nodded at him and drove off, the cruiser rolling slowly down Austin Drive, James no doubt keeping an eye out for trouble on his way out of the trailer park, because trouble often hid in the shadows of Little Texas.

By then it was past midnight and Kenny knew his mom was already in bed, that she'd been in bed for probably two or three hours, and he tried to be as quiet as he could as he opened the door.

Stupid bitches, he thought. Not just the one that had been talking to him all this time on the dating app—Ashley something—but those college girls at the bar who kept trying to avoid him and the other women around town who gave him the time of day only because he wore a badge and so they felt they needed to show him some respect.

And then there was Jessica Moore.

Kenny had never had any issues with the woman—and truth be told he almost felt sorry for her after what happened last year—but after what she'd said to him as James was leading him out of the bar?

Gee, Kenny, I can't imagine why anyone would stand you up.

Fuck. That. Bitch.

He detoured at the last second, swinging by the kitchen and grabbing a can of Coors from the fridge. Popping the top, chugging half the can, he stumbled down the short hallway to his bedroom, trying to be quiet so as not to wake his mom but knowing that she was a heavy sleeper anyway so it didn't matter how much noise he made.

In his room, he set the beer aside and got down on his hands and knees and crawled into his tiny closet and reached back in the far corner for the hole he'd chiseled out last year, fingers groping the darkness until his fingertips brushed the iPhone.

Soon he had it out, cracked screen and all, and he powered it up, watching the Apple logo as he took another long pull of the beer, and once the main screen came up he had no problem getting into the phone, what with the fact the passcode lock had been disabled. The phone wasn't connected to the network, either, so there was no way it could be traced.

He'd been entrusted with the phone because he'd been tasked to retrieve the girl's things from her house. The idea was to make it look like she'd decided to up and run away. Made sense, especially after what happened at the pep rally, and it turned out she may have already had it in mind, as most of her things were already packed in two large garbage bags waiting in her closet. There was even cash in an envelope stashed under her mattress that Kenny had coolly slid into his pocket and never told anyone about.

Kenny had needed to take the girl's phone along because the house had cameras, though he was told the cameras would turn off once Wyn Hayden or her mother came home. So that's why he'd been given the phone, though of course he'd been ordered to bring the phone back once he was done. And Kenny had planned to do just that, but then not long after he'd left the house—carefully driving the back roads to ensure nobody saw him—a bright idea had gone off in his head like a miniature atom bomb explosion.

It turned out the girl had the same kind of iPhone he did. All he needed to do was smash the screen, so it looked like hers, and then replace the cases, and so what was ultimately disposed of along with the girl and the car was really his phone (which was no big deal, because he ordered a replacement the next day), and so he'd kept her phone all this time.

Why?

Well, it was difficult to say. On the one hand, he liked the idea of having the phone. He'd already scrolled through all the pictures, and many of them were of Taylor Mitchell, who was one hot piece of ass. She'd been seventeen when she died, sure, but so what? It didn't make Kenny a pervert just to look at some pictures of a pretty girl, did it?

Of course, the other reason—the main reason—he'd kept the phone was to cover his ass. In case anything ever came back to try to bite him. That was what had occurred to him that night after leaving the girl's house, how if the poor girl's death was being covered up like this, what would happen if he were one day determined to be a loose end? This way he'd have something to use as leverage. Who the hell knew if he'd manage to stay out of prison if the shit ever hit the fan, but still it was something.

And now . . . well, now Kenny had an idea. A crazy, off-the-wall, batshit idea, but an idea nonetheless. An idea that he knew was so awful and stupid he would never actually do it, but still it made him chuckle all the same.

Some nights he'd get out the phone and scroll through all of Wyn's text messages to her friends, plus through what he'd come to think of as her diary. It seemed she'd been using the Notes app on her phone to write down her random thoughts, like the times she'd worried she was too fat or the times she'd masturbated thinking about Taylor Mitchell (hot!) or how she'd even told her mom the night before the accident how much she hated living with her.

He'd also become accustomed to the way she'd texted and typed out her notes. All lowercase. No commas or periods or question marks or apostrophes. She'd even disabled the autocorrect.

Wouldn't it be funny—wouldn't it be a fucking riot?—if tonight Jessica Moore received a text message from her missing daughter?

Kenny could just imagine the woman's expression. It made him giggle like a kid, and the more he giggled, the more he had to suppress a full-fledged laugh, and the more he had to suppress that, the more he needed to drink.

Three hours later, after several more beers, Kenny still hadn't put the phone away even though he kept telling himself he should. And the more he thought about Jessica Moore and what she'd said to him—*Gee, Kenny, I can't imagine why anyone would stand you up*—the more he remembered how those fucking people in that fucking bar had laughed at him . . . but no, he knew he couldn't do anything about it.

James was right: the first rule—the only rule, really—was to stay far away from Jessica Moore.

Then again . . . just who the fuck did she think she was? Honestly. Kenny might not be able to teach Ashley a lesson—he'd already sent her several angry messages through the app, for all the good it would do—but he could teach Jessica a lesson, and in doing so, he'd be teaching all those bitches a lesson.

And so it was at nearly four o'clock in the morning, Kenny drunk but still very well aware of his actions, that he connected the phone to the Wi-Fi and then sent a simple text.

mom

As soon as it went through, Kenny started laughing—but then stopped himself when he remembered this wasn't supposed to be fun and instead was meant to teach the bitch a lesson.

An idea had come to him—an excellent idea, an *amazing* idea—and so he texted:

please help

It was that expression on Jessica Moore's stupid face that kept him going. That look first of surprise and hope and then utter terror at what would come next.

i think he's going to kill me

Later, once he sobered up and reviewed the messages, he'd realize that the use of the apostrophe wasn't just his first mistake—the whole fucking thing was. He knew he'd get his ass chewed out big-time, and he would deserve it, but he also knew he was protected in a way, because he knew a secret hardly anybody else did, a secret that ensured he could essentially do whatever he wanted and get away with it.

"Stand this up, you cunt," he murmured, and pressed SEND.

48

Jessica

Now

At just after eleven o'clock that Thursday morning, I park in the back of the municipal building to avoid the handful of reporters camped out front and wait another ten or fifteen minutes until somebody comes out for a smoke break, and that's when I make my move.

The two women smoking recognize me, and at once their faces fill with emotion. They tell me that they've seen my video about Bronwyn and how shocked and sorry they are. I thank them and ask if I can sneak in the back to see Joe, and knowing the reporters are stationed out front, the women of course agree and soon I'm headed up to Joe's office.

The only person who tries to stop me on the way in is Joe's secretary. She's an older woman in her fifties. After replacing Emma, it makes sense Joe wouldn't want another attractive young secretary. Or maybe it was Emma who pushed for that.

"Jessica? Jessica, please, he's on the phone. Don't—"

I push open his office door and step inside, and as promised, Joe is on the phone. He's sitting behind his large oak desk, and he looks up at me in surprise, the phone to his ear, his electronic cigarette pinched between two fingers, and he says, "Ron, let me call you right back," and cradles the phone and then waves his secretary away when she starts to apologize.

He gestures at me to sit in one of the chairs in front of his desk. They're grander than the ones in his home office, look to be genuine leather, and even though I want to stay standing I find myself taking a seat.

"Thank you, Maureen," Joe says, smiling at his secretary until she finally closes his office door, and then the smile fades.

"What are you doing, Jess? Are you here to apologize? Good. The first thing you can do then is go outside and tell those reporters you made a mistake by posting that video. Maybe say the stress has become too much for you. That, I don't know, you've started drinking again, and maybe you've been staying up late watching movies, maybe something scary that put it in your head our daughter was abducted, and that—"

I cut him off.

"Where is she?"

He frowns. "Who? *Wyn?* I don't know. She could be anywhere by now."

"No more games, Joe. Tell me where she is, and I'll forget about everything else."

He stares at me, his mouth slightly agape. He's putting on a good show; I'll give him that. He's put on a good show these past two weeks. This past year. From the very moment he came to the house after I called, telling him our daughter was gone.

"Jess, I don't know what you're talking about."

"I'm serious, Joe. Cut the bullshit. Just tell me where she is."

"I don't *know* where she is! None of us do. The asshole who took her, he—"

"Enough!" I shout. "I said cut the bullshit, and I fucking mean it."

Joe stares at me again. Some understanding has entered his eyes. It's slight, but enough for me to confirm he realizes that I know more than I did yesterday.

Before he can say anything, though, the door opens and Stuart Colvin breezes into the room. He's paging through some papers, his focus on the text, and he doesn't realize I'm here until he looks up.

"Jess! Oh my God, how are you? I saw the video you posted. Joe told me that it's some kind of misunderst—"

"Does he know?"

I direct the question at Joe, not Stuart, and so Stuart stands there silent for a beat, looking confused.

Stuart says, "Do I know what?"

"The truth," I say.

Stuart's brow furrows at that. He looks to Joe for help, and Joe simply says, "Give us a couple of minutes, okay?"

The mayor of Bowden doesn't move at first. Just keeps standing there, those papers in his hands, looking lost.

Joe says, "Stuart, let me take care of this," and there's something in his voice, a commanding tone I've never heard him use before. It's enough to get Stuart moving, turning at once and hurrying out through the door. As soon as we're alone again, I almost laugh.

"I can't believe I never saw it."

"Saw what?"

"How Stuart is just a figurehead. The guy who has the right face for the campaign posters and who everybody likes. You're the real politician. The one in charge. Does he even know what you've done?"

Joe takes a pull on his electronic cigarette, that LED tip lighting briefly.

"I'm losing patience, Jessica. Tell me what you want, or else I'll call security."

"I told you what I want."

"And what is that?"

"For you to tell me where she is."

"Yes, and as I told you, I don't know. Our daughter was abducted. Her abductor works for law enforcement. Christ, Jess, you said as much on your insane video."

"It was Kenny who texted me that first time, wasn't it?"

Joe takes another pull on the electronic cigarette but says nothing.

"He was the first officer who arrived that night. My guess is James Healy and Carter Redcross arrived not too long after him. And Tony, of course. Maybe not all of them were there that night, but they were involved somehow. Just like you. Because nothing in this town happens without you knowing it, especially when it has anything to do with Stuart."

Still Joe says nothing.

"You were the only one who knew about the cameras at the house. How my phone or Bronwyn's phone turned them off. And so my guess is you sent Kenny to the house with her phone to gather her stuff. Maybe somebody else went with him, but he somehow managed to keep the phone. And he must have gotten pissed at me that night after I'd kicked him out of the Wonderwall. That's why he sent me those text messages. But who was I texting with the two other times? My guess . . . is you."

We stare at each other for a long moment, and then Joe's eyes shift down to the phone in my hand.

"Are you recording this?" he says, his voice quiet.

"No."

"Let me see the phone."

I place the iPhone on his desk. He picks it up and sees that the screen is locked but that there are countless notifications.

"Christ," he murmurs. "It looks like the whole world has been calling and texting you."

He sets the phone back down on his desk, stares at nothing for a beat, and then sighs.

"What's the point of all of this, Jess? What do you want?"

"The truth."

"The truth doesn't exist anymore. Everyone lives in their own realities. The trick is simply finding a reality that best suits you."

"You've lost your mind, haven't you?" When Joe doesn't answer, I say, "I want to know where my daughter is."

"I can't tell you that."

"You can't, or you won't?"

He doesn't answer. Just keeps staring back at me.

"Whose idea was it? Black Creek State Park. The cabin. The root cellar, the mattress, her backpack. The idea that we had *just* missed her by a few hours. Tony was already there by the time we arrived, and I hadn't thought about it much at the time, what with the fact, you know, I was terrified for our daughter, but there's no way he could have made it there that fast."

Silence.

"You destroyed her phone so now I'd have no more contact, and then . . . what, after a few months—after a few years—of silence, I would just forget the whole thing and move on with my life? Do you honestly think that would have solved everything?"

His expression has changed in the past minute or so, and when he speaks next, his voice is quiet.

"We needed to put an end to it. We couldn't keep the whole thing going forever. Or just never have her contact you again. You . . . you never would've let it go."

"You're damned right I wouldn't. So tell me, Joe: Where is she?"

"Just let this go, Jess. Please. I'm begging you."

"You make me sick."

His eyes have started to water.

"Don't you think I miss her every day? Don't you think I wish none of it ever would have happened? It was an accident, Jess, plain and simple. There was nothing that could have been done to save her. By the time I got there . . . she was already gone."

"So you decided to protect Aaron Colvin, whose father just happens to be your best friend and boss."

"Jess, you're not listening. She was dead. There was no changing that. So why . . . why destroy another young life—destroy the lives of an entire family—just to . . . what? Have some kind of justice? That wouldn't have been justice."

"Since when did you become judge and jury?"

"I'm sorry you've been kept in the dark this entire time. I truly am. But I did it for your own good, Jess. You have to believe that."

"You're a monster, Joe. What kind of father are you?"

Now tears roll down his cheeks. He wipes them away and takes a breath.

"A father who lost a child, and who never wanted anyone he knew to ever experience that pain. And now . . . now I'm a father who doesn't want to lose any more of his children. Which means I'll do whatever it takes to protect them."

"Gee, if only you'd felt the same way about our daughter."

"That's not fair, Jess, and you know it."

"No, Joe, what I know is that you covered up our daughter's death to protect yourself and your buddy and your delusional fantasy that Stuart is going to one day become president. Don't sit there and act otherwise."

Little by little, Joe's eyes have started to harden.

"How did you find all of this out, anyway?"

"What does it matter?"

"If I had to guess? I'd say Sean Heller told you. He would have been the only one who could have possibly known what happened."

This entire time my phone has been buzzing with incoming calls and text messages. I've been glancing at the screen every couple of seconds, waiting for one message in particular.

And now it comes in, one simple word from a phone number I saved in my phone just this morning. An answer to a question I'd tasked my new friend to find once other pieces of the puzzle had started clicking into place.

Yes.

I say, "One last chance, Joe. Tell me where she is."

"Let it go, Jess. I mean it. This time I'm not asking."

I stand up from the chair, grab the phone off his desk.

"Are you threatening me?"

"I'm just telling you to steer clear. To drop it. Otherwise you'll force my hand."

"Goodbye, Joe."

"You have no proof of anything. You realize that, don't you? So what if Sean Heller told you some crazy story? He's a pathetic has-been. Nobody in their right mind will believe him."

"Him, probably not. But I'm the missing girl's mother. People will believe me."

I start to turn away and head for the door and only pause when Joe speaks again.

"Are you sure about that?"

I turn back around.

He doesn't smile. Doesn't frown. Just stares back at me with no expression. His eyes are still red, but there are no more tears.

"The past year has been challenging for you. You've started drinking more than usual, and your *usual* was a lot. Let's face it, Jess—you're a drunk, just like your old man. Speaking of which, I can't believe you never told me you tracked him down."

"How—" I start to say, but then I see it and whisper, "Suzanne Walker."

Joe says nothing.

"You introduced us. So that . . . that you could spy on me?"

"I needed to keep an eye on you. To make sure you weren't spiraling out of control, but also to keep you in line."

"Does she even have a daughter?"

"I honestly have no idea. Suzanne Walker isn't even her real name. She was just a PI I hired."

I'm quiet for a moment, taking all this in, and then something else occurs to me.

"What about Steven Clark?"

"What about him?"

"Did you . . ."

But I can't say the rest. Not as images of that night from a year ago flash through my mind. Steven coming into the bar, asking me how I was doing. Sharing drinks with him as we talked and laughed. Then agreeing to go back to his place for a nightcap.

"I have no idea what Steven Clark has to do with any of this," Joe says.

So it had just been a cruel act of fate. Steven really had been looking for one last fuck before he got back together with his ex-wife.

I force a smile, because if I don't I might scream.

"Do you want to know how I spent my morning, Joe? I called the main office of Clegg & Hawthorne. I introduced myself and told them I owned and operated a bar and wanted to make a TV commercial and asked for the contact info for the ad agency they used. When I called the agency, I asked to be put in touch with the actor from the commercial, and then when I finally got him on the phone, he was excited at first with the idea of starring in a new commercial until he realized who he was speaking to."

Still smiling, I shrug.

"Apparently my name rang a bell. Especially after he saw the video I'd posted yesterday. But he said he couldn't tell me anything because he'd signed an NDA. The first time he'd ever needed to sign an NDA for any work, he told me. All he could say was that it was good money and that it helped the gig was at night, because otherwise he'd need to miss a day of teaching. You see, Joe, the FBI agent outside that cabin where our daughter had supposedly been kept? He's really a substitute teacher."

Still no expression on his face. His eyes flat.

Joe says, "Fake news. That's all we would need to say on our end. People don't believe what they're told anymore, Jess. They believe what they want to hear. Even when the truth is right in front of their faces. You could dig her up tomorrow and put her body on TV, and half the world still wouldn't believe it was true."

The smile on my lips is no longer forced. Now it's genuine. Enough so that Joe's eyes harden again.

"What?" he says.

"You just confirmed that she's buried somewhere. To be honest with you, Joe, that's more than I expected I'd get out of this whole visit."

And without another word I turn and leave his office, the phone in my hand buzzing with even more calls and text messages from a world interested in nothing more than being cruel.

I drive north through town, past Shepherd's Market and the post office, where the countryside opens up and homes dot either side of the highway.

Eventually I pull in to a turnaround and park behind Sean Heller's car. He gets out and limps over and climbs into the passenger seat.

"So he confirmed it?" I say.

Sean looks rougher than he did last night. He doesn't even look like he's taken a shower, and he still smells like beer.

Staring out his window as I pull back out onto the highway, he says, "Yeah, he confirmed it. Didn't want to at first. Kept trying to dodge my questions. But, you know, my dad's known Martin Jarrett forever, and Martin has even done work for him a bunch of times, and finally he did admit it."

"Thank you, Sean."

He's quiet for a moment, and then glances over at me.

"So we're headed there now?"

"Yes."

"I still . . . I'm not sure I want to do this anymore."

"You mean turn yourself in?"

"Yeah."

"That's up to you. But you said it yourself: the guilt's been eating away at you."

"Yeah, it has been eating away at me. But I'm not so sure prison is going to help."

"Look at it this way, Sean. If you come forward first, they might go easy on you."

He thinks about this, and then says, "But there isn't any guarantee."

I glance over at him, at the young man who in many ways is responsible for my daughter's death, and I say, "That's the thing about life, Sean. There are never any guarantees."

Then I flick on the turn signal as we slow to make the turn into Tony Parsons's driveway.

I park in front of Tony's barn and shut off the car, and we step out and look around the property. The sky is a clear pale blue, and the air is cold and crisp. Tony doesn't appear to be home, but a car is parked near the house that probably belongs to Carol's personal care aide. If the aide sees us, she might call Tony, but that's okay—I'm expecting the whole crew to get here eventually.

There's a lock on the barn door. But the door is old and flimsy, and Sean crouches down and peeks through the barest sliver of an opening. He issues a sigh as he nods.

"The backhoe's still in there. Just like Martin said."

"So Tony only borrowed it twice?"

Sean nods again. "Martin said last year Chief Parsons asked for it that homecoming weekend, but then he kept it a few weeks so he could dig out the pool. Then Martin said he asked for it again this past weekend."

"To get her backpack," I say quietly.

"What's that?"

"Nothing. Come on. Let's get this over with."

We start around to the back of the barn, and when we turn the corner, I gasp.

I remember the day my mother was buried. I'd gone back later that night just to cry alone, and the hole she'd been placed into had been filled in. All that was there was fresh dirt.

That's what the ground here looks like. A good square thirty feet or so of dirt that's been recently dug up and refilled. No way my daughter's car would take up all that space beneath the ground, but clearly the people who'd operated the backhoe didn't quite know what they were doing.

For the past half hour my phone has continued to buzz with notifications. I've ignored them all. Now I take out the phone and step back so I'll have enough room, and I snap a single photo, which shows the disturbed earth and rear of the barn and Tony's house on the hill.

I text the photo to Joe with the caption: How's this for fake news?

Carter Redcross is the first one to arrive.

He screeches up in his police cruiser but doesn't get out, just sits there waiting with the engine idling. It's unclear what he's waiting for until a minute later when James Healy and Kenny Gorman arrive.

Now that Carter has backup, he gets out of his car, just as James and Kenny get out of their cars. They slowly approach Sean Heller and me.

"Ms. Moore," Carter says, his low voice full of authority, "I'm going to need you to vacate the premises. This is private property."

"Really?" I say, my arms crossed as we lean against my car. "Is that the line you want to go with?"

"Don't make this harder than it has to be," Kenny says. "It'd be best for you and Sean to leave ASAP and act like this whole thing never happened."

"I didn't really think about it at the time, Kenny, but how did you know my daughter had butterflies painted on her bedroom walls? I suppose maybe one of these fine officers might have mentioned it—they'd seen her room during their quote, unquote, 'investigation'—but I don't see any reason why they would have. Which means the only way you would have known about them was because you'd seen them for yourself when you broke into my house the night my daughter died."

Kenny says nothing. Neither do the other two men.

"Honestly, Kenny, I'm surprised you're still breathing after what you pulled. Talk about a major screwup. You must have some good blackmail hidden somewhere that's kept you alive this past week."

Up at the house, the front door opens, and a woman calls out: "Is everything all right down there?"

That's when Tony arrives, followed by Joe. Tony climbs out of his pickup truck and waves up at the woman.

"Head back inside, Nancy! Everything is fine!"

"Did your grandson really slip and split his head open on the pool deck?" I say to Tony. "Or was that some bullshit story too? If it is true, you must feel *really* guilty. After all, you never intended to put in a pool, did you? You panicked when I saw the backhoe and so you came up with the pool as a cover story and then had to follow through."

Joe steps past the three police officers, who are standing yards away, and his face is pinched with anger.

"You don't know what you're doing, Jess."

"Oh, I know exactly what I'm doing."

"What do you think's going to happen here? You're making this worse than it has to be."

"How's that?" I say. "Are you going to kill Sean and me and bury us behind the barn with Bronwyn?"

Beside me, Sean stiffens, but he doesn't say anything.

"Sean won't say anything," Joe says. "Not if he doesn't want to go to prison for what he did to Taylor Mitchell."

Now Sean does make a noise, a soft inhale of breath.

Joe says, "That's right, Sean. We always suspected what happened to Taylor was a bit fishy. Especially when the autopsy came back that she was pregnant. Why else do you think we purposely suppressed that information? You were Bowden's golden boy. We needed to keep you out of trouble, just like it's been my job all these years to keep Stuart's kids out of trouble. So why do you want to get yourself in trouble now? You could still walk away from this scot-free."

Joe pauses, and then looks at me.

"As for you, Jess, I asked you not to force my hand. I *begged* you. But you . . . you just had to keep pushing, didn't you? Well, fine, we'll do it your way."

"What are you talking about?"

"Like I told you before: you're a drunk and everyone knows it. What they might not know is how you spent some time in a psychiatric facility when you were a teenager, right after your mom died. Had yourself a nervous breakdown. So it'd make sense that over the past year the stress has gotten too much for you. That and all the wine you drink, it's no wonder that suddenly you imagined getting text messages from your missing daughter. Let's face it, Jess: you're unstable, and Tony and I agree that it's in the community's best interest for you to be committed to another psychiatric facility until you eventually get your mind right."

I have to admit, I hadn't seen him playing the mentally unstable card. It was something I'd told him early in our relationship, something I'd confided in him because I knew I loved him and could trust him with all my secrets, and he'd held on to that secret all these years only to bring it back out now.

"So you knew," I say quietly. "The entire time you knew our daughter wasn't the one who was pregnant."

His eyes soften, just a bit.

"I didn't know for sure," he says. "Not at first."

"Well," I say, forcing a smile, "I forgot to tell you what else I did this morning. After I spoke to that nice young actor you hired to play an FBI agent."

"What's that?"

"Made a call to the state police. Told them that I would require their assistance later in the day. And right before you all showed up? I told them where to come. I even sent them that photo."

And right on cue, the first state police cruiser speeds up the long drive, followed by a second cruiser, their roof lights strobing red and blue like tiny fireworks.

49

Wyn

Day of the Pep Rally

Voices. Faint, indistinct voices. She could hear them, somewhere around her, but they were mostly background noise to all the pain. It was immense. Pulsing. She'd never even imagined pain like this could exist. She couldn't move her body. Could only lie there on the cold ground and stare up at the sky. The leafless branches towered over her, obstructing the view. Which was a shame, because all she wanted was to see the stars. Just one last time. A clear night sky in fall. What more could you ask for? Only . . . the pain kept getting worse. And it was hard to breathe. So very hard. Like she was underwater. Only she wasn't underwater; she was right here on the edge of Fox Lane, against the tree that she'd been flung into. Her entire body broken. Shattered. And then . . . who was coming toward her? Was that . . . was that her father? Already her vision was darkening but she could tell he looked sad. His face all bunched up. She wanted to say something to him. Ask him, Dad, why are you here? Say, Dad, help me. But she couldn't say anything and watched as he hurried toward her . . . only her vision was getting darker and darker by the second . . . and it was now almost impossible to breathe . . . and as her father crouched down next to her she started thinking, Dad, please . . . I don't want to die. I don't want . . . to die. I don't . . . want to—

50

Jessica

Now

It's just past nine o'clock in the evening when the state police detective drops me off at home.

He pulls into the driveway and parks the sedan and glances around. "Surprised reporters aren't camped out on your lawn. Though I suppose right now they've got bigger fish to fry."

When you have the mayor of a town—a man who's running for US Congress—embroiled in a scandal that includes conspiracy and manslaughter, that trumps the woman who posted a video that didn't go nearly as viral as she'd hoped it would. Several thousand views, yes, but somehow not nearly as many as the videos showing my daughter falling off the stage during the pep rally last year.

"Thank you for the ride," I say quietly. My eyelids are heavy, and I worry I might fall asleep right here in the car despite all the cups of coffee I've had over the course of the day, answering question after question after question.

"Of course. Someone will drop off your car tomorrow."

I gather my things—my keys and my iPhone, which has since lost power—and reach for the door handle but pause.

"Can I ask you something?"

"Certainly."

"Did any of them confess yet?"

He hesitates, then says, "Besides Sean Heller, no."

"But you need more than just Sean Heller's word to make a case."

"Well, it's complicated. The fact is one of them will most likely confess at some point. Hopefully sooner than later. We have your daughter's body. We have her car. Both were buried in Police Chief Parsons's backyard. There's no escaping the evidence."

"What about Edward Donovan? Is he really an FBI agent?"

"He works as a field agent for the FBI, yes."

"What's his connection to all of this?"

"From what we can tell, Chief Parsons has known him for quite some time. Our current theory is that he was offered something substantial for his cooperation in the hoax."

"Such as?"

"Well, it's still only a theory, but my guess is with Stuart Colvin's political aspirations, Agent Donovan was probably promised a plush assignment at some point in the future. Maybe even nominated to be the director of the FBI."

"For what it's worth, I never would have found my daughter without Sean Heller's help. Had he not forced me to go to Fox Lane last night and told me everything . . ."

"I understand that, and it's something that will certainly be taken into consideration."

I start to reach for the door but pause again.

"What about Aaron?"

"It's my understanding he'll be returning to the States shortly. He's currently stationed overseas."

"Thank you again, Detective."

"Anytime. You have my card, so if anything comes up, please don't hesitate to reach out. Otherwise, like I said, somebody will drop off your car tomorrow."

He waits for me to reach the front porch before he starts to back out. I wave to him and then let myself into the house and close the door and lock it. Press my forehead against the door, my eyes closed. I could very well fall asleep standing up.

But then I kick off my shoes and start toward the kitchen, my body moving as if on its own, fed up with all the coffee I've had today and wanting a few glasses of wine.

But no—not now. Maybe later. Or maybe never.

I head toward my bedroom. I get only a few paces when I hear the patio door open and quickly turn around.

Catherine Colvin steps into the kitchen, holding a key in her hand.

"Catherine?"

"Ms. Moore, I . . . I've been waiting for you to get home. I . . . I need to talk to you."

"What are you doing here? How—where did you get that key?"

She glances down at the key in her hand, as though she's never seen it before, and then she gives me a sorrowful look.

"I kept it after that night. The night . . . the night I hit Wyn with her car."

51

CATHERINE

Day of the Pep Rally

She watched Wyn push through the crowd, not sure where she was going, just that she needed to get out of there, and after a minute or so, when Catherine was sure everybody's attention had gone back to the party, she slipped down the same hallway Wyn had disappeared down moments earlier.

Wyn had gone into a bathroom, and Catherine glanced over her shoulder to make sure nobody was watching as she placed her ear close to the door. Somebody had increased the volume so the music was pumping again, making it almost impossible to hear what sounded like Wyn either retching or crying.

When Catherine stepped into the bathroom, Wyn spun around, her eyes wide, her hands up in front of her as if expecting to fend off an attack. Then, once she realized who it was, she lowered her hands.

"Cat, what are you doing?"

Despite the cramped bathroom—only the toilet and sink and some decorative towels hanging on a wall-mounted bar, the tight space smelling heavily of sandalwood—Catherine took a step toward her.

"I can't believe I used to think you were cool. I even liked your music. But you . . . you're a lying bitch."

Wyn didn't say anything. She simply tried to step past Catherine, but Catherine moved to block her path.

"You were gay this entire time, and you just, what, strung my brother along for no reason at all?"

"I'm sorry," Wyn said quietly.

Catherine's hands squeezed into fists as she took another step closer to Wyn.

"Don't say sorry to me. Say sorry to Aaron."

Wyn lowered her eyes, spoke quietly again.

"Please move out of my way."

"He's still in love with you, you know. You were his first serious girlfriend. You broke his heart and didn't even have the decency to give him a reason why."

Something flickered across Wyn's face, a note of understanding, and her gaze shifted up to meet Catherine's.

"You're Onyx Butterfly?"

Catherine nodded, feeling adrenaline surging through her now.

"That's right, you stupid bitch. Are you surprised?"

Wyn just stared back at her, silent, so Catherine pushed on.

"Aaron never had it easy, you know? He probably never told you how he struggled in math and science. He'd study nonstop, but he just couldn't get it. I had to tutor him, and even then it wasn't easy for him, but . . . well, he used to talk about you all the time when I was trying to help him with his work. He'd always had a crush on you. Then once you two started going out, he was the happiest I'd ever seen him. And when you broke up with him, I'd never seen him so depressed. And I . . . I told myself maybe if I learned what happened, why you had broken up with him, that would give him some kind of closure, and maybe he wouldn't be so depressed anymore. But I couldn't just walk up to you and ask you for a reason. So I created that Twitter account, the one named after your song, and . . . well, here we are."

Grinning, she spread her arms out wide, and that was when Wyn decided to step past her again.

"No," Catherine said, and pushed her back, hard, against the wall.

Wyn's eyes went wide, the first sign of fear Catherine had ever elicited from anyone, and here now—at this party where she'd admittedly had too much to drink, her pulse thudding in lockstep with the music—she felt a certain level of power as she glared hard at her brother's ex-girlfriend.

"What kind of person plays with people's emotions like that, huh? You . . . you're selfish. You don't care about anybody's feelings but your own."

Tears had started to well up in Wyn's eyes.

"That's not true," she whispered.

"The hell it's not. After what happened today, when you asked to meet, I thought maybe it was a chance for Aaron to show you just how much he cares for you. How he'd be there when you needed somebody. That you might, I don't know, actually give him a second chance. But he told me you were so cold to him. And you know what? Now it all makes sense, because you're a lying *bitch*."

Wyn shoved her away suddenly, even more tears in her eyes, and she pushed through the door into the hallway. If Catherine hadn't lost her balance and started to fall back into the sink, she might have taken a swing at Wyn, what with every muscle in her body tense and ready for a fight. But as it was, she grabbed on to the wall to keep steady, and then just stood there, catching her breath, staring back at herself in the mirror.

What more was she looking to get out of this? The truth was out now—Wyn was gay, which was obviously the reason she'd broken up with Aaron. But that knowledge wouldn't fix her brother's heartache, at least not right away; his depression had already started causing her parents to fight, and the more they fought, the more Catherine's perfect life felt like it had begun to unravel.

Still staring at herself in the mirror, feeling unsteady on her feet, she thought, *The bitch isn't getting off that easy.*

What Catherine intended to do next, she wasn't quite sure, just that she'd started something and would be damned if Wyn Hayden was the one who ended it. Maybe force Wyn back inside the house, make her apologize to Aaron in front of everyone. It might embarrass Aaron, but it would definitely embarrass Wyn even more, and in that moment, that was all Catherine cared about.

She turned away from the mirror and slipped out of the bathroom. She stared down the hallway toward the main hub of the party, then looked in the other direction and saw the back door.

Seconds later she was outside in the cold night air, scanning the backyard, and then she started around the house, toward where most of the cars were parked, and she spotted Wyn, who was now talking to somebody up on the front porch.

"I told you," Wyn was saying. "I saw you that night. You were in somebody else's car. You were coming from this place, if I had to guess. Taylor must have come here to tell Autumn the news, and Autumn had contacted you—I always suspected you were cheating with her behind Taylor's back—and somehow she managed to get her drunk. Then the two of you somehow managed to get her behind the wheel of her car down on Fox Lane and—"

"You. Don't. Know. What. You're. Talking. About."

It was Sean Heller up on the front porch. Catherine had heard his voice countless times before, but she'd never heard him this angry, not once.

Good, Catherine thought with a smile. *So I'm not the only one.*

Then she noticed something in Wyn's hand, held at her side, and it took Catherine an extra moment to recognize what it was . . . and as soon as she did, her smile faded.

What was that bitch doing with Aaron's Phillies cap?

The next thing she heard was Sean saying, "You're crazy," and then Wyn saying something about recording and uploading a song. Wyn held up her phone, held it high—and that was when fear flashed across her face. She turned at once and started running, and it was instantly clear why: Sean Heller had begun to chase after her.

Catherine followed them. She'd come out here to continue her confrontation with Wyn, but maybe she didn't need to bother, as it looked like Sean was going to beat the shit out of her instead.

She watched Wyn reach her car but fumble her keys. Watched as Wyn glanced up and saw that Sean hadn't slowed. Watched as Wyn made the split-second decision to forget the keys and keep running, straight for the woods.

By that point, Catherine was only a few cars away. She glanced around the front yard, saw that nobody else was outside to witness what was happening.

Part of her wanted to shout, *"Get her, Sean!"* but she worried that might spook him, and the very last thing she wanted to do right now was slow the momentum. This had turned out even better than Catherine could have possibly imagined.

But then Wyn disappeared into the trees, and so did Sean a few seconds later, and in the sudden stillness Catherine started to sober up.

What the hell was wrong with her? She was pissed off at Wyn, yes, and she had every right to be, but did she really want Sean Heller to physically hurt her?

Of course not.

Before she realized what she was doing, Catherine hurried to Wyn's car. The keys were in the grass, as was her brother's hat, and she scooped up both and got into the car and fired up the engine. She sped down the long drive, knowing that most likely Wyn and Sean would end up on Fox Lane, and that if Catherine drove fast enough, she might get there before Sean caught up with Wyn.

Wyn Hayden may be a lying bitch, but no woman deserved to be abused by a man.

And so that was what she was thinking as she slowed to squeeze through the barrier at the end of Fox Lane—how Aaron deserved retribution for having his heart broken, but not like this, nothing at all like this—and as she sped down the lane she stared off into the dark trees, having no idea where Wyn and Sean might appear and suddenly worried that maybe they wouldn't, that Sean had caught up with Wyn in the woods and was currently doing God knows what to her.

Catherine's stomach twisted at the thought.

Something suddenly appeared through the trees then, a flash of motion, and it took her a whole second before she understood what it was and slammed on the brakes.

But by then it was already too late.

52
Jessica
Now

For several seconds, I can't speak. All I can do is stand motionless, staring back at this young woman whom I've come to trust these past few months, this young woman who had reminded me so much of my lost daughter.

"You . . . it was *you*?"

Catherine nods, her expression still sorrowful.

"It was an accident, Ms. Moore. You've got to believe me. I didn't mean to hit her. I wanted to help her. Wyn just . . . she came out of nowhere."

I haven't gotten much sleep in the past couple of days. The world has already proved how unreliable it can be. Now, just when I've thought things might have sorted themselves out, everything has started to tilt again.

"Why are you here, Catherine?"

"Because I'm scared. I had nowhere else to go. The state police, they came for me at school today. I mean, now that I think about it, I guess they just wanted to talk to me. But my friend heard them ask if

I was there and texted me, so I took off. I called my mom and asked if everything was okay, and she was in tears, saying that my dad had been arrested. And for what? As far as my dad knows, Wyn ran away."

She shakes her head, fidgeting with the key.

"Anyway, my mom asked me where I was, and I panicked and hung up on her. I knew she could track my phone—that the police could track my phone—so I turned it off. Wasn't sure where to go, but then I thought . . . I should come here. I ditched my car a couple miles away and walked through the woods and have been hanging out on the patio waiting for you ever since."

"Why would you come here, Catherine?"

"I had nowhere else to go. And, well, you've always been nice to me. You *know* I'm a good person. So I was kind of hoping . . ."

"Yes?"

"That, you know, you might be able to vouch for me. To the police. And not just for me, but for Aaron too. I'm afraid they're going to try to blame him for what happened to Wyn."

"Sean Heller saw Aaron in the car that night, Catherine."

"No, that's not true. I mean, I get why Sean probably thought it was Aaron. When I'd grabbed the keys Wyn had dropped, I grabbed my brother's hat too. I tossed it on the passenger seat and didn't think anything of it until . . . well, until after the accident. And so I was sitting there, not sure what to do, and I remembered Sean had been chasing Wyn, that he was probably nearby in the woods. I didn't want Sean to see it was me when I got out to check on her. So I put on the hat and opened the door but, like, I only did it for a second, because then suddenly I realized there was just no way Wyn had survived. The car . . . it had hit her too hard. And so I called Joe."

"You called Joe," I say quietly.

"My dad always told us to call Joe if we ever got in trouble. Me and Aaron, I mean. My mom, too, I guess. But I'd never called him before.

Because, well, I usually stayed out of trouble. I mean, I got in trouble here and there, but nothing like *that*."

"What did he say?"

"He told me to wait where I was. To not get out of the car. All I told him was that I'd hit somebody and that I thought they were dead. I . . . I didn't tell him who it was."

She's still fidgeting with the key, staring down at it as she talks.

"Officer Gorman got there first. Officer Healy showed up not long after that, and then a few minutes later Joe showed up. And when he realized who I'd hit, it really messed him up. I was worried he'd be super pissed at me. But I told him it was an accident. That she'd come out of nowhere."

"Did you tell him about Sean Heller?"

"Only that Sean had been chasing Wyn, but I wasn't sure if Sean had seen anything. I remember looking into the trees but couldn't see any movement. I thought maybe he'd given up chasing her halfway through the woods. And besides, even if he had seen what happened, what was he going to do? I'd overheard him and Wyn talking. She had all but accused Sean and Autumn of killing Taylor. And based on how Sean had reacted, I'd say it was pretty clear they had something to do with it. So I knew that even if he'd seen what happened, he wouldn't do anything about it."

"How'd you end up with the key?"

"Joe told Officer Gorman to stop by the house to pack up her things to make it look like she'd run away. But he'd told him to drop me off at home first. On the way, I'd told Officer Gorman that he should let me help. Because, like, I'm a teenage girl, and I'd know what I'd pack to take with me if I was running away, and we needed to make it look convincing."

She shakes her head again.

"I could tell he had a thing for me. Or if not me, then just young girls in general. Officer Gorman, I mean. *Kenny*, he told me to call him. So I played it up. Worked his ego. And eventually he let me tag along."

"So you came here with Kenny."

"Yeah. I was the one who let us in through the back door. I'd told Kenny it made sense for me to come in first, just in case. Like, I could say I was looking for Aaron if anything went wrong. So he gave me the key. We had to bring the phone because of the cameras you have in here. Joe said that they were set up to turn off when either you or Wyn came home. Kenny was supposed to get rid of the phone after that night, but I guess he didn't."

"Why did you feel the need to come here in the first place?"

"Because I was worried Kenny might mess something up. And the idea that he might forget something or leave something behind . . . if we were going to make it look like Wyn had run away, everything had to be perfect."

"How did you even get access to my daughter's phone?"

"After Wyn broke up with my brother, I started paying closer attention to her at school. Just, like, watching her and stuff, trying to figure out what had happened to make her break my brother's heart. And, well, a few times I'd been nearby when she entered the passcode into her phone. Turns out it was Taylor's birthday."

"So you kept the key."

"Yeah, I did. Kenny forgot I had it."

"You were the one who broke into my house a few nights later."

"I was. I knew since you were home, I didn't have to worry about the cameras. You had just come to the house with that pregnancy test. Aaron was already all messed up after learning what had happened. I had to tell him. He was so upset, but he understood it was an accident and that nothing could have been done to help Wyn. He also knew if the truth got out, I'd go to jail, and that it would destroy our family. So I gave him back his Phillies cap, told him he needed to act like nothing had happened. But then, like I said, you showed up with that pregnancy test, and it messed him up all over again."

"But that doesn't explain why you broke into my house."

"I needed to shift the focus off Aaron."

It takes me half a moment, and then I say, "The note from Chad Murphy. That was *you*?"

Catherine nods, still fidgeting with the key.

"I felt sort of bad pointing the finger at him. He was the youngest teacher in the school, and he was always super friendly with the seniors, especially the girls . . . it just made sense he might have an inappropriate relationship with a student."

"How did you do it?"

"You mean the note? Forging his handwriting wasn't too difficult. Finding his cell phone number was a bit trickier. I knew when I hid the note in Wyn's room, I couldn't make it *too* easy to find, because you'd probably already searched the room. But you found it pretty fast."

I say nothing.

"You almost found me that night, too, you know. I was hiding behind the couch. I was so certain I was screwed. But then the cops showed up and you rushed outside, and I managed to slip out the back."

"You took the bottle of wine, didn't you?"

She lowers her eyes, looks almost ashamed of herself.

"I'd noticed all the empty bottles in the recycling, and I figured, well, you drank a lot. And, like, there was no guarantee you would find the note anytime soon, or at all, so . . ."

"You wanted me to feel like I was going crazy. There was only one bottle in the fridge, so of course I would know if it went missing. And then, when I said something to the police, they would think I was losing it."

"I'm sorry, Ms. Moore, really I am. But I had to protect my brother. I had to protect my *family*."

"Kenny searched the backyard that night," I say quietly, more to myself than to her.

"Yeah, he found me out there. He tried to make me give him back the key, but I told him no, and he grabbed my arm real tight and told me not to disrespect him or he'd go straight to Joe. I looked him right in the eye and told him that if he did, I'd tell Joe how he tried to feel me up the night he took me home. Kenny realized it would be my word against his, so he let me go."

I glance at the front door. My car isn't here. My phone is dead. My closest neighbor is a half mile away.

"Do you understand?" Catherine says. Her face is awash with emotion, her eyes glistening with tears.

"Understand what?"

"How it was an accident. How everything was never supposed to spiral out of control like this. I mean, my dad is probably going to go to prison, right?"

"I don't know, Catherine. Probably."

"But he didn't *do* anything! You . . . you're Wyn's mom. You could explain just how good a person I am to the police. Make them see that it wasn't really my fault. That my dad didn't know. That my brother wasn't involved."

I glance again at the front door. I wonder if I started to walk to it now how Catherine would react.

"Ms. Moore, please, won't you help me?"

I look at her again. There are even more tears in her eyes. Part of me wants to feel sorry for her, but another part can't get past the fact she's responsible for my daughter's death.

"You sent Aaron to the house that day, didn't you?"

"I'd seen you and Mr. Hayden at school earlier in the day. I knew the only reason you'd come was because you must have found the note. Plus, I saw Mr. Murphy leave the office, and he was all upset. But he was still teaching later that day, so I told Aaron that we needed to shift the focus now to Sean Heller. He didn't want to at first—he was still pretty rattled after you basically accused him of forcing himself on Wyn—but I finally convinced him. I mean, if you think about it, it mostly was Sean's fault. If he hadn't been chasing her through the woods that night, I never would have accidentally hit her."

I start to take a step toward the front door, but as soon as I do, Catherine moves in that direction as well.

"Ms. Moore, *please*. I'm begging you."

Something suddenly occurs to me, and I say, "You brought Kenny to the bar that night."

She lowers her eyes, again looking ashamed.

"I did. After that night when he grabbed my arm, I . . . well, he needed to be taught a lesson. On a hunch I found him on one of the dating apps. I started messaging back and forth with him. Talked him into coming to the Wonderwall that night. That's why I stayed so late. I wanted to make sure he learned his lesson."

She takes another step closer. Realizes that she's still fidgeting with the key. Sets it down on the counter, right next to a vase.

"Wyn's song—the one she was going to sing at the pep rally—is called 'Her Dark Secret.' Did you know that? It's kind of a love song. About a girl in love with her friend but not having the heart to tell her. About a girl knowing just how awful her friend's boyfriend is but not having the heart to tell her. And then how the boyfriend ended up killing the friend, and how the girl realized that in many ways she was responsible. Because she hadn't told her friend the truth, both about her feelings and how much of a monster the boyfriend truly was. It's such a heartbreaking song. It was on Wyn's phone. I guess she was going to upload it to the internet. That's why Sean chased after her. I managed to send the file to my phone before we deactivated all her social media accounts. Truthfully, I had always thought she was talented. I've listened to the song about a hundred times in the past year. It's honestly one of the best songs I've ever heard."

"That sounds amazing, Catherine. I'd love to hear it."

"I want you to hear it. I want everyone to hear it. It's such an amazing song. But . . . but you have to help me first. Help me *and* my family."

I shake my head slowly.

"No, Catherine."

Her face drops, and she practically wails, "What? Why not?"

"My daughter is dead, Catherine. It may have been an accident, but people covered it up, and those people need to be held accountable."

She just stares back at me, crestfallen. No, not crestfallen—devastated. I've never seen someone so crushed. Again, part of me wants to feel sorry for her, while another part knows better.

"I think you should leave now, Catherine. Go home to your mother. I'm sure she's worried sick wondering where you are."

Catherine doesn't move. Just keeps standing there, staring back at me. Then, little by little, her expression changes.

"I . . . I apologized to you. I told you everything. Things that . . . that nobody else knows."

Something in her expression shifts, an intensity flashing in her eyes. Suddenly I remember sitting across the table from Chad Murphy at school last year, how he'd looked trapped like a cornered animal.

And what does a cornered animal do when it feels threatened?

Whatever it takes to survive.

I quickly scan the living room, looking for something to protect me if and when the time comes. My eyes fall on the fire poker standing in the tray by the fireplace.

"Don't," Catherine says, her tone hard. "Don't . . . don't make this any harder than it has to be."

Her hands are trembling at her sides, tears in her eyes again.

"I wanted you to understand. I wanted you to *help* me. But you . . . you're not giving me a choice. I'm sorry."

Before I have a chance to pivot toward the fireplace, she grabs the vase off the counter and throws it at my head. I duck, and it shatters against the wall behind me. I jump over the easy chair and lunge for the fire poker. Catherine moves faster, shoving me to the floor. When I look up, she has the poker and is raising it above her head.

"Why couldn't you just *let it go*?"

I scramble to my feet as she swings the poker. I can just hear the tip whoosh over the back of my head.

"I *apologized*."

She swings the poker again, this time wildly.

"It was an *accident*!"

Again she swings the poker as she advances, backing me toward the hallway leading to the bedrooms. I can barricade myself in one of the rooms, but with the dead iPhone, there's no way I can call for help.

Except . . .

"The cameras, Catherine. They're still on. They've been on this entire time. Whatever you do to me, the police will see everything."

Catherine pauses. But only for a moment. Then, her face red, she issues a guttural cry as she rushes forward.

I turn away. Not to the right, which would direct me toward my room. But to the left, toward Bronwyn's room.

I don't have time to hit the light switch. It's much too dark in here, which may play to my advantage. But before I can take another step forward, Catherine swings the poker again, and this time it connects with my side.

Fortunately, the rake part of the poker is on the outside, so nothing breaks skin.

My arm comes down on the poker, and I try to pull it away, but Catherine grunts and tries to yank it from me, and then barrels forward to knock me off my feet.

We both hit the floor. I'm on the carpet, my arms outstretched. Bronwyn's desk is right next to us. I'm trying to reach behind the desk, right where I left—

Catherine hasn't let go of the poker, and she moves forward on her knees.

I reach farther, and yes, there it is, the wine bottle. My fingers curl around the neck, squeeze it tight.

"I'm sorry, too, Catherine," I whisper.

And swing the bottle at her head.

EPILOGUE

Nobody just disappears.

Not like in movies. Or on TV. Or in books.

People can't just one day up and vanish. Life isn't an elaborate magic trick. There is no magician standing in the wings whose fingertips are so powerful they can make a person disappear with one simple snap.

Your father didn't disappear. At least not entirely. You eventually found him. It took the help of a private investigator, but you proved that he hadn't simply vanished.

Just like how you proved your daughter didn't vanish.

That was a bit trickier. Took a lot more work. And a lot of people suffered. Many were put in prison, where they belong.

Some of those involved received harsher sentences than others. Other people—like the spouses and children—have suffered in different ways.

Part of you feels bad, but another part doesn't. That part just feels tired. Exhausted. Glad that the entire thing is finally over.

Your daughter didn't just disappear. She was killed.

But you found her. At least there's that. They dug up the car with her body in the trunk. You'd considered having her buried, but where were you going to bury her? Bowden no longer felt like home. So you decided to have her cremated. That way you can keep her with you wherever you go.

It's been several months, and you're finally ready to leave town. You've sold the Wonderwall. You've sold the house.

You don't quite know where you're going to go just yet, but you need to leave. Every day you spend in town is a reminder of what happened. How this was the place where you lost your daughter.

What few items you've decided to keep are loaded in the trailer hitched to your car. Everything else will be given away.

It's the first day of summer, and you decide to check the backyard one last time.

You stand on the patio and feel the light breeze on your face. The sky is clear, only a few clouds hanging around in all that deep blue like splotches on an artist's canvas.

You close your eyes and draw in a deep breath.

This is it, you tell yourself. This will be the last time you ever step foot in this town.

Then you open your eyes and freeze in place.

On the patio railing, right in front of you, is a butterfly. It's the first one you've seen in over a year. The first one you've seen since your daughter went missing.

Its coloring is violet. Not quite onyx but close enough that you find yourself smiling.

You don't move. Don't do anything that will spook the ethereal creature. You just stand there, watching it as its wing slowly pulse.

You whisper, "I heard your song. The one you recorded that night. It's beautiful. Heartbreaking. You were so talented, and I should have told you that every day. And . . . well, I uploaded the song a few months back. It went viral. The last I checked there have been over five million views on YouTube. Everyone loves it."

The butterfly's wings continue to pulse.

"I am so sorry for what happened. But I hope you're at peace now. I hope wherever you are, you're happy."

The butterfly still doesn't move.

"I miss you so much. I love you . . . Wyn."

The butterfly's wings pulse again, just a bit, and then it takes flight.

And as it does—as it lifts into the air and disappears into the summer breeze—you remember that day many years ago in Washington, DC. How you'd been so focused on your argument with Joe that you both didn't realize your daughter had gone missing. How you'd looked everywhere, calling her name, rushing through the crowd. And how you eventually found her, standing near a tree. How you'd dropped to your knees and taken her into your arms and told her that you'd been so scared and that she should never do anything like that ever again. And how your daughter, barely fazed, simply smiled at you and said, "It's okay, Mommy. I wasn't scared. I knew you would find me."

Acknowledgments

Thank you to my editor, Alicia Clancy, for guiding me in the right direction. To everyone at Lake Union, especially Gabe Dumpit. To David Downing, for his sharp eye, and to Maya Davis, for her insightful comments. To John Cashman, Kelli Owen, and Adam Perry for their feedback on early drafts. To Tess Callero, for her unending enthusiasm and support. And, as always, to Holly.

About the Author

Avery Bishop is the pseudonym for a *USA Today* bestselling author of more than a dozen novels.